the way.

ELLIE DARKINS
REBECCA WINTERS
LISA CHILDS

MILLS

First Published in Great Britain 2017
By Mills & Boon, an imprint of HarperCollins*Publishers*
1 London Bridge Street, London, SE1 9GF

BABY'S ON THE WAY! © 2017 Harlequin Books S. A.

Bound By A Baby Bump, Expecting The Prince's Baby and *The Pregnant Witness* were first published in Great Britain by Harlequin (UK) Limited.

Bound By A Baby Bump © 2015 Ellie Darkins
Expecting The Prince's Baby © 2014 Rebecca Winters
The Pregnant Witness © 2015 Lisa Childs

ISBN: 978-0-263-92993-5

05-1217

MIX
Paper from
responsible sources
FSC™ C007454

This book is produced from independently certified FSC™ paper to ensure responsible forest management.

For more information visit: www.harpercollins.co.uk/green

Printed and bound in Spain
by CPI, Barcelona

BOUND BY A
BABY BUMP

BY
ELLIE DARKINS

Ellie Darkins spent her formative years devouring romance novels, and after completing her English degree decided to make a living from her love of books. As a writer and editor her work now entails dreaming up romantic proposals, hot dates with alpha males and trips to the past with dashing heroes. When she's not working she can usually be found at her local library or out for a run.

For my family

CHAPTER ONE

LOOK UP.

He commanded her to feel his gaze on her skin, to glance over and meet his eye. To make a connection with him. He'd been watching her for hours, biding his time until he could have her complete, undivided attention. Since the moment he'd first seen her striding round the room, her tablet computer and Bluetooth headset at odds with her black silk evening dress and staggeringly sexy heels, he'd been transfixed.

The curve of her calves, the gleam of her skin and the fluid movement of her hair had caught his attention, but it was her fierce concentration that had held it. The way she'd managed the room and everyone in it with a gentle nudge here and a subtle pull there. With a glance at her watch and a whisper in the ear of a member of staff she'd averted disasters, negotiated tricky situations and ensured that every person she spoke to ended their conversation with a beaming grin. No doubt the charity the gala was fundraising for would make a fortune.

Under normal circumstances, the thought of a to-do list and a watch filled his belly with apprehension, an unwelcome reminder of school days that had tormented him at the time, and still threatened the occasional nightmare more than ten years later. But worn as an accessory by a woman who seemed so effortlessly powerful, it was suddenly incredibly sexy.

He'd waited for the perfect moment all night—watching groups where she was conversing, catching her eye across the room; at one point, he'd even headed towards her with a determined stride—only for her to abruptly change course and disappear into the kitchen. And now she was putting her head together with one of the other guests, consulting her tablet, tucking a curtain of shining hair behind her ear.

She laughed, and the sound reached him as clear as if the room had been silent. Her face creased, her head dropped back, and humour radiated from her like a wave. He wanted to make her laugh. He was unreasonably jealous of the person who had inspired the sound, a man with pure silver hair and a walking stick.

The string band had started playing in a corner of the ballroom, and a few couples were heading towards the dance floor. His eyes flickered towards them, and he wondered whether she'd accept an invitation to dance.

In the moment that his eyes left her, he felt her look at him.

He whipped around to try and catch her gaze, but her eyes had already dropped to her tablet, as she scrolled up and down. She glanced at him again, and this time he caught it. He turned, his hands in his pockets, and his body relaxed under her stare, turning his stance into something languid and louche.

He walked towards her, smiling, still refusing to look away. He would hold this contact until he could get his hands on something more solid.

Just a couple of steps away from her, he was hit with

unaccustomed nerves. It had been an age since he'd felt nervous talking to a woman. Things were pretty easy-come-easy-go in his love-life, much to the satisfaction of everyone involved. Nerves were thin on the ground when the most you were looking to gain or lose was a few nights or weeks of fun. The prospect of commitment, of expectations, of being caught in a situation with no simple way out—only the fix of her eyes on his kept a shiver from his spine.

'Hi, I'm Rachel Archer.' The words arrived in a rush as soon as he was within arm's reach and she stuck out her hand for him to shake.

'Leo.' He just managed the one word, though it felt as if all breath had left his body at the feel of her hand in his. He observed her closely, looking for any clue that she was as affected by this meeting as he. But she had dropped her eyes, pulling her hand back—was that a fraction of a hesitation?—and glancing down at her tablet.

'So, are you enjoying crashing the party?' She gave a throaty chuckle with the words, and he absorbed the sound, revelling in the delicious heat it inspired in his body. He was so focused on that sound that he almost missed the meaning of her words.

'Crashing?' he asked with a raised eyebrow and a smile. 'Says who?'

'Says me.' No laugh this time, though a perfectly polite smile was still on her lips. He wanted a real one. 'Tonight is strictly invitation only, though if you are here to con-tribute *generously* to the Julia House hospice, I'm sure we can make an exception.'

He returned his hands to his pockets; it was on the tip of his tongue to tell her that he was there in place of his father, who was unwell and couldn't attend. Normally, 'representing the family' wasn't something he was interested in, but his father had promised the organisers that the family would be there with a generous donation—for a good cause he had been known to make an exception. He was intrigued, though. How did she know he was crashing—had she been asking questions about him?

'I want to know more about why you think I'm crashing.'

'Well...' she said, pulling up another page on her tablet. 'I planned the guest list. I sent the invitations, checked the RSVPs and wrote the table plan. There wasn't a single Leo to be seen.' Her eyes left her screen, and she looked him up and down, her eyes travelling from his face to his shoes, faltering slightly at his belt and chest. Encouraging.

'Ah, so I must be crashing. I take it your lists are never wrong?'

'Never,' she agreed with a good-tempered nod, and just the merest hint of another chuckle.

'Then I suppose I've got some making up to do. What will it take?'

'Well, apart from your considerable contribution to Julia House, which I'm sure is already in hand...'

'Naturally.'

'I want an explanation.'

It was his turn to laugh. 'That's all?' But she didn't look equally amused. In fact a worry line had appeared between her brows, and she glanced again at her screen.

'Tonight has been planned and re-planned, checked and double-checked. I want to know how you're here, and how I didn't know about it.'

He wanted that line gone. Wanted any evidence of discomfort wiped from her face. He still wanted to make her laugh.

'I'll tell you everything. Every dark secret and trick of the conman's trade.' He raised his eyebrows, attempting melodramatic villainy, and was rewarded with a lift at the corner of her lips. 'All you have to do is dance with me.'

Rachel rested her hand stiffly on his shoulder as they started to move to the music, wondering—again—why she had agreed to this. She let her gaze travel up from his collar, over a tanned throat, blond stubbled jaw and endearingly crooked nose. Up to a pair of eyes as blue as a baking summer sky, and then remembered.

Somewhere along the line, somewhere between guest list and dessert, her system had fallen short. He was probably standing in for someone—she had a shortlist of faces she'd been expecting to see but hadn't. But how had she made it to eleven o'clock without realising something was wrong?

'So,' she prompted, trying to keep her mind on the job, rather than on the confident way Leo was leading her around the floor, or the scent coming from his skin. Something salty, natural and that had, she guessed, never been anywhere near a Selfridges counter.

She faltered for a second as she caught him looking at her, and felt her cheeks warming under the intensity of his interest. She stilled, suddenly hyperaware of the pressure of his hand around hers, of his arm at her waist, the sound of him breathing close to her ear. Only the subtle squeeze of his arm reminded her she was supposed to be dancing. Forcing her feet to move, she glanced over his shoulder and spotted her boss, Will, and for a moment she was worried she was about to be caught slacking. But one look at his face told her she had nothing to worry about. He had eyes only for Maya, his partner, and she smiled. She couldn't help but take a little credit for the happiness that was radiating from them both. She was the one who'd engineered Will into taking a cookery course he wasn't interested in, all because it was run by a woman he definitely was.

She'd watched that relationship blossom, from first meeting to their elation tonight, and felt a little pang of... what? Loneliness? No, that wasn't it. She had friends— she'd even shared a flat with her best friend, Laura, until she'd bought her own place a year ago—right on track for her five-year plan. Sometimes she even managed to schedule time for a date or two.

But she didn't have *that*, whatever it was that made it look as if half the light in the room were emanating from them.

So no, she wasn't lonely, but maybe she was curious. Intrigued enough by the possibilities that when the surfy-looking blond who'd been casting looks in her direction all night had asked her if she wanted to dance, she'd looked him up and down and considered it.

And she'd been intrigued enough by what she'd seen to fight down the urge to tell him that this wasn't in her schedule, but to send him a smile instead.

There wasn't actually much left of her schedule tonight. That was the benefit of being chronically well organised, she supposed. When everything was planned and prepared in advance, she could just sit back and watch all the results of her hard work fall into place. Like with Will and Maya: the consequences of her plan had far exceeded her expectations, and she'd only had to intervene a couple of times to keep everything moving in the right direction. Better still, her boss had barely even noticed her involvement. The sign of a great executive assistant, she told herself. Her work was practically invisible.

She was so engrossed with watching the results of her meticulous planning she almost, *almost*, forgot where she was and what she was doing.

That was until a warm, rough fingertip found its way under her chin and tilted her face upward.

'Should I be worried about the competition?' Her eyes snapped back to his, and she was taken aback again by their intense colour, and the way he looked at her, as if there was some part of her he was trying desperately to see.

'So who were you watching?' he asked, reminding her of his question.

'Jealous?' She drew out the word with a smile, enjoying for a moment the control that it gave her. She didn't even know yet what she wanted to do with this blatant expression of interest, other than enjoy it for a moment. 'I'm just enjoying a plan coming together.'

'You planned that?' he asked, as her boss leant down and kissed Maya gently on the lips. The kiss itself was chaste enough, but the blatant bedroom eyes on both sides nudged it towards obscene.

'I may have helped a little.'

'Well, I prefer your attention here,' he said, attempting to soften his words with a cheeky grin.

'Demanding, much?' Okay, so her attention wasn't such a ridiculous thing to expect. But she didn't want him thinking he could just demand what he wanted and expect her to deliver. And she still wasn't sure how she felt about his attention. Attracted, sure. But meeting a party crasher with a cute smile and a devastating way of watching her hadn't featured in her plans for tonight. She'd had no advance warning, no time to think about what she wanted to do.

'Absolutely.' He remained completely straight-faced and Rachel recognised the challenge. 'But I think if you're going to agree to dance with me, it's only fair you give it your full attention.'

'Perhaps. But you're not holding up your end of the bargain. The dance was in exchange for an explanation. So spill. How did you get in without me knowing about it?'

'Grappling hook,' he replied, deadpan and with no hesitation. She let out a laugh, leaning back against his arm, letting the humour arch her body and soften her indignation.

He teased and she laughed, until she could feel the tension of the night leaching from her body. She'd not checked her watch since he'd led her to the floor, and she had no idea how long they'd been up there. And she was dangerously close to not caring. His humour, the naughty light in his eyes, was forcing the strain of preparing this evening from her limbs, demanding she enjoy herself. That she enjoy *him*. Eventually, when she'd laughed off his latest suggestion for how he'd joined the party—something about an international jewel thief—he leaned in close, until she could feel his warm breath disturbing her hair, and the minutest brush of his lips against her ear. With a little shiver, she suspected the time for games was coming to an end. 'Someone asked me to attend on their behalf. I couldn't say no. Are you going to throw me out?'

His reply prompted a hundred questions in her mind,

but the one that sprang unguarded to her lips surprised even her: 'Where would you go if I did?'

His lips parted slightly and he chose his words carefully, she guessed, not wanting to break the connection crackling like electricity between them. 'That depends.'

Of course she was meant to ask 'on what', but the blatant suggestion in his eyes made her falter, suddenly aware they weren't playing any longer.

'Would you come with me?' he asked, deadly serious. He had given up on the dancing, too, and his hand had drifted up to her cheek, his thumb skittering across her skin. She had pulled her gaze away, unable to bear the close scrutiny of those huge, clear blue eyes, but now it snapped back up as she took a little half step away from him.

'I can't. I'm working.' She didn't even think before she spoke. The words came to her lips automatically as her heart rate spiked and her breath hitched. Her arms tensed where they rested against his body as she started to register the risk she'd taken coming up here with him. This man was chaos. She could see it in the haphazard drape of his tie and his mismatched cufflinks. The fact that even without being invited to the party he had got her away from her to-do list and onto the dance floor.

Her whereabouts and every action had been meticulously planned for the whole evening. She'd been in the right place and at the right time, with the right files and figures for just about every one of the past eighteen hours. She was currently partway through the hour that she'd marked 'Networking, socialising, misc.' And when it came to an end, she had planned to run through a couple of details with the venue manager before leaving for the night. Alone.

Leo smiled at her, cool and relaxed.

'So you want to,' he said, as if he'd just gained a small victory.

She narrowed her eyes. She hadn't said that.

'You said you can't leave because you're working. But you never said you don't want to. I've been watching you all night. Waiting for the right moment to catch your attention; wanting to know what's on that tablet of yours. How you keep a party like this moving with just a whisper and a look in the right direction. I've been completely hypnotised by you and all I want for the rest of the night is to find out more.'

Her eyes widened in surprise; she was completely taken aback by his words.

She'd spotted him early in the night, and wondered which name his face belonged to. As she'd worked round the room, meeting and greeting, discussing the practicalities of donations, nudging Will in the right direction, and keeping the company CEO, Sir Cuthbert Appleby, happy, her thoughts had drifted to the guy in the slightly crumpled suit, his wavy hair resisting any attempt at a style. But the more her gaze had been drawn to him, the more she'd fought it, forcing her eyes to her work, her schedule and smartphone. She'd recognised the danger in that pull, the need to stick to her plan and see out the night as she'd intended. But now? This dance was perfectly in line with her itinerary. She'd always expected to do *some* socialising. And after that? She had ten minutes' work to do—tops.

So she could tell him she wasn't interested, that she had barely noticed him and didn't need to know any more than that. But it would be a lie. Because ever since his arm had captured her waist she'd been trying *not* to think about all the wicked things she'd like to do with his body. Her brain had thrown a dozen different suggestions at her, each one making her blush more than the last. Top of the list being to get his shirt off, so she could see if the contours of his body looked as good as they felt.

But she couldn't just take off with him. She had responsibilities here, she thought, her heart rate picking up again, though from desire or panic she couldn't tell. She had work she had to finish up. She couldn't just take off because—

Ooh.

His thumb continued its exploration of her jaw, and dipped into her collarbone in a way that made her melt.

When she looked up and met his eyes, the danger there was obvious. But he spelled it out for her, anyway.

'I want to make you shiver like that again,' he said slowly. 'I could try here, but...' He stroked that magic spot again and she bit the inside of her cheek to stop herself groaning out load.

'You see the problem?'

She nodded, but... 'I can't do this.'

'You can't? Or you don't want to?'

Did it matter? 'I have a plan for tonight.' She took another half step away from him, knowing she needed distance. 'This isn't it.'

He pulled her back in and rested his forehead against hers. 'Rachel, you're killing me. At least come somewhere we can talk.' His arm dropped from her waist abruptly, but before she could mourn its loss her hand was engulfed by his and she was striding with him across the ballroom.

When they reached the lobby, he whirled around, his lips stopping just inches from hers. Was he doing it on purpose? Tempting her until she lost her mind and gave in?

'Help me here,' he said, his voice soft and enticing. 'You're attracted to me.' The lilt of his voice was just charming enough to compensate for his lack of modesty. 'So what's stopping you?'

She took her hand back, and a step away from him, understanding that being so close was doing nothing for her decision-making skills. This wasn't a question of what she wanted; she couldn't just drop everything and leave on a whim.

'Nothing's stopping me,' she said, keeping her voice carefully even. There was no need for him to know the nagging dread that would start in the base of her brain if she decided to embrace spontaneity. No need for him to know that she'd not done anything without a plan, a back-up plan and a contingency plan since she was a teenager. 'I'm working. I had some free time scheduled, and thank you for the dance, but now I have to get back.'

He looked at her carefully, and she held his gaze. 'Do you always have a plan? A schedule?'

'I do. What's wrong with that?'

'Oh, you mean except for the claustrophobia, the inflexibility, the stifling—' Wisely, he stopped himself, probably remembering he should play to his audience. 'So I wasn't in your plan for tonight. But what if something unexpected comes up? That must happen sometimes, right? Meetings get cancelled, things run late. Contracts get lost in the post. What happens to your plans then?'

'I make a new one,' she said, wondering what was behind his cut-off outburst, the flash of panic she'd seen on his face.

'You adapt to the circumstances—just like that. No stress. No panic.'

'Of course.' Working with Will could— and frequently did—send crises her way. She smoothed each problem until it fitted neatly into her existing plans, and all without anyone seeing that below the surface she was paddling like a racing swan.

Leo smiled at her as if he'd just scored a point. 'So make a new plan for tonight. Nothing serious, no reason to change tomorrow's plans, or any day after that. Just reschedule a couple of hours tonight to fit me in.'

'A couple of hours?' She raised an eyebrow at that: one night suited her just fine—her life was too full for anything more—but she had ideas enough already to fill more than a couple of hours. If she was going to do this, she was going to be sure it was worth her while.

And she was intrigued, because he was right. She'd altered plans before. She'd adapted to circumstances. Allowed for last-minute changes. So why shouldn't she do that tonight? Through the window into the ballroom she caught sight of Will and Maya dancing and remembered what she'd felt earlier, that stab of curiosity, or loneliness, or... Perhaps the fact that she didn't even know what it was made a good enough reason to do this.

'I have a few things I have to finish up before I—'

With a smile, he swooped in and pressed a quick, hard kiss to her lips. 'Just tell me when.'

CHAPTER TWO

LEO CRACKED AN eyelid and spotted a tangle of brown hair on the pillow beside him. Relaxing his head back, he was assailed by a stream of memories from the night before. Rachel meeting him outside the ballroom, belting her coat, telling him a cab was waiting for them. Him pressing a kiss to her neck as she unlocked her front door, too impatient to wait until they were inside. Her peeling off the silk of her dress with a teasing glint in her eyes.

He should be getting going, he thought, knowing that waiting round till breakfast could build unreasonable expectations that he might stay till lunch, and then dinner and then... His shoulders tensed, reminding him why breakfast was always a bad idea. Before he knew it, he could find himself trapped by expectations, unable to see his way out. The weight of claustrophobia sat on his chest as he remembered that feeling, of being stuck in a situation he couldn't escape. Locked in a dorm with people who only wanted to cause him hurt. But that wouldn't happen with Rachel, he reminded himself. She didn't want to lock him into anything. They were both happy with just one night. It had been hard enough to persuade her to find a few hours.

A snuffling noise came from beneath the mass of hair, and he smiled, despite himself. Running out of the door might be the safest option—and he wanted that Exit sign well in sight—but as he was hit by more flashbacks, he realised staying could definitely have its advantages.

He glanced around the bedroom, half lit by the summer sun fighting the curtains, and noticed for the first time the neatly arranged furniture, coasters on the bedside tables, books on the shelf organised by size, not a hairbrush or handbag or discarded running shoe in sight. The only items out of place were the trail of clothes from door to bed. So she'd not been faking the control-freakery. He felt a twist of unease again in his belly at what that might mean, whether that control would be heading his way. But he'd been pretty clear last night that he was only after a bit of fun—and she'd been equally frank about not being able to clear more than one night from her schedule for him.

Then a smooth calf rubbed against his leg, and any thoughts of running for the door vanished. Rachel turned her head on the pillow, and he watched her face as her eyes blinked, waiting for the moment when they finally opened properly and focused on him.

'Hi.' The sensation of her skin on his was making him impatient, and he wondered if it normally took her this long to come round.

'Morning.' She spoke the word quickly, shaking her head and blinking, as if rapidly assessing the situation and devising several different scenario-dependent plans. And she pulled the duvet up higher, tucking it tight against her breasts. A bit late for that, Leo thought. There was nothing he hadn't seen last night. More memories washed over him. Her skin, her taste, her smell.

'Forget I was here?' he asked, with a grin, propping himself up on one elbow.

'I thought maybe…' She flipped over and rubbed at her eyes, still sending him cautious looks, in between glancing at the door. Which told him exactly what she was thinking—the same as he'd been thinking not long before. 'Never mind.' She smiled, a little shyly, and glanced at the window. 'I need to be getting up.' She sat up properly and reached for her phone beside the bed, checking the time. At least he hoped that was all she was checking. He wasn't sure he could take it if she was kicking him out so she could deal with email.

'It's the weekend—what's the rush?' He wrapped his arm around her waist under the cover and pulled her back to him, grinning as she relaxed slightly. He took advantage of her momentary acquiescence and leaned over her, pinning her in place with an arm either side of her.

'I think you should stay,' he murmured soothingly, suddenly feeling as if nothing was as important as convincing her to spend a few more hours with him. It must be the sex, he told himself—the promise of a repeat performance—that had him so desperate to stay. Nothing to do with the cold and hurt he'd felt when she'd pushed him away—emotionally, if not physically—just now. He leaned in closer, brushed his lips softly against hers. When he thought he had her attention, he tucked a lock of her hair behind her ear.

'We could pretend it's not morning yet.' He glanced at the window, where the sun was still making a concerted effort to reach them. She held his gaze for a long moment, and he could see that light in her eyes that told him she was coming up with a plan. He grinned, suddenly excited to know what she would come up with.

'Well, maybe I could do with a little more sleep,' she said with an exaggerated yawn.

He laughed. 'Minx. Shut your eyes, then. Pretend it's still night.' Instead of closing them, she gave him a shrewd glance. Evaluation, he guessed. Assessing what this loss of control would cost her, and what she might stand to gain. Amending those plans of hers. He trailed a hand up the silky skin of her thigh, reminding her.

The moan that escaped her lips soothed his ego and brought a smile to his face.

Her eyelids drifted softly shut.

'Still feeling sleepy?'

'Maybe not quite sleepy…'

Afterwards, he held on to her tight. It was only as his eyes were drifting shut again that he remembered he'd planned to leave after…well, after.

'Ahem.'

At the clearing of her throat he forced his eyes open, drank in the colours of her hair, mahogany, chestnut, teak, which pooled in the hollow above her collarbone.

'Don't you need to…er…?'

He raised an eyebrow. Was she trying to kick him out? Again? He tried to pull her closer, made an indiscriminate soothing noise, but she wriggled from his grasp.

'I'm getting up. If you want the bathroom first…'

'Right.' No cuddling, no morning-after awkwardness or expectations. This was what he wanted, he reminded himself, fighting a sense of disappointment.

She watched his back, well, more specifically, she ogled his bottom, as he walked to the bathroom. Then dropped her head back on the pillow and draped her arm across her face, blocking out the world. Okay, so she'd made some slight adjustments to her plans last night—and this morning. But there was no reason not to get back on schedule now.

And she and Leo knew where they stood—they'd both been very clear last night exactly what was on the table. Now it was morning, properly morning, they could go their separate ways and enjoy the memories. Apart. Safe. With no plans to meet again. Because adapting to change once was just plenty, thank you, however nice the results might have been; but the thought of approaching more than one night with Leo, and the chaos and disorder she was sure followed him everywhere, started a cool mass of dread deep in her belly. It had been years, longer than she could remember, since she had approached life without an itinerary—and even contemplating what that might feel like now made sweat prickle on her forehead.

Hearing the flush of the toilet and not wanting to be in bed when Leo came out of the bathroom, she grabbed clothes from the dresser, hiding herself away in soft black yoga pants and a draped sweater.

By the time the shower stopped she'd picked up and folded their clothes, straightened the nightstand on his side of the bed, and stripped the sheets. She was just about to grab a fresh set when the bathroom door opened and Leo appeared, wet from the shower, his face grim.

'We might have a bit of a problem.'

'What sort of a problem?' Though she could guess from his serious look that she wasn't going to like what he had to say.

'The condom—it broke.'

'Broke?' She tried to keep her voice below a screech,

but wasn't sure that she managed it. 'What do you mean it broke?'

'I mean the condom had a tear in it. I thought you would want to know.'

She dropped the pillow she was holding and sat down heavily on the bed. Rubbing her fists against her eye sockets, she tried to take the information in and formulate a plan for what to do next. When she finally looked up, Leo was still standing in the doorway, watching her, a concerned look on his face.

'Are you on the pill?'

'No,' she said firmly, picking up her phone and jabbing at the screen. 'I'm not. But I'll stop at a pharmacy on my way to work and get the morning-after pill.'

She then nudged him gently out of the bathroom doorway with her hip.

'The door's just on the latch,' she said, desperate to be alone to gather her thoughts, and sure that Leo must be wanting to leave by now. She hadn't expected him to stay even this long. 'You can just pull it closed on your way out. Last night was lovely.' She turned and reached up to kiss him gently on the cheek then shut the door behind her.

She went about her Sunday-morning routine with meticulous precision, determined to banish the butterflies left over from her going off-plan last night with the familiarity of her routine. Shower, exfoliate, hair mask, face mask, cuticle oil. The appearance of a slightly scruffy-looking man with the ability to keep her awake half the night didn't mean her pores or her nails had to suffer.

It served as a timely reminder that she probably should have stuck to her plan A last night. Having a plan B was all good and well, but that didn't mean one always had to use it. Responding to change was part of her job, but a plan was meant to create order, not the chaos that threatened at the edges of her morning.

She emerged from the bathroom half an hour later with face, body and mind scrubbed smooth. And nearly dropped her towel at the sight of Leo stretched out on her unmade bed, eyes shut, breathing heavily, with two cups of coffee and a plate of toast on a tray beside him. Looking outrageously tempting. If it wasn't for the unease that gripped her shoulders, she might have been tempted to join him for round three. Instead she closed the door loudly, trying to wake him. He didn't stir. Clutching her towel more tightly, she walked over to the bed and reached out to shake him. But his fingers captured her wrist before she could touch him.

'What are you doing here?' she asked, too genuinely surprised to try and sugar-coat her words.

'You asked me back here. You had a plan, remember?' She smiled, trying to convince her shoulders there was no reason for them to tense and bunch up.

'No, I mean, why are you *still* here?'

'How about because I'm enjoying your company?' He reached and stretched behind him, then propped himself on his elbow, watching her from the bed as if he had every right to be there.

'I've not been keeping you company. I've been in the bathroom.'

'For an *age*. I know. What were you doing in there?'

'Grooming,' she replied with a quick, accidental glance at his tangle of hair, the stubble on his chin, the wrinkled shirt.

'Meow.' He laughed as he sat up on the unmade bed

and reached for a coffee. 'Are you always this mean in the morning?'

'Are you always this annoying?'

Her scowl cracked into a grin as she sat beside him.

'This will help.' She reached for the other cup of coffee and took a long gulp. 'And then I really do have to go. I have things to do at the office.'

'The office? You know it's a Sunday, right? I saw your boss last night. I bet he's not going to be racing out of bed to get to work.'

'Quite. All the more reason why I have to. I had to put a few things on the back burner in the lead-up to the fundraiser. I want to get them moving again.'

'They'll still be there tomorrow. I, on the other hand...'

'Will be long gone—you were quite adamant about that last night, I remember. And yet here you are, holding me up when I want to get to work.'

'You work too hard.' The deliberate change of subject wasn't lost on her.

'Do you work at all?' she asked, genuinely curious, and realising now how little she knew about him. Other than that he likely had a rich benefactor, of course.

He nodded as he took a gulp of coffee. 'Sort of.'

'Sort of? Anyone I know who "sort of" has a job has mainly been occupied spending a trust fund.'

He winced, she noticed.

'So when you say "sort of", you don't have an actual job.'

'You could say that.' His grin told her that he was enjoying frustrating her, refusing to spill the details of his life. Not that it mattered to her what he did or didn't do, she reminded herself. It was just she was curious, having spent the night with a man to whom the very idea of a plan near on brought him out in hives.

'So how do you fill your days? When you're not attending gala dinners, that is.'

He gave her a carefully nonchalant look. 'I spend it at the beach.'

She nearly snorted her coffee with a good-natured laugh. 'Well, I should have guessed that,' she said, draining the dregs.

She hunted in her drawers for underwear and grabbed a simple shift dress from the wardrobe and then headed into the bathroom. When she emerged, dressed and perfectly coiffured, Leo was leaning against the kitchen counter, jacket and shoes on, the smile gone from his eyes.

'I didn't want to just disappear. I could walk you to the train? I have to get going.' He hoped his voice sounded less conflicted than he felt. That he wasn't giving away his battle between regret and impatience. Leo Fairfax didn't do regrets. He was walking away because it was the only way to be safe. The only way to ensure he didn't find himself in a situation that was intolerable, as he had at school. As much as last night and this morning had been exhilarating, wonderful, this had to end now.

He'd been perfectly frank last night that she shouldn't expect anything lasting from him.

'A walk to the station would be good. Are you ready to go?'

Leo reached for her hand as they walked along the leafy street, and wound his fingers with hers. It was only when he felt her hesitation, the tension in her muscles, that he realised what he'd done. He didn't do holding hands. He didn't do *Shall I walk you to the station?* because that led to expectation, and that was the very last thing that he wanted.

One morning like this led to another and another, until it became impossible to escape. But her hand felt right in his, her delicate, smooth palm lost in his huge, calloused, weather worn grip. This was a choice, a pleasure, and he couldn't make himself take it back or regret it. He let go briefly as they passed through the ticket barrier, and had to stop himself from wrapping an arm around her waist as they walked through the station.

'I go north here,' she said eventually, when they reached the stairs. 'You want the southbound train, right?'

'Right.' He hesitated, no more willing to walk away from her now than he had been earlier in the morning. He tightened his hand around hers for a moment, the thought of waving her off causing an unexpected and unfamiliar pang. How could he want to keep hold of her and yet fear being tied to her at the same time?

Rachel wouldn't settle for someone drifting in and out of her life on a whim or desire. Whoever she decided to share her life with, she'd want him as predictable as the tide—she'd never stake her luck on waves and weather.

If he wanted more of her, it would mean dates and calendars and plans. And contingency plans and comparing schedules and an itinerary agreed months in advance. The thought of those constrictions, of being tied into someone else's expectations, demands…suddenly it was hard to breathe.

Since the day he'd left school, he hadn't encountered anything, whether it was a woman, a job, or the thought of family, that had made him want to tie himself down, to trap himself into any situation where he didn't have a clear and easy way out. He'd spent too many years in a hell he couldn't escape, trapped in a boarding house with his bullies, and no one to listen to him, to believe him. And all the time, the person he should have been able to go to for help, the person who should have been unquestionably on his side, had been the ringleader.

He'd counted down the days until he could leave school on his calendar, and then had never used one again. He'd sworn that he would never allow himself to be trapped as he was at school. Never find himself in a situation where someone had the power to hurt him, and he couldn't get away. So why was he gripping Rachel's hand as if she were a life buoy to a drowning man?

When he looked over at her fidgeting on her heels, all the reasons he knew he should walk away seemed to fade. He knew the dangers, knew that he couldn't hold on and expect to live untethered. He couldn't *want* a future with her in it, but his body refused to accept it. He turned to her, until they were shoulder to shoulder and toe to toe, just millimetres separating their bodies. He could feel the draw of her skin, pulling him towards her, and his fingertips brushed against her cheekbones of their own accord. As his hands moved to cup her face, to turn her lips up to meet his, a screech of brakes broke into his thoughts. He glanced across and saw the train pull up to the southbound platform.

'I have to go.' The words came from his lips, though he couldn't make himself believe them. But the train doors were closing, and with every piercing electronic beep he felt the walls of the station draw closer, his escape window closing.

With a wrench that he felt deep in his gut, he swept his lips across hers, pulled his hands away and then jogged down the stairs and through the doors of the train before either of them had a chance to say another word.

Rachel stood at the top of the stairs, watching as the train, and Leo, left the station. It was what she had wanted—him gone, and everything back to normal. But watching his train pull out of the station, she recognised the panicky feeling in her chest. He was gone, and she had no way of getting in touch with him. Despite everything, all the reasons she'd given herself that letting him into her life was a bad idea, despite the sense of panic that the thought of that man in her life caused, she wanted more of it. More of him.

Something caught her attention from the corner of her eye, and she started when she realised her train had already pulled up to the platform. She raced down the stairs, but the doors shut and locked with her on the wrong side. Even on his way out of her life Leo was disrupting her schedule. On second thought, she mused, maybe it was a good thing she wasn't in touch with him. He'd caused quite enough chaos in the one night she'd known him. She glanced up at the information screen, wondering how long the next train would be. Typical Sunday service. She'd be stuck on the platform for an hour.

But maybe she could do something useful with the time. A quick search on her phone showed a pharmacy just around the corner that should be open. Walking quickly, she headed to the chemist—a few minutes and several rather personal questions later, she had emergency contraception and a bottle of water. She read quickly through the information on the packet as she waited in a quiet corner of the station. Ninety-five per cent effective. Not ideal—but in the circumstances, the best she was going to get. She swallowed the pill then forced the issue from her mind, and looked through both hers and Will's schedules for the next week.

There were a couple of things she'd need to look into once she got to the office. Meetings that had been added at the last minute, when she was too busy with organising the fundraiser to pull together all the research and paperwork that she knew Will would need in order to prepare.

She worked through a few of her emails, making adjustments to her plan for the week as she went and slotting in new items for her Monday morning meeting with Will.

After the meeting she'd be able to plan out the rest of her week almost to the last minute. And her regular 'contingency' and 'AOB' slots meant that even the unexpected would have to bend to her plans and not the other way around.

She'd come to rely on that order, needed those careful plans to make her feel safe. Because without them what else was there?

It had been the only way for years that she'd been able to quiet her feelings of chaos and panic. The men who'd broken into her childhood home hadn't planned to hurt anyone, the court had heard: they'd thought the house would be empty, had no idea that a fourteen-year-old Rachel was home alone. So when she'd startled one of them as he'd been rifling through the video collection, he'd panicked and lashed out at her. It was a pretty unpleasant knock to her head, but nothing serious. And eventually the nightmares she'd suffered had stopped, but that hadn't stopped her parents' guilt at leaving her at home. They'd fussed and smothered and, on occasion, wailed, insisting that Rachel inform them of her whereabouts at all times. Curfews were to be observed to the minute, unless she wanted to afflict a full-on panic-attack melt-down on her parents.

So she could be flexible if she had to be. 'AOB' and 'unexpected' had their own places in her plans, and that was all last night had been. But perhaps she shouldn't do it again. Those slots should be kept strictly for emergencies. Not for blonds who were hard to forget in the morning.

CHAPTER THREE

RACHEL SCROLLED THROUGH the next two weeks of Will's schedule, looking for a half-hour slot. She knew that she'd pencilled it in somewhere, knowing that this phone call would come at some point. Ah, there it was. The seventeenth. How could she have forgotten that? She put the details into the calendar, added links to the relevant paperwork on the servers, made sure that everyone involved in the project was copied into the invitation and saved everything. She smiled to herself, satisfied with her work. She'd been an executive assistant at Appleby and Associates, a financial services company in the city, for more than five years and prided herself on always knowing what Will needed before he did. If only everything was that easy, she thought, glancing again at the date. It won't change, she told herself. It doesn't matter how many times you look at it. She sat still and shut her eyes for a moment, concentrating on her body, not sure what she hoped, or even wanted to feel. Anything other than the hint of queasiness in her stomach and tiredness in her bones that had started to feel permanent. For the past week, seven full days since her period should have arrived, every day had been a whole load of nothing. And this after a half-hearted, barely-there appearance last month.

How long did she wait? she wondered. A week wasn't that big a deal, was it? She'd been busier than ever since that night—with Will's eye somewhat off the ball now he actually had a personal life. And then he and Maya had started coming up with more and more fundraising ideas to support the charity, and it felt as if she hadn't had a moment to herself since then. It was just the stress. Except she wasn't stressed. She'd just worked the new projects into their routine and it had been fine. She wasn't stressed; she was just late. And it seemed like a little too much of a coincidence that the first time she'd ever been late coincided with her first ever sexual wardrobe malfunction. That ninety-five-per-cent figure had been haunting her thoughts for six days now.

She should probably talk to Leo, she thought. But she hadn't asked for his number that night—could she face calling his father, whose gala invitation he had taken, to try and get hold of him?

At least at the moment she had nothing to tell. But she couldn't leave it that way for long. She needed to know what she was dealing with. If—and it was still a big one—but if she was pregnant, then the sooner she knew, the sooner she could formulate a plan. It was twelve-thirty now, which gave her enough time to nip to the chemist's around the corner, grab a pregnancy test and a sandwich, and be back at her desk well before Will's two o'clock meeting. She locked her computer and grabbed her bag from her drawer, then headed out of the building.

Twenty minutes later she locked the cubicle door and sat on the lid of the toilet, reading through the packet instructions.

Pee, wait, read. And then she'd know.

She peed. She waited. The seconds on her phone stopwatch ticked by slowly, as if the whole universe wanted to put this off as much as she did.

At twelve fifty-nine she took a deep breath, closed her eyes for that last, long second, and then looked at the stick.

Pregnant.

She could barely see as she walked—dazed—out of the bathroom. She stopped at the coffee machine, as was her habit after lunch, and as she was about to select her usual order she stopped herself, blinked a couple of times, and selected decaf instead. She reached for the cup and took a sip, and felt the relief and comfort of her routine in place of the caffeine rush.

'Got the jitters?'

She whipped around at the sound of that familiar voice and felt the blood drain from her face.

'Leo, what a—'

She couldn't finish the word, never mind the sentence. What was he doing here? Why today? Why right now? Why did he have to look even better than she remembered? Sun-bleached, tanned and twinkling with humour.

He was watching her with careful eyes. And he reached out and took the cup from her shaking hands. 'Are you okay?' he asked. 'I didn't mean to startle you. But you looked as if you were in a world of your own.'

'No, it's… It's… Leo?'

He gave her a smug grin, and that helped her regain her senses somewhat. He wouldn't be looking at me like that if he knew what I knew, she thought. If he knew that in a few short months he'd be dad to a bouncing baby boy or…

She felt her blood drain lower still, and had to lean back against the counter in the small kitchen to keep her balance. Leo took a step closer and set the coffee down beside her, before taking her hand and looking closely at her face.

'You're white as a sheet,' he said. 'I'd love to take the credit for you swooning and all, but I'm worried. Are you ill? Should I call someone?'

'No, no,' she said, trying to regain composure amid the rush of her thoughts and the swirl of sensation from his fingertips. 'I'm surprised, that's all. And in need of a coffee.'

'So why are you drinking decaf?'

Great, she thought. Walked straight into that one. 'Because I've already drunk too much today, and know that I'll need a proper one before this afternoon's over.' Hopefully that would allay any more questions. She moved forwards tentatively, moving her weight from the counter to her feet, and almost smiled before she felt herself sway slightly. She really should have eaten that sandwich before taking the test, she thought. Because right now, despite her achingly empty stomach, and rather light head, she was sure she wouldn't be able to keep even a mouthful down.

'That's it, you're not well,' Leo declared, eyeing her carefully. 'You need to take the afternoon off.' She gave a shaky laugh, tensing slightly at this reminder of Leo's cavalier attitude to a nine-to-five.

'I'm fine, honestly. I've just not had lunch yet.'

'Then let me walk you to your desk, at least.'

'Leo, please, just leave it.'

This wasn't fair. She was careful. She was always careful. And then when events had conspired against her, she'd gone straight to the pharmacy and taken that pill. Why did *she* have to be that five per cent?

She had to tell him. He had a right to know. They had a right to make any decisions that needed to be made together. But did she have to do this just now, before she'd even had a chance to get used to it herself?

Leo was standing in front of her, close, too close, and she needed space to think about this. But she couldn't do that, because her calendar was full all afternoon. And all of tomorrow, and the day after that. Every minute of every day was accounted for. And she liked it like that; she just wished that she'd known to schedule in time to adjust to pregnancy, to becoming a mother. At that thought her knees went, and even though it was only for a second she knew that Leo had seen it. He slipped his arm around her.

'Where's your desk?' he asked.

She laid her hand on his at her waist, grateful for the support, but well aware that she couldn't be half carried through her office. She took a deep breath, let it out slowly, and grabbed hold of her self-control. She pushed Leo's arm away gently and stood up, forcing her heels into the floor, and walked across to her desk. Leo followed beside her looking concerned, but not trying to touch her.

'So what are you doing here?' she asked when she was safely back at her desk, looking for any excuse to draw the conversation away from herself. 'You probably should have called first—I try and keep my personal life away from work.'

He gave her an assessing look and then leant back against her desk.

'One, I couldn't have called because you didn't give

me your number. And two, as delightful as it's been running into you, I'm not here to see you.'

'Oh.' Just when she'd thought this day couldn't get any worse. She thanked her forethought in ordering a perfectly fitted ergonomic chair that wouldn't allow her to slump with disappointment even if she'd wanted to. Which, she told herself strictly, she absolutely didn't.

'Seeing you is just a very pleasant bonus,' he added with a hot smile that softened her disappointment, reminded her of that night and reached right to her belly. 'And as you haven't eaten, can I take you for lunch?'

'I've...I've already taken my lunch break. And if you're not here to see me, then surely you have plans.'

'Right,' he said slowly, as if only just remembering. 'I have a meeting with Will.'

'No, you don't.'

He laughed out loud. 'I promise you I do. I called him this morning, told him I was in town unexpectedly. He wanted a chat about something I mentioned at the fundraiser so we said we'd grab a few minutes this afternoon. I'm sorry, should I have checked with you first?'

'No, of course not. Will, however—'

'Is the boss—last time I checked.'

She spun round at the sound of Will's voice.

'And entirely dependent on my secretarial talents. And knows how much I *love* surprises.'

'Well, that's me told.' Will laughed, reaching out to shake Leo's hand. 'Sorry I'm a few minutes late, and, as I'm sure Rachel has already told you, I have another meeting in twenty minutes. But we can talk through a couple of ideas if you like and then follow up over Skype?'

'Perfect,' Leo said. 'And then Rachel and I are going

to head out for a bite to eat. Assuming that's not a problem with the boss.' Her eyes whipped to him, and her jaw dropped open at the sheer cheek of it.

'No problem at all,' Will said, with a raised eyebrow in her direction. 'I assume everything's set for my two o'clock?'

Professional pride forced her not to snap at either one of them. 'Files are on your desk, electronic copies are attached to the calendar appointment. The access codes for the teleconferencing are in there, too, but I can dial in for you if you need me to.' She fought the urge to tell Leo to sod off. Because much as his heavy-handed interference with Will rankled, if she didn't go now, then when was she going to tell him? It needed doing, and she'd be surprised if she was presented with a better opportunity than this.

'No, it's fine. I'm sure I can manage on my own for a couple of hours, despite what you might think. You go, enjoy yourself,' he said with a smirk that told her she was definitely not forgiven for interfering with his love-life.

Rachel looked pointedly at the clock. 'Your next meeting is in fifteen minutes, Will. Do I need to contact everyone and let them know it'll be late starting?'

He laughed, and she cursed the permanent good mood he'd been in since the night of the fundraiser. He had been so much easier to manage before. And she had no one to blame but herself.

'Come on through, Leo,' he said, with a smile in his voice that matched the grin on his face.

Rachel busied herself working through straining inboxes, her own, Will's, as well as one of the generic admin accounts. Then she flicked through her hard-copy inbox, separating out her own items from Will's, checking that the assistants had marked the correct pages for him to sign, adding sticky tabs where they hadn't. Finally she tackled the outbox, dividing up the signed documents into the recipients they needed to be sent to next. The second hand on the clock above Will's door crawled round, until she was certain that physics was working against her.

Except this was what she wanted, wasn't it? To put this off—for ever, if that were an option. She didn't want to see Leo. Didn't want to have lunch with him. She wanted to never see him again, never feel the loss of control that she'd experienced that night. And that had had consequences just as frightening as she'd ever imagined.

A baby. Where was she meant to fit a baby into her life? The Friday-afternoon 'catching up with the trade press' hour? She wasn't exactly experienced at motherhood, but she was pretty sure that a baby needed more than an hour a week. Even if she pulled together every single one of her contingency and emergency hours it was less than a day a week. No, having this baby meant ripping up everything that made her feel safe and secure, and starting over completely. She leant back in her chair, surveying the piles of paperwork covering her desk. What was the point to this? Because it wouldn't matter how neat the piles, how precise and efficient her system. At some point, this would all fall apart.

She had choices. She didn't have to do this, to have this baby. But even as she thought it, the tearing pain in her heart told her that it wasn't the right choice for her.

She was having this baby.

Now she just had to tell Leo.

She glanced up at the clock again—one-fifty-eight—and wondered if Will would remember his call. Should she buzz through and remind him? So that he didn't run late or so that she could get to lunch with Leo? She didn't want to think too hard about the answer to that.

At two minutes past two the door opened and Leo walked out, a grin still on his face. But then what did he have to worry about? Who wouldn't be happy if they could spend all day at the beach or dipping into their trust fund? Well, he might have to think about getting a little responsibility after today.

If he wanted to be involved, that was. She should really have used this time to think about what she was going to tell him, what she was going to ask him. What she wanted from him. She didn't need him to do this. Frightening as it was, she knew it could be done alone. There were plenty of single mothers out there who balanced parenthood with careers. No doubt all that was needed were killer organisation skills, and she had that one wrapped up nicely.

She refused to look up at him, still annoyed with Leo for his heavy-handedness. Instead she kept her eyes firmly on her monitor as she continued with her work. But she hadn't counted on a blond head with tanned skin and insanely blue eyes intruding into her field of vision.

'Ready to go?' Leo asked as he leaned nonchalantly forward and against her cubicle.

'Su-u-u-re,' she replied, buying herself extra milliseconds by dragging out that one syllable for as long as she could without seeming ridiculous. She saved and closed her documents, backed everything up, flicked through her inbox to make sure that nothing urgent had arrived in the past five minutes, and then logged off. She took a sneaky deep breath as she reached under her desk for her handbag and braced herself. She was going to tell him.

That was non-negotiable. What happened after that, how Leo reacted, she had zero control over.

Her stomach churned and she wished that she could blame it on morning sickness, but this was just good old-fashioned nerves.

'Will told me about this great place around the corner,' Leo said as they walked out of the door and onto the street. Great. He was definitely interfering and it was definitely on purpose.

How was she supposed to do this? Did she just blurt it right out over starters? Ply him with wine beforehand to soften the blow? Maybe she should tell him before they even sat down—that would make it less embarrassing if he did a runner straight off.

And she couldn't even have a glass of wine to steady her nerves.

Before she had a chance to realise how far they had walked they were passing through the doors of the restaurant and being shown to their table. Somehow in their fifteen-minute meeting, either he or Will had found a moment to call ahead. Perfect.

Now she sat trying to surreptitiously watch him over the top of her menu. He was in a good mood, and a smile was lighting up his face. She wondered at the reason for it. Was it the meeting with Will that had made him happy, or was it sitting here with her? She wasn't sure she wanted to know the answer. She didn't want to enjoy this, or for him to. Relationships meant chaos; they meant accommodating another person—something she generally didn't do outside a boss-employee relationship. And even then she only worked with people who were really looking for her to manage them, rather than the other way around. So she indulged in friendships and occasional casual dalliances, knowing that she could get out the minute anything approaching chaos started to impinge on her life. Short flings were satisfying and easy to manage. Leo fitted beautifully into that first category, but was failing miserably with the second.

He looked up and caught her eye.

'So, anything you fancy?' he asked with a cheeky grin. She rolled her eyes at the lazy innuendo. He slouched back in his chair and she took a moment to really look at him, in a way she hadn't allowed herself since the hazy early-morning hours after the fundraiser. She was desperate to smooth the chaotic curls that tumbled rebelliously over his forehead, but was aware at the same time he'd lose something of his charm if she were to do it.

Drawing her eyes away from him, she toyed with a breadstick as they waited in silence for the main courses to arrive. This was bad. This was a bad date. *She* was a bad date. How had she spent hours with this man, making love as if it were the most natural thing in the world, and now she was struggling to make small talk?

'Is everything okay?' Leo asked.

So her complete state of panic hadn't gone entirely unnoticed. Well, the worried glances he'd been throwing at her for the past fifteen minutes should have been her first clue. She'd chosen to studiously ignore them, worried that acknowledging them would lead to talking about what was wrong. But still, she was surprised by the serious note to his voice, feeling his concern, the connection between them, all the way to her core. She remembered the way she had felt that morning at the railway station, watching his train pull away from the platform and knowing that however much she felt for him, she'd missed any opportunity to explore it. And then he'd waltzed back into her life on the day when exploring any connection between them seemed more impossible than ever.

She had to tell him, and now was as good a time as any. Actually, no, that wasn't true. Now was the best chance she was going to get. She took a long, fortifying sip of her mineral water, wishing it could have been an ice-cold glass of Sauvignon Blanc, and opened her mouth to speak.

'Leo, there's something—'

'Here we go—two *tagliatelle al ragu*? Would you like parmesan? Black pepper?'

She hid her frustration behind a smile as the waiter bustled and chatted at them good-naturedly. And then watched his retreating back in panic, flailing.

'You were—'

'I'm pregnant.'

She blurted the words out before Leo could finish his sentence, and instantly regretted it as Leo snorted his red wine.

'Pregnant?'

'Keep your voice down,' she hissed, hoping that Will hadn't told anyone else at the office about this place.

'How can you be— I thought you were going to— What does— *Pregnant?*' She waited out his rambling until he could form a complete sentence. 'It's not even been that long,' he said. 'Only a few weeks. Can you even be sure? I mean, how do these things work?'

'It's been seven weeks. I'm late, I took a test, it was positive,' she said, trying to keep her temper, trying to remember that she'd not exactly been level-headed when she first found out, either. She couldn't be disappointed that he'd not taken it well—she'd not expected beaming smiles. But perhaps some tiny part of her had hoped for something…more. More than this obvious horror.

'Did you take the morning-after pill?'

'Does it matter? I'm pregnant.'

He leaned back in his chair and she tried to remind herself that actually, yes, it wasn't such an unreasonable question. After the condom fail, the contraceptive ball had been entirely in her court—there was nothing he could have done.

She softened her voice. 'Yes. I took it that morning, about half an hour after your train left. I followed the instructions and did everything right. But it's not a hundred per cent effective.' She gave him a minute to absorb this, but then found she didn't have anything else to say. She just waited for him to process.

'Are you okay?' he asked eventually, and she cracked a tiny smile, touched at the softness in his voice. She remembered it from that night.

'I'm still trying to take it in,' she said honestly.

'When did you find out?'

She checked her watch. 'A couple of hours ago. Right before—'

'Right before I surprised you at the coffee machine. Jeez, no wonder you were a mess.'

'A mess?'

'You know, all…' He waved a hand in the air, and she told herself it was probably better to be charitable and not to try and translate it.

'Have you thought about…?' From the careful way he spoke the words, and wouldn't look up to meet her eye, she knew what he was asking.

'I'm keeping it.'

As she said the words, she felt their truth. Felt that she

could never give a different answer to that question. Parallel shivers of excitement and fear raced up her spine.

'You're keeping it,' he repeated, his intonation just hinting at a question. 'Isn't this something I should expect to have a say in?' he asked.

Rachel dropped her head into her hands and rubbed at her hair, unable to bear the intensity of his stare. 'I'm not sure it's the sort of thing you can compromise on. It's sort of an either-or situation.'

'Still,' Leo said, his expression bordering on haggard when she peeked up through her fingers. 'When did you decide this, if you only just found out? You can't have had time to think it through.'

'I haven't. I don't need to. I know some people would choose something different, and I totally respect the right to make that choice. But it's not what I want.' She couldn't explain the fiercely protective instinct that told her she had to keep this baby, but that didn't mean she didn't recognise it. It had been there, lurking, since the minute she'd read the word 'Pregnant' on the test. It was the reason she'd had decaf coffee, and the reason she'd told Leo now, without needing time to think through their options.

'Did you plan this?' Leo's question snapped her out of her thoughts in an instant, and cut straight to her heart. She gaped at him, affronted.

'Why in God's name would you think I *planned* this?' He sat back against his chair again, letting it take his weight as if he were no longer able.

'You plan everything else.' His expression was hard and guarded—she flinched from the anger and the hurt she could see simmering below the surface. She wouldn't stand for this. This was not her fault. They had both played their part in getting them to this point, and they would both have to deal with the consequences. She opened her mouth to tell him that, but he spoke first. 'What was it—a big birthday on the horizon got your biological clock ticking? Did you reach the entry in your calendar that read "Start a family" and just pick up the next willing donor?'

She dropped her fork in shock, her mouth open as she tried—and failed—to put words to her hurt.

'Do you really think I'm capable of that?' Rachel asked, her voice low and throaty as she fought down tears, disbelieving that he could be capable of such cruelty. Of course she knew that she didn't know him *well*, but she'd thought after that night she had a pretty good measure of him. Nowhere had she seen the capacity for such heartlessness. 'Because I'm cutting you a hell of a lot of slack here by not throwing something.'

'No. I don't know. God.' He ran his fingers through his hair. 'I honestly don't know what to think. I turn up at your office hoping for a smile and a flirt and maybe— if I played my cards right—a repeat performance of that night. And you tell me that I'm going to be a father, whether it's what I want or not. I tell you, I've thought about you since that night, thought about you a lot, actually, but I never imagined...*this*.'

Rachel let out a long sigh. 'How could you? I can barely imagine it now, barely believe that it's true.' She took another long sip of her water and picked disconsolately at her congealing pasta. 'What are we going to do?'

She gave a little shudder at the sudden realisation she had no answer to that question. The next few months, years, decades of her life—which this morning had a predictable, reliable pattern—suddenly blurred, as she saw her plans for the future evaporating. To be replaced with…what? She had no idea what the next few days looked like now, never mind anything beyond that. A fist of fear gripped her lungs, and she struggled to draw in a breath. When she finally managed to drag in a couple of gasps of oxygen, she found that they were stuck there. She tried to force them out, but the effort tightened her chest further. One hand flew to her shirt, pulling at the collar as if it would somehow help the air move.

Her movement must have startled Leo, because his gaze flew from where it had been locked on the table-cloth to her face, and she saw her alarm reflected there. 'Rachel?' he asked urgently. 'What's wrong?' His hand reached for hers across the table.

'Can't…breathe…' she managed to gasp.

'Did you swallow something?'

She shook her head and saw realisation dawn in his eyes. He gripped her hand harder and pulled her from her seat, throwing some notes on the table and leading her quickly to the door. Once outside, he pulled her through the gates of a small park and down beside him onto a bench. He placed his hand firmly on her face, his palm cupping her cheek.

'Look at me,' he ordered her, his voice steady and un-derstanding. 'Rachel?' Her darting gaze locked onto him.

'You can breathe just fine,' he told her, his eyes fixed on hers, his voice calm but firm. 'I'm going to count and you're going to breathe out. Then you're going to breathe in.' She nodded, willing herself to believe him, listen-ing to his voice rather than the racing of her mind as he counted 'one…two…three…' With her lungs so full she thought they might burst, she looked at his eyes, fo-cused on his words, the simplicity and predictability of the numbers, and let her chest relax, let go of the solid tightness of her shoulders and the terror in her mind. As she gradually felt her body return to normal, she slumped back on the bench, and Leo did the same.

'Thanks,' she managed eventually.

'Okay,' Leo said. 'I think one thing we have to agree on right now is that neither of us is particularly able to make important decisions at the moment.'

'I—'

'Just had a panic attack. Forgive me if I take that to mean we need a little time.' She nodded slowly, unable to dispute his words. This might be easier if she were doing it alone, she thought. If she could make a plan exactly as she wanted, and then stick to it.

She knew without question that life couldn't happen that way with Leo. He would throw her plans off course from the first possible moment, and insist on chaos as often as possible after that. Just the thought of it made her chest feel tight again.

'Do you have to go back to the office or can I see you home?' Not words to help her to breathe normally.

'I have to get back,' she said, thinking of her and Will's schedule for the afternoon. She couldn't just not turn up.

'We need to talk, properly,' Leo said, and reached for her hand—a spark of something half remembered flickered between their skin. Her first instinct was to snatch her hand back—his touch was too dangerous—but his fingers clamped around hers before she could. His other hand tucked her hair behind her ear, and smudged away a tear that was trickling over her cheek. He turned her to look at him, and she relaxed, thinking how easy it would be to lean forward, to brush her lips against his, to lose herself for a moment. Leo's breathing quickened, and she knew he'd thought it, too. But, she told herself, the last thing this situation needed was more complications.

She dropped her gaze and pulled back slightly.

'Perhaps we should talk in a few days, when we've had time to think…' Her voice tailed off as she tried to re-shape her view of the world to imagine how that conversation would go. 'Are you coming up to London again?'

'No,' Leo said, with a small shake of his head. 'Not for a while. But you could come down to my place in Dorset, get away for a few days.'

Rachel opened her mouth to protest, but he held up a hand to stop her. 'Just hear me out. There's space, fresh air and distance from your office. I'm not promising sea air has all the answers, but maybe a change of perspective…?'

'I'm not sure that's a good idea.'

'And I'm not sure what choice we have. I can't see that getting to know each other is optional, now. I know where you live—where you work. I've even seen you in action. Don't you think it's fair that you see a little of my life, too?'

She nodded. 'Perhaps I could come for the day.'

'Honestly, by the time you've travelled, you'll want to stay longer,' Leo said. 'Plan to come at the weekend. Stay Saturday night. I have a guest room,' he added, no doubt noticing the refusal that was about to leave her lips.

She tried hard to think of some way to skewer this logic, some way to get out of this scenario that had her holed up with a man she found dangerously irresistible—the man who had got her pregnant. But whichever way she looked at it, she could see that he was right.

'Okay,' she said eventually. 'I'll come.'

CHAPTER FOUR

LEO COLLAPSED ONTO the sand, chest heaving and limbs comfortingly heavy.

A baby. He still couldn't quite connect that concept with his life. How had that even…? Okay, so it wasn't as if he needed a diagram, and it wasn't as if he didn't believe Rachel when she said she'd taken the morning-after pill. They were just that tiny fraction of a per cent that the maths for a double contraceptive fail worked out as. Maybe at the end of this weekend—he glanced at the sun; Rachel would be here in a few hours—it would feel more real.

He rubbed the heel of his hand against his forehead as he tried to think, the rhythmic crash of the waves on the sand soothing in its familiarity. Was *real*—knowing that there was absolutely, definitely no way of getting out of this—going to feel better? How could it? He'd all but walked away from his family. Had been happy managing on his own. But what could he do now? He'd enjoyed every minute of what had got them here, and he would take responsibility for what they'd done.

His head should be spinning. These past few days he should have wanted to scream, or run, or, God, *faint* or something. But instead, he felt nothing. A blank, empty space filled his brain, keeping feelings at bay.

But as he sat, thinking, he noticed a warm yellow glow creeping around the edges of that numb void. A hint of some emotion that was waiting, just out of reach, but heading closer.

He flopped back onto the sand, covering his eyes from the intense glare of the sun with his arm. Part of him wanted to go. To turn around and walk away and just imagine he'd never laid eyes on Rachel. Pretend that one night, one night that had tied him into a lifetime of commitment, had never happened. But then a flash of memory assailed him—a gentle, lazy smile on Rachel's lips in the dim early-morning light. Too tired for games, too sated for self-protection, he'd seen for the first time the real, unguarded woman, with no barriers, no motives, no second-guessing. He couldn't make himself regret that moment, that instant connection.

And there went the 'numb' phase, as the memory of his desire and passion that night was chased from his body by nausea-inducing fear. He let out a long, unsteady breath. God, he wished he'd appreciated 'dazed' more.

For a moment the thought of that commitment, the inescapable permanency of it, threatened to paralyse him, bringing back every nightmare and the sleepless nights between. The last time Leo Fairfax had been this frightened of the future.

But he was going to be a father. He and Rachel—that fascinating, maddening, excessively disciplined woman he'd been unable to shake from his mind for *weeks* now, had somehow, against all her best-laid plans, and his lack of them, created a new human life. The magnitude of the realisation stole his breath for a few long moments as he looked up and out across the water, trying to imagine who he was, this whole new person that they had created. But the vision remained hazy, too unformed to be anything more than broad strokes of a life.

Rachel stepped out of the taxi—she'd insisted to Leo that she could, and would, get to his place under her own steam—and gasped in horror. He'd warned her on the phone that he was doing some renovations, but this was…it was ramshackle. The ground all around was either churned up or covered in bags of building materials, and the windows were still covered by plastic sheeting. Most concerning of all, the roof seemed to consist of a couple of blue tarpaulins, flapping gently in the breeze. She glanced up further, relieved to see that the sky was still a clear, sunny blue, without a cloud in sight.

Thank goodness she had a list of practically every hotel in Dorset, sorted by distance from the coastal village Leo's postcode had directed her to. And a list of taxi companies, too. And train times back to London. As she'd saved them all on her tablet, just in case she found herself out of network coverage, she'd hoped that she wouldn't actually need them. She wanted to use her time here to get to know Leo better—it was essential, in the circumstances. And staying in a hotel the whole weekend would mean less time together. But she wasn't sure that a building site was the best place to get to know each other, either.

She'd give it a chance, she told herself, but double-checked that she had signal on her mobile, just in case. Tentatively, she picked her way along the path from the road, and as it passed around the corner of the cottage she stopped and dropped her bag. Okay, so *this* she could stay for. The cottage was perched on top of a rocky cliff, with views all around the bay, from majestic, prehistoric coastline at one end to brightly coloured beach huts and umbrellas at the other. The clumpy grass she'd been cursing for catching on her heels gave way to sand and rocks, and a path meandered down to the narrow sandy beach.

She breathed in a couple of good lungfuls of sea air, but her brief moment of tranquillity was interrupted by a mechanical scream from inside the house. The noise made her jump, but—curious—she ventured towards the door, certain that a whole crew of builders must be in there to make such a racket. A troop of roofers, she hoped, casting another glance at the tarp.

'Hello?' she shouted, once she'd grappled with her bag and made it to the door.

But when she caught sight of Leo, she fell silent, leaning against the door frame to enjoy the view. He wore jeans—faded and worn, moulded to his body in a way that told her they were well loved and often worn. His T-shirt was white, damp down the back and clinging in all the right ways. The powerful swimmer's muscles of his shoulders and back were outlined by the soft cling of the jersey, and rippled as he handled planks of wood and an electric saw with ease.

All day her thoughts had flip-flopped between terror and excitement at the thought of seeing Leo again. They had drifted his way often in the weeks since she'd seen him, reliving that night over and over again. But it wasn't just the sex that had stuck in her mind. It was the way he'd smiled at her on the dance floor as he'd figured her out, and found which buttons to press to help her change her mind. The sparkle in his eyes as he'd watched her figure him out, and find a way to take him home.

It was the way she'd let go as she'd moved in his arms, following his lead, taking it back, following her body and his, improvising. Exploring every possibility thrown up by this totally unplanned—she could admit it to herself, if not to him—encounter. But the things she'd found with him that night were exactly the reason she was nervous now. How would she keep control over the rest of her life when she'd failed so spectacularly to keep control even over her own body?

Well, she told herself, the first defence was easy—no repeat performances. She had to keep her head. Which meant she had to put the brakes on this little ogling session and somehow get his attention. Not easy when he was wearing ear protectors and making an unholy racket.

It didn't seem wise to sneak up on a man when he was communing with the power-tool gods. But how long was she meant to stand there? How long could she watch him like this before her resolve began to falter? She was about to take a step forward when her gaze dropped from where it had been fixed on Leo, and her brain caught up with what her eyes were hinting was wrong with the picture. The floor—where was it? She hadn't noticed it immediately because Leo was standing on a large piece of board, but between the door and him—nothing. Well, not quite nothing. A few joists, the odd floorboard balanced across them. Otherwise, just bare earth a few inches down.

She snatched her foot back and switched to plan B. While she waited for him to finish what he was doing with the saw, she pulled her phone out of her pocket and found his number. As soon as the whine of the tool stopped, she hit Dial, hoping that he had his phone on him, and set to vibrate. It gave her the perfect excuse to look at his bottom at least—trying to see if it had started buzzing, of course.

As she watched, Leo straightened and stretched his muscles, and then reached into his back pocket. Was it her imagination, or did his shoulders tense when he lifted the phone and saw the display? Regardless, hers tensed, too—sympathy stress. When Leo wrenched off the ear protectors, she cleared her throat and he finally turned to look at her.

She tried to read his expression—in business, a degree of mind-reading came in handy. And while she hadn't quite cracked full-on ESP yet, she'd got pretty good at reading people. So she knew that the smile was genuine—but what he was feeling was more complex than his sunny grin implied. His mouth said he was happy to see her. The line of his shoulders and slight stiffness in his arms told her he was wary. Of her? Of the baby? Was there a difference any more? They came as a package deal—literally—for the next seven or so months.

But he was still smiling at her as he walked across the room—balancing on the joists like a gymnast on a beam.

'Hi,' he said as he got to the door. 'I wasn't expecting you yet. Sorry, I thought I'd be done for the day before you got here.' She glanced at her watch. According to her travel schedule, which she'd sent over to him yesterday, she was right on time. But perhaps it was a little early in the trip to bring that up. She remembered the way he had stiffened when he'd seen she was calling and almost flinched herself. It was hardly flattering, knowing she was the cause of such trepidation. And she had no desire to kick off with anything other than small talk just yet. She'd put in a lot of thought, time and energy over the past few days, trying to come up with a plan that would suit both of them, all three of them, for the foreseeable future. There were a few scenarios for them to choose from, but she was satisfied that between the notes on her tablet and the scenario-planning charts she'd printed and bound she'd come up with something that they could work with. All she had to do now was convince Leo of that fact, and in doing so she was going to have to tread lightly.

'Oh, it's fine,' she said, trying to be breezy about the lack of flooring. 'So…new boards?'

'It's kind of a work in progress,' Leo said, glancing about him, apparently unconcerned. 'We found some rot and had to rip the old ones out. Then I found these incredible boards at a rec yard.'

She smiled and nodded, feeling the tension in her shoulders travel down her arms until her fingers were fighting against tight fists.

'But isn't it a little…inconvenient—not having a floor?'

'It's only temporary.' He shrugged. 'And it's only one room—the rest of the house is fine. Are you coming in?'

Fine? From what she'd seen from the outside, this floor was the least of her worries. But she forced herself to take a deep breath, and keep her smile stuck on a little longer.

'Sure.' She grabbed the handle of her suitcase and looked at the floor in anticipation, mapping out the shortest and quickest route.

'Leave your case—I'll grab it. Isn't there a "no heavy lifting" clause in this pregnancy thing?'

Her eyes flicked to his face, trying to read his expression. It was the first time either of them had mentioned the baby, and his voice hadn't exactly sounded sure, almost as if he were testing the words, not quite believing them. She didn't answer. She couldn't, yet. Couldn't face up to all the uncertainties that lay ahead of them.

She set a foot on the joist by the door. A couple of steps in she started to wish she'd kicked off her shoes as she wobbled a little on her stiletto heel. But just as she started to worry that she might not get that wobble back under control, Leo's hand grabbed hers and held her steady. A shiver spread through her body at the feel of his hand, and she squeezed it tight, suddenly feeling less steady on her feet, not more. He swung the door open in front of them and she jumped across the last gap.

As she landed, she wobbled again, and this time Leo's arm caught her around the waist. She'd put out a hand to break the fall she'd been sure was inevitable, but instead of hitting the floor it hit solid, warm muscle. She should have snatched it back, of course. Should definitely not have stretched her fingers and pressed her palm a little tighter against him, remembering the night she had spent held against that chest, the salty taste as she'd kissed it, how she'd pressed her palms to it as she'd…

Leo's arm tightened around her and she wondered if he was remembering, too. She looked up and found his gaze intent on her, his eyes serious and the smile gone. Her lips parted, and her body begged her to stretch up, to press her lips against his, to lose herself in his body. But her brain screamed warnings thick and fast. Caught in the middle, she wavered, leaning back slightly against Leo's arm as she met his gaze. Over his shoulder, she caught a glance of the room they had just left—the chaos, the power tools, the almost complete lack of *floor*—and she took a deliberate step backwards. Her life was chaotic enough. One night with Leo had shaken up everything she thought she knew about the future and dumped it back around her. The last thing she needed at the moment was for that to happen again.

Leo gave her a long look, his expression neither regretful nor pleased, but hovering somewhere around wary. After a beat, he turned from her and strode back across the joists to rescue her case from outside. Rachel dragged her eyes from him and, determined to distract herself, took a moment to look around the room she'd landed in so inelegantly. The contrast between the front room and this kitchen couldn't be greater. From chaos, she'd stepped into a lifestyle magazine. Sunlight spilled in through wide windows with views out towards the bay, reflecting off the polished wooden worktops. A huge table, made of boards similar to the ones Leo was laying in the next room, occupied one half of the kitchen and an enormous range cooker occupied an inglenook fireplace. Glass doors opened out onto a small garden and a staircase wound up the wall in the corner of the room. It was beautiful, and when she looked at Leo it was with admiration for more than his well-developed lats.

He arrived back at the door to the kitchen with her case slung effortlessly over his shoulder. Okay, she was still admiring the lats, she realised, that perfect diagonal of muscle between underarm and waist—and reminded herself that all her future plans for her life came with a big fat *No Repeat Performance* clause. If she wanted to stay on track, she had to get her ogle under control.

'Luckily for you, the kitchen and bathrooms were finished first,' he said with a grin.

'This is beautiful.' She was still slightly taken aback by the contrast of this room with the building sites she'd seen so far, but determined to stay focused. 'Did you do all the work yourself?'

He nodded. 'Everything I legally can—an electrician did a couple of bits, but most of it was me.'

'You've done a great job.'

'Thanks.' He smiled and nodded, without false modesty or undue pride. 'Can I get you anything before I go and clean myself up? Coffee? Tea?' He glanced down at his sawdust-caked jeans and T-shirt as he spoke.

She brushed off his offer, instead getting him to point her towards coffee and mugs. When he'd disappeared up the stairs, Rachel turned to the cupboard and started on the coffee, almost squealing with delight when the tin next to the kettle turned out to contain cake and biscuits. Her eyes threatened to fill with tears—stupid hormones. But she guessed he wasn't the type to keep cake in the cupboard, and that meant it was only there for her sake. Butterflies were still causing havoc in her tummy, and she reluctantly admitted to herself that her nerves were more about the man, today, than the baby.

Once the initial gigantic I-don't-know-what-the-hell-is-going-to-happen-next panic had receded slightly, the day after she'd taken the pregnancy test, she'd started to think more and more about the baby growing inside her. About bringing a new life into the world, and excitement had grown and grown. Her thoughts about Leo? Still bound up with an almighty warning sign. And seeing his home, the centre of his disorder, hadn't helped. She rubbed her belly, thinking soothing thoughts, not wanting to inflict her worries on her baby. It seemed important already that she didn't allow her concerns to become his, or hers. Not as her parents had with her.

She turned as she heard Leo's footsteps on the stairs,

and he appeared around the curve of the staircase in clean jeans and a black T-shirt, his hair a little damp.

'Sorry to abandon you like that. I looked in the mirror and thought I'd gone prematurely grey so I jumped in the shower to get rid of the dust.'

She smiled as she transferred coffee pot, mugs and cake to the table. 'And here was me thinking the shock had sent you all Marie Antoinette.'

He raised an eyebrow, questioning.

'Hair went white overnight? Never mind, obscure reference. Coffee and cake?'

'Sounds good,' Leo said, pulling out a chair and dropping into it. She watched his hands as he hacked a couple of wedges of cake, impressed and wondering whether she now had a pregnancy get-out clause when it came to denying her sweet tooth. She pulled up the chair beside him and poured the coffee, sending him sideways glances, wondering if he was finding this sudden domesticity as strange as she was. Bizarre, she thought. That she could find something so ordinary as coffee and cake new and nerve-racking when they were already somehow a family.

Rachel sipped the coffee and flinched when it scalded her lips. But it was worth it for the familiar caffeine buzz. The smell, even the taste, made her feel more comfortable. More herself. And the act of sitting at a great big table with a hot cup of coffee was all she needed to get her brain in gear, and have her reaching for her tablet. She grabbed her handbag, which she'd left propped by the chair, and pulled out all the plans she'd made since she'd first read *Pregnant* on that test. They had a lot to discuss, and it made sense to start work, she thought. She pulled herself up slightly on the word *work*; technically this was personal. But her—their—new life was going to take so much organising that it might as well be work. It was easier to think of it that way. To slot Leo and their child and all the changes they represented into her life as she would any other project. Because what was the alternative—chucking out everything she thought she knew and starting again?

But when she'd spread out her tablet and binders and looked up, she found Leo staring at her, a grimace on his face. She faltered slightly at the hard lines of his brows. The white knuckles of his fists.

'What are they?' The words were forced through his teeth, none too friendly. She glanced down—a little confused about how this had caused so much hostility. It wasn't as if he even knew what her plans contained. He'd gone white even at the thought of them.

'It's a tablet.' She spoke slowly, treading carefully in light of his sudden shift in mood. Not wanting to upset things further. 'And some charts. I had a few ideas about how we're going to make this work. I thought you might want to talk them through.'

'Oh, you did?' He took a long sip of his coffee—diversionary tactic, she guessed. 'And here was me thinking you were about to present me with a finished plan.' She dropped her eyes and felt her cheeks warm—it had never occurred to her to wait until she'd spoken to him before drawing up their options. But now they were laid out in front of her, and Leo was so obviously fighting to keep his annoyance under control, she could see that he was right.

'Did you just expect me to go along with everything you'd decided?'

Well, it wasn't as if he'd made any suggestions—it had been all down to her.

But when could he have contributed? She'd not seen him since they'd found out the news; she hadn't given him a chance. 'I'm sorry. I should have spoken to you first.' Her plans were good, though, thorough. They covered myriad scenarios with timetables, budgets and schedules. And of course Leo had a say. But *she* was the one carrying the baby. *She* was the one who would have to take time off for the birth. *She* was the one who would have to decide whether, and how, she could return to work.

She was the one who would have to put what little she recognised of her life back together after the baby was born.

And it wasn't as if she hadn't considered what Leo wanted. She'd given him plenty of options, with his involvement ranging from full-time parenting to 'financial contribution only'. Even—though nothing she'd seen of Leo so far told her that she'd need it—a 'no involvement' plan.

'I thought we were going to have a coffee.' Leo's tone was still harsh, and he gripped his mug as if struggling to keep his temper.

'Can't we drink and talk?'

'Sure, we can drink and talk. But that's not what you're suggesting. You want to drink and *work*.'

He was beyond tense now, and heading directly for angry. His body language was defensive, closed, and she could see from the lines of fear on his face that she'd stumbled into deeper waters than she'd thought. He wasn't just angry at her for doing this without him. Her temper had lit in response to his, but she forced it down, trying to keep neutral. Trying to understand what had him so wary. If she blew up, too, they'd never talk this through.

'We don't have to do this all today. But I'd like to make a start, if we can. We've got quite a lot to get through—'

'Get through?' He slammed his mug onto the table, and hot coffee spilled onto the wood, creeping towards her papers. She pulled them back, eyeing Leo, suddenly realising she'd completely underestimated how badly she'd read him, how much distance there was between them. How impossible it was going to be to create a family out of this mess. 'I'm not a project, Rachel. I'm not a client or a boss or someone you're giving a presentation to. This isn't going to be solved over a working lunch and a follow-up email.'

'But—'

'No!'

Rachel set her cup down slowly, willing herself to remain calm in the face of his raw emotion, wishing she could understand what was making him react this way. She hadn't expected this to be *easy*, but she hadn't expected such vehement opposition, either. She shut her eyes and counted to ten, hoping that when she opened them again Leo would've lost the frightened, cornered, *angry* look that twisted his features—usually so effortlessly sexy—into something ugly.

She looked up. He had calmed a little, the redness draining from his face, but there were still deep creases between his brows, and his mouth was set in a harsh line.

'I'm sorry, but I cannot have your plan dictated to me and just go along with it.' The clipped consonants and snappy vowels gave away the effort that near-civility was costing him. 'I know you need this. I know you want everything decided, booked, settled. But it's not just you

now. Can't you see that?' He could see it, and he didn't
know how to get away from it. 'If we decide something,
we have to do it *together*. I will not let you plan and
schedule and itemise my life just because I happened to
get you pregnant. That doesn't give you the right to come
in here and tell me how it's going to be.'

'I've given you choices…options.' Finally she couldn't
keep the anger from her own voice. With the venom contained in his, it didn't seem optional—it was a necessity.
A way to fend off his biting accusations.

'You don't get to *give* me anything. That's not how
together works.'

'What's made you so scared?' she asked. 'Tell me
why my having a plan freaks you out. Because as far as
I can see, with us barely knowing each other, and living
hours apart, and having an actual *baby* together, some
idea of how we're going to cope seems like a good idea.
So why is it you blanch, pretty much start shaking and
bite my head off?'

He scraped his chair backwards, leaving a good couple
of feet between him and the table, the space acting like
a force field around him. 'I can't do it like this, Rachel. I
won't. I can't sit here, backed into a corner with no way
out of what you've decided for us. I won't be trapped.'

And with that he headed straight out of the door, leaving her sitting at the kitchen table wondering what the
hell had just happened. Her heart was hammering in her
chest, tears pricked at her eyes, and her fingers shook
slightly when she reached for a cloth to mop up the spilled
coffee.

How had they got here? They'd gone from almost kissing when she'd arrived to the point where they couldn't
be in the same room together.

And now she was scared—because nothing he had said or done made her believe that he was in any way glad about the fact they were having a baby. In the days since she'd found out she was expecting, she'd started to look forward to being a parent. Feel joy at the prospect of meeting the new life they had created. Of course there was an enormous dose of full-body-paralysis fear, not least when she tried to think about how she could possibly spend the next eighteen—or eighty—years trying to maintain some sort of contact with Leo.

The thought of having to live with the disorder and randomness that Leo so clearly needed threatened to bring on another panic attack. But when he had headed for the door just now, her stomach had dropped and her heart had felt as if it had stopped. She had been filled with an overwhelming dread that he might not come back. That he was leaving her to have this baby alone. She knew that she could do it if she had to. But in the second that she thought that Leo might be walking away, she wanted him by her side. Chaos and all. They had made this new life together, and she wanted to find a way for them to be a family.

She cleared away a few pieces from the table—for no reason other than that she didn't want to be just sitting waiting for him when he got back. So when she heard his footsteps at the door, she had her back to him, running something under the tap and holding her breath.

'I'm sorry,' he said eventually, in a shaky voice redolent of raw emotion.

She stared into the sink a little longer, gathering her thoughts, and fighting down the swell of tears that seemed to be climbing her throat. She couldn't account for them, couldn't reason why the croak of his voice made hers swell with sympathy.

'I'm sorry, too.' She turned off the tap and slumped back against the sink, relief washing through her. 'I shouldn't have made those plans without you.'

'And I shouldn't have snapped at you like that. I'm genuinely sorry. But there are some things we need to talk about if we're going to make this work. I know you like to have everything all worked out, but I can't do that.'

'So what am I meant to do? Just wait and see if you turn up at my office again?' She tried to laugh, to pretend she could live like that, but it sounded hollow even to her.

'Would that be so bad? I'd make sure I was there when you—when the baby—needed me. Does everything need to be planned months in advance?'

Her spine straightened again; Leo's presence was seemingly anathema to serenity. 'And is that what I should tell my doctor? Oh, I'll definitely come along at some point. An appointment? No. I'll just arrive when I'm ready.'

'And what about the baby—is he allowed to arrive when he's ready, or are you going to hold him to whatever due date the doctors pull out of the air? I hope for his sake he isn't late.'

She was about to snap back, when her train of thought faltered and her voice failed. 'Wait, he?' she asked, with the beginnings of a smile tweaking her lips. 'Who says it's a boy?'

His face softened, and for the first time she saw the hard expression around his eyes ease, and his usual humorous glint return. She found she was relieved to see it, had been worried for a few moments that she and the baby had caused its disappearance to become permanent.

It had been his determination to make her laugh that had drawn them together that first night, and she was worried that without that humour between them the very foundations they were working on were unsteady.

'I don't know. In my head, when I think about how things will be, I just always see a boy.'

'You've thought about it?'

His eyes bugged.

'Have I thought about it? What else am I meant to think about? Have you thought about anything else?'

'No,' she admitted. 'So what do you?'

He raised an eyebrow by way of a question. 'What do I...?'

'What do you think, when you think about it?'

He crossed to the table and dropped into a seat, reaching for his abandoned cup of coffee. A smile was creeping across her face at the sight of the hint of a grin on his. He thought about their baby. The knowledge glowed inside her. 'I don't know. Just flashes of things, I suppose.'

'Good things?'

'Mostly.' They shared a long look, mutual happiness turning both their mouths up like a mirror. But they couldn't leave it there. If they wanted this to work, they had to dig deeper than that. Learn to trust one another.

'And the bad?' she asked.

'This.' He motioned towards her colour-coded papers. 'This is pretty much every bad thing I've imagined since Wednesday afternoon. I want you to know, Rachel, that I'm here for you and for the baby. But I will not do this entirely on your terms. We're *both* going to have to compromise.'

'And the first thing that's got to go is any attempt at a plan?' She couldn't help her defensiveness—he was threatening the only thing that was keeping her in any way connected to sanity.

'This plan? Yes. We didn't discuss a single thing before you made it. Of course it has to go.'

She felt a wave of nausea as she realised what he was saying. Every plan she had made in the past few days. All the words and the numbers and the tidy tick-boxes that had soothed her mind—were going to be thrown out. Already panic was making the edges of her thoughts fuzzy, and that wave of nausea was starting to feel more like a tsunami. With a shock, she realised it was more than just nausea. She must have looked pretty green, because as her hand flew to her mouth Leo was already by her side, grabbing her free hand and pulling her to the stairs.

CHAPTER FIVE

LEO LEANED AGAINST the landing wall, trying not to hear the noises emanating from the bathroom, and wondering whether he was relieved or annoyed that Rachel had so easily brushed away his offer of help and slammed the bathroom door shut with him on the outside. Not that it sounded a particularly appealing place to be right now, but the knowledge that she was perfectly happy doing this alone—was happier doing it alone—made his chest uncomfortable. Because at the moment, it felt as if any involvement in his child's life depended entirely on this woman's opinion of him, and was entirely on her terms. He'd been terrified, was still terrified, when she'd told him that she was pregnant; but the thought of his child out there in the world not even knowing him was more frightening still.

He'd have to apologise for snapping at her like that. Losing his cool definitely didn't help him get what he needed—but he had to get her to see his point, and to agree with it. Of course there were parts of this situation that he couldn't avoid planning in advance—he was perfectly prepared to understand that a doctor's appointment had to be made for a particular time. And though the thought of those appointments stretching out for years in the future didn't do brilliant things to him, it didn't fill him with the same queasy dread he'd felt when he'd glimpsed the plan she'd drawn up. Just the headings told him he was in trouble. Timing. Finance. Schooling. *Schooling?* He didn't even know when the baby was due, and they were talking schooling already? Did she even know yet when it was due? Had she been to the doctor? Probably things he would know already if he hadn't walked out on her. The bathroom had gone quiet, and he leaned back against the door.

'Rachel?' he shouted through the wood. 'All okay in there?'

'Fine,' she replied and he could hear tears in her voice. Was that the sickness or something else?

'Can I get you anything?'

'No, I'm fine. I just need to catch my breath.'

He heard her lean back against the door, and he followed her down, until the old oak was supporting them both.

'Then can I ask you a question?'

He took the mumble he could hear as a yes.

'Tell me about the plans. Why do you need them? Help me understand.'

He held his breath, hoping that she would trust him. See that he was reaching out to her, and wanting her to reach back. He needed to understand her. To try and find out how they were going to manage to get along, now that they were tied together.

'I don't need them. I just like to have an idea of what's going on. What's wrong with that?'

'There'd be nothing wrong with that. But that's not how you felt downstairs just now, was it?'

He listened through the door, wishing he could see her

face, wishing he could at least see her expression. Just as he was giving up hope that she would ever speak…

'It makes me feel safe.'

He was almost tempted to laugh at that, the quirk of fate that had brought him together with a woman who could only feel safe if he felt bone-chillingly terrified. Instead he heard the trepidation in her voice, the hint of tears. He wanted to break down the door, wrap his arms around her and tell her that they would be okay. Or, failing that, tease and kiss her until the tension left her shoulders, until her limbs were heavy and languid, wrapped around him. Instead, he asked another question, hoping that the pain now would be worth it eventually.

'Why?'

He pressed his head back against the solid wood of the door, wondering if she could feel how close he was. Whether she wanted him closer, the way he wanted her.

The memories of the night they had spent together had often played on his mind in the weeks after. Flashbacks, scents, snatches of songs all reminded him of the hours they'd spent wrapped around each other. And he couldn't deny that these memories had something to do with why he'd been so keen to meet with Will and discuss the idea he'd had—to create a sculpture for the Julia House charity. They could keep it in the grounds, or auction it for money. Whatever they thought would benefit their patients most. He'd floated a couple of ideas to Will the night of the fundraiser—always with half an eye for whether Will's assistant would take an interest in the conversation.

Then after he'd left Rachel at the station, the momentary relief he'd felt as his train had pulled away had faded quickly, leaving him dissatisfied, feeling as if he'd missed an opportunity. Maybe he'd been too hasty running from her then, he'd thought as he'd made the phone call to Will. Maybe they could have had a few more nights like the previous one before they inevitably went their separate ways. As he'd taken the train up to London, he'd let himself imagine how she'd react to seeing him again. And then a little longer thinking of everything they could get up to if she was of the same mind.

The shock of a baby in the works had seemingly done nothing to quell his fierce imagination.

He jumped up at the turning of the lock and was brushing off his jeans when the door opened and Rachel appeared, looking a little pale. 'Morning sickness, I guess,' she said as she walked out. He nodded as if he understood, but beyond the fact that he knew pregnant women were sick sometimes he was pretty much clueless. For a start, shouldn't it happen in the morning? He didn't know the exact time—he hadn't worn a watch since he was a kid. It was probably past eleven when he left his workshop. And he'd laid floorboards and half carried a pregnant woman up a flight of stairs since then. It was definitely well past morning.

'Sorry, it took me by surprise. It's not happened before,' she continued, as clipped and professional as if he'd called by her office. He stopped her with a hand on her shoulder and gently turned her face up to him.

'I borrowed your toothbrush,' she blurted, and he guessed from the rosy blush of her cheeks she'd not meant to confess. He laughed, the re-emergence of her human side relaxing him.

'No worries.' He smiled at her. 'I think we're a little past worrying about a shared toothbrush.' He was gratified by her small smile, but a little uneasy at how his own insides relaxed at the sight of it.

'So what now?' she asked as they hovered on the landing. She looked lost, smaller somehow, as if she was losing a grip on what it was that allowed her to present her usual polished, professional, vibrant face to the world. He knew what she was missing—her plan—but he couldn't bring himself to look at it yet. Not even for her. But he could offer her a distraction, a plan for the next hour or so. He hoped it would be enough.

'What about a walk on the beach? An ice cream and fish and chips—if you're hungry.'

She nodded and he remembered the night they met, when he'd heard the clear chime of her laugh and seen it as a challenge to get her to make that sound as many times as he could. The prospect seemed a distant one right now. But he'd made a connection with her before. Felt her relax in his arms. If they could do that again, find the connection that had strung between them that night and held strong until the next morning.

'A walk and an ice cream,' she repeated. 'I think I can manage that. I just need to change. Where…?' She glanced around the landing and he felt a stirring heat inside him. He wanted to curse the gentlemanly instinct that had made him tell her that he had a spare room, and had him working through the night for the past couple of days to get it ready for her. Even if it meant that he was sleeping on a mattress on bare floorboards.

He shook away the tempting image of sharing a room with her, and concentrated on their maintaining civility for the time being. That they couldn't even make it through a cup of coffee without fighting had shown him all too clearly how fragile this relationship was—how easily it could fall apart around them. He'd had no ulterior motive in inviting Rachel to come and stay. He really did want to get to know her better. Now he was starting to realise that he'd been hoping to get her to do things his way. To show her his way of life and hope that she would want it. This had shown him how precarious their situation was.

He pushed open the door to the guest room and stood back to let her past him. 'This is yours,' he said, even as he was turning away. He tried to brush past her—suddenly unable to think of being alone in a bedroom with her, and cursed the narrow doorway as he found himself pressed against her. He dropped his hands to her hips as he attempted to get by, but kept his eyes on their feet—determined not to be drawn in, not yet.

But the press of her body was electric against his, and her hair beneath his face smelt fresh and fruity. On impulse he lifted a lock of it, twisting it around his fingers. Rachel's eyes snapped up to his, and for a long moment their gazes held. All sensible considerations threatened to fall away in the onslaught of her body on his senses. But he couldn't give in to it. Couldn't lose sight of all the reasons getting any more involved with her was an impossibility. Dropping her hair, and pulling his eyes away, he jogged down the stairs and leaned back against the wall as he reached the kitchen. It was starting to look as if his bright idea had been a huge mistake.

He returned upstairs with her suitcase and a glass of water. Reaching out to knock on the open door, he caught sight of Rachel, silhouetted by the window, looking out over the water. The light was catching her hair, highlighting every shade of chocolate and chestnut, and a subtle smile turned the corners of her lips. She looked almost dreamy, and at that moment he would have given just about anything to know what she was thinking. But his foot hit a creaky floorboard, and she turned around, her relaxed expression replaced by something more guarded.

'This is beautiful,' she said, glancing round the room as she took in the furniture he'd found, sanded, painted and waxed. The light he'd sculpted from a block of driftwood, and the seascapes painted by a local artist friend, mounted in frames he'd made in his workshop. But her eyes hovered on the evidence of his labour only briefly. Because they were drawn inexorably to the window, and out over the water. The window itself was an exercise in love and commitment. The product of arguments with planning authorities, and then wrestling with metres-long expanses of timber and glass, all to create this huge, unbroken picture of the sea. It was calm today, just a few white-crested waves breaking up the expanse of ever-shifting blue-green.

If he'd known beforehand, though, what it would have taken to get the thing finished—the hearings and the plans, and the revised plans and rescheduled hearings—he wasn't sure that he could have started.

He handed Rachel the glass of water, and his gaze rested on her face rather than being drawn out to sea. Her eyelashes were long and soft, and brushed the skin beneath her eyes when she blinked. There were faint shadows there, he realised. He wondered whether they were new, or whether he'd just not seen them before. But he was struck by a protective instinct, the desire to look after her, ensure she was sleeping. Her hair had been pulled back into a loose tail—a style that owed more to her morning sickness than anything else, he guessed. The navy dress she wore wouldn't have been out of place among the stiff suits at her office. His eyes finally dropped to her belly—still as flat as he remembered it, but where her child, *their* child, was growing. It seemed almost impossible that a whole life could be growing with no outward sign.

She turned, and must have caught the direction of his gaze, because her hands dropped to her tummy. She spread her fingers and palms, stretching the fabric flat against her, and then looked up and caught his eye.

'Nothing to see yet,' she said with a small, cautious smile. 'It'll be a couple more months before I start to show.' He nodded again, as if he had the faintest clue about any of this. As if at the sight of her hands on her belly he wasn't remembering the last time he'd seen her fingers spread across her skin like that. He held her gaze, wondering if she remembered, too. But she gave a little start, pulling back her shoulders and straightening her posture—leaving him in no way uncertain that if she was remembering, she wasn't too happy about it.

'I'll see you downstairs,' he said, giving her the space her expression told him she needed.

CHAPTER SIX

As THEY STROLLED along the beach, Rachel felt the tension of the past few hours draining from her limbs, being replaced by the gentle warm glow of summer sunshine. They'd walked down the coastal path from the cottage, barely exchanging a word, but somehow the silence felt companionable, rather than awkward. She was taken aback, as she had been at the window upstairs, by the beauty of Leo's home. It perched on a cliff above the beach, and even with the tarpaulin for a roof, and the building materials dumped in the yard, the way it nestled into the rock and sand, shutters on the outside of the window, even the way the front door reflected the colour of the sea all helped it look as if it were a natural part of the landscape, as if it had emerged from the Jurassic rocks fully formed and—almost—habitable.

With the sun warming her hair, and the gentle exercise distracting her from the slight queasiness still troubling her stomach, she reached a decision. They were never going to be able to be friends if they didn't understand each other. Leo had asked her a question, one she'd avoided answering up till now, but he wanted to know why she needed a plan so badly, and if she was to stand any chance of him cooperating with it, then she at least had to expect to tell him why.

'You asked me why I need a plan,' she said, as they stopped momentarily to step over a pool of spray that had gathered on the rocks.

'To feel safe, you said.'

She nodded, wondering how she could explain, where to start.

'When I was fourteen, my parents left me home alone while they went out. It wasn't anything special, just cinema and dinner, I think. I'd gone to bed, but woke up when I heard a noise from my dad's study. I went downstairs and disturbed a burglar.'

Leo had stopped on the sand, and turned to face her. 'I'm so sorry,' he said, his face lined with genuine concern. 'That must have been awful for you.'

'I got a nasty bump to the head—he lashed out as he tried to get away—but I recovered pretty quickly. Not that you would have believed that if you'd listened to my parents.'

She dropped to her bottom in the sand, shielding her eyes from the sun and looking out over the water.

'They blamed themselves,' she explained. 'Thought that they never should have left me, that I'd been in huge amounts of danger and that I'd been lucky to survive.'

'They must have been so relieved that you hadn't been more seriously hurt.'

She shook her head, trying not to get drawn back into the suffocating anxiety her parents had forced on her.

'It never felt that way. They spent so much time concentrating on all the terrible things that could have happened, it got harder and harder to remember.' She fell quiet as she watched the waves, and glanced up a couple of times, following the path of the seagulls above the water. The sand was warm beneath her thighs, and she turned her face to the sun, letting the rays soak into her skin. Because she'd still not got to the difficult bit.

It had never occurred to her before that her planning might be a problem. That her need to know when and how the events in her life would unfold had become something that held her back, rather than helped her. It wasn't until she'd seen the revulsion in Leo's face when he'd glimpsed her plan that she'd realised how others might see her, how far from 'normal' her life had become. But it didn't really matter what anyone else thought about it. Even when that person was the father of her child, because she didn't know how to live any differently.

'I understand it must have been a difficult time...' Leo had dropped to the sand beside her, looking out over the water, as she was, so she didn't have to worry about his intensely blue eyes following every emotion that fluttered across her face. She wanted him to understand, because she wanted, needed, them to be friends. So she fought away the instinct to hide what had happened next, to protect herself and her family, by skirting around the behaviour that had locked them all into their fears.

'It was, but what happened next was harder.' It was the first time she'd admitted that. That the love and care that her parents had shown her in the weeks after the burglary had been more difficult to cope with than the initial trauma.

'My parents wouldn't let me out of the house.' She really hadn't meant for that to sound so dramatic. And she knew from the way that Leo had turned sharply to look at her that he'd misunderstood. 'They didn't lock me in or anything,' she clarified quickly, imagining a bevy of policemen or social workers or other officials turning up on her parents' doorstep and accusing them of crimes they'd never committed. 'They were just worried about me, and they liked to know where I was. They became anxious if I was out of the house too long, so I was never allowed to friends' houses or after-school clubs—I didn't really have any hobbies outside of home.'

'I still don't see what this has to do with the plan you presented this morning,' Leo said. His voice was soft, and his hand twitched in the sand, as if he wanted to reach for her. For a moment, she wished that he would. That he would thread his fingers with hers. Somehow she thought that it might be easier, to draw on his strength, to face her past together. Ridiculous, she told herself. They had only known each other a few weeks. Had really spent only a few waking hours together. There was no reason she should feel stronger just for having him there. But she couldn't deny how that twitch of his hand had affected her, how much she wished for the contact.

'I'll get to it, I will. It's just all tied up with everything else. I don't know how to tell you *just* that, if you see what I mean.' She turned to look at him and he nodded. 'I was still in school, they at least thought that I could be safe there, but I could see how much I was missing. I was losing touch with my friends, having to go straight home every night while they were meeting in parks and shopping centres and fast-food places. I was lonely, and I knew that things couldn't carry on as they were, with me speaking to no one outside school but my parents. So I negotiated a system. I would be allowed out with my classmates and friends if I provided my parents with a schedule of where I would be and when. They would have the landline numbers of anywhere I would be so that they could call and check I was really there. I had a mobile as well, of course, so that they could always get hold of me.

'If I was going out at the weekend, I'd plot out exactly what I'd be doing and when, give the itinerary to my parents, and then stick to it like my life depended on it. If they called and I wasn't where I was supposed to be, I knew that all hell could break loose. It wasn't just that they'd ground me—I knew that they would be terrified. And much as I didn't agree with the way they were wrapping me in cotton wool, I knew that they were only doing it because they loved me. Everything they did was because they were terrified of me getting hurt and they only wanted the best for me. I would never do anything that would upset them. They'd been through enough. Or felt that they had, at least. I didn't want to add to it.'

'So how long did it take?'

She looked at Leo in confusion.

'How long did what take?'

'Until it rubbed off. Until you started to believe that the schedule kept you safe, the same way your parents did.'

She started a little, surprised that he'd understood so clearly.

'Well, my friends all thought it was a little odd, that I had to be where I had to be and exactly on time. But when I was living at home, it wasn't easy to see where my parents' need ended and mine started. It wasn't until I went to university full of ideas of living on the edge, of being spontaneous and pleasing no one but myself, that I realised that I needed the schedule as much as they had.'

'Leaving home. I guess that was hard on you all.'

'It was. Painfully so. I had no idea before I left just

how hard it would be. I'd known all along that it would be for them. But I could also see how strong the apron strings were, how they would get harder to break as I got older. So I managed to convince them that I had to have a normal life. And I was eighteen—there was nothing much they could do about it anyway. I think perhaps they worried that if they didn't let me go, I'd take myself off and they might lose contact with me. If I went with their blessing, I was more likely to keep in touch.'

'So how was it?' Leo's voice was still low, gentle, but probing. Encouraging her to share, leaving her nowhere to hide her secrets.

She let out a long, slow breath as she remembered those first few weeks, when she'd clung to her class schedule and the fresher's week itinerary as if they were a lifeline.

'Hard. Really hard. I didn't know anyone, and my teen years had been pretty sheltered. The only way I knew how to cope with the confusion, the novelty of it all, was to make a plan and stick to it. So I mapped out the weeks and the months. Looked ahead to the career that I wanted and the life that I wanted, and started filling in the days in my calendar. Fast forward a decade or so, and here I am, right on track. Or was, until...'

'Until you met me.'

She nodded, but something about the familiar intimacy in his voice, the hint of remembered laughter, made her smile.

'So your first instinct was to make a new plan. You need it.'

'I...I do,' she admitted. 'It seemed the only way to make sense of this whole situation. But seeing it through your eyes, it's clear I need it a little too much, that there

are times when going with the flow or being more flexible can have their place. But it's not something I can just
turn off. And trust me, I've never felt more like I need a
plan than I have this week.'

'So we'll work something out together. Enough of a
plan for you to feel comfortable and enough flexibility
that it doesn't feel like a prison to me.' His voice sounded
rough, low, and she looked up to catch the concern on
his face, mixed with a distance she hadn't felt from him
before. He shook his head, and when he looked back at
her his expression was lighter, sunnier.

'When do we start?'

He laughed, and leant back on his arms, one of them
nudging slightly behind her back. 'How about not right
this minute? If we say we'll make a start today, is that
enough of a plan for now?'

'It'll do.' She grinned.

'Good, because I'm starving, and I'm guessing after
your spell in the bathroom you could use a big portion
of fish and chips. What do you say?'

'I say you're a mind-reader. Where's good?'

Leo pushed to his feet and reached down to help her
up. As she felt her hand disappear between his huge,
roughened palms, her body shuddered. Pulled to her feet,
she realised that—without her heels—Leo towered over
her. He'd pulled her up to him, and now she was probably
standing a little too close. She should take a step back,
she thought. But seeing Leo here, there was something
hypnotising about it. Until now, she'd only ever seen him
in her world: her party, her flat, her work. Here, by his
home, surrounded by the beach and the sea that he loved
so much, it added an extra dimension of sexy. It brought
out the gold shining in his hair, made his slightly wind-

chapped cheeks more attractive, like a good wine bringing out the flavours in food.

The wind had caught her hair, and was playing it around her temples, tickling at her face. She was reaching up to tame it when Leo caught it and tucked it behind her ear. His hand rested there, and for a moment Rachel was more than tempted to turn her face into his palm, to press her skin against his, to re-find the pleasure of that night. But she held her breath and stepped away. There was too much at risk; she could get too hurt. They needed to be friends and there was no surer way to ruin a friendship than a disastrous romance.

His eyes lingered on hers for a moment as she moved back, and his expression told her he knew exactly what she had felt between them just now, told her exactly what had been on offer, had she wanted it. And that he knew she'd deliberately stepped back from it.

CHAPTER SEVEN

LEO SAT LISTENING to the kettle coming to the boil, wondering whether he should wake Rachel. After a long walk down the beach yesterday afternoon, and a portion of fish and chips for dinner, she'd crashed almost as soon as they'd arrived back at the house. And had been asleep more than twelve hours. He wondered whether she'd been working too hard. Weren't pregnant women meant to take things easy? Perhaps she'd been overdoing it. Should he say something?

But what right did he have to even ask her that? Did the fact that she was carrying his child give him a right to question what she was doing? He shook his head. There were still so many things they hadn't discussed. But discussing meant deciding. And deciding meant getting it in writing, laminating and deviating only on the point of death.

He made a coffee and decided to leave her. She'd wake when she was ready. And maybe he could subtly ask her later whether she thought she should be taking things easier. He really needed to know more about pregnancy, about *babies*. He'd never given any thought to starting a family; it had always seemed a distant, uncertain thing. And he'd never imagined he'd be facing it with someone he barely knew. Perhaps he could ask his mum these questions. He'd have to tell her. And his dad, too.

He gave a shudder as he acknowledged what he'd been trying to ignore since he'd first found out about the baby. He'd have to see his family. His brother. He'd avoided him for years, had barely seen him since he'd left school. He knew that he was hurting his parents, that they despaired of ever seeing their family all together again. But what else could he do—sit down to a happy family dinner with him? The man who had made his life miserable—who had led the school bullies. So miserable that when he'd left school, escaped them, he'd sworn that he'd never again find himself in a situation he didn't like without an escape route. Which was why the news that Rachel was pregnant had terrified him. Because if there was any situation more impossible to escape than this one, he didn't want to know about it.

She would want to make a start on that plan this morning. Even when she'd been falling-over tired last night she'd mentioned wanting to do it. It was only the interruption of an enormous yawn that had made her listen to him and finally take herself off to bed—and a promise that they could talk about it today.

He only knew one thing for certain—no child of his would be subjected to the experience he'd had. He wanted a better life for him, or her.

What were the other headings in Rachel's magnum opus? Finance? She obviously knew—or thought she knew—that he was well off. After all, he'd made the generous donation she'd not so subtly hinted at the night of the fundraiser. But that was family money, not his. He'd always been happy to send his trust-fund proceeds the way of those who really needed them—but had never used it for himself.

He'd seen the damage done when people inherited money without responsibility. Stick a load of those with an inflated sense of self-worth together, with insufficient supervision, and you had a recipe for disaster— and emotional torture in his case. If Rachel thought that she'd found herself a meal ticket she would be sadly disappointed. But he didn't really think that was what she was interested in.

Creaking floorboards upstairs told him that she was awake. He gave a start, half pleased at the thought of seeing her, half dreading the discussion he knew would inevitably come. Remembering the hour she'd spent in the bathroom the night he'd stayed at her flat, he expected a little more grace before he had to face her, but then he heard her footsteps on the stairs.

For half a second, he wondered if he'd be treated to the sight of her in some sort of skimpy nightwear. The sight of her perfectly prim jeans and soft sweater reminded him she'd come here prepared for a business meeting. At least she wasn't clutching her tablet. In fact, he couldn't even see her phone on her. Though looking for it gave him a brilliant excuse for thoroughly checking out the pockets of her jeans.

'Morning,' he said, standing up from the table. Once he was on his feet, he wasn't sure why he had done it, except that it seemed impossible not to react to her, not to want to get close. 'Can I get you anything?'

He bit his tongue to stop the flood of questions filling his mouth. She had more colour in her cheeks than she had the previous afternoon, but he was still worried. As he reached her side, he rested a gentle hand on her shoulder, turning her to face him. 'Did you sleep well?' he asked, looking for any sign that she wasn't completely recovered from yesterday. An overwhelming need to protect her swept over him, and the hand on her shoulder slipped to her waist, pulling her closer. Once her body was near enough that he felt her magnetic pull, all thoughts of protecting her flew out of his mind, and were replaced with something hotter, more urgent. He pulled the arm around her waist tight, and dipped his head. His eyes were already closing as his body remembered the feel of hers, as his lips tingled with remembered sensation.

And then he was cold, his body left bereft as Rachel turned and pulled away until his arms were empty.

'I'll make the coffee,' she said, the shake in her voice at least showing that she wasn't completely immune to him. 'And I could murder some carbs. What is there for breakfast?'

He pulled his brain back to the real world, the one where they weren't a lust-filled couple shacked up together for a fun weekend. To the world where an ill-thought-through night had led to a baby, a lifetime of commitment, and he was momentarily glad that her self-control had outwitted his libido. 'Toast? Cereal?' He tried to keep his voice level, to take her cue and pretend that his clumsy attempt at a kiss hadn't happened. But he couldn't forget it, couldn't forget how it felt to be fractions of a second from bliss, and then left cold and wanting her.

She nodded, her body stiff, her smile a little forced. He threw bread into the toaster, dug around in the cupboard and put together a carb-loaded platter: muffins, crumpets, toast and cereal, anything to keep mind and body busy and away from her. They feasted on the breads, slathered in honey and jam, and conversation eventually started to flow between them almost as smooth.

He remembered the challenge he'd set himself that night. The way the sound of her laugh had so entranced him he was determined to make it happen again and again. The effect hadn't worn off. Every smile and chuckle became a challenge to make it grow. He felt himself relax as she slouched a little more in her chair, as her words flowed easy and her smiles grew. Every chime of her laughter swelled a light in his chest, something primal and basic, something he couldn't control, or make himself want to.

As they finished up with breakfast, he was tempted to hold his breath, to hold on to these moments of happiness, because something told him that this was borrowed contentment. That it wasn't real. Maybe this was in her plan all along, softening him up before she started. No need to spook him by hitting him with talk about the plan the minute she was up. Instead she lulled him into a false sense of security, waiting until he entered a food coma until she made her move. With the prospect of having to make some sort of plan on the horizon, he couldn't see what was real and what was his fear manifesting as paranoia.

She was fidgeting as they cleared the table, clearly getting more and more uncomfortable. There was tension in her shoulders and a tightness in her muscles that he didn't like. And he knew the only thing that would get rid of it. She was still flailing after he'd ripped up her plan. Writing a new one would ease her worries, make her feel safe.

Of course he'd discovered one other way of finding the relaxed, happy, free Rachel. And he knew which of the two—drawing up a schedule for the rest of his life, or a long, languorous morning of lovemaking—he would prefer.

But he also knew which of the two Rachel needed today. So he swallowed the very tempting suggestion and did what he hoped was the right thing. 'I think we should take a look at this plan.' He ran his hands through his hair and left them at the back of his head. He supposed he was hoping for 'oh, we don't have to do that now,' or, 'maybe we could leave it for a bit'. Though of course what he actually got was a sigh of relief, a smile and darting glances at the stairs. 'Grab whatever you need,' he said, suddenly feeling distant and uncomfortable around her, with her need for control—and his fear of it—sitting between them like a threat. 'I'll make some more coffee.'

She hesitated at the bottom of the stairs. 'Do you have any decaf?'

'Sorry, I didn't think.'

He leaned back against the kitchen counter as she went upstairs. Decaf? Another pregnancy thing, he assumed. Just one more part of this whole situation he was completely clueless about. Every good feeling he'd had when they'd shared breakfast had abandoned him, and even the house seemed darker and colder this side of the meal. Rachel re-emerged from the stairs a few moments later, clutching her bound-up papers, a notebook and her tablet.

'Old-fashioned or new-fangled?' she asked as she sat neatly at the table and set everything out in front of her. Death by fire or water? What did it matter?

But the smile had returned to her lips, her arms hung loosely at her sides, and she had lost the drawn, haunted look that told of a frightened woman.

'You choose.' He tried to keep the weighty, quavery feeling fluttering in his belly out of his voice. 'You're the expert here.' He hoped it didn't sound snarky. He didn't mean it to. Didn't mean to blame her for how uncomfortable he was. It didn't make sense to be angry at her for the situation they found themselves in. It wasn't her fault they were pregnant. It wasn't her fault that the way she wanted to live her life was the opposite of his. They just had to find a way to make this work for both of them. All of them.

'Old-fashioned, then.' She opened the notebook out to a blank double spread and reached for her pen. He could tell she was itching to write her headings across the top of the page but seemed to be waiting for his okay to do so. 'So…where do you want to start?'

He took a deep breath. She'd obviously spent a lot of time thinking about this. And to be honest her plan was probably as good as anything that they could come up with together. As he'd said—she was the expert here. But if he didn't have his say now, then when would he? Would he find himself in ten years' time on a path that she had chosen, and that he had never had any idea of where it was going? If he didn't rein this in, if she couldn't learn to live a little less rigidly, he'd find himself stifled and trapped. And if she couldn't start compromising now, then he couldn't see how this was ever going to work.

'Perhaps we could start with the next few weeks,' he said eventually, thinking that even he could manage with planning that far out, if he had to. 'And anything that needs a specific date. Appointments, travel plans, that sort of thing.'

Rachel nodded and he could tell from the small smile on her face she already knew exactly how she expected the next few weeks to pan out. She probably had appointments lined up, time blocked out, and knew exactly where he should be and at what time. But she said none of this and instead waited for him to make a suggestion. At least she seemed willing to try as hard as he was to make this work.

'Do you have any doctor's appointments scheduled? I'm not really sure how this works but I'd like to be there if that's what you want.'

'I've an appointment with my GP in a few days. Probably won't be much to tell at that stage, from what I've read. But generally they want to schedule the first scan at some point around twelve weeks.'

'Twelve weeks?' He raised a brow in question.

'The twelfth week of the pregnancy. Not twelve weeks from now. Or, in fact, twelve weeks from when we...' He smiled a little at her embarrassment. 'The counting is weird,' she continued, a light blush colouring her cheeks. 'Right now I think I'm about nine weeks pregnant, even though it's not that long since we... They count from the first day of your last...'

'Are you going to finish a sentence today?' He laughed at the sudden appearance of this bashfulness. 'Or is there always going to be so much guesswork?'

'I'm sorry. It seems stupid to be embarrassed talking about any of this when you're the one, well, we're the ones... Sorry.'

She laughed, too, and Leo relaxed into his chair as the tension in the air palpably lightened. What was it about her laugh that reached his spine and his heart?

'I'm doing it again, aren't I?' He nodded. 'They count from the first day of your last period, which means today is week nine of the pregnancy even though it's not been that long since we...met. Which means they'll want to schedule the scan for around three weeks' time.'

'I'd like to be there.'

'Me, too.' They both smiled, and he breathed a sigh of relief, glad that they'd found this common ground at last. Maybe they *could* do this. Maybe they could find a compromise to make them both happy. And if they did that, what next? What more could there be between them when they weren't both terrified of what the other craved?

Rachel drew a column on the piece of paper and wrote the heading *Appointments* at the top; then clicked through the screen of her phone with one hand and wrote the date in the column with the other. She glanced up at him. 'Do you want to make a note of the date?'

Or maybe they couldn't. 'What date? You haven't got an appointment yet.'

'No, but I'm sure they'll make it that week. You could…'

'Rachel, this is one of those times when you're going to have to let me make a decision for myself. I'm perfectly capable of keeping in my head the fact that I will have to make some time approximately three weeks from now to attend the scan. It's not something I'm likely to forget. Just because I'm not doing it your way doesn't mean I'm doing something wrong.'

She concentrated hard on the page; going over and over one word with her pen until he feared the paper would dissolve. But she didn't argue with him. The best he could hope for, for now, he supposed.

'Okay, so that's the appointments sorted for now. What next?'

'I want to have the baby in London.'

'Makes sense, considering you live there.'

'So you'll have to make arrangements to be up there, if

you want to be around when it happens.' He nodded, able to see the logic in that. He waited, wondering whether she'd want him to make some more definite plans, but she seemed happy—or at least reluctantly willing—to leave it at that for now. Though he did notice the way her pen ripped through the paper slightly as she wrote the next word.

'Fine.'

'Seems to me like we can't really decide anything to do with dates until you've seen a doctor, though,' Leo said. 'So how about we leave that for now and move on to another part of the plan? What else is on your list that needs deciding now?'

When she didn't reply, he looked up from where his eyes had been following her pen scoring into the paper, to find her sitting with her mouth open and a hesitant look on her face. 'What?'

'You're right. We don't need to decide everything now.' She started to close the notebook, but Leo reached out and laid a hand across the page, trying not to notice the way that his skin tingled when it accidentally brushed against hers.

'Something's worrying you. Why don't you tell me what it is?' He tried to catch her eye, but she seemed determined not to meet his gaze. An alarm bell, deep in his belly, started ringing. 'What's the problem?'

'It's not a problem. It's just—' she took a deep breath and spat the words out '—I had all this worked out with scenarios, and different options and choices, and now that I'm sitting here at your kitchen table it feels weird.'

'What? Now that I'm a real person and not just an item in your schedule? Now that I get a say?'

She nodded. 'I am sorry. For turning up with it all finished and ready to present to you. I didn't mean to cut you out, to tell you this is the way it has to be. I just had to see for myself how I was going to make this work. And the only way to do that was to work it all out and write it down. I can see how it must have looked, as if I was dictating the whole of the rest of your life to you. But I didn't mean it that way.'

Her honesty eased that little knot of tension from his stomach, and he couldn't tell her how grateful he was for this acknowledgement that maybe she didn't have it all worked out after all. Funnily, her apology for creating the schedule in the first place made him want to help her with a replacement more than ever; he wanted to do whatever it took to make this work for them, even if it felt like seeing Exit signs being ripped down in front of him. Because what was an escape to him now? Sure, he could run. He could get far away from Rachel, throw money at the situation to keep the lawyers happy and have nothing to do with this woman and her child ever again. But he wouldn't. He couldn't.

And just like that his relaxed feeling was gone. He sat a little straighter in his chair, the tension in his neck and shoulders not allowing him to lounge. There was no escape now. Nothing for it but to plough on, into whatever it was his life held for him. He couldn't escape the facts: he was going to be a father. This woman, her plans and her notebooks, would be in his life for ever.

But not every part of his life. Rachel's presence had become an accepted fact between that Italian lunch and her turning up here. But just because he had her in his life, didn't mean he couldn't keep parts of it for himself. Keep part of himself safe. So she would be the mother of his child. He couldn't change that. But that was all she would be. He would stop these daydreams and night-time fantasies about that night. Forget the feel and taste of her lips and skin. He wouldn't fall into a relationship with her just because she was carrying his child.

'Let's just get this over with,' he said, forcing out the words. 'We have to talk about it some time, and we're both here now. What else did you have written down before?'

'Well…there was one part of the plan I had trouble with,' she admitted. 'Without knowing your financial position it was difficult to be accurate, so I came up with a number of different scenarios.'

'You should know, I'm not as well off as you might think.' He wasn't sure why he just threw the words out like that. Best defence perhaps, hoping to scare her off. Instead, he could see from her scowl that he'd offended her. He cursed under his breath. How could they misstep at *every* turn?

'And how would you know what I think about your financial position?'

'Well, we met at a fundraiser where the tickets cost two hundred quid a plate. It would be reasonable on your part to assume that I was loaded. I'm not,' he added, watching her carefully to see her reaction. She didn't even look surprised, never mind disappointed.

'If you remember, I thought you were crashing. So the price of the ticket is neither here nor there.'

She was impossible to second-guess this morning, Leo realised. But nothing he'd seen so far screamed gold-digger. He was cautious of money, and those who wanted it. And he had every reason to be. He'd grown up surrounded by it, rich and miserable. When he'd turned twenty-one, and for the first time could decide for himself how much of the family money he wanted to use, he'd decided the answer was 'none of it'.

He'd been selling his artwork since school, and when he'd left had set up a website and taken a few commissions, still trying to decide what he wanted to do with his life. When the paperwork had come through authorising his access to his trust fund, he'd decided once and for all that he didn't want a penny of it for himself. So he'd set up donations to charities, funded a few local projects he was interested in, and left the remainder in the bank, waiting until he could decide the best place to send it.

He'd saved almost every penny he'd earned, and as the commissions for his work increased, so did the nest egg he was building up. He'd wanted to buy a home, somewhere completely his, where he could feel safe. All he could afford was this wreck, a shell of a place when they'd exchanged the contracts, but it was his, and he loved it. He worked the renovations around his commissions, and the time that he spent in his studio, so progress had been slow, but he had relished every minute of the work.

His art had gained a reputation now, and it had been a long time since he'd had to worry where that month's mortgage payment would come from. And he could certainly support a child.

But he wouldn't see his son or daughter grow up with the sense of entitlement—to money, to people, to anything they wanted—that he'd seen from the boys at school.

'I'm not loaded, and I can't give you a specific figure right now,' he said eventually. 'I pretty much just turn everything over to my accountant and let him worry about it. But I'll do my bit, I can promise you that.'

* * *

Rachel reached down and pulled off her flip-flops; she threaded her fingers through the straps as she walked along the beach, swinging her arms and enjoying the feel of the sand between her toes. Well, Leo didn't seem to be in any hurry for her to see whatever he wanted to show her, she thought, as they ambled down across the sand. The tide was out, and the beach stretched before her, flat and vast. A dark stripe of seaweed bisected the view, and as they grew closer she detected its smell— raw, salty, and not entirely pleasant. She couldn't help but notice that Leo seemed to be getting more interested the closer they got. His eyes scanned the beach.

'Looking for something?'

'For *any*thing,' he corrected, though Rachel wasn't any the wiser for this clarification.

'Looking for anything.' She spoke seriously and nodded as if this made perfect sense to her.

'Come on, I'll show you.'

Leo grabbed her hand and towed her the last few yards across the sand, dragging her, as far as she could tell, to the largest pile of stinking seaweed.

'Ah, now I understand,' she lied, looking down and laughing, still completely clueless about what they were doing here. She could hardly be expected to play detective when her hand was trapped in his. When her every nerve ending and neuron seemed intent on those few square inches of skin where their bodies were joined. 'You love the seaweed. You think a city girl like me will be impressed by its…pungency?'

He laughed. 'Exactly. I brought you all the way down to the coast to enjoy the finest seaweed this country has to offer. No, don't be daft.' He threw her another smile, and gestured to the stinking pile with their joined hands. 'Let's get stuck in.' Abruptly, he dropped her hand and to his knees, before picking up a huge handful of the slimy green fronds and throwing it to one side.

She let out a bark of laughter, unable to hide her amusement at this grown man's pleasure at rooting through rubbish. 'And what exactly are we looking for?' She crossed her legs and dropped beside him, gingerly picking through the nearest weeds.

'Whatever the sea has sent us.'

She sat with the idea for a moment, trying to see if she could leave that statement as it was. If she could accept it. Nope.

'You're sure you're not looking for something in particular.'

'I'm sure. I've found all sorts down here. You never know what will turn up.' He looked up and his gaze met hers. When he saw that she still didn't understand, he rocked back on his heels. 'If it helps you to have a bit more of a plan, look out for driftwood. Something big, rubbed smooth by the sea.'

She frowned a little. His answer had taken her by surprise, and she didn't like the feeling. 'What do you want it for?'

'To make something beautiful. Something for the house, or something to sell. I've found all sorts out here,' he went on—he must have seen she wasn't yet convinced. 'Jewellery, pottery, beautiful rocks and shells. Just have a dig around.'

Sitting on the sand, she couldn't do more than pick through the pile directly in front of her, so she clambered up onto her knees, getting used to the feel of the weeds slipping through her fingers. She snuck a glance at Leo from the corner of her eye, still trying to see where this exercise was leading. As if there was some part of him that was a complete mystery to her. He was wandering along the line of debris, kicking it with his toes at times. Unable to see anything but weeds and the odd carrier bag, she decided to catch him up.

'Any luck?' he asked as she reached him.

'Not—' She started to speak but then a glint of something on the sand caught her eye. She dropped to a squat on her heels like a toddler and carefully pulled the glass out from under the detritus. As she cleaned it off, an antique bottle emerged in her hand. She stared at it, taken aback by the appearance of this beautiful object. Leo came to stand behind her and peered at the bottle over her shoulder.

'Very nice.' He reached out to take it. 'May I?'

She handed it over and he turned it in his hands, brushing off a little more sand and scrutinising the lettering.

'It's been in the water a long time, I think,' she said, just making out the figures '1909' on one side. She took it back from Leo and tested its weight in her hands. 'No message, though.' She peered into the neck, wondering if it had once carried a slip of paper.

Energised by her find, hitting gold her first time beachcombing, she started walking again, stopping often to pull aside some stone or vegetation, offering up shells and rocks for Leo's admiration.

Before long, she had pockets full of pretty shells, and her bottle tucked safely under her arm. She could feel the waves and the sand working their magic on her and Leo, as an easy chemistry and camaraderie grew between them. 'Do you find a lot of stuff out here?'

'Enough to keep me in hot meals and building materials.' She raised an eyebrow in question, too relaxed to be frustrated by his cryptic answer. But then she'd been so…abrasive, that first time they'd met, she couldn't blame him for being reticent about telling her about his life.

'You know, you never really explained what you do. I know I wasn't helping, being snippy about a trust fund and everything. I realise I got it wrong, then.'

He halted suddenly, evidently taken by surprise. When he started walking, there was something a little stiffer about his stride. 'Not entirely wrong.'

'But you said—'

'I said I'm not loaded. What I didn't tell you is that it's out of choice.'

Her brows drew together in confusion, and she glanced at Leo, encouraging him to continue.

He sighed before starting to speak again. 'My family has plenty of money. Pots of it, in fact. Too much. And I do have a trust fund.' Not something that would normally cause such distress, she thought. 'But I haven't spent a penny of it for years.'

'Why not?' It was none of her business, but she could tell this was something big, for Leo. Perhaps the tip of an emotional iceberg, something he didn't often talk about. And she wanted to know him.

'It's hard to explain. I want you to understand. I want you to know why I find it hard for you to pull out that plan… I'm not making life hard for the sake of it. It's all connected.'

Her heart ached at the note of vulnerability in his voice, the pain that he was clearly hiding. And it soared a little, too, at the fact that he was sharing this with her. Opening up to her. But Leo's shoulders had fallen forward, and a haunted look had crept over his face. She reached for his hand, refusing to acknowledge what that contact might signify, but needing him to know that she was there to support him. 'I want to understand, Leo. Tell me anything you want.'

'The money,' Leo said. It seemed as good a place as any to start. He led them both away from the water, to the very edge of the beach, with the cliff creating a natural shelter around them. He sat on the warm sand, and pulled gently on Rachel's hand until she was sitting beside him. 'I grew up with people who had it—lots of it. Far too much. It didn't make them happy, and it didn't make them good. And there were people who thought I needed it, desperately...' He paused but she didn't say anything, just waited for him to continue. 'I went to a very good school—and it was hell.'

He gripped her hand, and she squeezed it back. The warmth and comfort of her touch flowed from her skin to his—he couldn't have let go of her at that moment if he'd had to. He wanted to pull her close, to bury his face in her hair and his body in hers. Forget everything about his past; ignore everything about their future. He wanted her lips on his, wanted to hear her chuckle with pleasure and sigh with satisfaction.

But he also wanted her to understand him. Wanted her to see why any hint of feeling trapped scared him so much. He needed her to know why he would never allow himself to be trapped in a relationship he couldn't get out of. And he knew he had to tell her everything.

'For some reason the other boys saw me as an easy—and early—target. To start with it was whispers about money. People accusing me of stealing from the other boys. Suggesting that money had gone missing from pockets and dorms. I tried to ignore it, thinking it would pass. And then they started talking about my mum. Insinuating that my "greed" ran in the family, that she was a shameless gold-digger who'd ensnared my dad for his money.

'She's from a different background from my dad, her family wasn't well off and his is loaded, and she married him when he was a widow with a three-year-old. That seemed to be all the evidence the boys needed.

'I couldn't ignore these whispers. I started to fight back, to defend my mum and myself, and it escalated. The older boys were determined to show me that answering back would get me nowhere. It turned violent, and nasty. I hadn't told anyone what was going on, but after a beating that left me bruised and heaving, I knew that I had to do something. My older brother—half-brother— was at school with me.'

'Did he help?'

Leo steeled himself to answer, but found his throat was thick, and his eyes stung. Even after all this time, he still couldn't think about what had happened without being close to tears.

'I'm not sure I understand,' Rachel said gently. 'I'm sure it must have been terrible, but it was a long time ago. You left that place—'

'Yes, and I will never go back.'

'Of course not, Leo. You're a grown man. No one can make you go back to school.'

He snatched his hand back, frustrated that after explaining the parts of his past that still caused the occasional nightmare, she could brush it off with 'you don't have to go back to school'.

'But I had to go back *then*.' The words burst out of

him, just short of a roar. He'd had to go back time after time, year after year. Stuck in that place every day with the boys who hated him. Who thought up new and different ways to torture him.

'Couldn't you have left?'

'You think I didn't want that? Even when I eventually told my father what was going on he didn't take it seriously. The bullies closed ranks when my parents spoke to the school. Told the headmaster that the bruises were from rugby. Or that *I'd* started a fight. They were so convincing. All the teachers fell for it. Sometimes even I found myself wondering if I was imagining it all. If I was going mad.

'I was trapped. Every morning I'd wake up in that dorm, and knew how my torture would pan out for the day. Taunts in the bathroom during break. Starving at lunch, too scared to risk the dinner hall. A few kicks in the changing rooms after games, somewhere it wouldn't show when I was dressed. And at night, I was locked in with them.

'The days the school knew where I would be and when, they would know, too. And ever since—I've needed a way out. The thought of being trapped—' He stopped abruptly. 'It terrifies me, Rachel.'

'You think I trapped you?' Her voice was flat and sad, more disappointed than angry.

'It doesn't matter, does it? Whether you did or not, it doesn't change the fact that—'

'That you want to escape and you can't.'

He rubbed his head in his hands, fighting against the fear to find the logic in his argument. 'I don't even know if I want to escape. What I would want if I wasn't...'

'Stuck.'

He nodded. 'You probably think I'm a complete jerk for telling you all this.' He felt like one. For admitting all the reasons he was terrified of what their lives were going to become.

She shook her head, though her expression was grim. 'I don't. I'm glad you told me how you feel. You can't help thinking the way that you do. I just wish it were... different.'

He reached past her to pluck a small piece of driftwood from the sand. The light played on it as he turned it over, and he kept his eyes focused on that, rather than meeting Rachel's gaze.

'How did you cope—at school?'

He looked across at her now, surprised she wanted to know more after what he'd just told her.

'I spent a lot of time at the beach.'

'Surfing? Swimming?'

'Some of the time. I was lucky in a way— the school was only a couple of miles from the coast, so I was able to spend a lot of time there. When I had to be on campus, I escaped to the art studio.' She looked at him in surprise. For some reason, he enjoyed that, throwing off her preconceptions of him. He was even able to crack a smile at her gaping expression.

'The art studio?'

'Yes—I'm an artist, didn't I mention that?'

'An artist.' She said the word as if it were something alien, obviously not believing him. He nodded, still playing with the driftwood as he took in her dropped jaw, her hands indignantly planted in the sand either side of her. 'You're an *artist*.'

A laugh escaped him, surprising him as much as her. 'I'm sure I mentioned it before.'

'And I'm certain that you didn't. What sort of artist?' She still hadn't wiped the incredulity from her face and he wasn't sure whether to be amused or annoyed that she found the idea of his occupation, vocation—whatever you wanted to call it—so laughable.

'A successful one, thankfully. That's what I wanted to show you this afternoon—my studio's down here rather than up on the cliff.'

'Right.' She drew the syllable out, as she examined his face, looking for hints of his artistic temperament perhaps. 'And the beachcombing, where does that fit into this?'

He breathed a sigh of relief that they were back on safer conversational ground. That she'd listened to his painful story, offered support, but moved on when he needed to. And his work he could talk about for hours. 'It's one of my favourite ways to find inspiration for my work and materials for the house. I've incorporated a lot of driftwood in the build. It's an ecologically sound way of working.'

'But doesn't it leave you at the mercy of the tides, or the water gods, or whatever force it is that throws up driftwood onto beaches? Wouldn't it just be easy to order the whole lot at once? I'm sure that there are suppliers with good green credentials.'

'I could do, I suppose, but I'm happy just taking opportunities as they arise. You never know what you're going to find. Like the floorboards for the living room. They just turned up in a reclamation yard. I could have bought brand-new timber last week and would have missed out on all that gorgeous character.'

'Yes, but you would have had a floor for a week by now.' He threw her a grin and nudged her with his shoulder. 'What is it, princess? Upset that the place wasn't perfect for you?'

'Oh, don't give me "princess". I just think that while your way of doing things sounds lovely, in theory, when you have no real responsibilities, sometimes practical matters have to take a higher priority. Like a roof that doesn't leak. And a floor beyond the front door.' Not in the mood to joke about the house, then, he surmised.

'Well, then, I count myself lucky that you don't get a say in how I renovate my house.'

He stared her down, daring her to argue with him, so that he could remind her again that he would not be tied down by her. She might be carrying his baby, but that didn't mean that she could come down here and start telling him how to live his life, any more than he would dream of going up to London and telling her how to live hers.

She didn't take the bait. Instead she stood and started brushing sand from her jeans, and then walked back to the cliff path. He watched her for a few moments; then jogged to catch her up.

'Wait, I'm sorry. That wasn't fair of me. If you still want to, I'd like to show you the studio.'

She paused and glanced up at the house. Then looked back at him and softened. 'I'd like to see it. I can't believe I didn't know you're an artist. You didn't finish telling me how that happened.'

He started down the twisting path that led along the bottom of the cliff to his studio and workshop, wondering whether he could talk about his introduction to the world of art without reliving more of the pain he'd suffered at that time. He'd try, for her, for them.

'I told you I used to hide out in the art studio… None of the other boys seemed too keen to follow me there. Perhaps something to do with the belligerent old teacher who rarely left the room, Mr Henderson. I found it peaceful—it had these huge windows that let in the light, and you could see the sea in the distance. I'd spend lunchtimes hiding out in there and playing around with whatever materials the professor had in that week. One week, when I arrived, this huge hunk of driftwood was sitting on one of the tables. When I walked in the room, Mr Henderson looked at me, then at the wood, and then walked into the store room and left me there with it. Does that sound weird?'

She raised her eyebrow slightly. He'd take that as a yes.

'Okay, so it sounds kind of weird. I'll warn you, it might get weirder. I just wanted to touch the wood. It was as if I could see, no, *feel*, something beneath the surface. So I got some tools and started carving. It was as if the wood came to life under my fingers, and I found something beneath the surface that no one else could see until I revealed it.'

'You're right. Weird.'

He laughed.

'In a good way,' Rachel clarified, bumping Leo with her hip as they walked along. 'Weird, but cool. And there's a market for this? Secrets lurking in driftwood.'

'I know, it surprised me, too.' Leo smiled, thrilling at the energy Rachel's smile and teasing could create in him. 'But there is. A bigger one than I'd imagined, actually. Enough for me to put down a deposit on a shell of a house and to keep me in tarpaulin until I stumble upon some roof tiles. Anyway, we're here,' he declared as they rounded a corner and the studio came into view.

She ran a hand along the workbench, and enjoyed the sensation of the wood—warm, dry and gritty on the soft pads of her fingers. It was like meeting Leo afresh, see-ing this room, and for the first time she was aware of how much she'd underestimated him. One glance at his beach-ready hair and surfers' tan and she'd written him off as a beach-bum trust-fund kid.

But this room showed her how wrong she'd been. It wasn't just the evidence of how much work had gone into the place—hours to fit out the studio: floor-to-ceil-ing window panels, cupboards and work surfaces. It was the art itself, each piece like a little peephole into Leo's character. Almost every surface carried pieces in various states of completion. The centre of the room was domi-nated by an enormous piece of wood. It must have been three feet across, and was nearly as tall as she was. And it seemed to be moving. It wasn't, she saw as she moved closer. It was just light playing over the wave-like carv-ings that made it seem that way. Constantly changing; constantly keeping her guessing. As she took another step closer she realised that it wasn't just one piece of wood, it was many, woven and flowing together. She wanted to glance across at Leo, to tell him she thought it was beautiful—more than that, it was astonishing—but she couldn't drag her eyes away. At last she reached out, wanting to feel the waves and light beneath her fin-gers, but Leo gently grabbed her wrist and stopped her.

'I'm sorry. I shouldn't have just—'

'Normally I'd say touch away. But I treated the wood this morning. So, what do you think?'

She finally managed to pull her eyes away from the piece and flicked her gaze up to his face. He looked a little anxious, she realised, as he waited for her verdict on his work.

'Leo, it's beautiful. I had no idea.'

'Ah, well, you know, I only come down here when the waves are rubbish.'

He was still standing close, his fingers still wrapped around her palm, and she pushed him lightly with her other hand. 'If I remember rightly, you told me you "sort of" had a job. I'm sorry, but this isn't sort of anything. You *are* an artist.'

He nodded. 'Like I said back on the beach. This is worth the scavenging, then?'

She nodded, her gaze fixed back on the waves, trying to see what it was that made the solid wood seem to shift before her eyes. Leo finally nudged her with his hip—'Earth to Rachel. I'm glad you like it. Really, I am.'

Suddenly she was aware how close he'd stepped to stop her touching the sculpture. How his hand still gripped hers, although it must be minutes—longer—since she'd dropped it away from the driftwood.

Though she'd felt hypnotised by the piece, it slowly filtered through to her that it and Leo couldn't be separated. The beauty of his work was part of who he was. And something about that made her feel as if she didn't know him at all. Didn't understand him. As if she no longer understood the situation they found themselves in.

She turned her face up to his, and tried to see the Leo she thought she knew in the features of this talented, passionate artist. She thought back to how quickly she'd written him off as spoiled and undisciplined when he'd told her he "sort of" had a job, and could have kicked herself for that lazy assumption. If she'd taken the time and care to actually ask him more about himself, she wouldn't be so blindsided now.

She'd turned her body when she looked up at him, and could almost feel the attraction pulling them to-

gether. He seemed taller—much taller—when she was
in her flats, and from here she had a perfect view of his
broad chest and shoulders, courtesy, no doubt, of hours
in the water. Leo seemed to be studying her as closely as
she was him, though she wasn't sure why. He wasn't the
one who'd just had his entire perception of their circumstances change again. But the intensity of his gaze was
intoxicating, and she found that once her eyes met his
she couldn't look away.

'I'm sorry—' Rachel hoped that speaking out loud
might break the dangerous connection. Help her to re-
establish some sort of calm. But Leo laid a gentle finger on her lips.

'You don't need to apologise.' The finger was replaced
by a thumb, which rubbed across her lower lip, bringing
sensation and longing with it. She felt her flesh swell-
ing beneath his touch, ready for his kiss, begging for it.
And Leo was reading the message loud and clear. He
dipped his head, and Rachel let out a little sigh, remembering all too clearly exactly what one of Leo's kisses
promised. As she breathed in, and got two lungfuls of
his salty, sea-tanged scent, she was tempted—God, so
tempted—to forget the last point she'd made in her plan.
The one she'd set in red, bold and underlined: *NO SEX*.

Leo's lips brushed against hers and she turned her
head, so his kiss grazed across the corner of her lips and
her cheek. She stifled a groan, half kicking herself for
writing that into the plan, and half impressed with herself for making a decision when she was thinking more
clearly than she was right now. Because she strongly
suspected if she hadn't had a plan to follow in that moment, she would have been in serious danger of repeating past mistakes.

She took a deliberate step away from him, still not quite able to trust her commitment to her plan. Leo raised an eyebrow in question when she finally lifted her face to meet his gaze.

'I'm sorry. I should have been clearer before now.' Rachel took another step away and leant back against one of Leo's workbenches to steady herself. 'I enjoy your company, and I'm glad we're getting to know one another. I hope that we can be friends. But that's all that's on the table—friendship.'

Leo's hands dug into his pockets and he watched her from under heavy brows. 'You enjoy my company?' She could sense embarrassment washing over her features at the slow, deliberate way he spoke the words, conjuring memories of every pleasurable moment of their first and only night together.

His voice was low and gravelly as he spoke again. 'I would have thought a decision as important as that would have been in your plan.'

She opened her mouth to tell him that if he'd made it to the last page, he would have seen, would have known that it was. But he obviously read her expression too well and finally lost his serious look, bursting into an unexpected laugh.

'You did! You wrote "no sex" into the plan. You astound me, Rachel, honestly.' Except he looked more amused than astounded, what with the laughing and everything.

'It's important to know where we stand,' she told him, a little offended, if she was honest, that he could laugh so soon after their aborted kiss.

'Well, consider me well informed.'

Shouldn't he be a bit more...disappointed? Rachel

thought as Leo walked over to the other side of the studio and started sorting through a stack of driftwood and bric-a-brac in one corner. It didn't make sense, the hollow, sinking feeling in her belly. Because a purely platonic relationship was exactly what she'd wanted. But Leo's easy acceptance of her rejection was as good as a rejection in itself.

'Here they are. I knew there were a couple in here.' From the pile he pulled two glass bottles, similar to the one she'd just plucked from the beach. 'They look nice together, don't you think? Perhaps for the windowsill in your room?'

He lined them up on the bench, but she was more interested in why he'd been so keen to walk away from that kiss. He was the one who'd started it, wasn't he?

'So you're happy to just be friends. You're not interested in anything more.' She tried to keep the words casual. To show only the friendly interest her head told her was reasonable, and not the roiling discomfort her heart demanded. 'Because I think if there's anything we need to talk about, we should do it now.'

The smile actually dropped from his face, and he looked a little worried, she realised.

'"More" is an interesting concept.'

Interesting? Of all the words she would use to describe what happened when they went for 'more', *interesting* would not be high on her list.

'If "more" is another night like that one back at your place, then I'm all for "more". As much "more" as is on offer.'

She actually felt her cheeks warm again—she'd not blushed like this since she was a girl.

'But I suspect that for you, "more" is something,

well…more than that. If we can't do one without the other, then you're right. Friends is best.'

And again with the sinking disappointment. So he wouldn't mind more sex, but he didn't want a relationship with her. Well, then, they were in perfect agreement.

'Back to the house?' she asked, faking a jollity she didn't feel. 'My train's in an hour, so I probably need to make a move.'

'Of course. Don't forget your bottles.' She scooped up the antique glass and with a last look at the sculpture in the centre of room, she swept out.

'What's the hurry?' Leo jogged up the path behind her, lagging behind because he'd had to lock up the studio.

'Oh, I didn't realise I was.' A lie, of course. Because much as she knew that she couldn't allow herself to want a relationship with Leo, as much as the thought of being involved with someone who was happy to live with no roof till the right tiles came along filled her with dread, she still wanted a little time and space to lick her wounds. Just because she'd decided not to want him didn't mean she didn't want him to want her—however ridiculous that might be.

As they turned the corner and the house came into view, the sight of it made her feel better and worse at the same time.

'So the roof,' she said, as Leo overtook her along the path and held out a hand to help her over a small crop of rocks. 'Is there a…?'

'A plan?'

'Yes.'

'No.'

Not exactly what she wanted to hear. No, she didn't technically get a say in how he wanted to renovate his home. But if she were to come back here—and they were having a baby, how could she not?—it would be nice if the place was watertight. And there would be a baby before next summer. She was reassessing the way she made decisions, the way she relied on her plans, but was it unreasonable to expect that there might be a roof to sleep under?

'Don't worry, Rachel. The roof should be done any time now. I can absolutely promise it'll be finished by the next time you visit. The floor, too.'

She laughed, though still wasn't convinced. 'Sounds like luxury. So…I'll see you in London in a couple of weeks, for the scan? Do you want me to book you a hotel? I don't have a guest room. But you're welcome to my couch.'

'Don't worry; I'll sort somewhere to stay.'

'Are you sure? Because I—'

'I don't need you to organise anything. Relax. I'll take care of it. Do you want a lift to the station?'

'Oh, no need. I've already arranged a cab.'

He gave her a smile she wasn't sure how to interpret. 'Of course you have.'

CHAPTER EIGHT

'So this "no-sex" thing. Remind me again, what kind of a rule are we talking about—a law, guideline or EU directive?'

Rachel shot Laura a look over her decaf Americano. It still took her by surprise sometimes that her slight, quiet, almost mousy best friend could cut to the chase quite so sharply. Laura had been thrilled for Rachel when she'd seen how happy she was about the baby, but too fascinated by far by her relationship with the father. 'Why are you bringing this up now? It's whichever one of those means that it's not happening. Ever.'

'I'm bringing this up because I'm about to meet him for the first time and you still fancy him.'

She took a couple of deep breaths, until she was sure she could speak impassively. 'He is quite attractive.'

Laura rolled her eyes. 'He got you home from that party. I'm willing to put money on him being pretty special.'

Okay, so she was crazy to think she could pull the wool over her best friend's eyes. 'He's gorgeous, all right. I freely admit that he's gorgeous. But that wasn't why...' She trailed off, not wanting to incriminate herself by admitting to anything other than the most carnal feelings about Leo.

She glanced at her phone again, wondering what was taking him so long. All he had to do was show up. How hard could it be? So hard that the last time they'd had a scan appointment he'd called with a barrelful of excuses and then missed the first look at their baby.

With ten minutes to go before their previous appointment, she'd hit redial again and again. Voicemail. It had gone straight through to his messages ever since Leo had lost signal as he'd passed through a tunnel the last time he'd called. Two hours before. He couldn't have still been in that tunnel, so there was no reason for it not to have rung. She had tried to fight her anger down— it hadn't been Leo's fault that floods had closed all the train lines from the south-west. That the motorways had been clogged. That trees had been blown down and were blocking roads. But none of that changed the fact that she had needed him, and he hadn't been there. She needed a partner, her co-parent. She'd been excited for weeks about the scan, counting down the days until she would get a first glimpse of her baby. But in those past few hours since Leo had called with the news about the trains, all she'd been able to think about were her fears—what if the stick had lied to her, and she wasn't pregnant after all? What if they saw there was something wrong with the baby, if there wasn't a heartbeat? What if she had to face bad news without him?

She had hit redial again—and still there had been no response.

Checking the time as she'd hung up, she had taken a deep breath and squared her shoulders. She had to do this one on her own. Not that she'd had a choice; those last few hours had taught her something she should have faced long before then. She couldn't rely on Leo. It didn't matter how enthusiastic he was about the pregnancy, how good his intentions had been, she had to rely on herself, and no one else.

She'd gone into the ultrasound room alone and upset. The first glimpse of her baby should have filled her with complete joy, and it had; it was magical, emotional. But she hadn't been able to help but feel the loss of Leo by her side. When he'd finally arrived, Leo had promised her that he'd tried everything humanly possible to get there, but now, with less than five minutes to go until she was meant to meet him for their second scan, she was becoming nervous. What if he let her down again? What would she do if she couldn't trust him to be there when she—when they—needed him?

This time she'd asked Laura to come with her, to give her the support she knew she couldn't rely on Leo for.

'Oh, now, this is interesting.' Laura dragged her thoughts back to their conversation. 'This *is* new. If you didn't take him home because you were mad for his body, then this is something else entirely. I thought you told me that it was a moment of lust, not to be repeated.'

'It was!'

'No.' Rachel waited as Laura took a long sip of her coffee, and could practically see the words flying behind her eyes as she picked through them carefully, analysing, choosing an angle. 'You just said, or didn't say, that isn't true. So, what was it about him that caught your eye, other than his "quite attractive" looks? I know you, remember, and I know you don't make decisions like that at the drop of a hat.'

Rachel thought back to that night—the way Leo had teased her and made her laugh, made her relax. Fooled her into thinking that just for a night she could change her plan with no repercussions.

'He made me laugh; we were having a good time. I didn't expect—'

'For him to start baking in your oven.'

Rachel coughed as her coffee made a bid for escape through her nose.

'Thank you. Beautifully put.'

'Seriously, though.' Laura placed her coffee carefully on the table and held her gaze with a shrewd look. 'Are you sure that "just friends" is really the answer? You *like* him.' She held up a firm hand to stop Rachel's blustering protests. 'You can deny it all you want and I still won't believe you. And you have no reason to think that he doesn't like you, either. But you're not going to even explore what there is between you?'

'The baby—'

'Is the perfect excuse to give it a go, not run from it. So what is it that scares you about him?'

She stared into her drink for a long minute, trying to capture everything that Leo made her feel. The exhilaration of that night, the glimpse of a more relaxed life, the freedom when he made her laugh. The terror of everything she knew, understood and believed about her future suddenly being ripped away. 'Be honest with me. Do you think there's something...not right...about the way I like a plan, a schedule?'

Laura didn't drop her shrewd expression, though her eyes softened. 'Yes. Truthfully, I don't think it's healthy how anxious you are without one. And if you're starting to see that, too, perhaps now is a good time to be thinking about making changes. I hate to break this to you, darling, but there's no hiding from chaos now. You're going to have to find a way to—'

'No.' Rachel choked the word out of instinct, her gut revolting at the thought of that inevitability. And then felt instantly bad for snapping at her friend. 'Yes. I'm going to try. But the baby's enough chaos. Leo's just too much, and I can't trust him to be there when I need him.'

'You really are nervous.' Laura smiled, giving no hint that she was offended by her best friend snapping at her. 'It's cute. I don't think I've seen you nervous before.'

'I'm not nervous.'

'So the father of your child, the man you found literally irresistible five months ago, is going to show up in this coffee shop in ten minutes' time, and you're not even slightly nervous? Rubbish.'

Leo raced across the pavement, determined to get to Rachel before the second hand hit twelve, to prove to her that he could be the partner, and the parent, that she needed him to be. He'd barely seen her since the last scan. A couple of lunches in London, that was all, the last time just a coffee when he'd been in the city to meet with Will about the Julia House sculpture.

She claimed she hadn't been able to get a weekend off since that first time she'd been down in Dorset. But he knew the real reason, that she was still angry and upset that he'd missed that scan. And of course he could understand that. But he'd tried everything he could to get there on time. He'd hired a car when all the trains were cancelled. He'd waded through floodwater when the car had got caught in a soaked back lane and had conked out. He'd begged and bartered for lifts into the city, and when he'd finally made it, fourteen hours after leaving his house, he'd apologised until his voice was hoarse and she'd told him to stop. He just wanted to make things right, which, despite her assurances the last time he saw her, he knew they weren't.

He swung open the door to the coffee shop, and there she was. Her hair shiny and straight around her shoulders, a mug clasped in her hand, and, framed by her propped elbows, a neat little bump. His breath stopped at the sight of her. And then he saw that she wasn't alone, and his heart sank.

'Hi,' he said, as he walked up to the table, sending Rachel a questioning glance. He looked at the other woman and held out his hand. 'I'm Leo.'

She'd brought a friend to their ultrasound? There was only one reason he could think of that she would do that, and it made him cringe in regret. She couldn't trust him to be here. He'd let her down, and she wasn't ready to forgive.

'Leo, this is Laura.'

He watched the loaded look that passed between Rachel and her friend, and tried to translate it. *You want me to leave now he's here?*

He stood awkwardly as they gathered bags and finished coffees. The silence between him and Rachel stretched out onto the street, through goodbyes with Laura, down the corridors of the hospital, and into the waiting room. She maintained a clear foot of space between them, and every time he tried to close it, it pushed her further away. It was a relief when the sonographer appeared, breaking the tension in the hushed waiting room.

'Rachel Archer?'

He risked a small smile at her as they walked into the ultrasound room, and then didn't know where to look when Rachel pulled up her top and the technician tucked blue paper into her waistband. The sight of her skin gave him goose bumps, as he remembered how soft it had been under his lips and his body. Looking up at the ceiling, he took a deep breath, reminding himself that this really was not the right time to be thinking those thoughts. In fact, Rachel had made it more than clear in every strained silence since he'd let her down that there was no right time for those thoughts—and he had agreed with her, at least at first.

Because he shouldn't want anything more than friendship from her. He was already getting so much more than he had wanted. One night with this woman had already brought one lifelong commitment. A thought that still made him breathless—and not in a good way. It was crazy to embark on anything romantic, because what else could that bring other than more commitment? They could hardly date and see how it went. Because where did they go when one of them realised that it wasn't going to work out? Or what happened if she started thinking about a future and a ring, and he started to sweat? They should just concentrate on being the best parents that they could be, and try to be friends, as well.

But, God, she looked delicious. Her body curved in new places, her breasts were bigger, and her belly rounded. His child was growing in there, he thought, his mind boggling. He dragged his eyes away, though, realising suddenly that it probably wasn't brilliant form to ogle someone while they were in hospital, whatever the reason.

That thought sobered him. Because this scan wasn't just a chance to wave at the baby and hope that he or she waved back. He'd been reading up about what they should be expecting. And so he knew that the ultrasound was done for serious reasons, that it was for the medical professionals to check for health problems. That thought gripped him with a twist of anxiety and without thinking he reached for Rachel's hand. She flinched, though whether it was from him gripping her hand or from the gel being squeezed on her belly he couldn't be sure. But she squeezed his hand back and looked up to meet his eye. When she gave a little smile, he realised that she was as nervous as he was.

He watched the screen as the technician manipulated the ultrasound wand, and saw black and white shadows moving. He squinted, trying to make out what was what, but it wasn't until the technician pointed out the tiny head and limbs that he finally understood he was looking at his child. His son or daughter.

He'd spent so long thinking about all the ways his life had to change now, about the fact he'd woken up one morning and found himself painted into a corner, forced into fatherhood whether he wanted it or not, that he'd never stopped to consider that he and Rachel had done something so…so…miraculous. It was the only word he could grasp as he looked at the tiny life on the screen. A whole new life, created from nothing but the urgent, overwhelming desire of that night.

And seeing that miracle, and the one on Rachel's face as she saw it, too, the undisguised incredulity and rush of happiness, he couldn't help but be deliriously happy with her. Or help the tear that slid from the corner of his eye. It wasn't that he wasn't stomach-churningly terrified still, he just realised that that fear didn't have to be all-consuming. He could be worried to his bones about what effect this little child would have on his life, but still be absolutely, unbelievably happy that they'd made their baby.

He squeezed Rachel's hand a little harder, and she turned her face towards him, her eyes and cheeks lit with happiness and wet with tears.

As he watched, another tear snuck from the corner of his eye, and he smudged it away with his thumb.

'Everything looks good here,' the radiographer announced, breaking the silence and passing Rachel a tissue to clean off the gel.

The intimacy between them suddenly lost, Leo turned away, offering her some privacy.

They strolled from the hospital into the park opposite still dazed with happiness.

'Rachel, you know I'm sorry, don't you, that we didn't get to share this before? That I would have given anything to have been here.' He reached for her hand, needing the physical contact, desperate to know that they were back to being friends. That everything was right between them again.

To his surprise, she smiled, looking up at him, her eyes still a little damp. 'I know. I know that you tried, and I should have forgiven you a long time ago. I thought that I…that the baby…that we didn't mean enough to you. But I know that I was wrong.'

Didn't mean enough to him? He didn't know how it would be possible for anyone to mean more. Somehow his whole world had shrunk and expanded until Rachel was the shape of his whole future. He stopped walking, and held onto her hand a little tighter.

'Rachel, you have to know, you and the baby, you're everything. There are still days where I feel like I've got no idea how we got here, but I wouldn't change it for anything. Wouldn't wish for anything but what we have.'

His free hand brushed away another tear, just sneaking out from the corner of her lashes.

'I felt so alone—'

'And it kills me even thinking about it.'

'I know,' she said, 'I didn't say it to make you feel worse. It just made me realise how much I wanted you there. How much I wanted us to see our baby together. How much it means to me that we get to share this. It wasn't that I wanted *someone* there, Leo. I wanted you.'

He drew her close, swiping another tear as she hid her face in his chest.

'I feel the same,' he said into her hair. 'And it's frightening and exhilarating and it reminds me how much there is still to learn about this whole family thing. But we can do this, Rachel, and we can be brilliant at it. Be parents. Be more than that to each other.'

He dipped his head and pressed his lips to her mouth. It was quick and soft and sweet, and as he rested his forehead against hers he couldn't think of a moment in his life when he'd been more content than this. With his baby's heartbeat echoing in his ears, with Rachel's skin warm against his and the memory of her lips smiling against his fresh in his mind. All the reasons he'd fought this romance seemed to slip away. Every objection to keeping this woman at the centre of his life—the space she'd occupied since the moment they'd met—faded. The important thing, the only important thing, was that they faced their lives together. 'You're right,' she murmured, and he could hear her smile in her voice. 'We'll be brilliant.'

CHAPTER NINE

RACHEL EYED THE encroaching black clouds and glanced at the ETA on the taxi satnav. Four minutes. She crossed her fingers and hoped she could get inside before the storm broke. It was going to be a big one, and her jacket was buried in the bottom of her bag, stowed out of reach in the boot of the car. Either running up the pathway—she glanced at her patent pumps doubtfully—or digging through her bag, she'd be soaked in seconds.

The weather had been beautifully clear in London, and had only clouded over slightly on the train journey down. But once she'd climbed into the taxi from the station it had turned so dark it seemed like night. And the clouds just kept on gathering. It was almost impossible not to consider it an omen. Not that she had any reason to think this weekend would go badly. After the last scan she and Leo had spent a joyful afternoon together, laughing and joking, talking tentatively about the arrival of the baby, and generally being full of generosity and joy. There was no reason to think that today would be any different.

Except that when he'd called her at lunchtime—inviting her down to Dorset for the weekend—there had been something in his voice that worried her. Behind his words had been an edge of something nervy and taut.

Why didn't she take the afternoon off, he'd said, and come straight down to the cottage? She'd bitten down on the word *no*, and thought about it for a second, glancing at her calendar. It would mean moving her Monday around, but there was really no reason she couldn't... It was the perfect chance to put her new life decisions in action and try something spontaneous for a change. To ignore her plan for just a few hours and see where the afternoon took her.

She'd cleared it with Will and treated herself to a cab straight to her flat and then the station, her belly fluttering with the excitement of her first spur-of-the-moment action in years.

But as the car turned the final corner and the cottage came into view, Rachel's stomach sank, and she felt the cool damp fingers of fear and disappointment trickling down her collar, as icy as the imminent rain. The pile of builders' material in front of the house had shrunk considerably, but Rachel's eye was drawn to the roof, where a bright blue tarpaulin stood out like a flag against the grey sky. The tile-less corner of the house was very small, but very bare nonetheless.

And just like that she felt the significance of that omen grow. He'd promised. She'd trusted him that the house would be more habitable now—that it would at least be watertight. She was here, trying to live a little freer, trying to make their family work, and he had let her down before she'd even stepped inside. A crack of thunder threw her eyes to the sky and she knew that she'd have to run to the door. She just had to hope that she would be drier inside than she would be out here, as the first marble-sized drops of rain reached her.

Leo, umbrella in hand, swung open the front door

when she was halfway up the path. 'I'm so sorry,' he shouted as he ran towards her, umbrella aloft and reaching for her bag. Another peal of thunder tore across the sky. 'I only just saw the taxi—'

'I'm fine,' she said as they reached the front door and Leo stood back to let her through. She glanced around her at the living room as she wiped the water from her face and brushed down the front of her sweater. At least he'd lived up to his promise of a floor.

'You're not fine. You're angry,' Leo said, looking at her.

Of course she was angry. How could she be expected to trust a man who didn't think a house in a thunderstorm needed a roof? Who couldn't see that something like the small issue of your home being watertight might be important? Especially when he had a guest. Who was pregnant—with *his* child.

'What's up?'

She shouldn't bite. They needed to be civil to one another if they were going to make parenting together work. She would just have to learn. 'What's up? The house still doesn't have a roof!'

'Oh, that. Most of it's finished, but there was a slight problem with the calculations, and there weren't enough tiles. I've got some more on the way. You're really annoyed about the progress of the building?'

'I'm really annoyed that it might rain indoors tonight.'

'Don't worry about that. It's only a small patch, and your room's on the good side. The roof's lined with plenty of tarps. The ceilings are all totally dry. I can't see any water getting in.'

'That's not the point.' Her hair was dripping cold water down the back of her neck, and she shivered. She pulled it into a ponytail and bundled it up onto the top of her head, using the distraction to try and temper her anger. 'You said that it would be finished by now.' The words came out icily cool, and she prided herself on keeping her fury under wraps.

'So I'm running a little late. It'll be done soon. There were a couple of other jobs that I wanted to do first. Wait.' He stopped his pacing, which had taken him from her side and back to the window, checking on the progress of the storm. 'Why are you so annoyed?'

With his casual disregard, she finally lost it. 'In case you hadn't noticed, you're going to be a father in a few months. Which means—I hope, or I hoped—that you might want your child to visit. How can I bring a baby into a house that doesn't have a roof?'

He stared at her, his eyes wide and his body language heading towards guarded as he planted his hands on his hips. 'The baby isn't due for months. There's plenty of time before then. I promise it'll be done by the time—'

'Another promise! How am I meant to believe this one, when the last one meant nothing?' She pulled her sweater over her head as she was talking, scattering raindrops everywhere, and forcing icy water from her hair down her back. Her shirt underneath was damp, too, and she shivered.

'It'll get done when it needs doing! Can't you trust me to know when that is?'

She rolled her eyes in disbelief, and dropped her voice as the fight left her and disappointment set in. 'I'm standing in a roofless house in the middle of the storm. Of course I can't trust you.' She shivered again, water still dripping down the back of her neck, her skin turning chilly and rising with goose bumps. She just wanted to get warm, and dry. And away from Leo and his empty promises. She grabbed her bag, brushing off Leo's offers of help, and headed for the kitchen and the stairs. She stormed up to her room and then dropped on the bed. Rubbing the heels of her hands into her eyes, she forced down tears. Why hadn't she expected this? Why did her disappointment make her feel so utterly broken?

Pulling herself together, she dug in her bag for dry clothes, and headed to the bathroom. When she walked back into her room, wrapped in cosy cashmere and with her hair turbaned into a towel, it was to find Leo on his hands and knees on the floor.

'You looked cold.' He glanced over his shoulder as he spoke. 'I thought you might like a fire.'

Rachel dropped down on the bed and gave Leo a long look. Her eyes darted to the ceiling, looking for damp, or any other sign of the storm that was shaking the windows. It looked dry, as Leo had said, and the heavy, guilty feeling in her belly made her wonder whether she'd been slightly hasty with her temper.

Suddenly, the fire caught, and Leo sat back on his heels, his face fully caveman smug. As the flames licked from the kindling to the wood—which looked suspiciously like the floorboards downstairs—she dropped onto the floor between the bed and the fire, sneaking her bare toes towards the heat.

Leo sat next to her, and nudged her shoulder with his. 'I know I said it would be done by now. And it almost is. But I'm sorry I disappointed you.'

'And I'm sorry for snapping the minute I arrived.' She let her shoulder rest against him, his heat adding to that of the fire, making her feel drowsy.

'You know these things take time. The materials don't

just appear when I click my fingers. I can't do this according to your plan.'

She sighed, seeing how far apart they still were on how their lives would unfold. 'I know I said I'm going to be more flexible, but some things have to be done to a plan. Some things aren't safe, or sensible, or reasonable without one.'

'And some things work better. Sometimes we're happier.'

'Sometimes *you're* happier.'

He nodded. 'You're right. I am. But we need to meet somewhere in the middle. We need to find a way to do things that keeps us both happy. So if you're prepared to accept my apology for the roof not being finished, then maybe we can take another look at that master plan of yours. See what else we need to work out.'

She agreed, feeling a bit dreamy by the fire with the warmth on her face, the carpet soft between her toes and the bedspread squidgy behind her back. Those first few months of feeling exhausted had faded, but now six months pregnant and still keeping her usual unsociable hours—in the office by seven in the morning, often still there late in the evening—afternoon naps had become a standing fixture of her weekends.

She didn't move when Leo reached out to pull the fire guard back across, or when he reached above her to pull back the bedspread, even though it was more than tempting to turn into his shoulder, soak up more of his warmth and his smell. She was cold again when he stood, leaving her on the floor, but then he reached for her hands, pulled her to her feet and then back towards the bed. 'You look like you need sleep more than you need an argument.'

She couldn't disagree with that, and tucked herself between the sheets, wondering, for a fleeting second, what would happen if she kept hold of his hand and pulled him in after her. Disaster surely, probably, but just for now it would be... Perhaps it was best that sleep was pulling her eyelids closed, taking the decision from her hands.

She woke to the sound of pans clashing in the kitchen, and glanced at the clock on the bedside table. She'd slept for more than an hour. She stretched out under the bedspread, savouring the warmth in her limbs and on the side of her face. The fire in the grate was still burning strong, and it was no easy thing to drag herself out of bed, and pad downstairs to a man she'd practically fallen asleep on mid-argument.

'Hi.'

As she reached the bottom of the stairs, Leo was standing across the kitchen, his back to her, stirring something on the hob. But what caught her eye was the spread of papers on the table. Coloured pencils were scattered across pages peppered with arrows, exclamation marks and doodles. When she looked closer, she recognised the headings from her own plan, each one in the centre of a sheet of paper. And a couple she'd saved to talk about later: names, visitation, nursery.

She remained standing, astonished that Leo had started to plan for this baby, and admiring the beauty of what he'd produced. Most of it was indecipherable to her. Scribbles and arrows and more question marks than answers, from what she could see. But the doodles were what held her attention. Though that wasn't really the right word for them. They were miniature works of art, tucked into corners, and they told her more than she'd ever thought she'd know about what was going on in the mind of the man who had drawn them. A baby's head cradled in a muscular arm, unmistakably Leo's. A shadowy sketch that looked remarkably similar to the picture of their ultrasound. A woman sitting on the edge of a bed, her naked back covered by a fall of shiny hair. Rachel blushed, recognising herself.

'Afternoon.' Leo turned to her, holding a couple of mugs.

'There's chicken and vegetables as well, but I wasn't sure what you were up to these days…'

'Chicken sounds great.' Her belly gave a roll of thunder to back up her words. 'Thanks. This is brilliant.'

Leo set the plates down on the table, sweeping aside his papers. He subtly tucked away the one with the sketch of her, she noted, from the corner of her eye.

'You saw my plans, then.'

'I did. They're beautiful…'

They'd taken to talking a couple of times a week. At first she'd thought that it was to sort out practical stuff, but gradually this had turned instead into a brief catch-up, and then they had spent long, lazy evenings and Sunday afternoons discussing the latest fundraising for Julia House, what the tide had thrown up, how the guy at the rec yard had found the perfect tiles for the kitchen. Face to face, conversation flowed more easily still, as she relaxed into his company.

'It's mostly what we've already talked about. It just all fell into place, and I could look at it in a way that made sense to me.'

'You've made it beautiful.'

She soaked up the smile he gave her, as warm as the fire upstairs.

'Eat first, talk second?'

'Perfect,' she agreed, digging into her dinner.

Once their plates were cleared away, she couldn't help her eyes wandering to Leo's plans, keen to see what he'd come up with and how it would fit with what she'd written. Leo must have spotted her not so subtle perusal.

'All right, then, get your notebook out. I know you're dying to.'

Why bother to deny it? She nipped up to the bedroom and grabbed her plans, and was back at the table before Leo had the chance to brew another coffee.

She pulled out her A3 plan as Leo placed a cup of black coffee in front of her. She flicked her eyes up and parted her lips to ask a question. 'Decaf,' Leo said, preempting her. She held his gaze a moment longer, before letting her eyes drift back to her plans.

She shuffled their papers and tried to match up Leo's to her own. Most of the practical stuff was covered: the dates of her midwife appointments; which hospital she was planning for the birth; due date, maternity leave and annual leave. So when she looked down at her plan, all the easy questions were dealt with, which left them with the tricky one they'd been skirting around for months now: access and living arrangements.

Leo was entitled—and deserved—to see his son or daughter as much as possible; she had no intention of ever denying that. But that didn't make it easier. They lived hundreds of miles apart, and their careers kept them there. And that meant that their child would have two homes, and that as parents they would be constantly shuttling between the two. The idea of a newborn was terrifying enough. When you added a three-hour train journey into the mix, it was suddenly more terrifying still.

'I think we need to talk about what happens after the

baby's born,' she started. 'I need to be in London for the birth, and I can't see that it would be good for the baby to move around a lot in the first few months. From the advice I've read for separated parents, the best thing for a new baby is a consistent routine when it comes to see-ing the secondary par—'

'Secondary?' She sat back in shock at the sudden hint of anger in Leo's voice. 'I'm sorry, when—exactly—did I get demoted?' His shoulders were fixed into a straight, solid line, and his face was flushed with emotion.

And this was why they'd put it off for so long, she thought. It was a minefield. She tried to keep her own voice calm, to defuse the situation.

'You've not been demoted, Leo. Please don't think that's what I'm trying to do. But unless you've suddenly grown the apparatus to feed a child then I'll have to be the primary caregiver. It would be the same if we were a couple, if we were married. It's just a word.'

He glared at her, and she realised that it wasn't just a word. Not to him at least.

'You're pushing me out.' His shoulders were still up and his face tense, and she realised he had been build-ing up to this. She'd sensed it occasionally on the phone, an edge of concern and suspicion whenever they skirted around the issues of access and contact. She reached for his hand, wanting to calm the situation, but the contact of his skin on hers made her anything but.

'Leo, trust me. We are going to find a way that we are *all* happy. All three of us.'

'And how exactly are we going to do that when you hold all the cards and get to call all the shots?' He al-most hissed the words as he pulled his hand away from hers, and then sat back in his chair and crossed his arms.

'We make this plan together. Tell me what you want and we will find a way to make it work.'

'Fine.' He ground the words out through gritted teeth. 'I want to be there. I want half the time, half the responsibilities. Half the holidays and Christmases. And I want it legal and in writing.'

'I don't understand where this is coming from.' Bewilderment kept her voice gentle, questioning. 'For months you've baulked at even the thought of a plan or a schedule. Now you're demanding it? What's changed?'

'What's changed is you demoting me to a secondary parent! What's changed is you pushing me out.'

'And you refusing to trust me.'

She rested her head in her hands and took a couple of long, calming breaths. Parents at loggerheads didn't help any child—they would have to find a way through this.

'Let's start from the beginning,' she suggested. 'I go into hospital and the baby is born. When do you want to visit?'

'Visit? I don't want to visit.'

So starting from the beginning was no help. Was there nothing that they were going to be able to agree on? Leo's anger had been so sudden and unexpected she had no idea how to handle it.

'I want to be there for the birth. I want to be a part of everything. I thought I'd made that clear.'

She viscerally recoiled at the thought of it, of him seeing her groaning and exposed. 'No way. I know we're going to share a lot, for the rest of our lives, in fact. But can't you grant me a little dignity?'

'You don't want me there.'

'You're putting me on the spot,' she countered, trying to keep up with his arguments. 'I never even considered you might *want* to be there. I'd already thought—'

'You've already planned. What a surprise. Tell me, then, what have you planned?'

'I'd like Laura to be there during the birth, and she's said that she'll do it.'

He shook his head as if she'd disappointed him, and he'd expected it all along.

'And where do I fit into any of this? Or am I meant to just miss out on the first few weeks?' His voice broke, betrayed the fear and despair she sensed behind his anger. If he'd just tell her what was wrong, why he was finding it so hard to trust her, maybe they'd have a way of working this out.

She placed a hand over his, trying to soothe. 'So let's agree on something we're both happy with.'

'I want to be at the birth.' For a few moments, all she could see, hear, smell was blood, guts and embarrassment. She swallowed down her automatic refusal.

'Head end only. If I change my mind on the day you respect my privacy. And I want Laura, too.'

He looked up in surprise. 'Okay, I can live with that. But when we get home, it's just the three of us.'

She nearly choked on her coffee. 'Oh, no, you can't think that you're moving in with me.'

Hurt twisted his features again. 'How else am I meant to be a father? Of course I'll be there. I'll sleep on the couch, if that's what you're worrying about. I'm not assuming that we'll…'

She shook her head again. Already able to see the argument she was walking into, and starting to feel shame colour her cheeks. This was something she should have talked to him about. She shouldn't have assumed that she could decide this without him. But the damage was already done. She hadn't meant to hurt him, but he seemed to be blindsiding her at every turn, wanting things she'd never imagined he would.

'I'm sorry, Leo, but I don't think it will work. For a start, there's not enough room.'

'It's a pretty small couch, you're right. I'll buy one of those blow-up mattresses or something.'

'That's not what I meant. I mean there's no room because my mother's going to be on the couch.'

'Your mother?' The words whipped out of him, stinging Rachel with their sharp edges of disappointment and distress. 'Let me get this right. So far your friend's going to be at the birth of our child, and there's no room for me to care for our newborn baby after you come home because you've invited your mum to stay. And you still don't think you're pushing me out.'

The worst part was, he was right. She had pushed him out. Regret swelled in her chest, and tears threatened at the corners of her lashes. She hadn't intended to do it, to plan without even making room for him. 'I'm sorry. I didn't think of it that way. I just…I just needed a plan. And I knew I couldn't push you. And my mum was offering help, insisting really. I didn't know what to do, so I took it.'

'This isn't meant to be about making either one of us happy, Rachel. Or your mother—or Laura, for that matter. It's meant to be about what's best for our child.'

'You really think you have to tell me that? That I'm not thinking about what's best for him every single minute? I can't believe you would accuse me of that.'

'And you don't think that what he needs is *both* his parents? Unless you can give me a very good reason why my being there is bad for our child, I'll be moving into your apartment. If there's not room for your mother, too, then she can book into a hotel. But my need to be with my child, and my child's need to be with his parent, trumps hers.'

She rubbed her face in her hands, knowing that he was right.

'I can see from your face that you agree with me.'

'I'm sorry. Of course you can stay. I'll speak to Mum.'

And with that concession, the fire fell out of both their arguments. Leo's shoulders softened, and he reached out a hand for hers. 'Thank you. I just don't want to miss anything. Not a minute.'

'I know, Leo. But I'm not the enemy. I don't know why you can't trust that I just want what's best for our child.'

'I do.'

'That's not what you were saying a minute ago, when you were talking solicitors and formal access.'

'Then don't make plans without me.' He grabbed a sheaf of his sketches and spread them out on the table. 'Here. Everything that was in your plan, as I remember it. Well, almost everything.'

She looked over the sheets and realised what he meant. There was nothing about 'no sex' here. She glanced up at him. Was it not here because he didn't want it to be? Or because they had both been so vehement about it before that he thought they didn't need it. She wasn't sure what she had to say about it anyway. She was still bristling a little from his accusations.

'So you've told your parents about the baby.'

She looked up at him, shocked by his question. 'Of course I've told them. He'll be here in a few months. I wasn't just going to turn up with him after he's born.'

And then something occurred to her. 'Don't tell me you haven't told yours…'

He held up his palms in a sign of defeat. 'I haven't really known where to start.'

'How about, *Mum, Dad—I've got some brilliant news…?*'

He raised an eyebrow. 'Is that how the conversation went with your parents?'

'Actually, I used those exact words.' She'd chosen them carefully, hoping that they might pre-empt her parents' concern.

It had taken her a couple of weeks to build up the courage to call her parents, knowing how much they were going to worry over her, sensing how that worry was going to threaten her own peace of mind. But eventually she had picked up the phone.

Once her mother had regained the power of speech, a flood of concern had followed. Why hadn't they met this man? Were they in a relationship? Had someone taken advantage of her? Had she informed the police?

Rachel had moved the phone away from her ear, trying to let their worries fall between the phone line and her brain, not letting them in. It was only when they started talking about getting in the car and coming to support her through this 'traumatic time' that Rachel realised that she had to put a stop to this.

'Mum, Dad. Please listen. I didn't take unnecessary risks. I wasn't taken advantage of. I'm thrilled about this baby, and I'd like it if you could be pleased for me, too.'

Stony silence.

Eventually they'd given muted congratulations, but Rachel had known as she'd hung up the phone that they would let their concerns about how their first grandchild was conceived spoil their excitement.

But Rachel wouldn't. She'd told them that it was brilliant news, and she'd meant it. Because however she might feel about Leo, she was in no way confused about what she felt about their baby. She supposed it was too much to hope that her parents would see it the same way.

But at least she'd told them. And apparently Leo hadn't even bothered to do that.

'You've told them nothing?'

His body language closed up, his arms crossing over his chest as he pushed his chair back from the table. She wondered what it was about his family that made him so…defensive. Like an animal that had been hurt before and was determined to avoid it happening again. Did this all come back to his brother, and school? 'It's not like we talk a lot.'

'And you didn't think that the fact that you're expecting a baby is something worth phoning home about?'

'You don't understand, Rachel.'

'Then tell me.' She leaned forward, making it impossible to escape into the space he'd created for himself. Impossible for him to run from her. 'Explain what's going on, because I don't understand, and if I don't understand, then how can we make it better?'

'There's nothing to tell.' The arms folded tighter. 'It's not a big deal.'

'Of course it's a big deal.' She couldn't let this drop, couldn't see something causing him pain and walk away from it as if she didn't care. This man had been on her mind every day for the past six months. Every day since they'd met, her heart had grown a little closer to his, as their lives had entwined, until she wasn't sure where hers ended and his began. And every day, she'd cared a little more, and her hurts and his were as tangled as their lives.

'We're having a baby in three months' time, and you haven't told your family about it. It makes me worry about you. That there's something wrong that I don't know about. Something hurting you. Is this something to do with what happened at school? Because your father wouldn't pull you out?'

He sighed, and when he spoke his voice shook a little. 'That's part of it. But I wasn't going to put it off for ever.'

The tremble in his voice nigh on broke her heart, seeing this big tough guy, moments ago demanding to be put through the trials of the birthing suite, cowed and afraid of talking to his family. 'But ignoring it isn't helping, either. When are you planning on telling them?'

'Tomorrow. It's Mum's birthday. She called this morning and told me she's having a family lunch tomorrow. Wouldn't take no for an answer. She asked me if there was anyone I'd like to bring and I thought that this might be as good a time as any...'

She snorted a gentle laugh at his naive plan, that they would just walk in there with her big belly and that would be that, while trying to fight down her panic at this sudden swerve to their weekend. But Leo's serious face and lines borne of worry and fear firmed her resolve. He needed her there with him. She couldn't let him down just because she was uncomfortable with surprises.

'This is your family, your problem, so we can do this your way. No plan required. I'm not going to tell you what you should do. But I think talking with them could be a good thing. The very fact that you don't want to makes me think that it's a bigger deal than you're letting on.'

'Sometimes you're too smart for your own good. You know that?'

He spoke with a smile, and she held his gaze for a moment longer than was strictly friendly. And then she couldn't look away. She could feel something building between them. Something warm and strong that started in her belly and reached out through her fingertips, jumping the distance he'd put between them and pulling her in. His fingertips stretched out on the tabletop and just brushed against hers. She held back a gasp at the prickle of awareness concentrated in the pads of her fingertips, and pushed them a little harder into the grain of the wood. Schooling them not to grab him. Because that was what every hormone-fuelled impulse in her body was screaming at her to do. To grab that hand, seize the heat simmering between them and bury the remnants of their harsh words and misunderstandings in a kiss. Or, preferably, more.

But when Leo reached a little further, and buried her palm in his, his touch wasn't sensual. His eyes shifted, and it was pain, not desire, in his features. Her own momentary desire morphed into compassion as she read his change in mood.

'It was my brother,' Leo said baldly, the words barely inflected. 'At the very centre of it all. The bullying. He started it, he encouraged it, and he's no less cruel now than when we were children. When Dad spoke to the school, Nicholas somehow convinced the teachers, and in turn my parents, that there was nothing wrong. That I was attention-seeking. In the end Dad thought it would be character-building for me to stay.'

It was disgusting, made her feel physically sick. She could never imagine being treated that way by her family, and her heart ached for Leo. She squeezed his hand back. 'Leo, I'm so sorry. I can't believe your father—'

'No, it wasn't him. He had no idea what was really going on. You don't understand. Nicholas is…well, he can be very charming. And very convincing. I really do think that my father thought he was doing what was best. And it wasn't until later that I discovered Nicholas was at the root of everything. By then I'd left school and left home and it didn't seem worth tearing the family apart by bringing it up. My mother is happy as things are. She loves my father and he adores her. As long as Nicholas and I can keep our distance, she stays happy.'

'And I'm guessing it's mostly you who keeps your distance. It doesn't sound like your brother would be so considerate. You must love your mum very much, to do that for her.'

'Of course I love her. She's my mother.'

'Do you think she's going to be excited to be a grand-mother? Is it her first? Nicholas doesn't…'

'No. Thank God. And yes, she's going to be thrilled. That's why I thought…at her birthday…'

'Whatever you decide. Whatever you need. Let me know.'

He turned her hand over in his and pressed a kiss to her palm. She shivered as his lips brushed her skin, and cupped her fingers around his jaw, just brushing against the ends of his hair.

But seeing him so upset, it was impossible not to try and help him. Not to reach for him and offer comfort. It sounded better that way, she told herself. Convincing herself that this was a selfless act, purely to make him feel better, and not to satisfy the ache that had travelled between heart and belly for the past few months. Ever since the night she had first met Leo.

As she reached across the table to him she felt their baby shift inside her, and dropped her other hand to her belly, rubbing at the elbow, or heel, or whichever body part was giving her belly a corner.

She remembered the first time it had happened, as she had lain on the couch, laptop balanced on her almost flat belly. Just a little flutter, almost nothing, but *everything*. The first time she'd truly felt pregnant. She'd dropped her work and reached for the phone, thinking of nothing but sharing this moment with Leo. Wanting him to share the rush of adrenaline and emotion.

Now his eyes followed her hand, watching closely as her hand moved over her tummy.

'Can I...?'

The yearning in his face was as strong as she had ever seen it. But this time it wasn't her body he wanted. Well, not exactly.

'Do you want to feel?' She pushed her seat back from the table at the same time as he stood. But standing over her, he hesitated. So she gently took his hand and guided it to where she could feel the baby kicking.

Rachel tried to keep her feelings motherly as Leo gently rubbed her stomach, following the kicks and movements of the baby. But with him standing over her, reaching down, she was surrounded by his body. Everywhere she looked there was tanned forearm, broad chest. That salty smell that was so unmistakably him. And this was wildly inappropriate, she told herself. He'd only come over here, was only touching her, because she was carrying his child. As far as she knew, he saw her as nothing more than an incubator right now. It had certainly been weeks, months, since they had even spoken about the fact that they had once been so intimate with one another. She had no reason to think that he wanted anything other than friendship from her. So she should just pull these pregnancy hormones of hers in line and stop fantasising about the other parts of her body that hand could be touching right now.

Rachel looked towards the ceiling, still trying to find a safe place for her gaze to rest. But it collided with Leo's intense blue stare. His hand remained on her belly, but, somehow, the touch changed. No longer curious, it was suddenly sensual. Caressing rather than exploring. His other arm rested along the back of her chair, and he leaned on it a little further. Bringing his face fractionally closer to hers. Just enough to fill her entire field of vision with the clean lines of his face and the coarse chaos of his hair. And her nose with his scent. And every single nerve-ending with the memory of how he could make her body sing. She tipped her head and closed her eyes.

His lips brushed against hers. Soft, but not hesitant. Deliciously assured and practised. Familiar but new, teasing her with all he had learnt about her since the moment they'd met. As Leo's hand found her waist, or what was left of it these days, she parted her lips with a moan, and twisted in her chair, snaking her arms up around his neck and pulling his body closer. He wasn't the only one who wanted to touch.

Somehow all the reasons this had seemed like a bad idea faded to nothing in the face of this connection with their child. With the passion that she felt for him and the love that they shared for the life growing inside her. And the love she felt for him, she realised. The love that had been growing alongside their child as she'd learnt more and more about its father. An artist who saw beauty in everything, the sublime in the ordinary. A son who sacrificed his own happiness to protect his mother. A brother who endured rather than confronted to save tearing apart his family. And the man who had helped her face her fears, and realise that not everything that terrified her should be avoided. Not this. Especially not this.

But she *was* afraid. She was afraid that Leo didn't feel the same way. That their differences still amounted to more than what kept bringing them together. But not so afraid that she was going to run.

God, she tasted incredible. He nipped out his tongue, tasting and teasing, as he desperately tried to catch his brain up with his libido. But it wouldn't cooperate. It was so flooded with sensation and need that there was no room for anything rational.

His hands cupped beneath Rachel's elbows and he pulled her to her feet. She was stretching up on tiptoe to reach his mouth, and it arched her body into his, their child pressed firmly between them.

'God, I've wanted to do this for so long.' He ground out the words between kisses, capturing her every gasp and moan with his lips. 'This—more—everything.'

At the word 'more', she pulled back, concern clear on her face.

'More?' His mind was thrown back to that day she'd told him there could be no sex between them, because she could never be happy with something just physical. He'd been an idiot. He wanted her in every way, in every part of his life. As he'd sat and sketched out their plans, he'd come to see that they all revolved around her. She was at the centre of his every hope and desire for the future.

'Not just that kind of more,' he said, too far gone to sugar-coat, to look for pretty words. 'I want you, Rachel. In every way possible. More. More of everything.'

His ego thrilled at the smile on her lips as he led her upstairs.

CHAPTER TEN

He stroked a strand of her hair as it pooled on his chest, his eyelids heavy and his body sated. 'Morning,' he said with a yawn, glancing at the curtains and guessing the time. 'I could stay here all day.' He kissed her gently awake and pulled his arm tighter round her. 'But we have to go tell my mum she's going to be a grandma.' He wanted to share their news, their joy, with his parents. Wanted to make Rachel a part of his family. Being so close to her, after months of denying how he felt, didn't seem like enough. The only way forwards from here was to face the demons from his past so that the three of them could move on. Together.

Because he wasn't scared any more. He was walking into this relationship with his eyes open. He couldn't be trapped somewhere he'd gone voluntarily. They were in charge of this situation, and no one else. And they could take this relationship anywhere they wanted.

'You're right, you know. I should have told them ages ago. So let's go and do it together.'

She smiled at him, reached up and brushed a soft kiss on his lips. 'Let's do it.'

As the car advanced up the driveway, Rachel's eyes widened. Leo tried to imagine seeing the house for the first time. The driveway wound through the grounds to show off every beautiful angle of the building. It offered views of leaded windows, grand entrances, and a glimpse of formal gardens. The redbrick building sat proudly in the landscape, its turrets and chimneys reaching up towards fluffy white clouds. It was staggering, he knew. But it wasn't home. Nothing would ever persuade him that his modest house was in any way inferior to this.

And then that sleek black car came into view, and the lump in his stomach started to grow and curdle. Nicholas. He reached automatically for the gearstick, intending to stick the car straight in reverse and get out of there as quickly as possible. But Rachel turned towards him.

'Leo? What is it? You're shaking.'

'Maybe this is a bad idea. We could still go. It's not too late.'

But the front door opened, and he glimpsed his mum standing inside, shielding her eyes from the low winter sun. He saw the moment when she realised that it was him in the car, because her face broke into a broad grin. And he hit the brakes.

He reached for Rachel's hand and held tight. 'Nicholas is here.'

'Still want to do this?' She stretched an arm across his shoulders, and drew herself closer.

He hesitated, but nodded. He couldn't leave now that his mum had seen him. Maybe it was better to get this done.

He glanced down at Rachel's belly, and realised that his mum would guess their news the second that they stepped out of the car. Perhaps this wasn't such a good idea. He should have spoken to his parents first, in private. Let them get used to the idea before he introduced

Rachel. This probably wasn't fair on Rachel, either. Throwing her into the middle of his family dramas. But they were here now and there was no going back.

Rachel watched as all the colour drained from Leo's face, and he gripped the car door handle as if he never wanted to let go.

She walked around the front of the car and stopped in front of him. 'If you're sure you want to do this—' she laid a gentle hand over his white knuckles '—then let's go in. No point putting it off any more. And I think we owe your mum an explanation.' She'd seen the way the other woman's eyes had widened to take in her bump, and the blatant curiosity that had followed.

She tangled her fingers in his as he shut the car door and pocketed the keys, and squeezed his hand as they walked towards the door. His mum, a short, plump woman, with pink cheeks and brightly blonde hair, stood leaning against the door frame, her expression beaming pride and happiness.

'Hi, Mum. Happy birthday.' Leo's voice was solemn as he leaned in to kiss her on the cheek. 'This is Rachel. Rachel, this is my mum, Michelle. Mum, we have some news for you.'

Rachel flinched. It didn't exactly set the jubilant tone that news of a baby should bring.

She followed them through the house to the kitchen, suddenly feeling nervous and awkward, as Leo's mum called to the rest of the family. 'Francis, Nicholas, are you there? Leo's here and he has some news for us!'

Leo gripped her hand a little harder, and she squeezed back, letting him know that he wasn't doing this alone, that she would face down his brother with him.

When she looked up, Michelle was watching them expectantly.

'Right then, Rachel. Can I get you anything? Something to drink? Leo, are you hungry yet?'

'No, thanks.' Rachel tried to smile, but Leo's nerves were rubbing off on her, travelling up from his tight-gripped hand to make her shoulders tense, her posture awkward. Her belly was the elephant in the room while they waited for the family to gather in the kitchen.

Two men walked in through the door on the opposite side of the kitchen, and she thought that Leo might actually bolt. His whole body tensed and she looked up and saw fight or flight playing out on his features. His forehead was shining slightly and his limbs were stiff and tense, ready to run or strike. She wished she could reach out and hold him. She knew that facing his brother was painful for him, clearly almost unbearably so.

But he hadn't reached for her. And if that was what he wanted then surely he would.

'So what's this new—' Leo's father's voice boomed, before he caught sight of the bump and stopped mid-sentence.

Nicholas—or at least that was who she guessed he was; Leo wasn't exactly making introductions—sent her a charming smile from behind his father's back. She remembered what Leo had said about how he used that charm, and sent a subtle scowl back.

'Leo?' his father prompted him, but Leo seemed frozen. Unable to move or speak.

Rachel stuck out her hand. 'I'm Rachel, a friend of Leo's,' she introduced herself. Using the movement to cover a quick squeeze to Leo's hand. His arm moved, and, just slightly, the rest of his body followed as he ushered her across the centre of the room towards his family.

'Rachel, this is Nicholas. My brother.'

'How do you do?' She forced the words out, though they felt rotten in her mouth. Well, this was awkward. She wished she'd known that Leo was going to freeze like this. She could hardly blame him, knowing everything that he'd gone through because of his brother. But at some point they had to spill the beans about this baby.

'So, this news...' Michelle prompted, her eyes flashing again to Rachel's bump.

She glanced up to Leo again, wondering whether he was going to step in—but no. He was no nearer composure than he had been before. They were facing things together, were stronger together. And if he needed her to, she would do this for the both of them.

She glanced up at him in a question, and he nodded fractionally in response. All she really wanted to do was disappear with him for a few minutes, get the smile back on his face and his softness back in his body.

She forced a smile to her lips instead. 'We're expecting a baby,' she announced.

Michelle flew at her across the kitchen and wrapped her in a hug. 'That's wonderful news! Oh, a baby in the family. Brilliant.' Overwhelmed by this reaction, so much warmer than the one she'd received from her own mother, Rachel felt tears gathering in her eyes. There was nothing to worry about here. Until she looked over Michelle's shoulder and saw a knowing half-grin on Nicholas's face. She glanced up at Leo and realised that he was looking at his brother, too, eyes locked together with decades-old hostility. It was unbelievable his parents didn't know something was wrong.

'I've got so many questions,' Michelle said. 'When did you two meet? When's the baby due?' She must have spotted the conspiratorial glance that passed between Rachel and Leo, because she blushed, and moved the conversation swiftly on. 'But you can fill us in on all the details later. Let's just open a bottle of something fizzy now and celebrate.' When she turned to the fridge, Leo looked over at Rachel, and she gave his arm a quick squeeze. His dad returned with a handful of champagne flutes, which he deposited on the worktop before clapping Leo into a hug, and kissing Rachel on the cheek.

'A baby. Marvellous news,' he declared. 'Don't you think so, Nick? You'll be an uncle, of course. Really wonderful news.'

Rachel eyed Nick carefully, trying to see the cruelty behind this affable exterior. And there it was. The slight lift of his eyebrow changed his smile to a smirk. It gave him a slight air of superiority, as if he had guessed exactly how planned this pregnancy was. She could practically see the X-rated guessing games playing across his brain. Pervert. Michelle handed her a cold flute of champagne and she took it, wishing she could gulp it down.

'To the new Fairfax,' Michelle toasted. And then stopped when she saw the look that Rachel threw at Leo—they definitely hadn't decided on a surname yet. 'And there's my foot in my mouth again. Here's to the new baby, whatever his or her name might be.'

'Cheers.' Rachel clinked glasses and allowed herself a sip of champagne, closing her eyes to savour the taste.

She kept an eye on Nick for the rest of the afternoon, as the family chatted in the kitchen while Francis cooked. Her heart ached for Leo, seeing how uncomfortable he was around his brother, and the selfless way he put his mother's feelings above his own by being here. But he wished he weren't—that much was evident from the way his body had grown more and more tense and his words more and more terse.

Michelle had noticed it, too, she realised: she became more watchful, glancing at Leo more and more often, though never drawing attention to it by asking him what was wrong. How long had she suspected? Rachel wondered. How long had she been aware of the fractures in her family without knowing the cause?

Rachel could see that Nick's accusations about Michelle being a gold-digger were unfounded. The mutual adoration between Leo's parents was clear to anyone who cared to see it. Perhaps jealousy was the root of all Nick's behaviour. It couldn't have been easy to see his mother replaced so fully in his father's affections. But to take that out on his innocent brother was inexcusable. Was it unforgivable, as well? Was there any way back from animosity for these brothers? But she wasn't so naive that she thought that she could bring about a reconciliation.

By the time they sat down to dinner, her shoulders had followed Leo's, fixed into a stiff line. It was impossible to relax with Leo tense beside her, and she felt every moment of his discomfort with him. His parents were smiling and upbeat, but they weren't as oblivious to the tension between the brothers as Leo had told her they were.

Her moment of relief when dinner was finished vanished in the second when Michelle casually suggested, 'You boys will sort out the kitchen, won't you? It will give you a chance to catch up. And your father and me a chance to interrogate this lovely young woman.' Her horror at the prospect of Leo being stuck alone with Nick must have shown, but fortunately was misinterpreted. 'I was only joking, Rachel, lovey. Absolutely no embarrassing questions.' She shoved a stack of empty plates into Leo's hands, giving him no choice but to take them through to the kitchen.

Rachel tried to follow Michelle's questions while keeping half an ear out for signs of physical altercation in the kitchen. She told her about due dates and scans, and a highly edited version of how she and Leo had met, and then spotted a couple of empty wine and water bottles on a side table. She stood abruptly, grabbed the bottles and headed for the door, brushing off Michelle's protestations that she wasn't to help.

She slowed as she approached the kitchen door, expecting to hear raised voices. But it was ominously quiet. She paused before she pushed it open, and heard the low murmurs and hisses of men who didn't want to be overheard. But not so quiet that she couldn't hear what they were saying.

Nick's voice, low and vindictive: 'She's after your money, is that it? Can't think why else she'd be interested. Maybe she heard that your mother slept her way into a nice house and a fat bank account and thought she'd try the same. Or maybe you cooked it up between you. A way to get a bigger slice of Dad's inheritance.'

'Don't you dare speak about Rachel that way.' Leo's voice was a hiss. 'Or Mum. After all these years can you still not see—' She could hear the venom packed into the tight syllables, the years of hatred he was trying to keep from spilling out into a shout.

'But maybe the little bastard isn't even yours. She wouldn't be entitled to a penny then. You'll be getting a paternity test, I assume. Stupid not to with a girl like that.'

Through the crack in the door she saw Leo's hand tighten into a fist. She opened the door with a bang and strode into the room, shoving the bottles on the worktop and turning to Nick with a scowl.

'Actually there was no need. But obviously we're grateful for your concern for your new niece or nephew.'

'Rachel, stay out of this,' Leo hissed. 'I'm handling it.' Turning to his brother, Leo spoke with low menace. 'Apologise. Now.'

But she didn't need him to fight her battles for her. Nick had been allowed to get away with bullying for years, and she had no interest in being his next victim. 'I think it was Nick who involved me, Leo. Is there anything else you'd like to know about my personal life, Nick? Because you obviously think who I sleep with is your business. Perhaps you want to see my medical notes and employment history. Or are facts less fun than snide accusations?'

'Rachel…' After just one word his voice had slipped into the smooth honey of a serial liar, using practised charm to cover his misdeeds. Good job she was much too smart, and too angry, to fall for it. 'I don't know what you think you heard—'

'You know what you said, you bastard. Now apologise.'

'Bastard?' Nicholas raised a mocking eyebrow at Leo. 'I hardly think your little family is in a position to throw stones.'

'That's enough!' Rachel looked at Leo in shock. She had never heard him raise his voice before. He'd always wielded quiet authority and humour to get what he wanted, without needing to shout about it.

'What's going on here? Boys?'

Rachel turned on the spot, to find Michelle and Francis behind her.

'It's nothing, Mum,' Leo said, painting on a smile that would convince no one. 'We were just on our way back.'

'It didn't sound like nothing; it sounded to us as if Nick said something to upset Rachel. Nick?'

He smiled, smirked, and raised his palms in innocence. 'A complete misunderstanding. Hormo—'

She saw anger flash again in Leo's eyes, and his fist reach back. She grabbed his hand and threw him a warning look. The last thing this situation needed was to escalate into violence.

'Finish that word and you'll live to regret it.' Even as she said the words, she was aware of the damage that she was doing, that Leo had tried for years to keep the family oblivious to the problems at the heart of it, and here she was hanging out dirty laundry for anyone to see. But Nick had bullied and intimidated for too long. She wasn't a scared child and she wouldn't stand for it.

She locked eyes with Nick, refusing to be the first to look away. She didn't want him thinking he could cow her, that she would back down from him as she was sure that many others had done in the past. She was at an advantage—had known his capacity for malice before even meeting him—and she had no intention of falling for his charming shtick.

Leo's voice broke the heavy silence. 'Mum, I'm sorry but I think we need to be going. Don't worry. Everything's fine.'

'But, Leo,' Michelle protested. 'There's something you're all hiding and I don't like it. We should talk about this.'

'It's between me and Nick. It wasn't fair of us to bring it up now and spoil your birthday. We'll sort it out another time.'

'Rachel?'

She hesitated, wanting to help. Leo was allowing Nick to drive a wedge into the heart of the family. However much he thought he was helping his mum, he wasn't hiding from her the fact that something was wrong. But it wasn't her story to tell—the most she could do was be there for Leo when he decided it was the right time.

'I think we should go, Michelle. But it's been so lovely meeting you. And I'll speak to you soon. I'll email you the pictures from the scan.'

'It's been lovely meeting you, too,' Leo's mum replied, though the wary look she gave her sons told them all she wasn't happy about them leaving before this was sorted. 'I can't tell you how excited we are about the baby. And you being part of the family, of course.'

Leo hustled her out of the house so quickly she barely had a chance to kiss Francis on the cheek and throw Nicholas an 'I know your game' glare.

The silence in the car was thick and heavy, and lasted for far longer than Rachel liked. Past cross, past angry and heading to furious. With every minute that went by with Leo not saying a word, the dread in her belly grew thicker and the chance of the day ending without another argument disappeared.

They sat in silence for a moment longer after the car pulled up outside the house. And Rachel wondered what Leo was working up to. She could see from his white knuckles on the steering wheel and the solid tension from left fingertip to right, through the stiff lines of his arms and shoulders, that it was something big.

He was angry. And although she knew how much he
hated his brother and how angry he was at him, she also
knew he was mad at her. She'd told herself on the drive
back that the reason his eyes had been fixed so deter-
minedly on the road was an overzealous adherence to the
Highway Code. But the fact that his eyes remained fixed
through the windscreen, even now they were stationary,
confirmed her worst fear. He couldn't even look at her.
Perhaps she had been rash confronting Nick like that,
when she knew how much history there was between Leo
and his brother. And how Leo had kept their problems
secret from the rest of the family for years. But was she
meant to ignore it? Let Nick get away with hurting and
provoking Leo, because that was what he always did?
Perhaps. It was what Leo had wanted. He'd never asked
her to jump to his defence. But when someone hurt him,
it hurt her. It hurt their family, and she hadn't been able
to stand it.

'I'm sorry.' She reached out a hand and brushed it
against Leo's, hoping to soften the tension there. But he
flinched away from her. She caught her breath, shocked
by the pain his rejection had caused in her chest. 'I didn't
mean to cause a scene.'

'Well, you still did a good job of it. You know I didn't
want my parents to find out about the problems between
me and Nick. I don't want them to have to deal with our
issues. You knew that and yet you went ahead anyway.'

'How was I supposed to let him say those things about
you and me—and let him get away with it?'

'I wasn't going to let him get away with it.' He turned
to face her now, and his rage showed in his every fea-
ture, his skin flushed, his forehead lined, his mouth thin
and hard. He had retreated to the far side of the car, arms

crossed again, putting every distance and barrier he could between them again. She was desperate to reach out to him, to feel his arms wrapped around her as they had just a few hours ago. 'There are ways of dealing with this that don't involve my parents.'

'Yes, and those ways have led to you suffering in silence for years. I couldn't add to that, couldn't stand by and watch you hurting. Again.'

'I told you not to interfere, Rachel. It's not worth tearing my family apart for. However much he may have dented your ego.'

'It's not about my ego, Leo.' Her voice was raised now, too, frustrated that he thought this all came down to her wanting to defend her reputation. It was nothing to do with her. She wanted to defend Leo. To protect him. 'He can say what he likes about me. I don't care about his opinion. But I won't let him get away with bullying. And I can't believe you think your parents don't know what's going on. Are you really that blind? They must have known for years if that's how you normally behave when you're at home. Your mother watches you like a hawk. If you'd just talk to them—'

'And say what? My brother bullied me when we were children. He made me miserable, and I avoid seeing you if it means seeing him. There is no easy solution to this, Rachel. I don't want to have to make my parents choose. Can't fix this on a schedule. I'm sorry that my family won't bend to what you want.'

'That's not what I was trying to do, Leo.' The heat went out of her voice, as she realised how badly Leo had misunderstood her, how big a hole she had dug for them. 'I've apologised for being rash. He was rude; I pulled him up on it. That's all.'

'That's enough! That's enough to keep Nick happy, for him to be satisfied that he's got to me again. I specifically told you that I didn't want a confrontation. What happened is in the past, and I want it to stay there. I'm happy with how I've moved on, and I don't need to relive the worst years of my life just because you want to play happy families. Especially when your own family is so messed up. You think you can come to my parents' home and dig up issues that have been dealt with, but you can't even face your own problems. Can't tell your parents that they've suffocated you with their overprotection. That you're crippled because of the way they have treated you.'

His words hit her like a slap, and she sucked in a breath, tried to recover from their sting. All she had done was try to help him, and he threw her own failed family life back in her face. 'I—'

'You trapped me,' he said. 'And now there's nothing I can do. I can never be free of you.'

She counted to ten very, *very* slowly, reminding herself that murdering the father of her unborn child was in nobody's best interest.

'We're obviously both emotional. I think we need to cool down and talk about this tomorrow. Let's just go to bed and get some sleep.'

She reached for the door handle but turned back when she realised Leo hadn't moved. 'Aren't you coming inside?'

'I don't think I'm going to want to talk about this tomorrow.'

She sighed. 'We'll talk about it tonight, then, if that's what you want. But either way you're going to have to get out of the car.'

She let out a relieved breath when he finally let go, and turned to look at her.

But when his eyes met hers, she wished she'd let him sit there a little longer. Because what she saw made the dread she'd felt earlier seem like the lightest of butter-flies. What she felt now was a lead anvil, heavy despair just waiting to crush her.

'I don't want to talk about it tonight. I don't want to talk about it tomorrow. Rachel, I don't want to talk about this at all. I realised something, driving back here. We've both made a mess of our family lives. And still we think we're doing the right thing creating a new family out of two people who barely know each other and have noth-ing more in common than an ill-advised night in bed to-gether. We're making a mistake.'

'Leo, I don't understand.' Tears broke her voice, but she forced words out anyway, trying to find a way to fix this. 'What mistake?'

'This!' A sharp, sweeping hand movement took in the two of them.

'You've changed your mind about the baby. About wanting to be involved?'

'No. Not about that. I want this baby. I want to be a good father. But I don't want to do it like this. With you and me playing happy families. It's impossible. We have to face facts.'

She pushed open the car door and shambled out onto the path, not wanting to believe what she was hearing. She'd spent six months redrawing her picture of her life, trying to see the shapes and contours and details of her future. In the last weeks, she'd finally started to under-stand it. To see the picture emerging from the chaos. To push the fragments of her old life into this new scenario with Leo and the baby and make sense of it all. And in the last days she'd felt the pleasure and delights of falling into bed with him, of feeling his arms around her, and knowing that whatever big, scary, overwhelming emotions she'd felt in the past six months, he returned them. He felt for her as much as she did for him.

And that was what was driving the knife of hurt into her chest. The complete corruption of her life plans was nothing compared to the pain of him pushing her away. That not only did he not love her, he wasn't even interested in trying. She pushed away from the car, stumbling slightly as she headed up the path. She wasn't even sure where she was going; all she knew was that she had to get away from him.

She wrapped her arms around her belly, protecting her baby from his harsh words and her own hurt. He was just striking out because he had seen his brother. She stopped for a moment and almost walked back. And then she saw the hard, uncompromising expression he wore and hesitated. But they were expecting a child. They couldn't just give up. She took another step back to the car and spoke. 'Leo, please. I don't believe that you can just walk away—'

He climbed out of the car and leant against it, keeping the hulk of metal between them. 'And that was what you wanted all along, wasn't it? Me completely unable to walk away from this. Trapped. No way out. You planned it.'

His words struck her like arrows. The injustice biting at her. Each word's sting sharper than the last.

'I—'

'I can never be free of you.'

It wasn't the words that hurt the most; it was the expression on his face. The pain, fear and resignation that told her he meant every one of them. He was broken, afraid and angry—and he blamed her entirely. She walked to the door, grabbed the spare key from beneath a plant pot and let herself in, not looking back to see whether Leo was following her. Upstairs, she swept her clothes from a drawer with one hand while ordering a cab from her smartphone with the other. By the time she returned to the front door, packed and ready to go, she'd already had a text to tell her the car was on the way.

She took a deep breath, steeling herself to see Leo.

She couldn't believe that he'd accused her of trapping him on purpose. Couldn't believe that this man, with whom she'd felt so close just a few hours before, could believe her capable of deceiving him. No crappy childhood made it okay to treat her like that.

He wasn't in the house. She'd listened for him when she'd left the guest room, not quite sure whether she wanted him to be there or not. But as she'd tiptoed through the cottage it had become clear to her that there was no need to be quiet. He wasn't there. When she opened the front door, the car was still there. Doors closed and locked, with no sign of Leo.

He must have walked down to the beach, she surmised. Either to walk by the water or work in his studio. She considered walking down there to find him. But even if the prospect of walking down an uneven and unlit coastal path at night while six months pregnant hadn't seemed like a stupid idea, she wouldn't have gone. Why should she chase after him, after what he had said to her? Why should she give him the courtesy of letting him know that she was going, when he could stand there and accuse her of lying to him, of deliberately getting pregnant? Of manipulating him.

As she looked out of the front door, her taxi pulled up. And with one last look down the path to the beach, she opened the door and slipped inside.

Leo laid his hands flat on his workbench and let out a long breath. His skin felt tight and itchy, as though it were too small for his body. He'd watched Rachel walk into his house and shut the door and then suddenly it had seemed impossible to stay still. Adrenaline had flooded his body and demanded that he move.

He'd stalked off at a tearing pace down the path to the beach, not knowing why he was going, where he was going. And already regretting his words to Rachel. But he had felt trapped in the situation and in that second he had hated it. It didn't matter whether he would choose to be with her, whether if circumstances had been different they could have found a way to be together. All that mattered was that the baby had locked them together for life, and he'd had no choice about it. About any of it. It had seemed so important, in that moment, to have a choice about something. To control the nature of their relationship, now that he knew that she would be in his life for ever. Even if it meant hurting Rachel, hurting himself, in the process.

He held on to the bench, trying to anchor himself, trying to suppress the energy coursing through his muscles, forcing him to keep moving. He grabbed a block of wood and a file and started hacking away at it, willing some form to emerge. Some shape or texture to distract him from the tempest in his mind.

It wouldn't come. Of course it wouldn't. He was in no mood to create. His body was so filled with rage and sadness and regret that he could barely make his hands move where he wanted them, never mind let them find beauty in something.

He threw the block of wood down, angry with himself for the waste of something that had so much potential, and which had been sacrificed for no reason other than that he couldn't think of any other way to rid himself of these overwhelming emotions.

Where could they go from here? He'd told Rachel that they were making a mistake. That they shouldn't try to be a family. But this baby was coming, and he'd not for a second wished it weren't. This wasn't about the baby. His heart still felt a little fuller, his spine a little straighter and the corners of his mouth a little higher when he thought about his child growing inside Rachel. He could not and would not walk away from his responsibilities as a father.

That wasn't what scared him. It wasn't the prospect of being a father that had made him panic—that had made him feel as if the structure of the car were closing in on him, as if he'd inadvertently driven into a crusher at a scrapyard.

It was the prospect of a lifetime with Rachel. Because however much they might tell themselves that they didn't need to make decisions like that now, however much they thought that they could take things slow, like other people, date, get to know one another, find out what these feelings they had for one another meant, this situation was different. In their lives, you didn't get to walk away if things became hard. If she hurt him—if she betrayed him—he would still have to endure a life with her in it, and he wasn't sure that he could bear that.

And how could he know that she wouldn't hurt him? He'd thought he was safe, once. Thought that as long as he had people around him that loved him, he would be okay. When the bullying had started at school, he'd told himself that it would be all right. That his brother would look out for him. That his dad would intervene if it got too bad.

And the day that he'd found out that Nick was at the heart of his being tormented, his faith in family, and trust, and love, had shattered. If he couldn't trust his own brother not to hurt him, then how could he ever trust anyone else?

He could never trust her. And if he couldn't trust her, they'd never be happy. They were best off acknowledging that now. Trying to find a way to get along with neither of them getting involved emotionally. With neither of them getting hurt.

He'd got too close already.

He glanced out of the window, saw that the fingers of light that were still tinting the sky pink when he'd left the car had long left the beach, which was now pitch dark. The stars and moon were eerily bright and reflected in the still, flat sea. He locked up the workshop, faltering over the action, stretching out the task, unwilling to return to the house. Would she be there? He didn't deserve for her to be, that was sure. He didn't even know if he wanted her to be.

But he wanted her. That much was true. He wanted to lose himself in her body. Comfort himself with her nearness and warmth. To bury his face in her hair and forget about the world. To enjoy her just for now without having to think about tomorrow. It wasn't fair, it wasn't right. But it was the only thing he could think of that would ease the ache in his chest.

CHAPTER ELEVEN

TAP-TAP-TAP. Tap-tap-tap-tap.

Rachel hit the end of her pencil on her desk as she scrolled through her inbox, trying to locate the email she needed. She knew it was here somewhere. She just needed to focus. But there was the problem. With her personal life in chaos, it was impossible to concentrate.

She needed to fix it. Any other problem in her life she considered the options, found the best solution, implemented it. Christmas had come and gone with barely more than a text from Leo, leaving a heavy lead feeling in her belly, somewhere low and hard to hide from. Leo had apologised for his harsh words. For the fact she'd felt she had to leave. But there was more to say. The days were crawling by in a grey fog, and she'd had enough of the uncertainty. She couldn't begin the new year sitting doing nothing, not knowing. She wanted answers, and she'd have to go and get them.

The office would be closed for the weekend and bank holiday, giving her the perfect break in her schedule.

The shrill sound of her mobile grabbed her attention, and she groaned as she glanced at the screen. Mum.

Christmas with her parents, the first time she'd spent more than a day with them since she'd met Leo, had been

something of a challenge. Far from the unquestioning
support she'd hoped for from her mum and dad, every
conversation about the baby had been so full of doubts
and worries that she'd found herself driven crazy before
the end of Boxing Day. And now, no doubt, her mother
was calling to ask her—again—if she was sure that
she wouldn't come to them for the new year. She should
be taking it easy, she'd been told a thousand times in the
last week. Shouldn't be out partying with her friends, or
schlepping down to Dorset. She should be at home where
she could be looked after—wrapped in cotton wool and
stifled till she couldn't breathe, more like.

She took a deep breath and hit answer, preparing for
another heavy round.

'Hi, Mum.'

She rubbed the heel of her hand against her forehead
as she listened to her mother repeat everything she'd
heard over Christmas. Get lots of rest…we'll be able to
look after you…won't have to lift a finger…London so
unpleasant on New Year's Eve.

For a moment, she considered telling her that she
wasn't planning on being *in* London for the rest of the
day, but somehow she didn't think that the idea of her
getting on a train down to Dorset was going to do her
mum's nerves any favours.

Eventually, when her mum had exhausted all possible
worries for that weekend, she turned the subject to her
current favourite: asking Rachel to reconsider having her
come and stay after the birth.

'I really think that it would be best, darling. I know
that Leo wants to be there, but what does he know about
babies? There are so many risks in those early days. So
much to learn. Keeping the temperature moderated,

getting those feeds done right. And if something goes wrong…have you seen the statistics of sudden infant deaths?'

'Mum, that's enough.'

Rachel found that she was standing at her desk, having stood up on impulse. Her mum was only worried. But her worrying was so far over the top it was unbelievable. And the last thing that Rachel needed in order to be a calm, capable mum herself was scaremongering.

'Leo and I have made a decision together, and you're going to have to accept it. Of course we'd love you to visit. But this is our child, our decision, and you're going to have to let us make our own mistakes. All these years you've been trying to protect me, it's made things worse. Made it so that I can't recognise which dangers are real and which I've created. I won't go on that way, and I won't have my child growing up as afraid as I am.'

She sat back down, and concentrated on softening her voice as she spoke again. Her mum's shocked silence on the other end of the phone spoke volumes, and Rachel felt guilty, knowing her mum had only ever wanted what was best for her.

'I'm sorry, Mum, I didn't mean to shout. But you have to let me do this my way.'

There was another long silence at the end of the phone, and then a sniff. But Rachel held her ground, knowing that she had to stand by her words if she wanted this relationship to work. Eventually, her mum spoke. 'I'm sorry, darling. I didn't know you felt that way. We've only ever wanted…'

'What's best for me. I know.' Rachel breathed a long sigh, relieved that her mum was still talking to her, and more importantly could see her point of view. 'But really, truthfully, Mum, what's best for me is letting me make my own mistakes, my own decisions. And trusting me to know what I want.' After a few more minutes, Rachel made her excuses, knowing that if she was going to get down to Dorset she would have to head off soon.

She looked back at her emails, and finally found the one she'd drafted to Leo, letting him know she was coming. She'd held off sending it, not sure whether warning him was the best thing to do. Because giving each other time to think about what they were going to say to each other wasn't working so well right now. Leo had retreated into a polite, distant, paler version of the man she'd known. Sending careful words over email and text, not the funny, impulsive, challenging humour she'd grown to love. And the only way she could think of to shake them out of this stalemate was to turn up at his place and have it out with him. She hovered over Send, before making up her mind. Better just to turn up. She hit Delete instead and shut down her computer.

Pulling on a scarf and fleece-lined gloves, she approached the revolving doors to the street, using her teeth to pull on the second glove—why did no one warn you about the third-trimester swollen fingers? Juggling the handle of her wheeled case and lifting the strap of her handbag over her head, she pulled harder on the glove, and nearly lost her balance when she walked straight into something tall and solid.

She swayed, trying to re-find her centre of gravity, not as easy as it used to be, but a big, heavy hand found the middle of her back and held steady until she got her footing.

She drank in his damp hair, the heavy wool coat and the familiar blue sparkle of his eyes. For the past few weeks she'd been convinced that he never wanted to talk to her again. And given the way they'd left things, if they weren't expecting a child together her wounded pride might have tempted her to leave things that way. She'd thought that it would be a challenge even getting him to speak to her tonight. Now he was at her office, wearing an open expression and a tentative smile, and she had no idea what to make of it.

But, what if he wasn't here to see her? She felt a little flush of colour rising on her neck as she remembered the last time he'd surprised her at her office. She'd mistakenly jumped to the conclusion then that he was here to see her, and she wouldn't make the same mistake twice. Wouldn't show her cards before she knew what he wanted. There had been enough humiliation and hurt.

'Leo? What are you doing here?'

'What do you think? I'm here to see you. To apologise for…for the last time I saw you. And to show you something. Something important.'

There was a time that knowing he wanted to see her would have started a fizz of desire and anticipation. Today, there was too much still standing between them, too much doubt and distrust weighing on her emotions. Seeing him still halted her breath in her throat, made her want to reach for him, but when she didn't know what she wanted from him, what she wanted for herself, then she couldn't know if that was a good thing.

He glanced down at her case. 'Going somewhere?'

She dropped the handle, had almost forgotten she was holding it. For a split second, she thought about lying. But what would be the point? Ten minutes ago she was set on going to see him to talk things through. What good would chickening out now do?

'To see you, actually.'

His face broke into a full smile, lips turned up, eyes twinkling, cheeks creasing into fine lines with the breadth of his grin. She remembered all the times one of these full-wattage smiles had created a mirror image on her own face. Today, it made her shoulders tense. He was practically bouncing now, exuding barely repressed energy. He was so different from the silent, icy man she had left seething in his car, and the change in him was unsettling. She had been prepared to do battle with taciturnity and now he was grinning at her. What had happened?

'I was coming to talk,' she told him, keeping her voice carefully neutral. 'We can't leave things like we did last time. There's too much at stake. Too much for us to decide.'

'Absolutely.' His expression turned serious, but the sparkle didn't leave his eyes. 'There's so much I want to say. I wasn't sure whether you'd listen.'

She glanced around her. People were still milling about in Reception, the atmosphere festive and full of anticipation.

'Okay, but I don't want to do this here.'

Rachel lowered herself onto her couch, letting out an involuntary sigh of relief as the weight left her feet.

'Long day?' Leo asked, dropping beside her.

'They're all feeling long lately.'

His eyes held hers for long moments, and as she watched they softened from frantic energy to something gentler and more intimate. 'Were you really coming down to my place?'

She nodded and looked away. His gaze was too intense; he saw too much.

'You wanted to talk?'

'I think there's a lot we need to say.' She shifted on the couch, trying to get comfortable. She shoved a cushion or two behind her back to combat the ache there, but they pushed her closer to Leo. She could have moved to the armchair, or could have asked him to move. But sitting close to him was making her body glow in ways she'd forgotten about in the past few weeks, drowned out by the hurt of his words and withdrawal. She stayed put, telling herself that as long as they weren't actually touching, then she was in no danger.

She focused inwards, trying to block out the quickening of her pulse, the way his scent was tickling at her senses. Eventually she spoke, repeating the words she'd rehearsed before she'd left for work that morning. 'Leo, we need to talk about what we're going to do. How you want to be involved with your child. We can't go on like the last few weeks.'

She'd thought long and hard about what she was going to say to him. Whether pushing him to talk was the right thing to do. But Nicholas Fairfax had been allowed to get away with too much for too long. She wasn't going to let him ruin her life from a distance without fighting for what she wanted. And she'd sworn she couldn't walk away from the wreckage of her and Leo until the ashes were cold and there was no hope of them reigniting. Now, faced with a Leo so different from the man she'd last seen, her carefully thought-out plan didn't seem to apply. No change there, then.

'I need to apologise. I know I've already said it, but I need you to understand how sorry I am for what I said.

I should never have attacked you, or your family, like that, and I'm sorry. I don't think we're making a mistake, having this baby, and I think that we can be wonderful parents.'

She was so shocked by this speech that it took her a few moments to gather her thoughts and translate them into words.

'Thank you for apologising.' She had to stop a sigh of relief escaping her lips as he spoke. She had told herself ever since that horrendous afternoon that he had been lashing out because seeing his brother had brought up more bad memories than he could handle. But deep down she'd wondered if that was all there was to it. Whether seeing his family had merely provided the excuse that he'd been looking for to escape from her and their child. The future that they promised.

But seeing Leo here, looking happy and open in a way she'd never quite seen him before, she felt as if her worst fears were quietened, and she let herself hope, for the first time, that they could find a way back to that steamy night after the gala, the intimacy and tenderness they'd shared that night in his house by the sea.

'I'm sorry, too, Leo.' Because the blame wasn't all his. The way that she had interfered with his family, when he'd specifically asked her not to, had played on her mind since that afternoon. If she'd gone into that confrontation less determined to make Nick pay for what he'd done, had helped Leo, rather than forcing the issue, then they could have found a way to change things without reaching breaking point. 'I made things worse with Nick.'

Leo shook his head.

'No, you did exactly the right thing.'

She wished that she could believe him, but that hadn't

been what he'd said when he'd left her alone in a dark, cold house, and told her that he didn't believe in their new family.

'I don't understand…'

'Nick. I should have faced him down years ago. You were right about my parents. They knew something was wrong. I went home for Christmas. Ignored Nick's usual behaviour on Christmas Day, Boxing Day. And then I couldn't take it any more. I thought about the way that you faced him. How you pulled him up on his insinuations and snide remarks and decided that he shouldn't get away with it. I confronted him and my parents practically applauded.'

Rachel smiled, imagining the scene, unbelievably proud of Leo for doing the one thing he'd feared most. 'That's brilliant, Leo. I'm so glad you were able to talk to your parents about things.'

'But that's not all.' He reached across the sofa for her hand, gripped her fingers and pulled her a little closer to him. 'After I'd done it, all I could think about was how I'd let you down. How I'd let Nick get to me until I barely knew what I was saying. I'd let him spoil what we had, and I had to fix it. I want you back, Rachel.'

'Leo…' The change in him was so obvious that there was no point disputing that his confrontation with his brother had resolved so many of his issues. But Leo suddenly deciding that he wanted to try again wouldn't be enough to make this relationship work. Maybe he'd been right. They were crazy to think that they could just try and mash their two lives together and think that they could make a family from it. 'I'm really pleased things are better with your family. But I don't think that us as a couple is going to work.'

'Don't you want it? Because I can promise you I've never wanted anything more. I know that I can't fix this overnight. I know that it will take time to trust again, but I want to work at this. I want to deserve you again.'

'I want it, too.' She could never say otherwise. How could she when her body craved his, when she missed the way that he made her laugh, relax, be the version of herself that wasn't constantly afraid of something going wrong? 'It's just not that simple, Leo.'

'I know it's not simple,' he called over his shoulder as he reached into the holdall he'd thrown on the floor earlier. 'Trust me, I know that. But it's not impossible. If we want to try, we *can* do this. And I can prove it.'

He turned back to her with a boyish grin, and held out a dog-eared sketch pad. On the front, in a hand-drawn cursive script, were the words 'Archer Fairfax Family'.

She looked up at him in surprise. 'Leo? What's—'

'It's a plan!' The boyish excitement was back, and he bounced the sofa cushions with his energy. She laughed in response—it was contagious. 'Not a plan for everything. But what we agreed, a compromise. A plan for the big stuff, the stuff we have to decide in advance. The rest of it we explore as we go along.'

Stunned into silence, she opened the cover and flicked through the first pages. Like the plans she'd once seen on his kitchen table, they were beautiful. Sketched line drawings and scatterings of bullet points and script. His house. Her flat. A baby swaddled in blankets. From the pictures, and a scattering of jottings, a picture of their lives started to emerge. Living together in her flat in London, the baby in a cot by their bed. In the city in the week, close to her work with rented studio space for Leo. Weekends at the coast. The three of them looking out to sea.

She laid the pad in her lap, resting her hands on it, tracing the lines of the sea with a finger.

'You think we can do this?'

'I do. I love you, Rachel. I love the way you laugh, and the way you are so utterly unfazed by the most terrifying things I can think of. I love that you stood up to my idiot brother. I love that you've been an incredible mother to our child before he—or she—is even here. The past few weeks, not speaking to you, have been the worst that I can remember. I think we already know how to do this; we've just been fending for ourselves for so long that we have to remember how to let someone else in.'

'And you'd do it? You'd live in the city?' The sea, the beach, his workshop were so much a part of who he was she couldn't imagine him without them. Would she be enough to make him happy? Could he be content with her?

'I'd live with you, if you'll have me. City, sea—we can do both. As long as we're together.'

'But your studio…'

'Is not as important to me as you are. There's studio space in London. Your office is here—it makes more sense for me to move. And the house isn't going anywhere. Weekends, holidays by the sea. It's the best of both worlds.'

She was still staring, she knew. But she could hardly let herself believe this: it was so far from what she had been expecting. Leo was still grinning at her, and her lips turned up in response.

'Tell me you feel the same. Tell me you want to try.'

'I don't know what to say, Leo. Last time I saw you…'

'Last time you saw me was the worst day of my life. I was angry and scared, and when I realised that you'd gone, that I'd driven you away, I was heartbroken. I swore to myself that I would never let that happen again. That's why I went home for Christmas and faced my nasty little bully of a brother. And that's why I'm here, begging you to give us another chance.'

She glanced down again at the sketchbook, the image of the two of them, arms entwined around each other's bodies, looking out to sea with their baby safe between them. It was everything she wanted. He was everything she wanted.

From the minute she'd met him, she'd been rewriting the plan for her life, rethinking her future. For months it had been a hazy mass of maybes and what-ifs, but now she knew, without doubt, what she wanted. She wanted him, with all the surprises and madness that he brought her. For the way that he made her laugh, made her take risks, made them a family.

She reached up, and cupped his face in her hand. Drawing him close, she pressed a soft kiss to his lips. 'I love you, Leo. And you're right, I know we can do this. It's going to be terrifying and thrilling, and—at times— it's going to be downright confrontational. Which sounds to me like just about every other family on the planet. But you're going to make me happy, every day, even when you make me exasperated; and I promise I'm going to spend the rest of my life trying to make you happy, too.'

With his hand tangled in her hair, he kissed her back, wrapping his arm around her until he had his whole little family, his whole world, where he wanted them.

EPILOGUE

LOOK UP.

Rachel leaned against the bathroom door frame, watching Leo sprawled out on the bed. A tray of toast and coffee lay on the duvet beside him, and she had to fight the déjà vu. Nine months ago, she'd stood in this exact spot, and held her breath when she'd seen Leo still in her bed long after she'd thought he'd gone. This morning the picture was almost identical, apart from the precious bundle tucked into the crook of Leo's arm.

Their daughter. Three days old, and already the centre around which their whole world revolved.

Suddenly, Leo looked up and caught her eye. His face broke into a vast grin, his eyes shining; still with that disbelieving expression they'd both worn since the midwife had placed the baby on her chest and announced that they had a daughter.

She moved the tray to her bedside table, and slipped into the bed beside her lover and their baby girl, and breathed a sigh of contentment as she curled under Leo's other arm. 'Is this real?' she asked, looking up at him.

'I hope so, because I'm not letting her go. Or you.' Leo gazed from her to their daughter, his eyes still dreamy.

As Rachel reached across for the toast, her eye was

caught by the corner of a sketch pad peeking out from
under the bed. Just one of the many things she was getting used to since Leo had moved in: the propensity of
belongings to show up anywhere and everywhere. That
first morning, it would have driven her mad. Today it
made her smile, evidence all around her of her new life,
her new family.

She pulled the sketch pad up beside them and leafed
through the familiar pictures as she ate her breakfast,
lingering on the picture of them looking out to sea, the
image that had spoken to her heart the day Leo had
turned up asking her to trust him, to love him.

There were new pictures since then; she'd seen Leo
scribbling away in the evenings as she'd scrolled through
spreadsheets and handed over the final projects at work.
There were sketches of her, her vast belly, her sleeping—
or trying to. And over the past three days the most precious drawings of all. Their daughter's first hours. The
first time she'd nursed, the first time she'd snuggled up
in her Moses basket beside their bed. Her face screwed
up with tears.

As she turned the page again, she started with surprise. A piece of paper had been pasted in. A drawing
not of her or the baby. But of a hollow circle of wood, the
grain spinning around the outside and through the centre. Her forehead creased as she turned the book through
ninety degrees, trying to see where this picture fitted
into the story. A new sculpture Leo was working on, perhaps, pasted into the wrong book? But when she turned
the page, there it was again. The grain slightly different
this time, more delicate. And the dimensions were different, too. The outer circle slightly narrower, the space
inside larger.

When she turned the page again, the same image greeted her. This time with scribbled dimensions in millimetres, and fractions of millimetres, and something sparkling and glinting at the very top of the arch.

She dropped the book.

It was a sculpture, or a plan for one. A tiny sculpture, about the size of...

She looked up at Leo in surprise. 'A ring?'

He smiled down at her, shuffling the baby in his arms as he reached under the duvet and pulled out a small wooden box, carved with a question mark on top, and unmistakably Leo's work.

As he handed it to her, she held his gaze, looking long and intensely into his eyes, trying to calm the galloping of her pulse and the hitches in her breathing. The box was smooth and warm in her hand, and she took a moment to trace the inscription on the lid with the pad of her finger.

She opened it slowly, pulling her eyes away from Leo's now, a smile playing at the corner of her lips.

A diamond gleamed at her, nestling in the wood-grained platinum as her antique bottle had nestled in the sand.

'Leo, it's beautiful.' She was so taken aback by its delicate beauty that for a moment its greater significance was lost on her. All her brain could process was the care and attention put into this exquisite item. Until Leo reached for her left hand, and pulled it towards him.

'Rachel, you've already made me happier and luckier than any man alive deserves to be. And I want you for ever. Will you be my wife?'

She grabbed his hand harder and hauled herself up on the bed until she was kneeling in front of him.

'Yes, Leo. Of course, yes. I love you. I will always

love you, and everything you've given me, and I can't wait to spend the rest of my life with you.' She slipped the ring onto her finger, lifted the baby out of Leo's arms and into her basket, and leaned over to kiss her fiancé.

* * * * *

EXPECTING THE PRINCE'S BABY

BY
REBECCA WINTERS

Rebecca Winters, whose family of four children has now swelled to include five beautiful grandchildren, lives in Salt Lake City, Utah, in the land of the Rocky Mountains. With canyons and high alpine meadows full of wildflowers, she never runs out of places to explore. They, plus her favourite vacation spots in Europe, often end up as backgrounds for her romance novels, because writing is her passion, along with her family and church.

Rebecca loves to hear from readers. If you wish to e-mail her, please visit her website: www.cleanromances.com.

I dedicate this book to my angelic grandmother, Alice Vivia Driggs Brown, who made my childhood a constant enchantment. She was so romantic she called the home she and my grandfather had built 'Camelot.'

CHAPTER ONE

VINCENZO DI LAURENTIS, thirty-three-year-old crown
prince of the Principality of Arancia, stood before the
camera on the balcony of the royal palace overlooking
the gardens to officially open the April Fifteenth Lemon
and Orange Festival. This was his first public appearance since the funeral of his wife, Princess Michelina,
six weeks ago. He waved to the crowds that had come
out en masse.

His country was nestled between the borders of
France and Italy on the coast of the Mediterranean.
Eighty thousand people lived in the city of the same
name. The other thirty thousand made up the population that lived in the smaller towns and villages. Besides tourism, it had depended on the lemon and orange
industries for centuries.

For the next two weeks the country would celebrate
the mainstay of their economy with marching bands in
the streets, food fairs, floats and statuary in the parks
decorated with lemons and other citrus fruit.

Vincenzo had just gotten back from a series of visits
to three continents, doing business for the monarchy
with other heads of state. It felt good to be with his
father, King Guilio, again. On his return, he'd forgot-

ten how beautiful Arancia could be in the spring with its orchards in full flower. He felt an air of excitement coming from the people that winter was over. As for himself, the darkness that had consumed him over the last six weeks since Michelina's death seemed to be dissipating.

Their marriage had never been a love match. Though betrothed at sixteen, they'd spent very little time together before their wedding fourteen years later. When he'd walked into their apartment earlier this afternoon, more than any other emotion, he was aware of a haunting sense of guilt for not having been able to love her the way she'd loved him.

Romantic love never grew on his part for her, only respect and admiration for her determination to keep up the image of a happily married couple. They'd suffered through three miscarriages hoping for a child, but it hadn't happened.

His passion had never been aroused when they'd made love because he hadn't been in love with her, but he'd done his best to show her tenderness. He'd known passion with other women before he'd married Michelina. But it had only been a physical response because he was never able to give his heart, knowing he was betrothed.

Vincenzo suspected Michelina's parents had undergone the same kind of unfulfilled marriage. He knew his own parents had struggled. It was the rare occurrence when a royal couple actually achieved marital happiness. Michelina had wanted their marriage to be different, and Vincenzo had tried. But you couldn't force love. That had to spring from a source all on its own.

However there was one thing he *had* been able to do that had brought them their first real happiness as man and wife. In fact it was the only thing that had gotten him through this dark period. Just a few days before she'd died, they'd learned they were pregnant again. Only this time they'd taken the necessary steps to prevent another miscarriage.

Relieved that his last duty for today was over, he left the balcony anxious to visit the woman who'd been willing to be a gestational surrogate for them. Abby Loretto, the American girl who'd become his *friend*. Since twelve years of age she'd been living on the palace grounds with her Italian father, who was chief of security.

Vincenzo had been eighteen, with his own set of friends and a few girlfriends his own age, when Abby had arrived on the scene. Yet Abby had become the constant in the background of his life, more like a younger sister flitting in and out of his daily life. It was almost like having a sibling. In a way he felt closer to Abby than he'd ever felt to his sister, Gianna, who was six years older.

The two of them had played in the sea or the swimming pool. She was fun and bright. He could be his real self around her, able to throw off his cares and relax with her in a way he couldn't with anyone else. Because she lived on the grounds and knew the inner workings of the palace, she already had the understanding of what it was to be a royal. They didn't have to talk about it.

When his mother had died, Abby had joined him on long walks, offering comfort. When he didn't want anyone else around, he wanted her. She'd lost her mother, too, and understood what he was going through. She asked nothing from him, wanted nothing but to be his friend and share small confidences. Because they'd been in each other's lives on a continual basis, he realized it was inevitable that they'd bonded and had developed a trust.

She'd been so woven into the fabric of his life that years later, when she'd offered to be a surrogate mother for him and Michelina, it all seemed part of the same piece. His wife had liked Abby a great deal. The three of them had been in consultation for several months before the procedure had been performed. They'd worked like a team until Michelina's unexpected death.

He'd gotten used to their meetings with the doctor and the psychologist. While he'd been away on business, it had felt like years instead of weeks since he'd seen or talked to Abby. Now that she was carrying Vincenzo's son or daughter, she was his lifeline from here on out. He needed to see her and be with her.

All he could think about was getting back to make certain she and the baby were doing well. But accompanying this need was an uncomfortable sense of guilt he couldn't shake. Less than two months ago he'd lost his wife. While still in mourning over the marriage that had been less than perfect, he now found himself concentrating on another woman, who was carrying the baby he and Michelina had made.

It was only natural he cared about Abby, who'd agreed to perform this miracle. Before long he was going to be a father, all because of her! Yet with Michelina gone, it didn't seem right.

But neither was it wrong.

While he'd been traveling, he hadn't had time to dig deep into his soul, but now that he was back, he didn't know how to deal with this new emotional dilemma facing him, and he left the balcony conflicted.

Abigail Loretto, known to her friends as Abby, sat alone on the couch in her apartment at the palace, drying her hair while she was glued to the television. She'd been watching the live broadcast of Prince Vincenzo opening the fruit festival from the balcony of the palace.

Abby hadn't known he was back. Her Italian-born father, Carlo Loretto, the chief of palace security, had been so busy, he obviously hadn't had time to inform her.

She'd first met Vincenzo sixteen years earlier, when her father had been made the head of palace security. The king had brought him and his American-born wife and young daughter from the Arancian Embassy in Washington, D.C., to live in the apartment on the palace grounds. She'd been twelve to his eighteen.

Most of her teenage years had been spent studying him, including his tall, hard-muscled physique. Instead of a film star or a famous rock star, she'd idolized Vincenzo. She'd even kept a scrapbook that followed his life, but she'd kept it hidden from her parents. Of course, that was a long time ago.

The crown prince, the most striking male Abby had ever met in her life, had many looks depending on his mood. From what she could see now, he appeared more rested since his trip.

Sometimes when he was aloof, those black eyes and furrowed brows that matched his glistening black hair made her afraid to approach him. Other times he could be charming and fun, even a tease. No one was immune from his masculine charisma. Michelina had been the most fortunate woman alive.

His picture was always on the cover of magazines and newspapers in Europe. The camera loved the handsome thirty-three-year-old son of Arancia, with his olive skin and aquiline features. Dogged by the press, he made the nightly news on television somewhere on the continent every day of the year.

The knowledge that he was home from his travels sent a wave of warmth through her body. Six weeks without seeing or talking to him about the baby had felt like an eternity. She knew he'd get in touch with her at some point. But after being away, he would have so much work to catch up on at home, it might be another week before she heard his voice on the phone.

Now that he'd left the balcony and had gone back inside the palace, the station began showing a segment of the funeral that had been televised on every channel throughout the kingdom and Europe six weeks ago.

She would never forget her father's phone call. "I have bad news. Before Vincenzo and Michelina were due to return to Arancia today, she went for an early-morning ride on her horse. Vincenzo rode with her. While she was galloping ahead of him, the horse stepped in a hole. It tossed her over end. When she hit the ground, she died on impact."

Abby froze.

Michelina was dead?

It was like déjà vu, sending Abby back to that horrific moment when she'd learned her own mother had died.

Poor Vincenzo. He'd seen the whole thing… She

couldn't stand it. "Oh, Dad—he's lost his wife. Their baby will never know its mother."

Before long she was driven to the hospital, where Dr. DeLuca had his office. "My dear Abby, what a terrible shock this has been. I'm glad your father brought you here. I'm going to keep you in the hospital overnight and possibly longer to make certain you're all right. The prince has enough pain to deal with. Knowing you're being looked after will be a great comfort to him. Excuse me while I arrange for a private room."

When he left, Abby turned to her father. "Vincenzo must be in absolute agony."

He kissed her forehead. "I know he is, but right now it's you I'm worried about. Your blood pressure is up. I plan to stay with you and will tell Signor Faustino you've caught a bad cold, but will be back to work in a few days."

"You can't stay with me here, Dad. Your place is at the palace. The king will want you there."

"Not tonight. My assistant is in charge, and Guilio wants to be there for his son. My daughter needs me, and I need you, so let that be the end of the discussion."

Her father's words had been final. Deep down she'd been glad he'd remained with her.

Abby kept watching the funeral she'd lived through once before. It was shocking to see how gaunt and shadowed Vincenzo's handsome features had been back then. His wife's death seemed to have aged him.

The most beautiful man she'd ever known in her life made a striking yet lonely figure in his mourning finery. Once again her soul shuddered to see his somber expression as he walked behind the funeral cortege toward the cathedral. He led Michelina's favorite horse from the palace stable alongside him. The chestnut mare was covered in a throw of his wife's favorite pink roses. The scene was so heart wrenching, Abby felt tears well up once again.

Behind him came the king, in his uniform of state, and his mother-in-law, dressed in a black mantilla and suit. They rode in the black-and-gold carriage with the siblings of both families. When the broadcast moved inside the cathedral, Abby listened once again to the scripture reading and remarks from the archbishop. When it was over and the bells from the cathedral rang out their mournful sound, she was once more a trembling mass of painful emotions.

"For those of you who've just tuned in, you're watching the funeral procession of Her Royal Highness Princess Michelina Cavelli, the wife of Crown Prince Vincenzo Di Laurentis of the Principality of Arancia. Earlier in the week she was killed in a tragic horseriding accident on the grounds of the royal palace on the island kingdom of Gemelli.

"In the carriage is His Majesty Guilio Di Laurentis, King of Arancia, her father-in-law. His wife, Queen Annamaria, passed away two years ago. Seated next to him is his daughter, Princess Gianna Di Laurentis Roselli and her husband, Count Roselli of the Cinq Terres of Italy.

"Opposite them is Her Majesty Queen Bianca Cavelli, mother of Princess Michelina. Her husband, King Gregorio Cavelli of Gemelli, was recently deceased. Also seated in the royal carriage is His Royal Highness Crown Prince Valentino Cavelli of Gemelli and Prince Vitoli Cavelli, the brothers of Princess Michelina.

"On this day of great sadness for both royal houses,

one has to speculate on the future of the Principality of Arancia. The world has been waiting to hear that their Royal Highnesses were expecting a child after three miscarriages, but tragically the love match between Michelina and Vincenzo ended too soon.

"Should the Princess Gianna and her husband, Count Enzio Roselli, have offspring, then their child will be third in line to—"

Abby shut off the TV with the remote and got to her feet, unable to watch any more. She shouldn't have allowed herself to live through that funeral segment a second time. Vincenzo's trip appeared to have done him some good. It was better to leave the tragic past behind and concentrate on the future.

She walked into the den to do some work at her laptop. Her dinner would be arriving shortly. Except for the occasional meal out with her best friend, Carolena, Abby normally ate in while she worked on one of her law briefs. But she had little appetite tonight.

How hard for Vincenzo to come back to the palace with no wife to greet him. His loneliness had to be exquisite and her heart ached for him.

After receiving an urgent message from his father that couldn't have come at a worse moment, Vincenzo had been given another reason to visit Abby. As he rounded the corner to her suite, he saw Angelina leaving the apartment with the dinner tray.

Angelina was Abby's personal bodyguard, hired to keep an eye on Abby, virtually waiting on her. She was the one who fed Vincenzo information on a daily basis when he couldn't be there himself. He stopped her so he could lift the cover. Abby had only eaten a small portion of her dinner. That wasn't good. He put the cover back and thanked her before knocking on the door.

"Yes, Angelina?"

He opened it and walked through until he found Abby in the den, where he could see her at the desk working on her computer in her sweats and a cotton top. The lamp afforded the only light in the room, gilding the silvery-gold hair she must have just shampooed. He could smell the strong peach fragrance. It fell to her shoulders in a cloud.

Instead of the attorney-like persona she generally presented, she reminded Vincenzo of the lovely teenager who'd once flitted about the palace grounds on her long legs.

"Abby?"

She turned a face to him filled with the kind of sorrow he'd seen after her mother had died. "Your Highness," she whispered, obviously shocked to see him. A glint of purple showed through her tear-glazed blue eyes. She studied him for a long moment. "It's good to see you again."

Because of the extreme delicacy of their unique situation, it frustrated him that she'd addressed him that way, yet he could find no fault in her.

"Call me Vincenzo when the staff isn't around. That's what you used to shout at me when you were running around the gardens years ago."

"Children are known to get away with murder."

"So are surrogate mothers." There was something about being with Abby. "After such a long trip, I can't tell you how much I've been looking forward to talking to you in person."

"You look like you're feeling better."

Though he appreciated her words, he wished he could say the same about her. "What's wrong? I noticed you hardly ate your dinner. Are you ill?"

"No, no. Not at all." Abby got up from the chair, rubbing the palms of her hands against the sides of womanly hips. To his chagrin the gesture drew his attention to her figure. "Please don't think that finding me in this state has anything to do with the baby."

"That relieves me, but I'm still worried about you. Anything troubling you bothers me."

She let out a sigh. "After I watched your live television appearance a little while ago, they replayed a segment of the funeral. I shouldn't have watched it." Her gaze searched his eyes. "Your suffering was so terrible back then. I can't even imagine it."

Diavolo. The media never let up. "To say I was in shock wouldn't have begun to cover my state of mind," he said.

Abby hugged her arms to her chest, once again drawing his attention to her slender waist. So far the only proof that she was pregnant came from a blood test. She studied him for a moment. "Michelina loved you so much, she was willing to do anything to give you a baby. I daresay not every husband has had that kind of love from his spouse. It's something you'll always be able to cherish."

If he could just get past his guilt over the unhappy state of their marriage. His inability to return Michelina's affection the way she'd wanted weighed him down, but he appreciated Abby's words.

Little did Abby know how right she was. In public his wife had made no secret of her affection for him and he'd tried to return it to keep up the myth of a love match. But in private Vincenzo had cared for her the way he did a friend. She'd pushed so hard at the end to try surrogacy in order to save their marriage, he'd finally agreed to consider it.

Needing to change the subject, he said, "Why don't you sit down while we talk?"

"Thank you." She did as he asked.

He subsided into another of the chairs by her desk. "How are you really feeling?"

"Fine."

"Rest assured that during my trip I insisted on being given a daily report on your progress. It always came back 'fine.'"

"It doesn't surprise me you checked. Something tells me you're a helicopter father already," she quipped.

"If you mean I'm interested to the point of driving you crazy with questions, I'm afraid I'm guilty. Since you and I have known each other from the time you were twelve, it helps me to know I can have the inside track on the guardian of my baby. Dr. DeLuca said your blood pressure went up at the time of the funeral, but it's back to normal and he promises me you're in excellent health."

Abby had a teasing look in her eye. "They say only your doctor knows for sure, but never forget he's a man and has no clue."

Laughter broke from Vincenzo's lips. It felt good to laugh. He couldn't remember the last time it had happened. "I'll bear that in mind."

"So what does the crown prince's *personal* physician have to say about the state of the expectant father?"

He smiled. "I was disgustingly healthy at my last checkup."

"That's good news for your baby, who hopes to enjoy a long, rich life with his or her daddy."

Daddy was what he'd heard Abby call her father from the beginning. The two of them had the sort of close relationship any parent would envy. Vincenzo intended to be the kind of wonderful father his own had been.

"You're veering off the subject. I told you I want the unvarnished truth about your condition," he persisted.

"Unvarnished?" she said with a sudden hint of a smile that broke through to light up his insides. "Well. Let me see. I'm a lot sleepier lately, feel bloated and have finally been hit with the *mal di mare*."

The Italian expression for sea sickness. Trust Abby to come up with something clever. They both chuckled.

"Dr. DeLuca has given me medicine for that and says it will all pass. Then in the seventh month I'll get tired again."

"Has he been hovering as you feared?"

"Actually no. I check in at the clinic once a week before going to work. He says everything looks good and I'm right on schedule. Can you believe your baby is only one-fifth of an inch long?"

"That big?" he teased. Though it really was incredible, he found it astounding she was pregnant with a part of him. He wished he could shut off his awareness of her. Michelina's death had changed their world.

Vincenzo suspected Abby was also having to deal with the fact that the two of them were now forced to get through this pregnancy without his wife. No doubt she felt some guilt, too, because they were treading new ground neither of them could have imagined when they'd had the procedure done.

A laugh escaped her lips. "It's in the developmental stage. He gave me two identical booklets. This one is for you. Anatomy 101 for beginner fathers."

Abby...

She reached in the desk drawer and handed it to him. The title said *The Ten Stages of Pregnancy at a Glance.*

"Why ten, not nine?"

"A woman wrote it and knows these things."

He appreciated her little jokes more than she could imagine. Her normally lighthearted disposition was a balm to his soul. Vincenzo thumbed through the booklet before putting it in his pocket. When he went to bed tonight, he'd digest it.

"Thank you. Now tell me about your law cases." A safe subject that intrigued him. "Which one keeps you awake at night?"

"The Giordano case. I have a hunch someone's trying to block his initiative for political reasons."

"Run it by me."

Her arched brows lifted. "You'd be bored to tears."

"Try me." Nothing about Abby bored him.

She reached in one of the folders on her desk and handed him a printout on the case, which he perused.

As has been stated, major constraint to import into Arancia is nothing more than bureaucracy. Import certificates can take up to eight months to be released, and in some cases are not released at all. However, if the procedure is simplified, an increase of imports could particularly benefit Arancia, providing high-value high-season products.

That made even more sense to Vincenzo since talking to important exporters on his trip.

At present, the hyper/supermarket chains do not operate directly on the import market, but use the main wholesalers of oranges and lemons as intermediaries. Signor Giordano, representing the retailers, has entered the import market, thus changing some long-established import partnerships. He's following a different strategy, based on higher competition, initial entry fees and spot purchases, thus bringing more revenue to Arancia.

Vincenzo knew instinctively that Signor Giordano was really on to something.

Signor Masala, representing the importers, is trying to block this new initiative. He has favored cooperative producers and established medium-to-long-term contracts, without requiring any entry fee. The figures included in this brief show a clear difference in revenue, favoring Signor Giordano's plan.

I'm filing this brief to the court to demonstrate that these high-quality products for fast-track approval would benefit the economy and unfortunately are not unavailable in the country at the present time.

Vincenzo handed her back the paper. Her knowledge and grasp of their country's economic problems impressed him no end. He cocked his head. "Giuseppe

Masala has a following and is known as a hard hitter on the trade commission."

Abby's brows met in a delicate frown. "Obviously he's from the old school. Signor Giordano's ideas are new and innovative. He's worked up statistics that show Arancia could increase its imports of fuel, motor vehicles, raw materials, chemicals, electronic devices and food by a big margin. His chart with historical data proves his ideas will work.

"I'd like to see him get his fast-track idea passed, but the lobby against it is powerful. Signor Masala's attorney is stalling to get back to me with an answer."

She had him fascinated. "So what's your next strategy?"

Abby put the paper back in the folder. "I'm taking him to court to show cause. But the docket is full and it could be awhile."

"Who's the judge?"

"Mascotti."

The judge was a good friend of Vincenzo's father. Keeping that in mind, he said, "Go on fighting the good fight, Abby. I have faith in you and know you'll get there."

"Your optimism means a lot to me."

She was friendly, yet kept their relationship at a professional distance the way she'd always done. To his dismay he discovered he wanted more, in different surroundings where they could be casual and spend time talking together like they used to. Her suite wasn't the right place.

Her bodyguard already knew he'd stopped by to see her and would know how long he stayed. He wanted to trust Angelina, but you never knew who your enemies were. Vincenzo's father had taught him that early on. So it was back to the business at hand. "The doctor's office faxed me a schedule of your appointments. I understand you're due for your eight weeks' checkup on Friday, May 1." She nodded. "I plan to join you at the clinic and have arranged for us to meet with the psychologist for our first session afterward."

"You mean you'll have time?" She looked surprised.

"I've done a lot of business since we last saw each other and have reported in to the king. At this juncture I'm due some time off and am ready to get serious about my duties as a father-in-waiting."

Laughter bubbled out of her. "You're very funny at times, Vincenzo."

No one had ever accused him of that except Abby. He hated bringing the fun to an end, but he needed to discuss more serious matters with her that couldn't be put off before he left.

"Your mention of the funeral reminds me of how compassionate you are, and how much you cared for Michelina. I've wanted to tell you why we decided against your attending the funeral."

She moistened her lips nervously. "My father already explained. Naturally, none of us wanted the slightest hint of gossip to mar your life in any way. Just between us, let me tell you how much I liked and admired Michelina. I've missed my daily talks with her and mourn her loss."

He felt her sincerity. "She cared for you, too."

"I—I wish there'd been a way to take your pain away—" her voice faltered "—but there wasn't. Only time can heal those wounds."

"Which is something you know all about, after losing your mother."

"I'll admit it was a bad time for Dad and me, but we got through it. There's no burning pain anymore."

When he'd seen Carlo Loretto's agony after losing his wife, Vincenzo had come to realize how lucky they'd been to know real love. Abby had grown up knowing her parents had been lovers in the true sense of the word. Obviously she could be forgiven for believing he and Michelina had that kind of marriage. *A marriage that had physically ended at the very moment there was new hope for them.*

"Did your father explain why I haven't phoned you in all these weeks?"

"Yes. Though you and Michelina had told me we could call each other back and forth if problems arose, Dad and I talked about that too. We decided it will be better if you and I always go through your personal assistant, Marcello."

"As do I."

It would definitely be better, Vincenzo mused. She understood everything. With Michelina gone, no unexplained private calls to him from Abby meant no calls to be traced by someone out to stir up trouble. They'd entered forbidden territory after going through with the surrogacy.

Vincenzo had to hope the gossip mill within the palace wouldn't get to the point that he could no longer trust in the staff's loyalty. But he knew it had happened in every royal house, no matter the measures taken, and so did she.

"I mustn't keep you, but before I go, I have a favor to ask."

"Anything."

"Michelina's mother and brothers flew in for the festival." It was an excuse for what the queen really wanted. "She would like to meet with you and me in the state drawing room at nine in the morning."

His concern over having to meet with his mother-in-law had less to do with the argument Michelina and the queen had gotten into before the fatal accident, and much more to do with the fact that he hadn't been able to love her daughter the way she'd loved him. He was filled with guilt and dreaded this audience for Abby's sake. But his mother-in-law had to be faced, and she had refused to be put off. "Your father will clear it with your boss so he'll understand why you'll be a little late for work."

"That's fine."

It wouldn't be fine, but he would be in the room to protect her. "Then I'll say good-night."

She nodded. "Welcome home, Vincenzo, and *buonanotte*." Another smile broke out on her lovely face.

"*Sogni d'oro*."

CHAPTER TWO

THE PRINCE'S FINAL words, "sweet dreams," stayed with her all night. Seeing him again had caused an adrenaline rush she couldn't shut off. She awakened earlier than usual to get ready, knowing Michelina's mother would ask a lot of questions.

Abby always dressed up for work. Since the law firm of Faustino, Ruggeri, Duomo and Tonelli catered to a higher-class clientele, Signor Faustino, the senior partner, had impressed upon her and everyone else who worked there the need to look fashionable. Though her heart wasn't in it this morning, she took her antinausea pill with breakfast, then forced herself to go through the motions.

Everyone knew she was the daughter of the chief of security for the palace, so no one questioned the royal limo bringing her to and from work. Except for her boss and Carolena, her coworkers were clueless about Abby's specific situation. That's the way things needed to remain until she took a leave of absence.

After the delivery, the palace would issue a formal statement that a surrogate mother had successfully carried the baby of their Royal Highnesses, the new heir who would be second in line to the throne. At that time Abby would disappear. But it wouldn't be for a while.

Vincenzo had been a part of her life for so long, she couldn't imagine the time coming when she'd no longer see him. Once the baby was born, she would live in another part of the city and get on with her life as a full-time attorney. How strange that was going to be.

From the time she'd moved here with her family, he'd been around to show her everything the tourists never got to see. He'd taken her horseback riding on the grounds, or let her come with him when he took out his small sailboat. Vincenzo had taught her seamanship. There was nothing she loved more than sitting out in the middle of the sea while they fished and ate sweets from the palace kitchen. He had the run of the place and let her be his shadow.

Abby's friends from school had come over to her parents' apartment, and sometimes she'd gone to their houses. But she much preferred being with Vincenzo and had never missed an opportunity to tag along. Unlike the big brothers of a couple of her friends who didn't want the younger girls around, Vincenzo had always seemed to enjoy her company and invited her to accompany him when he had free time.

Memories flooded her mind as she walked over to the closet and pulled out one of her favorite Paoli dresses. When Abby had gone shopping with Carolena, they'd both agreed this one had the most luscious yellow print design on the body of the dress.

The tiny beige print on the capped sleeves and hem formed the contrast. Part of the beige print also drew the material that made tucks at the waist. Her friend had cried that it was stunning on Abby, with her silvery-blond hair color. Abby decided to wear it while she still could. The way she was growing, she would need to buy loose-fitting clothes this weekend.

After arranging her hair back in a simple low chignon with three pins, she put on her makeup, slipped on matching yellow shoes and started out of the bedroom. But she only made it to the hallway with her bone-colored handbag when her landline rang. Presuming it was her father calling to see how she was doing, she walked into the den to pick up and say hello.

"Signorina Loretto? This is Marcello. You are wanted in the king's drawing room. Are you ready?"

Her hand gripped the receiver tighter. It sounded urgent. During the night she'd worried about this meeting. It was only natural Michelina's mother would want to meet the woman who would be giving birth to her grandchild. But something about the look in Vincenzo's eyes had given her a sinking feeling in the pit of her stomach.

"Yes. I'll be right there."

"Then I'll inform His Highness, and meet you in the main corridor."

"Thank you."

Because of Vincenzo, Abby was familiar with every part of the palace except the royal apartments. He'd taken her to the main drawing room, where the king met with heads of state, several times. Vincenzo had gotten a kick out of watching her reaction as he related stories about foreign dignitaries that weren't public knowledge.

But her smile faded as she made her way across the magnificent edifice to meet Michelina's mother. She knew the queen was grieving. Marcello met her in the main hallway. "Follow me."

They went down the hall past frescoes and paintings, to another section where they turned a corner. She spied the country's flag draped outside an ornate pair of floor-to-ceiling doors. Marcello knocked on one of the panels and was told to enter. He opened the door, indicating she should go in.

The tall vaulted ceiling of the room was a living museum to the history of Arancia, and had known centuries of French and Italian rulers. But Abby's gaze fell on Vincenzo, who was wearing a somber midnight-blue suit. Opposite him sat Michelina's stylish sixty-five-year-old mother, who was brunette like her late daughter. She'd dressed in black, with a matching cloche hat, and sat on one of the brocade chairs.

"Come all the way in, Signorina Loretto. I'd like you to meet my mother-in-law, Her Majesty the Queen of Gemelli." Abby knew Gemelli—another citrus-producing country—was an island kingdom off the eastern coast of Sicily, facing the Ionian Sea.

She moved toward them and curtsied the way she'd been taught as a child after coming to the palace. "Your Majesty. It's a great honor, but my heart has been bleeding for you and the prince. I cared for your daughter very much."

The matriarch's eyes were a darker brown than Michelina's, more snapping. She gave what passed for a nod before Vincenzo told Abby to be seated on the love seat on the other side of the coffee table. Once she was comfortable, he said, "If you recall, Michelina and I flew to Gemelli so she could tell the queen we were pregnant."

"Yes."

"To my surprise, the unexpected nature of our news

came as a great shock to my mother-in-law, since my wife hadn't informed her of our decision to use a surrogate."

What?

"You mean your daughter never told you what she and the prince were contemplating?"

"No," came the answer through wooden lips.

Aghast, Abby averted her eyes, not knowing what to think. "I'm so sorry, Your Majesty."

"We're all sorry, because the queen and Michelina argued," Vincenzo explained. "Unfortunately before they could talk again, the accident happened. The queen would like to take this opportunity to hear from the woman who has dared to go against nature to perform a service for which she gets nothing in return."

CHAPTER THREE

ABBY REELED.

For Vincenzo to put it so bluntly meant he and his mother-in-law had exchanged harsh if not painfully bitter words. But he was a realist and had decided the only thing to do was meet this situation head-on. He expected Abby to handle it because of their long-standing friendship over the years.

"You haven't answered my question, Signorina Loretto."

At the queen's staccato voice, Abby struggled to catch her breath and remain calm. No wonder she'd felt tension from him last night when he'd brought up this morning's meeting. Michelina's omission when it came to her mother had put a pall over an event that was helping Vincenzo to get up in the morning.

He was counting on Abby being able to deal with his mother-in-law. She refused to let him down even if it killed her. More time passed while she formulated what to say before focusing on the queen.

"If I had a daughter who came to me in the same situation, I would ask her exactly the same question. In my case, I've done it for one reason only. Perhaps you didn't know that the prince rescued me from certain death when I was seventeen. I lost my mother in that same sailboat accident. Before I was swept to shore by the wind, I'd lost consciousness.

"When the prince found me, I was close to death but didn't know it." Abby's eyes glazed over with unshed tears. "If you could have heard the way my father wept after he discovered I'd been found and brought back to the living, you would realize what a miracle had happened that day, all because of the prince's quick thinking and intervention.

"From that time on, my father and I have felt the deepest gratitude to the prince. Over the years I've pondered many times how to pay the prince back for preventing what could have been an all-out catastrophe for my father."

The lines on the queen's face deepened, revealing her sorrow. Whether she was too immersed in her own grief to hear what Abby was saying, Abby didn't know.

"The prince and princess were the perfect couple," Abby continued. "When I heard that the princess had had a third miscarriage, it wounded me for their sake. They deserved happiness. Before Christmas I learned through my father that Dr. DeLuca had suggested a way for them to achieve their dream of a family."

Abby fought to prevent tears from falling. "After years of wishing there was something I could do, I realized that if I could qualify as a candidate, I could carry their child for them. You'll never know the joy it gave me at the thought of doing something so special for them. When I told my father what I wanted to do, he was surprised at first, and yet he supported my decision, too, otherwise he would never have approved."

She took a shuddering breath. "That's the reason

I'm doing this. A life for a life. What I'm going to get out of this is pure happiness to see the baby the prince and princess fought so hard for. When the doctor puts the baby in the prince's arms, Michelina will live on in their child, and the child will forever be a part of King Guilio and his wife, and a part of you and your husband, Your Majesty."

The queen's hands trembled on the arms of the chair. "You have no comprehension of what it's like to be a mother. How old are you?"

"I'm twenty-eight and it's true I've never been married or had a child. But I won't be its mother in the way you mean. I'm only supplying a safe haven for the baby until it's born. Yes, I'll go through the aches and pains of pregnancy, but I view this as a sacred trust."

Her features hardened. "You call this sacred?"

"I do. During my screening process, I met a dozen different parents and their surrogates who'd gone through the experience and now have beautiful children. They were all overjoyed and agreed it's a special partnership between them and God."

For the first time, the queen looked away.

"The prince is a full partner in this. He and the princess discussed it many times. He knows what she wanted and I'll cooperate in every way. If you have suggestions, I'll welcome them with all my heart."

Quiet reigned.

Realizing there was nothing more to say, Abby glanced at Vincenzo, waiting for him to dismiss her.

He read her mind with ease. "I'm aware the limo is waiting to drive you to your office."

"Yes, Your Highness."

At those words Michelina's mother lifted her head. "You intend to work?" She sounded shocked.

"I do. I am passionate about my career as an attorney. After the delivery, I will have my own life to lead and need to continue planning for it."

Vincenzo leaned forward. "She'll stop work when the time is right."

"Where will you live after the baby's born?" The pointed question told Abby exactly where the queen's thoughts had gone.

Nowhere near the prince.

She couldn't blame the older woman for that. How could Michelina's mother not suspect the worst? Her fears preyed on Abby's guilt, which was deepening because she'd found herself missing Vincenzo more than she should have while he'd been away. He shouldn't have been on her mind so much, but she couldn't seem to turn off her thoughts. Not when the baby growing inside her was a constant reminder of him.

For weeks now she'd played games of *what if?* during the night when she couldn't sleep. What if the baby were hers and Vincenzo's? What would he or she look like? Where would they create a nursery in the palace? When would they go shopping for a crib and all the things necessary? She wanted to make a special baby quilt and start a scrapbook.

But then she'd break out in a cold sweat of guilt and sit up in the bed, berating herself for having any of these thoughts. Michelina's death might have changed everything, but this royal baby still wasn't Abby's!

How could she even entertain such thoughts when Michelina had trusted her so implicitly? It was such a betrayal of the trust and regard the two women had for each other. They'd made a contract as binding as a blood oath. The second the baby was born, her job as surrogate would no longer be required and she'd return to her old life.

But Abby was aghast to discover that Michelina's death had thrown her into an abyss of fresh guilt. She needed to talk to the psychologist about finding strategies to cope with this new situation or go crazy.

Queen Bianca had asked her a question and was waiting for an answer.

"I plan to buy my own home in another part of the city in the same building as a friend of mine. My contract with the prince and princess includes living at the palace, and that ends the moment the baby is delivered."

Vincenzo's eyes narrowed on her face. "What friend?"

That was probably the only thing about her plans the three of them hadn't discussed over the last few months.

"You've heard me speak of Carolena Baretti and know she's my best friend, who works at the same law firm with me. We went through law school together at the University of Arancia before taking the bar."

If a woman could look gutted, the queen did. "This whole situation is unnatural."

"Not unnatural, Your Majesty, just different. Your daughter wanted a baby badly enough to think it all through and agree to it. I hope the day will come when you're reconciled to that decision."

"That day will never come," the older woman declared in an imperious voice. "I was thrilled each time she informed me she was pregnant and I suffered with her through each miscarriage. But I will never view surrogacy as ethically acceptable."

"But it's a gestational surrogacy," Abby argued quietly. "Dr. DeLuca says that several thousand women around the globe are gestational surrogates and it's becoming preferable to going with traditional surrogacy, because it ensures the genetic link to both parents. Think how many lives can be changed. Surely you can see what a miracle it is."

"Nevertheless, it's outside tradition. It interferes with a natural process in violation of God's will."

"Then how do you explain this world that God created, and all the new technology that helps people like your daughter and Vincenzo realize their dream to have a family?"

"It doesn't need an explanation. It's a form of adultery, because you are the third party outside their marriage. Some people regard that it could result in incest of a sort."

Tortured by her words, Abby exchanged an agonized glance with Vincenzo. "What do you mean?"

"As the priest reminded me, their child might one day marry another of *your* children. While there would be no genetic relationship, the two children would be siblings, after a fashion."

Naturally Abby hoped to marry one day and have children of her own, but never in a million years would she have jumped to such an improbable conclusion. By now Vincenzo's features had turned to granite.

"There's also the question of whether or not you'll be entitled to an inheritance and are actually out for one."

Abby was stunned. "When the prince saved my life, he gave me an inheritance more precious than anything earthly. If any money is involved, it's the one hundred and fifty thousand dollars or more the prince has paid the doctors and the hospital for this procedure to be done." She could feel herself getting worked up, but she couldn't stop.

"I've been given all the compensation I could ever wish for by being allowed to live here in the palace, where my every want and need is taken care of. I'm so sorry this situation has caused you so much grief. I can see you two need to discuss this further, alone. I must leave for the office."

Abby eyed the prince, silently asking him to please help her to go before the queen grew any more upset. He got the message and stood to his full imposing height, signaling she could stand.

"Thank you for joining us," he murmured. "Whatever my mother-in-law's reaction, it's too late for talk because you're pregnant with Michelina's and my child. Let's say no more. I promise that when the queen is presented with her first grandchild, she'll forget all these concerns."

The queen flashed him a look of disdain that wounded Abby. She couldn't walk out of here with everything so ugly and not say a few last words.

"It's been my privilege to meet you, Your Majesty. Michelina used to talk about you all the time. She loved you very much and was looking forward to you helping her through these coming months. I hope you know that. If you ever want to talk to me again, please call me. I don't have a mother anymore and would like to hear any advice you have to help me get through this."

It was getting harder and harder to clap with one hand and the prince knew it.

"Again, let me say how sorry I am about your loss. She was so lovely and accomplished. I have two of her watercolors hanging on the wall of my apartment. Everyone will miss her terribly, especially this baby.

"But thankfully it will have its grandmother to tell him or her all the things only you know about their mother."

The queen stared at Abby through dim eyes.

Abby could feel her pain. "Goodbye for now." She curtsied once more. Her gaze clung to Vincenzo's for a few seconds before she turned on her low-heeled sandals and left the room. The limo would be waiting for her. Though she wanted to run, she forced herself to stay in control so she wouldn't fall and do something to hurt herself.

The queen had put Abby on trial. No wonder Vincenzo's wife had been frightened to approach her mother with such an unconventional idea. Only now was Abby beginning to understand how desperate *and* courageous Michelina had been to consider allowing a third party to enter into the most intimate aspect of all their lives. Facing the queen had to be one of the worst moments Abby had ever known.

But this had to be an even more nightmarish experience for Vincenzo. Here he was trying to deal with his wife's death while at the same time having to defend the decision he and Michelina had made to use a surrogate. He had to be suffering guilt of his own.

Abby blamed no one for this, but she felt Vincenzo's pain. How he was going to get through this latest crisis, she couldn't imagine. Probably by working. That was how *she* planned to survive.

Twenty minutes later Abby entered the neoclassical building that housed her law firm and walked straight back to Carolena's office. Her friend was a patent attorney and had become as close to Abby as a sister. Unfortunately she was at court, so they'd have to talk later.

Both Carolena and Abby had been hired by the well-known Arancian law firm after they'd graduated. Abby had been thrilled when they'd both been taken on a year ago. She had planned for this career from her junior-high days, and had been hired not only for her specialty in international trade law, but because she was conversant in French, English, Italian and Mentonasc.

Since the Mentonasc dialect—somewhere between Nicard and a dialect of Ligurian, a Gallo-Romance language spoken in Northern Italy—was currently spoken by about 10 percent of the population living in Arancia and its border areas, it gave her an edge over other applicants for the position, which required her particular linguistic expertise.

Abby's parents had cleverly directed her studies from a very young age. Thanks to them her abilities had taken her to the head of the class. However, this morning Abby's mind wasn't on her latest cases.

She felt disturbed by the revelation that Michelina had kept her mother in the dark about one of the most important events in her life. Abby had done her research. Since the death of King Gregorio, Queen Bianca become the ruler of Gemelli and was known to be rigid and difficult. Abby had felt her disapproval and didn't envy Vincenzo's task of winning his mother-in-law over.

Hopefully something Abby had said would sink in and soften her heart. At the moment, Abby's own heart was breaking for all of them.

* * *

Six hours later, Abby finished dictating some memos to Bernardo and left the building for the limo. But when she walked outside, she noticed the palace secret service cars had parked both in front of and behind the limo. One of the security men got out of the front and opened the rear door for her. What was going on?

As she climbed inside and saw who was sitting there waiting for her—in sunglasses and a silky claret-colored sport shirt and cream trousers—the blood started to hammer in her ears.

"Vincenzo—"

His name slipped out by accident, proving to her more and more that he filled her conscious and unconscious mind.

The tremor in Abby's voice made its way to every cell of Vincenzo's body. After she'd bared her soul to his mother-in-law that morning, he'd realized not only at what price she'd sacrificed herself to make their dreams of a baby a reality, but he'd been flooded with memories of that day when she'd lost her mother.

Abby had been a great swimmer and handled herself well in the sea. As some of his friends had pointed out years ago when they'd seen her in the water offshore, she wasn't a woman yet, but she showed all the promise.

By the time she'd turned seventeen, he'd found himself looking at her a lot more than he should have. She was one of those natural-blond American girls with classic features, noted for their long, gorgeous legs. At that point in time Vincenzo had already been betrothed to Michelina. Since the marriage wouldn't be for at least another ten years, he'd had the freedom to date the women who attracted him.

Abby had been too young, of course, but pleasing to the eye. She'd turned into a very beautiful girl who was studious, intelligent and spoke Italian like a native. He enjoyed every moment he spent with her; her enthusiasm for everything surprised and entertained him.

But even if he hadn't been betrothed, Abby had been off-limits to Vincenzo for more reasons than her young age or the fact that she wasn't a princess. Her parents had become close friends with Vincenzo's parents. That was a special friendship that demanded total respect.

Though her periwinkle-blue eyes always seemed to smile at him with interest when they chanced upon each other, there was an invisible boundary between them she recognized, too. Neither of them ever crossed it until the day of the squall...

As Abby had told Queen Bianca earlier, she and her mother, Holly, had been out in a small sailboat off the coast when the storm struck. Nothing could come on as rapidly and give so little time for preparation as did a white squall.

Vincenzo had been in his father's office before lunch discussing a duty he needed to carry out when they'd noticed the darkening sky. A cloudburst had descended, making the day feel like night. They hadn't seen a storm this ferocious in years and felt sorry for anyone who'd been caught in it.

While they were commenting on the fierceness of the wind, a call came through informing the king that the Loretto sailboat was missing from its slip. Someone thought they had seen Signora Loretto and her daugh-

ter out sailing earlier, but they hadn't come back in yet.
Several boats were already out there looking for them.

Abby—

Vincenzo was aghast. *She* was out there?

The sweet girl who'd always been there for him was
battling this storm with her mother, alone?

Fear like Vincenzo had never known before attacked
his insides and he broke out in a cold sweat. "I've got
to find them!"

"Wait, son! Let the coast guard deal with it!"

But he'd already reached the door and dashed from
the room. Driven by fear, he raced through the palace.
Once outside, he ran to the dock, where a group of men
huddled. He grabbed one of them to come with him
and they took off in his cruiser to face a churning sea.

The other man kept in radio contact with the rescue
boats. Within a minute they heard that the sailboat had
been spotted. Vincenzo headed toward the cited coor-
dinates, oblivious to the elements.

The rescue boats were already on the scene as Vincenzo's cruiser came close to the sailboat. It was toss-
ing like a cork, but he couldn't see anyone on board.
"Have they already been rescued?"

"Signora Loretto was found floating unconscious in
the water wearing her life preserver, but there's no sign
of her daughter yet," replied his companion.

Vincenzo's heart almost failed him.

Abby had drowned?

It was as though his whole life passed before him.
She *couldn't* have drowned! He couldn't lose her! Not
his Abby...

"We've got to look for her! She knows to wear a life
jacket. The wind will have pushed her body through

the water. We're going to follow it. You steer while I search."

"It's too dangerous for you, Your Highness!"

"Danger be damned! Don't you understand?" he shouted. "There's a seventeen-year-old girl out there who needs help!"

"Tell me where to go."

He studied the direction of the wind. "Along the coastline near the caves!" Vincenzo knew this coastline like the back of his hand. When a low pressure over the Mediterranean approached the coast from the southeast, the weather could change quickly for the worse and its clear sky change to an east wind. If Abby had been knocked unconscious, too, she could have been swept into one of the caves further up the coast.

When they reached the opening of the largest cave, Vincenzo dove in and swam through to the three hidden grottoes, where he'd been many times with his friends. In the second one, his heart had leaped when he saw Abby's body floating lifelessly, like her mother's. Quickly he'd caught hold of her and swum her out to the boat, where he took off her life jacket and began giving her mouth-to-mouth resuscitation. At first there was no response. Her face was a pinched white. Though terrified she was too far gone, he kept up the CPR.

At the last second there came sounds of life, and her eyelids fluttered. He turned her on her side while she coughed and threw up water.

"That's it, my precious Abby. Get rid of it."

When she'd finished, she looked up at him, dazed. "Vincenzo?"

"*Sì,*" he'd murmured in relief. "You were in a storm,

but I found you in one of the grottoes and you're all right now."

Abby blinked. "My mother?" she cried frantically. "Where is she?"

"With your father." It wasn't a lie, but since he didn't know the whole truth of her condition, he kept quiet.

"Thank God." Her eyes searched his. "I could have died in there. You saved my life," she whispered in awe. In a totally unexpected gesture, she'd thrown her arms around his neck and clung to him.

"Thank God," he'd whispered back and found himself rocking her in his arms while she sobbed.

Vincenzo had never felt that close to another human being in his life. She'd felt so right in his arms. When they took her to the hospital and she learned her mother had died of a blow from the mast, she'd flung herself into his arms once more.

That was the moment when he knew Abby meant more to him that he could put into words. Their relationship changed that day. His feelings for her ran much deeper than he'd realized. To imagine his life without her was anathema to him.

She'd been too inconsolable for him to do anything but let her pour out her pain and love for her mother. His only desire had been to comfort her. He'd held her for a long time because her father, overcome with grief, had to be sedated.

In front of the queen today, they'd both relived that moment. Abby's outpouring of her soul had endeared her to him in such a profound way, he could hardly find expression. Though he knew it was wrong, he'd decided to break one of his own rules and pick her up from work.

Bianca had put Abby through a torturous session.

Despite his guilt in seeking her out for a reason that wasn't a medical necessity, he couldn't let it go until he'd seen for himself that she was all right.

"I came to find out how well you survived the day."

The picture of her in that yellow dress when she'd walked in the room had made an indelible impression of femininity and sophistication in his mind. Bianca couldn't have helped but notice how lovely she was, along with her moving sincerity. It hadn't surprised him his mother-in-law had been so quiet after Abby had left the room to go to work.

"My worry has been for you." She sat down opposite him and fastened her seat belt. "For me, work is the great panacea. But it's evident the queen has been in absolute agony."

"She's flown back to Gemelli with a lot to think about."

"The poor thing. We have to hope she'll let go of her preconceived beliefs so she can enjoy this special time."

There was a sweetness in Abby that touched Vincenzo's heart. "You're the one I'm concerned about. It hurts me that you no longer have your mother to confide in." Until now he hadn't thought about how alone Abby must feel. Bianca's castigations had been like a dagger plunged into her, bringing out his protective instincts.

She flicked him a glance. "But I have my father, and I have you and the doctor. Who better than all of you to comfort me when I need it?" Except that Vincenzo wanted to do more than comfort her, God forgive him.

He held her gaze. "I'm sorry if anything the queen said has upset you, but I promise everything's going to be all right in time."

"I believe that, too. Did she say anything else?"

"No, but her son Valentino and I are good friends."
When he'd gone with the queen and his brothers-in-law
to visit Michelina's grave once, they'd eaten lunch before he'd accompanied them to their jet. "He's promised
to keep in close touch. Now let's change the subject."

"You're taking too great a risk, Your Highness. We
mustn't be seen out together like this."

"The limo protects us." Even as he said it, he was
trying to tamp down his guilt over pressuring her when
it was obvious she was afraid to be seen with him. He
ought to be worried about that, too, but something had
come over him.

"Please, Your Highness. The fact that there are so
many security men will cause the locals to speculate about who is so important, driving around in the
crowded streets. Have the car turn around and take me
back to the office."

"It's too late for that." Vincenzo had no intention of
letting her go yet.

"After my audience with the queen, surely you understand my fears."

"After the way she went after you, I have my own
fears where you're concerned. You didn't deserve that
and I want to make it up to you."

CHAPTER FOUR

"WE'RE GOING IN the wrong direction to the palace."

Vincenzo ignored Abby's comment. "Last night you didn't eat a full meal. This evening I intend to remedy that and take you to a very special place for dinner to celebrate the Lemon and Orange Festival. Don't worry," he said when he saw her eyes grow anxious. "We'll be arriving via a private entrance to a private dining room where my own people will be serving us. All you have to do is enjoy a meal free of caffeine and alcohol, with salt in moderation."

She kneaded her hands. "I know why you're doing this, Vincenzo, but it isn't necessary."

"Has being pregnant made you a mind reader?"

For once she couldn't tell if he was having fun with her or if her comment had irked him. "I only meant—"

"You only meant that you don't expect any special favors from me," he preempted her. "Tell me something I don't already know."

"I've annoyed you. I'm sorry."

"Abby—we need to have a little talk. Because of the sacrifice you've made for me and Michelina, any social life you would normally enjoy has been cut off until the baby's born. At this time in your life you should be out having a good time. I have no doubt there are any number of men who pass through your office wanting a relationship with you. Certainly I don't need to tell you that you're a very beautiful woman. My brother-in-law shared as much with me earlier."

"I've never met Michelina's brother."

"But he saw you this morning after you left the drawing room for the limo."

That was news to Abby. Vincenzo's words had shaken her. "Thank you for the compliment."

"Now you sound vexed with me."

"I'm not!"

"Good. Then try to understand that our relationship isn't one-sided, with me reaping all the benefits while you lie around like a beached whale, barefoot and pregnant, as you Americans tend to say."

Abby burst into laughter.

"I'm glad you think that's funny. We're making progress."

No one could be more amusing than Vincenzo when he revealed this exciting side of his nature. "I can't believe you've ever heard those expressions."

"I graduated in California Girls 101 during my vacation one summer in San Diego."

She rolled her eyes. "*That* school. I don't doubt it." She knew he'd traveled a lot in his twenties. "I guess you didn't need a booklet for the class."

He grinned, revealing a gorgeous white smile. "And the tuition was free. Why do you think most men congregate there when they get the chance?"

"Isn't it interesting that most women congregate in Arancia and Italy to attend Mediterranean Gods 101? They don't need booklets, either."

Vincenzo let go with a belly laugh that resonated throughout the interior of the limo. "You must be dynamite in the courtroom."

"Why don't you come up and see me some time?" she said in her best Mae West impersonation. *Why didn't he come to her apartment and stay...* It was a wicked thought, but she couldn't help it. The other night she hadn't wanted him to leave.

The corner of his mouth lifted. "Who were you imitating just now?"

"Someone you'd never know. She was in American films years ago. My mother loved her old movies."

"Tell me her name."

"I'll give you a hint. They named inflatable life jackets after her in the Second World War. If you still can't think of it, I'll do better and have a DVD sent to you so you can see for yourself."

"We'll watch it together."

No. They wouldn't watch it together. They'd done enough of that when she was much younger. He had his own theater in the palace, where she'd seen a lot of films and eaten marzipan with him. But that time was long gone and this idea of his had to be stopped right now. She was having too much fun and needed his company too much.

Thankfully they'd left the Promenade d'Or along the coast and were following a winding road up the hillsides above the city. In another minute they rounded a curve and pulled up to, of all things, a funicular railway.

Vincenzo got out of the limo and came around to help her. Together with some of his security people, they got on and sat on one of the benches. He told her to buckle up before it started climbing the steep mountain.

"There's a lovely little restaurant two kilometers higher that overlooks the Mediterranean. While we eat, we'll watch the festival fireworks being set off in town."

Once Abby was settled, Vincenzo had to talk to one of his security men, leaving her alone with her thoughts for a second. During her teenage years she'd had ridiculous daydreams about being alone with him, but none of them could match the wonder of such an evening. Without question this was the most thrilling moment in Abby's life.

However, there was one problem with reality intruding on this beautiful dream. While he was trying to give her a special night out to make up for her being denied a social life at present, Abby could never forget she was carrying the child he and Michelina had made. The wife he'd adored was gone, leaving him desolate, just like her father.

She remembered the night of Michelina's funeral, when she'd wandered out onto the patio of her apartment, not knowing where to go with her pain. Before her was the amazing sight of dozens of sailboats and yachts anchored offshore from up and down the Riviera with Arancian flags flying at half-mast in the breeze to pay respect to the prince.

While she stood there, her cell phone had rung, causing her to jump. She hurried inside to check the caller ID, hardly able to see through the tears.

"Carolena?" she'd cried after clicking on.

"Abby? When the announcer started speculating on the future of the monarchy, I had to call and see if you're all right."

She breathed in deeply. "Yes," she'd murmured, wiping the moisture off her cheeks with her hand.

"No, you're not. I don't know how you're handling this."

"Truthfully, not very well."

"Talk to me. I know you told me you can't leave the palace until tomorrow and I can't come over there today, so the phone will have to do. Have you even talked to Vincenzo since the accident?"

"Yes. He came for a minute last evening, worried about my welfare, if you can imagine."

"Actually, I can. To know you're carrying his child is probably the only thing keeping him from going under. I never witnessed anything more touching in my life than the sight of the horse covered in her favorite flowers walking alongside that incredible-looking man. Already I've seen one of the tabloids out in the kiosk bearing the headline The Prince of Every Woman's Dreams in Mourning."

Abby had closed her eyes tightly. "The media will make a circus of this." She could hear it all now: *Who will be the next princess? Will she be foreign? Will he wait a year, or will he break with tradition and take a new bride in the next few months?* Abby had a question of her own: *How will the next woman he chooses feel about the surrogacy situation?* All those thoughts and more had bombarded her.

"You really shouldn't be alone."

"All I have to do is get through tonight, Carolena. Tomorrow I can start living a normal life."

Now, seven weeks later, here Abby was with the prince of every woman's dreams, riding to the top of the mountain. But there was nothing normal about his life or hers. When she and her father had gone through all the *what if*s before she'd made her decision to be a surrogate, the idea of either Michelina or Vincenzo dying had only been mentioned in passing. But she couldn't have imagined anything so horrible and never thought about it again.

"Shall we go in?" sounded the deep, velvety male voice next to her.

"Oh—yes!" Abby had been so immersed in thought she hadn't realized they'd arrived. Night had fallen during their journey here. Vincenzo led her off the funicular and walked her through a hallway to another set of doors. They opened onto a terrace with a candlelit table and flowers set for two.

A small gasp of pleasure escaped her lips when she realized she was looking out over the same view she could see from her own patio at the palace. But they were much higher up, so she could take in the whole city of Arancia alive with lights for the nightly festival celebration.

"What an incredible vista."

"I agree," he murmured as he helped her to sit. Of course it was an accident that his hand brushed her shoulder, but she felt his touch as if she'd just come in contact with an electric current. This was so wrong; she was terrified.

Grape juice from the surrounding vineyard came first, followed by hors d'oeuvres and then a luscious rack of lamb and fresh green peas from the restaurant's garden. Abby knew the chef had prepared food to the prince's specifications.

She ate everything. "This meal is fabulous!"

His black eyes smiled at her. "Tonight you have an appetite. That's good. We'll have to do this more often."

No, no, no.

"If I were to eat here every night, I'd be as big as that whale you referred to earlier."

He chuckled. "You think?"

"I know."

While Abby enjoyed the house's lemon tart specialty for dessert, Vincenzo drank coffee. "Mind if I ask you a personal question?"

How personal? She was on dangerous ground, fearing he could see right through her, to her chaotic innermost thoughts. "What would you like to know?"

"Has there been an important man in your life? And if so, why didn't you marry him?"

Yes. I'm looking at him.

Heat filled her cheeks. "I had my share of boyfriends, but by college I got serious about my studies. Law school doesn't leave time for much of a social life when you're clerking for a judge who expects you to put in one hundred and twenty hours a week."

"Sounds like one of my normal days," he remarked.

She knew he wasn't kidding. "You and I never discussed this before, but I'm curious about something. Didn't you ever want to be a mother to your own child first?"

Abby stifled her moan. If he only knew how during her teenage years she'd dreamed about being married to him and having his baby. Since that time, history had been made and she was carrying his baby in real life. But it wasn't hers and that dream had come with a price. How could she be feeling like this when he was forbidden to her?

"Well—" She swallowed hard. "The desire to be a mother has always been rooted in me. I've never doubted my ability to be a good one. Despite the fact that Mother died early, I had a charmed and happy childhood. She was a wonderful mom. Warm and charming. Funny. Still, I never saw raising a child as my only goal.

"I'd always envisioned motherhood as the result of a loving relationship with a man, like my parents had. Carolena has told me many times that it's just an excuse because no man has ever lived up to my father. She said the umbilical cord should have been cut years ago. With hindsight I think she's probably right, but there's no one like him."

In truth, there was no one like Vincenzo and never would be. *He* was the reason she hadn't been able to get interested in another man.

"Your father has been a lucky man to have inspired such fierce love from his wife and daughter."

The comment sounded mournful. "Michelina loved you the same way."

"Yes."

"So will your child."

His eyes grew veiled without him saying anything.

The fireworks had started, lighting up the night sky in a barrage of colors, but she couldn't appreciate the display because of a certain tension between them that hadn't been there earlier. She was walking such a tightrope around him, her body was a mass of nerves.

"Maybe coming out to dinner wasn't a very good idea for you, Your Highness."

"What happened to *Vincenzo?*"

Again she had the feeling she'd angered him, the last thing she wanted to do. But it was imperative she keep emotional distance from him. "You're still mourning your wife. I appreciate this evening more than you know, but it's too soon for you to be out doing the things you used to do with her." *And too hard on me.*

She wiped her mouth with the napkin. "When was the last time you brought her here? Do you want to talk about it?"

That dark, remote expression he could get had returned. "Michelina never came here with me."

She swallowed hard. "I see." She wondered why. "Nevertheless, being out on a night like this has to bring back memories."

His fingers ran over the stem of the wineglass that was still full. "Today as I opened the festival, you could feel spring in the air. You can feel it tonight. It calls for a new beginning." His gaze swerved to hers, piercing through to her insides. "You and I are together on a journey that neither of us has ever taken. I want to put the past behind us and enjoy the future that is opening up."

"With your baby to be born soon, it will be a glorious future."

"There are a few months to go yet, months you should be able to enjoy. I want to help you. How does that sound?"

It sounded as though he didn't want to be reminded of his wife again because it hurt him too much and he needed a diversion. Naturally, he did, but Abby couldn't fill that need! She didn't dare.

"I'm already having a wonderful time enjoying this meal with you. Thank you for a very memorable evening."

"You're welcome. I want us to enjoy more."

"We can't, Vincenzo. The people close to you will notice and there will be gossip. If I've angered you again, I'm sorry."

Silence followed her remarks. They watched the fireworks for a while longer before leaving. The ride down the mountain was much faster than the ride up. It was much like the sensation when Dr. DeLuca had said, "Congratulations, Signorina Loretto. The blood test we did revealed the presence of the HCG hormone. You're pregnant!"

Abby hadn't believed it. Even though she'd wanted to be a surrogate mother and had done everything possible to make it happen, for the doctor to tell her the procedure had worked was like the first time she rode the Ferris wheel at a theme park. The bar had locked her in the chair, filling her with excitement. Then the wheel had turned and lifted her high in the air. That was the way she felt now, high in the air over Arancia. She didn't know if she wanted this descent to continue, but it was too late to get off. She had to go with it and just hang on. Only this time she wasn't on the Ferris wheel or the funicular and this ride would continue for the next thirty-odd weeks.

Abby hadn't been able to tell anyone about her pregnancy except Carolena. But she knew she could trust her best friend with her life, and that news hadn't been something she could keep to herself on that day of all days.

When she went to work on the day she'd found out she was pregnant, Abby visited with her gorgeous, fashionable Italian friend, who stopped traffic when she stepped outside. Carolena had worn her chestnut hair on top of her head in a loose knot. Though she didn't need glasses, she put on a pair with large frames to give her a more professional appearance.

She looked up when she saw Abby and smiled. "*Fantastico!* I've been needing a break from the Bonelli case."

"I'm so happy you said that because I've got something to tell you I can't hold in any longer. If I don't talk to you about it, I'll go crazy." She closed and locked the door behind her before sitting down in the chair opposite the desk.

"This has to be serious. You looked flushed. Have you settled the Giordano case already? Shall we break out the champagne?"

"Don't I wish! No, this has nothing to do with the law." She moved restlessly in the leather chair. In fact there'd be no champagne for her for the next nine months. "What I say to you can't ever leave this room."

Carolena's smile faded before she crossed herself.

Abby leaned forward. "I'm going to have a baby," she whispered.

Her friend's stunned expression said it all before she removed her glasses and walked around the desk in her fabulous designer sling-back high heels to hunker down in front of her. She shook her head. "Who?" was all she could manage to say.

The question was a legitimate one. Though Abby had been asked out by quite a few men since joining the firm, she hadn't accepted any dates. No on-site romances for her. Besides, she wanted to make her place in the firm and that meant studying when she wasn't in the office so she could stay on top of every case.

"Their Royal Highnesses."

Carolena's beautifully shaped dark brows met together in a frown. "You mean…as in…"

"Prince Vincenzo and Princess Michelina."

There was a palpable silence in the room. Then, "Abby—"

"I realize it's a lot to swallow."

A look of deep concern broke out on Carolena's expressive face. "But you—"

"I know what you're going to say," she broke in hurriedly. "It's true that I'll always love him for saving me from drowning, but that was eleven years ago when I was seventeen. Since then he has married and they've suffered through three miscarriages. The doctor suggested they look for a gestational surrogate mother for them."

"What?"

"His logic made total sense. Gestational surrogacy, unlike adoption, would allow both Vincenzo and Michelina to be genetically related to their child. Even better, they would be involved in the baby's conception and throughout the pregnancy, so they'd feel a total part of the whole experience."

"But you can't be a surrogate because you've never had a baby before."

"There are a few exceptions, and I'm one of them."

Carolena put a hand on Abby's arm. "So you just nominated yourself for the position without any thought of what it would really mean and threw yourself into the ring?" She sounded aghast at the idea.

Abby had hoped for a happier response from her friend. "Of course not. But I wasn't able to stop thinking about it. I even dreamed about it. The answer of how to repay him for saving my life came to me like a revelation. *A life for a life.*"

"Oh, Abby—despite the fact that you push men away, you're such a romantic! What if midway through the pregnancy you become deathly ill and it ruins your life? I can't even imagine how awful that would be."

"Nothing's going to happen to me. I've always been

healthy as a horse. I want to give them this gift. I didn't
make the decision lightly. Though I had a crush on him
from the time I was twelve, it had nothing to do with
reality and I got over it after I found out he was already
betrothed to Michelina."

Those famous last words she'd thrown out so reck-
lessly had a choke hold on Abby now. She adored him,
but had to hide her feelings if it killed her.

By the time she and Vincenzo had climbed in the
limousine, she realized her due date was coming closer.
In one regard she wanted it to get here as quickly as
possible. But in another, she needed to hug the precious months left to her, because when it was over,
she wouldn't see Vincenzo again. She couldn't bear
the thought.

When Abby's eight-week checkup was over, Dr. De-
Luca showed her into another consulting room, where
she saw Vincenzo talking with the psychologist, Dr.
Greco. Both men stood when she entered. The prince
topped him by at least three inches.

Her vital signs had been in the normal range during
her exam, but she doubted they were now. Vincenzo
possessed an aura that had never made him look more
princely. He wore a cream-colored suit with a silky
brown sport shirt, the picture of royal affluence and
casual sophistication no other man could pull off with
the same elegance.

The balding doctor winked at her. "How is Signorina
Loretto today, besides being pregnant?" She liked him
a lot because he had a great sense of humor.

"Heavier."

Both men chuckled before they all sat down.

The doctor lounged back in his chair. "You do have a certain…how do you say it in English? A certain bloom?"

"That's as good an English term as I know of to cover what's really obvious. I actually prefer it to the Italian term *grassoccia*."

"No one would ever accuse you of looking chubby, my dear."

Vincenzo's black eyes had been playing over her and were smiling by now. The way he looked at her turned her insides to mush. She felt frumpy in the new maternity clothes she'd bought. This morning she'd chosen to wear a khaki skirt with an elastic waist and a short-sleeved black linen blouse she left loose fitting.

The outfit was dressy enough, yet comfortable for work. Her little belly had definitely enlarged, but Carolena said you wouldn't know it with the blouse hanging over the waist.

Dr. Greco leaned forward with a more serious expression. "A fundamental change in both your lives has occurred since you learned the embryo transfer was successful. We have a lot to talk about. One moment while I scroll to the notes I took the last time we were together."

Abby avoided looking at Vincenzo. She didn't know if she could discuss some of the things bothering her in front of the doctor. Up to the moment of Michelina's death, when she'd been through a grueling screening with so many tests, hormones and shots and felt like a scientific experiment, she'd thought she'd arrived at the second part of her journey. The first part had been the months of preparation leading up to that moment.

Abby recalled the smiles on the faces of the hopeful royal couple, yet she knew of their uncertainty that made them feel vulnerable. The three of them had seen the embryo in the incubator just before the transfer.

It was perfect and had been inserted in exactly the right place. The reproductive endocrinologist hugged Michelina and tears fell from her eyes. Vincenzo's eyes had misted over, too. Seeing their reaction, Abby's face had grown wet from moisture. The moment had been indescribable. From that time on, the four of them were a team working for the same goal.

For the eleven days while she'd waited for news one way or the other, Abby had tried to push away any thoughts of failure. She wanted to be an unwavering, constant source of encouragement and support.

When the shock that she was pregnant had worn off and she realized she was carrying their child, it didn't matter to her at all that the little baby growing inside of her wasn't genetically hers. Abby only felt supreme happiness for the couple who'd suffered too many miscarriages.

Especially *their* baby, who would one day be heir to the throne of the Principality of Arancia. Vincenzo's older sister, Gianna, was married to a count and lived in Italy. They hadn't had children yet. The honor of doing this service of love for the crown prince and his wife superseded any other considerations Abby might have had.

But her world had exploded when she'd learned of Michelina's sudden death. The news sent her on a third journey outside her universe of experience. Vincenzo had been tossed into that black void, too.

"Before you came in, Vincenzo told me about the meeting with you and his mother-in-law," said the doctor. "He knows she made you very uncomfortable and feels you should talk about it rather than keep it bottled up."

She bit her lip. "*Uncomfortable* isn't the right word. Though I had no idea the queen had such strong moral, ethical and religious reservations against it, my overall feeling was one of sadness for Vincenzo."

"He feels it goes deeper than that."

Abby glanced at Vincenzo. "In what way?"

The doctor nodded to him. "Go ahead."

Vincenzo had an alarming way of eyeing her frankly. "When we went out to dinner the other night, you weren't your usual self. Why was that?"

She prayed the blood wouldn't run to her face. "Months ago we decided to be as discreet as possible. Since your wife's death I've feared people would see us together and come to the wrong conclusion. But you already know that."

"The queen put that fear in you without coming right out and saying it, didn't she?"

This was a moment for brutal honesty. "Yes."

"Abby—our situation has changed, but my intention to go through this pregnancy with you is stronger than ever. You shouldn't have to feel alone in this. I intend to do all the things Michelina would have done with you and provide companionship. I don't want you to be afraid, even if people start to gossip about us."

She shuddered. "Your mother-in-law is terrified of scandal. I could see it in her eyes. It's evident that's why Michelina was afraid to tell her the truth. The other morning I sensed the queen's shock once she heard you'd saved my life, and that I'd lived on the palace grounds since the age of twelve.

"It wouldn't be much of a stretch for her to believe that not only am I after an inheritance, but that I'm after you. I even feared she believes I've been your mistress and that the baby isn't her grandchild."

"I *knew* that's what you were worried about the other night," Vincenzo whispered.

"I wish Michelina had talked to her mother before the decision was made to choose a surrogate, Your Highness."

"So do I. It grieves me that my wife was always intimidated by her and couldn't admit she hadn't told her mother first, but what's done is done and there's no going back."

Abby was in turmoil. "Vincenzo and Michelina have broken new royal ground with my help, Dr. Greco. Unfortunately it's ground that Queen Bianca isn't able to condone. I'm half-afraid she's going to demand that the pregnancy be…terminated." The thought sickened Abby to the point that she broke out in a cold sweat.

"Never," Vincenzo bit out fiercely. "She wouldn't go that far, not even in her mind, but she's going to have to deal with it since the time's coming when people will know you're the surrogate."

The doctor looked at both of them with concern. "Vincenzo is right. I think it's good you've already felt the fire by dealing with Michelina's mother first. To my knowledge no other royal couple in the known world has undergone the same procedure. The situation involving the two of you is an unprecedented case, but a wonderful one since it means preserving the royal line."

"Here's my dilemma." Vincenzo spoke up once more. "Before Michelina's death I'd planned to keep a lower profile around you, Abby, but that's impossible now and I can't have you feeling guilty. Of course we'll try to be careful, but only within reason. Otherwise I'll be worried about the stress on you and the baby."

"Vincenzo makes a valid point, Abby," the doctor inserted.

She lowered her head. "I know he's right. The moment I decided to go through with this, I realized it would be a risk, but I felt helping them was worth it. But with the princess gone…"

"Yes. She's gone, but you still need to keep that noble goal uppermost in your mind. One day soon you'll be free to live your own life again and the gossip will be a nine-day wonder. Do you have any other issues you'd like to discuss with me in this session?"

Yes. How did she keep her emotional distance from Vincenzo when he'd just stated that he intended to be fully involved with her?

"I can't think of any right now."

"You, Vincenzo?"

He shook his dark, handsome head. "Thank you for meeting with us. I'm sure we'll be talking to you again." Vincenzo got to his feet. "Abby needs to get back to work and so do I."

The three of them shook hands before they left his office and walked out of the building to the limousine. Abby's office wasn't that far away from the hospital. When the limo pulled up in front of the entrance, Vincenzo reached over to open the door for her.

"Have you made plans for the evening, Abby?"

"Yes," she lied. "Carolena and I are going to enjoy the festival before it ends."

"Good. Be careful not to tire yourself out."

She didn't dare ask him what he was doing tonight.

It was none of her business. How on earth was she going to get through seven more months of this?

Vincenzo watched until Abby hurried inside before he closed the door and told his driver to head for the palace. For the moment he had an important meeting with the minister of agriculture. That would keep him occupied until Abby got off work.

If she'd been telling the truth and had plans with her friend, then he was in for a night he'd rather not think about. But she didn't make a good liar. He'd known her too long. He had the strongest hunch she would go straight back to the palace after work and dig into one of her law cases. If he was right—and he would find out later—he'd take her for a walk along the surf.

Incredible to believe that the girl he'd saved from drowning eleven years ago had become a gorgeous woman in every sense of the word, *and* was carrying his child. Even though Michelina had been the biological mother, Abby was now the birth mother.

Though there'd been other candidates, the second he'd heard that Abby was one of them, his mind was made up on the spot. Because she'd always lived on the grounds and they'd developed a special bond, he knew her in all those important little ways you could never know about another person without having had that advantage.

Abby was smart, kind, polite, thoughtful, intelligent, fun. In fact, he knew that he would never have gone through with the surrogacy process if she hadn't been on the list. Michelina had been determined to go through with it because she was desperate to fix their marriage. After her incessant pleading, his guilt finally caused him to cave about turning to the procedure for the answer.

No matter how hard they'd tried, theirs had been a joyless union they'd undergone to perform a duty imposed by being born into royalty. He'd driven himself with work, she with her hobbies and horseback riding. Part of each month she spent time in Gemelli, riding with her friends. They had been counting on a child to bring happiness to their lives.

Thanks to the pregnant woman who'd just left the limo, his baby would be born in November. It would have been the miracle baby his arranged marriage had needed to survive. Now that he was alone, he needed that miracle more than ever. His eyes closed tightly. But he needed Abby, too…

CHAPTER FIVE

"ABBY?"

"Yes, Bernardo?"

"You just received a message from Judge Mascotti's court. Your case for Signor Giordano has been put on the docket for June 4."

"So soon?"

"It surprised me, too."

"Wonderful. I'll call my client."

That kind of good news helped her get through the rest of the afternoon. At five-thirty Abby said good-night to Carolena, who was going out on a date with a friend of her cousin, and hurried out to the limousine. She needed to let go of any unwanted feeling of guilt for lying to Vincenzo over her plans for the evening.

Once she reached the palace, she walked to her suite with its exposure to the water. In her opinion, her new temporary home, set in the heart of the coastal city, was the jewel in the crown of the Principality of Arancia.

At a much younger age, Vincenzo had shown her around most of the palace and she'd adored the older parts. Nine weeks ago she'd been moved from her dad's apartment to the palace and installed in one of the renovated fourteenth-century rooms, with every convenience she could imagine. It thrilled her that Vincenzo had remembered this one was her favorite.

The maid had told her he'd had it filled with fresh flowers, just for her. When she heard those words Abby's eyes smarted, but she didn't dare let the tears come in front of the staff.

Her bedroom had a coffered ceiling and was painted in white with lemon walls up to the moldings. The color matched the lemons of the trees clumped with the orange trees in the gardens below. This paradise would be hers until the baby was born. Vincenzo had told her she had the run of the palace and grounds until then.

She'd marveled at his generosity, but then, he'd always been generous. Years earlier, when she'd mentioned that she wanted a bike to get around sometimes and hoped her parents would get her one for Christmas, he'd provided one for her the very next day.

They did a lot of bike riding on the extensive grounds and had races. He let her win sometimes. She wondered what the doctor would say if she went for a bike ride now. If he gave her permission, would Vincenzo join her? It was a heady thought, one she needed to squelch.

After a snack, Abby decided to take a swim in the pool at the back of the palace and told Angelina she wouldn't want dinner until later. She was supposed to get some exercise every day and preferred swimming to anything else in order to unwind.

Once she'd put her hair in a braid and pinned it to the top of her head, she threw on a beach robe over her bikini and headed out wearing thonged sandals. When she reached the patio, she noticed Piero Gabberino pulling weeds in the flower bed.

"Ciao, Piero!"

"Ehi, Abby!"

The chief gardener's nice-looking son, who would be getting married shortly, had always been friendly with her. They'd known each other for several years and usually chatted for a while when they saw each other.

When she'd found out he was going to college, she took an interest in his plans. Three weeks ago Saturday she'd invited him to bring his fiancée and have lunch with her on the patio. The young couple were so excited about the coming marriage, it was fun to be around them.

"Only a week until the wedding, right?"

He grinned. *"Sì."*

She removed her robe and got in the pool. The water felt good. She swam to the side so she could talk to Piero. "I'm very happy for you. Thank you for the invitation. I plan to come to the church to see you married." Both she and her father had been invited, but she didn't know if her dad would be able to take the time off.

Piero walked over to the edge of the pool and hunkered down. "Thank you again for the lunch. Isabella always wanted to come to the palace and see where I work."

"It's a beautiful place because you and your father's crew keep the grounds in exquisite condition."

"Grazie."

"Aren't you working a little late this evening?"

"I had classes all day today."

"I know what that's like. Have you and Isabella found an apartment yet?"

"Two days ago. One day soon you will have to come over for dinner."

"That would be lovely."

"*Buonasera,* Piero!"

At the sound of Vincenzo's deep voice, Abby's heart thudded. She flung herself around in the water at the same time Piero got to his feet.

"Your Highness! It's good to see you again. Welcome home."

"Thank you. You look well."

"So do you. May I take this moment now to tell you how sorry I am about the princess. We've all been very sad."

"I appreciate those kind words."

As long as Abby had known Vincenzo, he'd almost always gone swimming in the sea in the evenings and did his early-morning workouts in the pool. Now she'd been caught in the act of lying.

He looked incredible in a pair of black swim trunks with a towel thrown around his broad shoulders. Mediterranean Gods 101 could have used him for their model.

Vincenzo eyed both of them. "Don't let me disturb the two of you."

"I was just leaving. *Scusi,* Your Highness." He gave a slight bow to Vincenzo and walked back to the plot of flowers to get his things before leaving the patio.

Abby shoved off for the other side of the rectangular pool while she thought up an excuse why she hadn't gone out with Carolena. She heard a splash and in seconds Vincenzo's dark head emerged from the surface of the water next to her.

His unreadable black eyes trapped hers. "Why did you tell me you had plans with Carolena when it's obvious you wanted to rush home after work to be with Piero? My apologies if I interrupted something between the two of you. You both looked like you were enjoying yourselves."

Her heart fluttered out of rhythm. Coming from any other man, Abby could be forgiven for thinking he was jealous. But that was absurd.

"Before work was over, Carolena told me she'd been lined up with her cousin's friend, so we decided to do something tomorrow evening instead." That was partially a lie, too, but she would turn it into a truth if at all possible.

She could hear his brilliant wheels turning. "Have you and Piero been friends long?"

"Quite a few years. He speaks Mentonasc and has been a great teacher for me. I, in turn, have been coaching him in one of his first-year law classes, but he doesn't really need help."

His black brows lifted in surprise. "He's going to be an attorney?"

"That's been his hope since he was young. He has been influenced by his father to get a good education. Some kind of business law, probably. I've been helping him review appellate court decisions and analyze the judges' reasoning and findings. He's very bright."

Vincenzo looked stunned. "I'm impressed."

"Six months ago he got himself engaged and is going to be getting married next week. I met his fiancée the other day and we had lunch together out here. They've invited me to the wedding next week. I'm thrilled for them."

Vincenzo raked a hand through his wet black hair. "Apparently a lot has been going on around here, under my nose, that I've known nothing about."

"You have so much to do running the country. How could you possibly know everything? Don't forget I've lived on the grounds for years and am friends with everyone employed here. When I was young the gardeners helped me find my mom's cat, who went out prowling at night and never wanted to come home."

Vincenzo's smile was back, reminding her of what a sensational-looking male he was.

"Sometimes they brought me a tiny wounded animal or a bird with a broken wing to tend. Piero's father used to call me 'little nurse.'"

His gaze played over her features and hair. She saw a tenderness in his eyes she'd never noticed before. "All the same, I should have been more observant."

"Need I remind you that your royal nose has much greater worries, like dealing with your country's welfare?" He chuckled. "The word *multitask* could have been coined on your work ethic alone. Don't you remember the dead starling I found and you helped me plan a funeral for it?"

He nodded. "You were so broken up about it, I had to do something."

"It was a wonderful funeral." Her voice started to tremble. "You even said a prayer. I'll never forget. You said that some angels watched over the birds, but if they couldn't save them, then they helped take away the child's sorrow."

His black brows lifted. "I said that?"

"Yes. It was a great comfort to me." *You've always been a great comfort to me.*

"Your praise is misplaced, but like any man I admit to enjoying a little flattery."

"It's the truth. I have a scrapbook to prove it." Her confession was out before she could prevent it. Feeling herself go crimson, she did a somersault and swam to the deep end of the pool to cool down. When she came up gasping for air, he was right there, without a sign of being winded. If her heart didn't stop racing pretty soon, she was afraid she'd pass out. "Haven't you learned it's impolite to race a woman with a handicap, and win?"

His eyes grew shuttered. "Haven't you learned it's not nice to tease and then run?"

Touché.

"When am I going to see this scrapbook?"

Making a split-second decision, she said, "I plan to send it to you when your child is christened." She couldn't help searching his striking features for a moment. "The pictures showing you and your wife will be especially precious. I can promise that he or she will treasure it."

Abby heard his sharp intake of breath. "How long have you been making it?"

"Since soon after we arrived from the States."

"Clear back then?"

"Don't you know every girl grows up dreaming about palaces and princes and princesses? But my dream became real. I decided I would record everything so that one day I could show my own little girl or boy that I once lived a fairy-tale life.

"But now that you're going to have a little girl or boy, *they* should be the one in possession of it. The story of your life will mean everything in the world to them. If they're like me when I was young and poured over my parents' picture albums for hours and hours, they'll do the same thing."

Vincenzo was dumbfounded. Evening had crept over the palace, bringing out the purity of her bone structure, but he saw more than that. An inward beauty that radiated. It was that same innocent beauty he'd seen in her teens, but the added years had turned her into a breathtaking woman.

He wondered what she'd say if he told her that....

Of course he couldn't, but something earth-shattering was happening to him. As if he was coming awake from a hundred-year sleep. Vincenzo was starting to come alive from a different source, with feelings and emotions completely new to him. Not even his guilt could suppress them.

"I'm looking forward to that day, Abby."

"You're not the only one." But she said it with a charming smile. He liked her hair up in a braid. She wore it in all kinds of ways, each style intriguing.

"Shall we swim a couple of laps before we have dinner? When I talked to Angelina and she told me you hadn't eaten yet, I arranged for us to be served out here on the patio." While she was forming an answer he said, "I promise to let you set the pace."

"Thank you for taking pity on me." On that note, she started for the other side of the pool.

Vincenzo swam beside her, loving this alone time with her. There was no tension. A feeling of contentment stole through him. At the moment he was feeling guilty for *not* feeling guilty. He asked himself if he would feel this way if she weren't pregnant, but it wasn't a fair question. With Michelina gone, he naturally felt more protective toward Abby, who no longer had a female mentor to turn to for support.

To his surprise, he'd been disturbed to find her talking and laughing with Piero. *Why* had he felt that way? Was it the helicopter father coming out in him, as she'd suggested? Vincenzo frowned. Was he already becoming possessive?

Her comment about never finding a man who measured up to her father had been on his mind since they'd eaten at the mountain restaurant. He wondered if she'd ever been intimate with any of her boyfriends. If the answer was no, then in one respect he understood his mother-in-law's remark about the pregnancy being unnatural.

Just how would Vincenzo feel when Abby did get married, knowing she'd carried his child for nine months before she'd known another man? When she did get married one day—he had no doubt about that— how would the man she loved feel to know she'd given birth to Vincenzo's baby? Would that man feel robbed in some way?

His thoughts kept going. What if Vincenzo wanted to marry a woman who'd already given birth through surrogacy? It would mean she'd already gone through a whole history with some other man and his wife. Would that change the way he felt about her?

The more he pondered the subject, the more he couldn't answer his own questions.

While he succeeded in tying himself up in knots, Abby climbed the steps to leave the pool. For a moment he caught a side view of her lovely body. His heart clapped with force to see her stomach wasn't quite as flat as he remembered, but at this stage you wouldn't know she was pregnant. Dr. DeLuca had said that since this was her first pregnancy, it might be awhile.

That didn't matter. *Vincenzo knew.*

The day Abby had given him that pamphlet, he'd studied it and learned she would probably start showing by twelve weeks. Michelina had lost their three babies by that point, so he'd never seen his wife looking pregnant.

His excitement grew to imagine Abby in another month. Since he wasn't the most patient man, the waiting was going to be hard on him. And what about her? She was the one going through the travail that brought a woman close to death. Her patience had to be infinite.

He found himself asking the same question as the queen: What *did* Abby get out of this?

Vincenzo had listened to her explanation many times, but right now he was in a different place than he'd been at Christmas when they'd talked about surrogacy as an answer. His focus hadn't been the same back then. Now that he was no longer desperate for himself and Michelina, he had a hard time imagining this remarkable woman, who could have any man she wanted, being willing to go through this.

How did any surrogate mother who wasn't already a mother or who had never given birth leave the hospital and go back to her old life without experiencing changes, psychologically and emotionally? He could understand why it was illegal in many parts of the world for someone like Abby. He and Michelina must have been so blinded by their own unhappiness that they'd agreed to let Abby go through with this.

Though they'd discussed everything before the procedure, nothing had seemed quite real back then. Those same questions were haunting him now in new, profound ways. A fresh wave of guilt attacked him. He needed to explore his feelings in depth with Dr. Greco, because he was concerned for Abby's welfare. She was having to put off being with other men until the baby was born. That meant putting off any possible marriage. To his dismay, the thought of her getting married brought him no joy. What was wrong with him?

Abby put on her white beach robe over her green bikini and they sat down to dinner. "This cantaloupe is so sweet I can't believe it."

"I hear it's especially good for you."

"You're spoiling me, you know."

He gripped his water glass tighter. "That's the idea. You're doing something no one should expect you to do."

A wounded look entered her eyes. "I didn't *have* to do anything, Vincenzo. It was my choice."

"But you've never been pregnant before. My wife and I were entirely selfish."

Michelina because she'd wanted so much to have a child. Vincenzo because he'd wanted Abby to be the woman if they did decide to go through with it. The perfect storm...

After drinking the rest of his water, he darted her another glance. "Though I know you would never admit it to me, you've probably regretted your decision every day since the procedure was done."

She put down her fork. "Stop it, Vincenzo!" It pleased him she'd said his name again.

"You know the reason I did this and you couldn't be more wrong about my feelings now. Why don't we take Dr. Greco's advice and drop all the guilt? Let's agree that though this is an unprecedented case, it's a wonderful one that's going to give you a son or daughter. We need to keep that goal foremost in our minds."

Vincenzo sucked in a deep breath. "So be it! But I

have to tell you that you're the bravest, most courageous soul I've ever known."

"You mean after you. Let's not forget *you* were the one who dove into that cave looking for my body during the most ferocious storm I'd ever seen after moving to Arancia. It wasn't the men in the coast guard who'd performed that deed.

"Their first duty was to protect you. Instead they let you risk your life to save me. If Father hadn't been so devastated over losing Mother at the time, those men would have faced severe penalties, so I'd say we're equal."

There was no one like Abby when her back got up. "All right." He lifted his water glass.

"Truce?"

She did likewise. "Truce." They touched glasses.

After she drank a little and put her glass on the table, he could tell there was something else on her mind. "What were you going to say?"

"How did you know?" she asked, bemused.

"A feeling."

She was quiet for a moment. "Today a minor miracle occurred when I received word that Judge Mascotti is going to hear the Giordano case in less than a month. I was expecting it to be six at the earliest." She eyed him with blue eyes that sparkled with purple glints in the candlelight. "Who do you suppose was responsible?"

"I have no idea," he said in a deadpan voice.

"Liar." No one had ever dared call him that, but then, no one was like Abby. "I'm very grateful, you know. It's my biggest case so far with the firm."

"You've got a good one. My bet is on you to win it in the end."

"Please don't hold your breath."

He smiled. "In my line of work I'm used to doing it. Don't forget I have to face our constitutional assembly on a weekly basis, and they're *all* stars." Laughter bubbled out of her, but he noticed she'd drawn her beach robe closer around her. "It's cooling off, Abby. Since you have another workday tomorrow, I mustn't keep you up any longer."

She got up from the table before he could help her. "I've enjoyed the company and dinner very much. After your good deed in getting my law case heard sooner, I have to hope my side will prevail. *Buonanotte,* Vincenzo."

Her disappearance left him at a loss. As he walked swiftly to his apartment, Vincenzo phoned Marcello. "My mail included an invitation for the wedding of Luigi Gabberino's son. Can you give me the particulars?"

"Momento." Vincenzo headed for the bathroom to take a shower while he waited.

"Friday at four o'clock, San Pietro Church."

"Grazie. Put that date on my calendar. I intend to go."

"I'm afraid there's a conflict. You'll be in a meeting with the education minister at that time."

"I'll cut it short."

"Bene, Your Highness."

On Friday Abby left work at three-thirty in order to get to the church and be seated by four. She'd worn a new designer dress in Dresden-blue silk to the office. The top of the square-necked two-piece outfit shot with silver threads draped below the waistline. The sleeves were stylishly ruched above the elbow. On her feet she wore low-heeled silver sandals.

She'd caught her hair back in a twist with pins. Once she'd bid her latest client goodbye, she retouched her makeup before pulling the new floppy broad-brimmed hat with the silvery-blue rose from her closet. After putting it on, she grabbed her silver bag and left the office with a trail of colleagues gawking in her wake. Carolena had been with her when she'd bought the outfit, and now gave her the thumbs-up.

Outside the building she heard whistles and shouts of *bellissima* from the ever-appreciative male population of Arancia. She chuckled. What a gorgeous, sunny day for a wedding! There was a delightful breeze off the Mediterranean.

The limo wound through the streets until it came to a piazza fronting the church of San Pietro, where she was let out. Abby followed a group of people inside and found a seat in the assembled crowd of friends and extended family. She recognized several employees from the palace, and of course Piero's immediately family.

Before the Mass began, heads turned as a side door opened. When she saw Vincenzo enter surrounded by his bodyguards, she started to feel light-headed. The exquisitely groomed prince of Arancia wore a dove-gray suit. He was heartbreakingly handsome and took her breath away, along with everyone else's.

He sat off to the side. Piero's parents had to feel so honored. This was the second time Vincenzo had gone out of his way to perform a service that hadn't been on his agenda—the first, of course, being a word put in Judge Mascotti's ear to hasten Abby's court case hearing.

The prince was an amazingly thoughtful man. She'd

worked around a lot of men. No man of her acquaintance could touch him. Abby knew deep in her heart he was so grateful for her being willing to carry his baby, there wasn't enough he could do for her. It was something she would have to get used to. When he dedicated himself to a project, he went all out.

For the next hour Abby sat there eyeing him with covert glances while Piero and his bride took their vows. When the service was over, Vincenzo went out the side exit while she followed the crowd outside to the piazza to give the radiant couple a hug. But when she was ready to walk to her limousine, one of the security men touched her elbow.

"Signorina Loretto? If you would come with me, please."

With heart thumping, she followed him around the side of the church to another limousine, where she knew Vincenzo was waiting inside. The breeze was a little stronger now. As she started to climb in, she had to put her hand on her hat to keep it in place. At the same time, her skirt rode up her thighs. She fought madly with her other hand to push it down.

Vincenzo's dark eyes, filled with male admiration, missed nothing in the process, causing her to get a suffocating feeling in her chest. The hint of a smile hovered at the corners of his compelling mouth. After she sat down opposite him, he handed her the silver bag she'd accidentally dropped.

"Thank you," she said in a feverish whisper.

"Anyone could be forgiven for thinking *you* are the bride. That color is very becoming on you. We can't let such a stunning outfit go to waste. What is your pleasure?"

Her pleasure… She didn't dare think about that, let alone take him up on his offer.

"To be honest, it's been a long day. I'm anxious to get back to the palace and put my feet up. If that sounds ungracious, I don't mean for it to be."

"Then that's what we'll do." He let his driver know and the limo started to move out to the street. His arms rested along the back of the seat. He looked relaxed. "I enjoyed the wedding."

"So did I. Piero was beaming. I know he was a happy groom, but your presence made it the red-letter day in all their lives. That was very kind of you, Vincenzo."

"I have you to thank for reminding me of my duty. Now that it's over, we'll concentrate on taking care of you. When we get back to the palace we'll have dinner in your apartment and watch a movie I ordered."

Ordered? Her pulse raced. "I'm sure you have other things to do."

His black eyes glinted with a strange light. "Not tonight. It will feel good to relax. Tomorrow my father and I are leaving to visit my mother's sister in the French Savoie. We'll be attending another wedding and taking a vacation at the same time."

"That's right. Your father usually goes away this time of year."

He nodded. "I'm not sure how soon we'll be back, but I promise I'll be here for your June appointment with the doctor."

June… He'd be gone several weeks at least. She fought to keep her expression from showing her devastating disappointment.

The limo drove up to his private entrance to the palace. "I'll come to your apartment in a half hour, unless you need more time."

"Knowing that you have a healthy appetite, thirty minutes is probably all you should have to wait for dinner."

The flash of a satisfied white smile was the last thing she saw before he exited the limo. It stayed with her all the way to her suite. Her hands trembled as she removed her hat and put it on the closet shelf. Next came the dress and her shoes.

After Abby had put on jeans with an elastic waist band and a pink short-sleeved top, she redid her hair. While she fastened it with a tortoiseshell clip, she was assailed by the memory of Vincenzo's eyes as she'd climbed in the limo. They'd been alive and there was a throbbing moment when...

No. She was mistaken. The prince was a man, after all, and couldn't have helped looking while she was at a disadvantage. Furious with herself for ascribing more to the moment than was there, she lifted the phone to ring Angelina for her dinner tray, then thought the better of it. Vincenzo had made it clear he was orchestrating the rest of this evening.

If she wasn't careful, she could get used to this kind of attention. But once she'd had the baby, her association with the prince would be over. By November he could easily be involved with another woman, who had the right credentials for another marriage.

Her thoughts darted ahead to his trip with the king. Since Vincenzo had recently returned from a trip that had lasted weeks, she doubted he'd be accompanying his father because he needed another vacation.

In all probability there was someone the king and

his aunt wanted him to meet. With a baby on the way, he needed a suitable wife who was already situated at the palace to take over the duties of a mother the minute Abby delivered. But the thought of another woman being a mother to Abby's baby killed her.

This baby was Abby's baby. She couldn't possibly separate herself from it now. She'd been imagining the day she held it in her arms, the clothes she'd buy, the nursery she'd create. No other woman would love this baby as fiercely as the way Abby already did.

But Vincenzo was the father and he'd been born to fulfill his duties. One of them at the moment was to make certain Abby felt secure while she was pregnant with the next royal heir of Arancia. She knew better than to read anything more into what was going on. He was doing his best while trying to cope with the pain of his loss. There was only one way for her to handle this and keep her sanity at the same time.

He needs a friend, Abby. Be one to him.

A half hour later Vincenzo arrived at her apartment. He'd changed out of his suit into chinos and a polo shirt. He looked so fabulous, she tried not stare at him. He'd tucked a DVD under his arm. She flashed him her friendliest smile. "You're right on time."

"In the business I'm in, you have to be."

A quiet laugh escaped her lips. "Well, tonight you can forget business for once. Come right in and make yourself at home."

"If it's all right with you, I'll put this in the machine."

She closed the door after him and folded her arms. "Aren't you going to show me the cover?"

"I'd rather surprise you." In a minute he'd inserted it

so they could watch it on the living room couch when they were ready.

"All I have to offer you is soda from the fridge in the kitchen."

"I'll drink what you're drinking."

"It's boring lemonade."

"Sounds good."

She didn't call him a liar again. He was probably used to some kind of alcohol at the end of the day, but was going out of his way to make her comfortable. This man was spoiling her rotten.

"Excuse me while I get it." When she came out of the kitchen, she found him on her terrace leaning against the balustrade. "In the States we say 'a penny for them.'" She handed him a can.

He straightened and took it from her. "I'll give you one guess." He popped the lid and drank the contents in one go. Abby was thirsty, too, and followed suit, but could only drink half of hers before needing a breath.

"A name for your baby."

"It has already been picked, whether it's a boy or a girl. Actually, I was thinking about your plans after the baby's born," he said on a more serious note.

So had she... Since that terrible morning with the queen, she'd decided that living anywhere in Arancia wouldn't be a good idea after all. "You're giving me a complex, you know."

A frown marred his handsome features. "In what way?"

"You worry too much about everything, so maybe what I tell you will help. The other night my father came over and we had a long talk. Before Christmas, in fact, before I even knew you were looking for a surrogate,

Dad was planning to resign his position here and move back to the States. He says his assistant, Ernesto, is more than ready to take over."

Stillness enveloped Vincenzo for an overly long moment. "Does my father know about this?"

"Not yet. He plans to tell him soon. We have extended family in Rhode Island, where I was born."

"But your father has family here in Arancia, too."

"That's true, but he's been offered a position at a private firm there I know he will enjoy. He won't leave until after I have the baby. Though I had thoughts of living in Arancia and working at the firm with Carolena, I can't abide the idea of him being so far away. Therefore I'll be moving back with him and plan to study for the Rhode Island and New York bar exams. So you see? That's one worry you can cross off your long list."

During the quiet that followed, she heard a knock on the door. He moved before she did to answer it. Angelina had arrived with their dinner. Vincenzo thanked her and pushed the cart to the terrace, where they could sit to enjoy their meal while they looked out over the view.

Once they started eating, he focused his attention on her. "Are you close with family there?"

"We've all kept in touch. Mom took me for visits several times a year."

"I remember. The grounds seemed emptier then."

Abby wished he hadn't said that. Though it was nice to see family, she lived to get back to Vincenzo.

"After she died, Dad always sent me to stay with my mother's sister and her husband at Easter. I have a couple of fun cousins close to my age. It will be wonderful to live around all of them again. My aunt's a lot like my mom, so nice and kindhearted."

That part was the truth, as far as it went. These years in Arancia were a dream that had to end, but she wouldn't allow herself to think about leaving the country, about leaving *him*. Not yet.

"If you've finished," he said all of a sudden, "shall we go inside and start the movie?"

"Marvelous idea. I can't wait to see what you picked out. Something American and silly, I presume, like *Back to the Beach*."

A mysterious smile appeared to chase away his earlier somber look. She got up from the chair before he could help her and walked in the living room to turn it on.

CHAPTER SIX

ABBY'S REVELATION HAD put Vincenzo off the last of his dinner. He'd meant it when he'd told her he missed her presence during her vacations out of the country. Because of their situation, Abby had always been natural with him and treated him like a friend. No artifice. Though he'd been six years older, she'd been there in the background of his life for years. But when she went away next time, she wouldn't be returning.

The sense of loss was already hitting him. He was staggered by the depth of his feelings. When she'd opened the door to him awhile ago, he'd discovered her in yet another new maternity outfit. This time she wore flattering casual attire. Yet no matter how she played down her assets, nothing could disguise the fact that she was a very desirable woman.

Now that she was carrying his child, how could he not notice her or stop certain thoughts from creeping into his mind without his volition? Abby had become as precious to him as the little life growing inside of her.

Earlier, once he'd entered the church and scanned the guests, he'd spotted the hat and the face beneath it. For the rest of the ceremony he couldn't take his eyes off her. She'd lit up the interior like an exotic orchid among the greenery.

"My Little Chickadee?" The excitement in her voice was all he could have hoped for. She swung around to face him with a brilliant smile. "Trust you to manage getting hold of a copy of it. This was Mom's favorite Mae West film. W.C. Fields is in it, too. This movie is hilarious."

"While you stretch out on the couch and put your legs up, I'll sit in the chair with the ottoman."

"Vincenzo—I didn't literally mean I needed to do that. My feet aren't swollen yet!"

He took his place in the chair anyway. "From what I saw as you got in the limo, I couldn't detect any problem in that department, either, but as you reminded me a week ago, I'm only a man and don't have a clue about a woman."

While the film got underway, she curled up on the end of the couch. He saw her shoulders shaking with silent laughter. "You'll never let me live that down. Apparently you have a photographic memory. I bet Gianna could tell me what a maddening brother you were at times."

He grinned at her. "It's a good thing she's not here to reveal my secrets."

Abby flicked him a narrowed gaze. "Oh, I heard a few."

"Like what, for instance?"

"Like the time you and your friends brought some girls to the palace and sneaked them into the pool at three in the morning to go skinny-dipping. I know it's true because I heard about it from my father later. He'd been awakened in the middle of the night by some of the security men."

He spread his hands. "What can I say? My life has been an open book in more ways than one. Were you scandalized?"

"I was only fifteen at the time and wondered how any girl could be so daring."

"But not the guys?"

"No. It's in your nature, which has been written into your Roman mythology. Wasn't it the goddess Diana, Jupiter's favorite daughter, to whom he swore he wouldn't make her marry and allowed her to hunt by the light of the moon? She loved skinny-dipping, and naturally all the young men came to watch."

The laughter rolled out of Vincenzo. He couldn't help it.

Abby kept a straight face. "But sadly for them, when she caught them, she turned them into stags. Of course, that was centuries ago. Today it's the other way around. The teenaged girls are scandalized by prudes like me."

When he could find his voice, he said, "You mean I couldn't have talked you into it?"

"Not on your life!"

She could always make him laugh, and the film *was* hilarious. He'd been waiting for the famous line she'd impersonated. When it came, he realized Abby had sounded just like the legendary actress.

After the film ended, she got up and turned off the machine. "I wish I'd had an older brother. You and Gianna were lucky to grow up together. One day when you marry again, hopefully you'll be able to have another baby so your first one won't grow up to be an only child."

The thought of taking another wife sent a chill through him. He knew when his father had insisted Vincenzo accompany him on this next trip it had been motivated by an agenda that had little to do with the need for a vacation.

"Were you ever lonely, Abby?"

"Not in the sense you mean, because being the brightest light on my parents' horizon was my only reality. I knew nothing else. But when I think of you and Gianna, especially the two of you growing up in a royal household, I can see how great that would have been for you. She told me she went to bat for you when you got into trouble with your father. There's nothing like the power of sibling love."

With pure grace she curled her leg underneath her again and sat down. "Did you ever have to help her out of a spot?"

"Many times. She wanted money. When I didn't feel like carrying out some official function, I'd bribe her to do it for me."

Abby laughed. "At what cost?"

"Pocket money. Our parents kept us both on a strict allowance."

"Good for them! I always liked them, but that admission puts them on an even higher level in—"

Vincenzo's cell phone rang, breaking in on her. "Sorry." He pulled it out of his pocket and checked the caller ID. "Excuse me for a moment, Abby. I have to take this."

"Of course."

He moved to the terrace, out of earshot. *"Pronto?"*

"I'm sorry to disturb you, but the queen was insistent you call her back immediately."

"Do you have any idea why, Marcello?"

"No, except that she'd been talking to the king first."

He had an idea what this might be about. Something told him he needed to put out another fire, but first he needed to talk to his father. "I'll take care of it. *Grazie*."

When he walked back inside, Abby was waiting for him near the front door. "Duty calls, right?" She'd given him no choice but to leave. "Thank you for this lovely and unexpected evening."

"I enjoyed it, too. Keep the DVD as a reminder of your mother," he said when she was about to hand it him.

"You're too generous, but I'll treasure it."

"That's the idea," he murmured.

She put a hand to her throat. "As soon as you came in from the terrace, I could tell by your face something was wrong. I hope it's nothing too serious."

If his hunch was right, then it *was* serious. But for once, this had nothing to do with Abby. He could thank the Roman gods for that, at least.

Too bad he couldn't get rid of a certain dangerous vision in his mind of joining Abby the Huntress in that forest pool and making love to her before her father discovered them and *he* turned Vincenzo into a stag.

He ground his teeth absently. "So do I, Abby. I'll see you at the clinic for your next appointment. Though I know you'll follow the doctor's orders, I have to say this anyway. Take meticulous care of yourself." June sounded an eternity away.

Her eyes had gone a smoky blue. "You, too, Your Highness. Your baby's going to need you."

Vincenzo turned from her before he couldn't and took off for the other region of the palace at a fast clip.

When he reached his apartment, he decided it wouldn't do any good to call his father first. Without hesitation he phoned Michelina's mother to get this over with.

"Thank you for returning my call, Vincenzo."

"Of course. How are you getting along, Bianca?"

"How do you think? My world has fallen apart. I didn't believe it could get worse until I talked with your father. He informed me you're going on vacation tomorrow to stay with the *duc de Chambery*. If you hadn't chosen Michelina, you would have married his granddaughter Odile, who's still single. That would be a humiliation for our family if you choose her now. I'm telling you I won't—"

"Bianca?" he broke in on her. He had it in his heart to feel sorry for this woman who was grieving over her daughter. "You don't need to say another word. I know exactly how Michelina felt about her. I never considered marriage to Odile and I'll make you a solemn vow now that I never will. Does that answer your question?"

Her weeping finally stopped and all he heard was sniffing. "But you'll take another bride."

He'd braced his back against the door to his den and closed his eyes. "To be frank with you, I don't plan on marrying again. When Father is no longer alive, I may step down so Gianna can take over the business of ruling Arancia. My first duty is going to be to Michelina's and my child."

Her gasp came over the phone loud and clear. "I don't believe you."

"Which part?" he bit out.

"You don't fool me. We both know the only reason why you'd give up the throne..."

Her insinuation was perfectly clear. She'd all but accused Abby of going after Vincenzo. He'd been waiting for her to start in on him. This was just the first volley.

He heard the click, severing their connection.

"Congratulations, Signorina Loretto. You show no problems so far. It means you've been following directions to the letter." Abby could thank Vincenzo for that. "How is the nausea?"

"I hardly ever notice it anymore."

"Good. Your measurements are fine. Be sure to keep your feet up for a little each day after work."

"I will. How big is the baby by now?"

"Um, three inches. You're growing."

"I know. I already prefer lying on my side."

The doctor smiled. "I'll let the prince know that at your sixteen-weeks' checkup we'll do an ultrasound, which should reveal the gender of that special baby."

Abby didn't know if Vincenzo wanted to be surprised and wait until after the baby was delivered, or if he was anxious to know right away. But it was his business, not hers.

"You can get dressed now and I'll see you in another month. Be sure you keep coming in on a weekly basis for your blood pressure check. I'll give Vincenzo the full report when he's back. He'll be delighted. As for Dr. Greco, he said for you to call him when the two of you can come in."

"Thank you, Doctor."

Abby put on her white sundress with the brown-trimmed white bolero top and left for the office. Her father had told her the king had returned to the palace three days ago. That meant Vincenzo was still in France.

With a woman who might possibly take Michelina's place one day?

Abby was used to him honoring every commitment to her. The fact that he hadn't come today shouldn't have mattered, but it did. She missed him and would be lying if she didn't admit that to herself.

The show-cause hearing at the court yesterday had persuaded the judge to hear the Giordano case in August. Abby was thrilled with the outcome and knew his decision had frustrated Signor Masala's attorney. She wanted to share the good news with Vincenzo and thank him, but it would have to wait.

She was starting to get a taste of what it would be like when he wasn't in her life anymore. Not liking that he'd become the focal point of her thoughts, she phoned her father after she got in the limo and invited him to a home-cooked dinner at her apartment that evening. She planned to fry chicken and make scones, the kind her mom always made. He loved them. But to her disappointment, he couldn't come until the following night.

Once she got to work, she invited Carolena to the palace to have dinner with her at the pool. Abby would lend her one of the bikinis she hadn't worn yet. Thankfully her friend was thrilled to be invited and they rode home together in the limo at the end of the day.

"Am I in heaven or what?"

They'd finished eating and had spent time in the pool. Now they were treading water. Abby laughed at her friend. "I've been asking myself that same question since we moved here years ago." She was tempted to tell Carolena her future plans, but thought the better of it until closer to the delivery date. "I think I'll do one more lap and then I'll be done for the night."

She pushed off, doing the backstroke. When she reached the other side and turned to hold on to the side, she saw blood and let out a small cry.

"What's wrong?" Carolena swam over to her. "Oh—you've got a nosebleed."

"I don't know why." She pinched her nose with her thumb and index finger.

"I'll get a towel."

Abby followed her to the steps and got out.

"Sit on the chair." She handed Abby her beach towel. After a minute she said, "It's not stopping."

"Keep holding while I call your doctor. Is his number programmed in your cell phone?"

"Yes. Press three."

Angelina came out on the patio to clear the table, but let out an alarmed sound the second she saw the blood on the towel and hurried away.

By now Carolena was off the phone. "The doctor wants you to lean forward on the chair and keep pressing your nostrils together for ten or fifteen minutes. Breathe through your mouth. It should stop. Apparently pregnant women get nosebleeds, so not to worry. If it doesn't stop soon, we'll call him back."

"Okay." Before another minute passed, Vincenzo came running toward her. He was back!

"Abby—" Without hesitation he hunkered down next to her. The fear in his eyes was a revelation to her.

"I'm all right, Vincenzo. My nose started to bleed, but I think it has stopped now."

He reached for his cell phone. "I'm calling Dr. DeLuca."

"Carolena already contacted him for me. I'm fine, honestly!"

She removed the towel to show him the episode was over. Already she felt like a fraud.

"Don't move." He got up to get her beach robe and put it around her shoulders. His touch sent fingers of delight through her body. "It's cooler out here now."

"Thank you. I don't believe you've been introduced to my friend, Carolena Baretti. Carolena, this is His Royal Highness Prince Vincenzo."

"Thank heaven you were here for her, Signorina Baretti. I'm very pleased to meet you."

"The pleasure is mine, Your Highness. Dr. DeLuca said the increased blood flow with pregnancy sometimes produces nosebleeds. She's supposed to stay put for a few minutes so she won't get light-headed when she stands. He'll be relieved to know the bleeding has stopped."

"I'll call him and tell him right now."

While Vincenzo walked out of earshot to make the phone call, Carolena moved closer to Abby. Her brows lifted as she stared at her. "When he saw you holding that towel to your face, I thought he was going to have a heart attack."

"I know he was afraid something had happened to the baby."

Carolena shook her head. "From the look in his eyes, it wasn't the baby he was worried about," she whispered. "If a man ever looked at me like that…"

Abby's heart thudded against her ribs. "You're imagining things." But inwardly she was shaken by the look in his eyes. It was that same look he'd given her after she'd recovered on the boat that black day, as if she'd meant the world to him.

What a time for him to return from his trip! She looked an utter mess.

Vincenzo walked toward her. "If you feel all right, I'll help you get back to your apartment."

"I'm fine. Carolena will help me."

"We'll both help." The authority in his voice silenced her.

Together the three of them left the pool. Carolena brought all their things while Vincenzo stayed at Abby's side. When they reached her suite, her friend changed her clothes and announced she was leaving.

"I'll have a limousine waiting for you at the entrance, *Signorina*. Again, my thanks for your help."

"Abby's the best."

"So are you." Abby hugged her friend.

"Thanks for dinner. See you at work tomorrow."

The minute the door closed, Abby glanced at Vincenzo. "If you'll excuse me, I'll take a quick shower."

"Don't hurry on my account. I'm not going anywhere."

That fluttery sensation in her stomach had taken over again. It happened whenever he came near. She rushed into the bathroom and got busy making herself presentable once more. After drying her hair with a clean towel, she brushed it the best she could and put on a clean blouse and skirt.

The nosebleed had definitely stopped. Just one of the surprises brought on by the pregnancy. She couldn't complain. So far she'd been very lucky.

Again she found him out on the terrace, which was her favorite place, too, especially at night. He looked sensational in anything he wore. Tonight it was a silky blue shirt and khakis. "Did the doctor reassure you?"

He turned and put his hands on his hips, the ultimate male. "To a point. I'm much more relieved now that I see you walking around without further problem."

"Don't do it," she warned him.

Those black brows furrowed. "Do what?"

"Start feeling guilty again because I'm in this situation."

"If you want to know the stark, staring truth, guilt is the last thing on my mind. I'm worrying about the next time you get another one. What if Carolena hadn't been with you?"

"I had the usual nosebleed here and there growing up. They've always stopped on their own, as this one did tonight, even though she was with me. But if I'd been alone and needed help, I would have called out for Angelina. Don't forget that at work I'm never alone."

Her logic finally sank in and his frown disappeared. "I'm sorry I didn't make it back in time for our appointment with Dr. Greco. If I hadn't been detained, I would have been in the pool with you when this happened."

A thrill of forbidden excitement shot through her body to hear that.

"Everything's fine. We'll reschedule when it's convenient for you."

His dark gaze wandered over her. "Dr. DeLuca says you're in excellent health."

"You see?" She smiled.

"He's going to do an ultrasound on you next month."

"Is the helicopter daddy anxious to know if he's going to have a boy or a girl?"

"I'm not sure yet. For the moment all I care about is that you and the baby stay healthy."

"That's my prime concern, too. But maybe by then you'll have made up your mind and want to know if the kingdom can expect a prince or a princess."

"Maybe. Let's go back inside where it's warmer so you'll stay well."

When Abby had told her father that Vincenzo was a worrywart, he'd laughed his head off. If he could see them now...

She did his bidding and walked through to the kitchen, where she opened the fridge. He followed her. "Orange juice all right?" she asked.

"Sounds good."

Abby chuckled. "No, it doesn't. Why don't you have some wine from the cupboard? You look like it might do you some good."

"Soda is fine."

"A warrior to the end. That's you." She pulled out two cans and took them over to the table, where he helped her before sitting down. They popped their lids at the same time. The noise was so loud they both let out a laugh, the first she'd heard come from him tonight. A smiling Vincenzo was a glorious sight. "How was your trip?"

"Which one are you talking about?"

She almost choked on her drink. "You took two trips?"

He nodded. "I only flew in an hour ago from Gemelli."

Abby blinked. "I didn't realize you were going there."

"It wasn't on the schedule, but Bianca slipped on a stair in the palace and broke her hip."

"Oh, no—"

"Valentino phoned me after it happened. It was the day Father and I were scheduled to come home. We agreed I should fly to Gemelli to be with her."

Whatever Abby had been thinking about the reason for his absence, she'd been wrong and promised herself to stop speculating about anything to do with him from now on.

"Is she in terrible pain?"

"At first, but she's going to be fine with therapy. We had several long talks. If there can be any good in her getting hurt, it seems to have softened her somewhat in her attitude about the coming event. Despite her misgivings, the idea of a grandchild has taken hold."

"That's wonderful, Vincenzo."

"She's missing Michelina."

"Of course." Abby took another long drink. "You must be so relieved to be on better terms with her."

He stared at her through veiled eyes. "I am. But when Angelina told me about you—"

"You thought you were facing another crisis," she finished for him. "Well, as you can see, all is well. Did your father have a good vacation?"

Vincenzo finished off his soda before answering her. "No."

"I'm sorry to hear that."

"He brought his troubles on himself."

"Is he ill?"

"If only it were that simple."

"Vincenzo—" She didn't know whether to laugh or cry. "What a thing to say."

"Before I was betrothed, my parents arranged for me

to meet the princesses on their short list of candidates, carefully chosen by the extended family."

Abby lowered her head.

"It came down to two, Michelina Cavelli and Odile Levallier, the granddaughter of the *duc de Chambery*. Both were nice-looking at their age, but of the two, I preferred Michelina, who wasn't as headstrong or spoiled."

"I can't imagine being in your situation."

"When you're born into a royal family, it's just the way it is. You don't know anything else. If I'd had a different personality, perhaps I would have rebelled and run away. I was still a royal teenager at the time and knew I had years before I needed to think about getting married, so I didn't let it bother me too much."

Her head came up and she eyed him soberly. "Were you ever in love?"

"At least four times that I recall."

"You're serious."

"Deadly so. In fact it might have been seven or eight times."

Seven or eight?

"Those poor women who'd loved you, knowing they didn't stand a chance of becoming your wife. Did you spend time with Michelina over the years, too?"

"Some. When my father decided it was time for me to marry, I saw her more often. She had always been good-looking and smart. We enjoyed riding horses and playing tennis. She was a great athlete, and loved the water. I could see myself married to her."

"When did you actually fall in love with her?"

He cocked his head. "Would it shock you if I told you never?"

Never?

Shaken to the core, Abby got up from the table and put their cans in the wastebasket.

"I can see that I have."

She whirled around. "But she loved you so much—"

Quiet surrounded them before he nodded. "Now you're disillusioned."

Abby leaned against the counter so she wouldn't fall down. "The loving way you treated her, no one would ever have guessed."

He got up from the table and walked over to her. "Except Michelina, her mother, my parents and now you... We both wanted a baby to make our marriage work."

She couldn't believe it had never worked, not in the sense he meant. Talk about a shocking revelation....

So *that* was the real reason they'd gone so far as to find a surrogate and flaunt convention. It explained Michelina's desperation and her decision not to tell the queen until it was too late to stop it. No wonder Bianca feared another woman coming into Vincenzo's life. The pieces of the puzzle were starting to come together. She could hardly breathe.

"Obviously we were willing to do anything. Again we were presented with a short list. This time it had the names and histories of the women available and suitable to carry our child."

She lifted pleading eyes to him. "Will you tell me the truth about something, Vincenzo?" Her voice throbbed. "Did Michelina want me?"

"Of course. She'd always liked you. She said you had a wonderful sense of humor and found you charming. When she learned you were on that list of possible surrogates who'd passed all the physical tests, like me she was surprised, but happy, too. Our choice was unanimous."

Unable to be this close to him, she left the kitchen for the living room and sat down on the end of the couch. He again chose the chair with the ottoman. They were like an old married couple sitting around before they went to bed.

Abby wished that particular thought hadn't entered her mind. With Vincenzo's revelation, the world as she'd known it had changed, and nothing would ever be the same again. All these years and he hadn't been in love with his wife? He'd been in love seven or eight times, but they didn't count because they weren't royal. She needed to move the conversation onto another subject.

"You were telling me about your father."

Vincenzo let out a sigh. "He wants me to marry again before the baby is born." He came out with it bluntly, rocking her world once more.

"In the beginning Odile was his first choice, only because of his close association with the *duc.* It would be advantageous to both our countries. She hasn't married yet and he feels she would make a fine mother. If she's there from the moment the baby is born, then she'll bond with it."

Abby sucked in her breath. "Does Odile still care for you?" It was a stupid question. The fact that she was still single was glaring proof, but she'd had to say it.

"She thinks she does, but that's because no one else has come along yet whom her grandfather finds suitable. I told Father I couldn't possibly marry Odile because I don't have the slightest feeling for her."

Unable to stand it, she jumped up from the couch.

"This is like a chess game, moving kings and queens around without any regard for human feeling!"

One black brow lifted. "That's where you're wrong. My mother-in-law certainly has a lot of feelings on the subject."

"She knows why you went to France?"

He sat forward. "Every royal household has its spies. That's why she phoned me before I left to tell me she wouldn't stand for it if I ended up marrying Odile. Michelina had been frightened I'd choose Odile over her in the first place."

Incredible. "What did you tell the queen?"

"That there was no chance of it because I don't plan to marry again. For once I'm going to do what my heart dictates and be a good father to my child, period."

Abby started trembling. "I'm sure she didn't believe you." Abby didn't believe it either. He was too young to live out the rest of his life alone. But if he had to marry another royal he didn't love…

"No, but it doesn't matter, because I've made my decision."

"Don't you have to be married to be king?"

"That has been the tradition over the centuries, but Father's still very much alive. If the time comes when someone else must rule, my sister will do it. So in answer to your question, *that's* how my father's trip went. Why don't we get onto another subject and talk about your court case? How did it go?"

She sat back down, still trying to get her head around everything he'd told her. "You know very well how it went. The judge had it put on his calendar for mid-August."

"Excellent. That relieves some of your stress, which

can only be good for the baby. What other cases are you dealing with?"

"I don't know. I—I can't think right now," Abby stammered. She honestly couldn't.

"Let's watch a little television. There's usually a movie on this time of night." He got up from the chair and reached for the remote on the coffee table.

"You don't need to stay with me, Vincenzo. The doctor assured you I'm all right. I know you must be exhausted after being in Gemelli. Please go."

A fierce look marred his features. "You want me to?"

A small gasp escaped. She'd offended him again. "Of course not. It's just that I don't want you to feel you have to babysit me."

"There's nothing I'd rather do. Everything I care about is in this room, and I've been away for weeks."

Shaken again by his honesty, Abby felt his frustration and understood it before he turned on the TV and sat back down again. One glance and she saw that the prince was a channel grazer. Nothing seemed to suit him. On impulse she got up from the couch.

"I'll be right back. I've got something for you." She made a stop at the bathroom, a frequent habit these days. Then she went to the bedroom and pulled her thick scrapbook out of the bottom dresser drawer. She'd had the leather cover engraved in gold letters: *The Prince of Arancia.* She hoped this might brighten his mood.

"Here." She walked over to him. "I'll trade you this for the remote."

He eyed her in surprise. When he got a look at the cover, he let out an exclamation. "I thought this was going to be a gift for the christening."

"I've changed my mind." Abby had compassion for

him and his father, who wanted his son to be happily married and was trying to make it happen in the only way he could think of as king. "You need to see what an impact you've made on the life of your subjects."

Maybe this album would make Vincenzo realize what an important man he was. To live out his life alone wasn't natural or healthy.

"I know the court has a historian who records everything, but this is more personal, with some of my own photos and articles I've found interesting from various magazines and newspapers coming from the U.S. Dad's been receiving the Stateside news for years and I read everything right along with him."

From the moment Vincenzo opened the cover, he went away from her mentally. While she watched the news, he turned page after page, thoughtfully perusing each one. No sound came out of him for at least an hour.

Eventually he closed it and looked over at her. "For the first time in my life, I know what it feels like to have your life flash before your eyes. I don't know what to say, Abby. I'm speechless."

"You're probably tired from viewing all the good works you've done over the years. I hope you realize you've *never* received negative press. Do you have any idea what a great accomplishment that is?"

He studied her as if he'd never seen her before. "I hope *you* realize I've never received a gift like this. You've touched me beyond my ability to express," he said in a husky voice she felt all the way to her toes.

"I'm glad if you're pleased. I consider it an honor to be a friend of yours, and an even greater honor to be the person you and Michelina chose to carry your child. Only a few more months before he or she is here."

She had the impression he wasn't listening to her. "All these photos of yours. I wasn't aware you'd taken them."

"While I was darting around on the grounds with my little camera, I took a lot of pictures and sometimes you were there."

"You got me on my motorcycle!"

"If you have a boy, he'll be thrilled to find out you didn't always behave with perfect decorum. I daresay he'll love it that you were a daredevil. The skinny-dipping I missed, because I had to be in bed and asleep by eleven."

Low laughter rumbled out of him. "I can be thankful your father was the head of security and made sure his daughter minded him."

She smiled. "Do you think you'll be a strict father if you have a girl?"

He got up from the chair and put the album on the coffee table before staring at her. "Probably."

"But since kindness is part of your nature, she won't mind."

He rubbed the back of his neck, looking tired. "Have you had any feelings yet whether you might be having a boy or a girl, Abby? I understand some women instinctively know."

"I've heard that, too, but since I'm not the mother, that's not going to happen to me." Secretly she didn't want him to know how involved she really was with this baby and that she thought about it all the time. "However, there's no law that says the father can't feel inspiration about his own unborn child."

He shook his head. "No indication yet."

"Well, you've got a month before there's the possibility of your finding out. That is, if you want to."

"If it's a girl, Michelina wanted to name her Julietta after her grandmother on her mother's side."

"That's beautiful. And if it's a boy?"

Their gazes held for a moment. "Maximilliano, after three kings in the Di Laurentis line. I'll call him Max."

"I love that name!" she cried. "We had a wonderful Irish setter named Max. He died before we moved here."

Vincenzo looked surprised. "I didn't know that. Why didn't your father get another one when you settled in your apartment?"

"The loss was so great, neither he nor Mom could think about getting another one. They kept saying maybe one day, but that moment never came. Did your family have a pet?"

He nodded. "Several, but by my later teens I was gone so much, my mother was the one who took care of them and they worshipped her."

"That's sweet."

"Whether I have a boy or a girl, I'll make certain they grow up with a dog. It's important."

"I couldn't agree more. Whether you've had a good or bad day, they're always there for you and so loving. My cousin and I liked little creatures. I once kept a cockatoo, a turtle, a snake and a hamster. When each of them died—not all at the same time, of course," she said with a laugh, "Max helped me get through their funerals. Daddy used to say the best psychiatrist is a puppy licking your face."

"Abby..." There was a world of warmth when he said her name. "No wonder Piero's father called you the little nurse."

"It's a good thing he didn't get together with my father to compare notes. If you got him alone, Daddy would tell you I probably killed them all off without meaning to."

She loved the sound of his laughter so much, Abby never wanted it to stop. But for the sake of her sanity and her heart, it was imperative he leave. Quickly she got up from the couch and handed him the scrapbook.

"This is yours to keep. You once saved my life, and now you're taking such good care of me, my thanks will never be enough. Now it's time someone took care of you. Please don't be mad at me if I tell you to go to bed. You look exhausted." She walked to the door and opened it. If he didn't leave, she was on the verge of begging him to stay the night.

"Good night, Your Highness."

In the weeks that followed, Vincenzo made certain his schedule was packed so tight with work he wouldn't be tempted to spend every free moment at Abby's apartment. Though he phoned her every morning before she went to work to know how she felt, he stayed away from her.

The night she'd given him the album, she'd shown him the door before he was ready to leave. When he'd told her the true situation that had existed between him and Michelina, there'd been a definite shift in the universe. He didn't regret his decision to tell her. At this point in the pregnancy, they shared an intimacy that demanded she understand what his marriage had been like so there'd be honesty between them.

The day of the ultrasound was here. His greatest concern was the health of the baby. If something was wrong, then he'd deal with it. Vincenzo had gone back and forth

in his mind on the subject of gender and finally decided
he didn't want to know. That way both sides of his family would have to go on speculating until the delivery.
As for himself, he preferred to be surprised.

He had the limousine pulled around to his private entrance. When Abby appeared in a kelly-green dress with
flowing sleeves and a high waist, he lost his breath for
a moment. She was finally looking pregnant and more
beautiful than she knew with her silvery-gold hair up-
swept and caught with a comb.

Dr. DeLuca met them in his office first and smiled.
"This is the big day. Are you ready for it?"

"It's very exciting," Abby answered. Though she
seemed calm, Vincenzo knew she had to be nervous.

"Will you come in to watch the ultrasound, Vincenzo?"

"Yes!"

Abby looked stunned. "You really want to?"

Vincenzo caught her blue gaze. "I've been waiting
for this from the moment we found out you were pregnant."

"I—I'm excited, too," she stammered, rather breath-
lessly, he thought.

"Excellent," the doctor said. "If you'll come this way
with me. It won't take long."

They followed him through another door to the ultrasound room. The doctor told Vincenzo to sit at the
side of the bed while Abby lay down. His heart picked
up speed to realize this moment had come. He didn't
intend to miss a second of this whole process.

Abby's face had blushed when he'd said yes. He knew
she'd been trying her hardest to keep her professional

distance, but at this point in the pregnancy that was impossible. Having a baby was an intimate experience and she'd never been "just a surrogate" to him.

Over the last few months she'd come to be his whole world. It was miraculous that a sonogram could see inside her gorgeous body, where his baby was growing. The body he'd once rescued from the sea. How could he have known that one day she'd carry his child? He couldn't think about anything else.

Michelina was the mother of his child, but right now his focus was on Abby while the doctor put special gel on her stomach. For several nights he'd had trouble sleeping while his mind thought of all the things that might be wrong with the baby.

She shared a searching glance with Vincenzo as the doctor moved the transducer around her belly. Suddenly they both heard a heartbeat coming from the monitor. The doctor pointed to the screen. "There's your baby. The heart sounds perfect."

"Oh, Vincenzo—our baby! There it is!" In the moment of truth, her guard had come down, thrilling him with her honesty. As for himself, he couldn't believe what he was seeing and reached for her hand. She squeezed it hard. "It looks like it's praying."

The doctor nodded with a smile. "Nice size, coming along beautifully. No abnormalities I can see. So far everything looks good. This test can't detect all birth defects, but it's a wonderful diagnostic tool and tells me the pregnancy and your baby are both on the right track."

Relief poured off Vincenzo in waves. He looked into her tear-filled eyes. Without conscious thought he leaned over and kissed her mouth. "You're a wonder, Abby," he whispered. "You're giving me the world."

"I'm so thankful everything's all right."

The doctor cleared his throat. "Do you two want to know the gender?"

"That's up to Vincenzo," she said first.

He'd already made up his mind. "I'd rather wait and be surprised."

"Very well. Here are some pictures for you to keep." The doctor explained what Vincenzo was seeing, but he didn't have to, because the shape of the baby was self-evident and filled him with awe. If Michelina were here, the tears would be overflowing. "The fetus is four and half inches long and developing well."

Vincenzo put them in his jacket pocket. "Doctor? How's Abby?"

He removed his glasses. "As you can see, she's fine. No more nosebleeds?" She shook her head. "I'd say Abby is in perfect health. If she continues to do what I told her and rest a little more often after her swims, she should get through this pregnancy in great shape."

That was all Vincenzo wanted to hear, though it didn't take away his guilt that she was risking her life to give him this baby. "Thank you, Dr. DeLuca."

After the older man left the room, Abby got up off the table to fix her dress. "Can you believe it? Our baby's fine."

"I'm glad to hear you say *our* baby. It is our baby now, Abby. And I'm overjoyed to know you're fine, too." He got up from the chair. "This calls for a major celebration." As they walked out of the hospital to the waiting limo, he said, "After work, we're leaving for a weekend aboard the yacht. The doctor wants you to rest and swim and do whatever you like. I'll let you decide our destination once we leave port."

She looked startled. "How can you get away?"

"Very easily."

Once inside the limo, she turned to him. "Vincenzo? Do you think this would be wise?"

A dark frown broke out on his face, erasing his earlier happiness. "Obviously you don't."

"When I tell my father where we're going, he'll tell me it's not a good idea. Already he's talking about our move back to the States. I can tell he's getting nervous about you and me spending any more time together that isn't absolutely necessary."

Vincenzo's jaw hardened. "Has he spoken to my father yet about leaving?"

"Yes. Last night."

That was news to Vincenzo. "How did he take it?"

"He wanted to know the reasons and asked him about our extended family back home."

"Was my father upset?"

"No. He said he'd been expecting it for some time."

Vincenzo grimaced. "Then he didn't try to dissuade your father from leaving."

"No, and we both know why." Her voice trembled. "You and I have shared a unique relationship for many years. The baby's on the way and Michelina is gone. Guilio wants you to take a wife ASAP."

Vincenzo's dark head reared. "Father knows my feelings on the subject. I'm not planning to get married again and am already looking into finding a full-time nanny to help me with the baby."

"You're serious—"

His mouth tightened. "Do you think I would make that up? If so, then you don't know me at all."

"I don't think Guilio has any idea you mean it. The situation is even worse than I'd feared," she muttered.

"What situation?"

"You know exactly what I'm talking about. The only reason I felt all right about becoming a surrogate was because you and Michelina were a team. But she's not here anymore and *I* am."

He sat forward. "I still don't understand you."

"Yes, you do, even if you won't admit it."

"Admit what?"

"You and I have shared a unique relationship over the years. With Michelina gone and me carrying your child, our friendship is now suspect. The fact that your father isn't begging Dad to stay on tells me it will please him once we've left Arancia for good. He wants you to take Odile on the yacht, not me."

"You haven't been listening to me," he ground out.

Her heart thudded harder, because she could feel how upset he'd become. "Vincenzo, you're in a very rocky place right now and grabbing at what is easy and familiar because I've always been around. But you're not thinking straight. For us to go on the yacht could spell disaster. That's why I'm not going with you."

He said nothing while her guilt was warring with her heart, but her guilt won. "Your wife has only been gone a few months. Of course you haven't been able to figure out your future yet. You're in a state of limbo and will be until the baby is born."

"Have you finished?" came his icy question.

"Not quite yet." As long as she'd been this brave, she needed to get it all said. When she felt her lips, they still tingled from Vincenzo's warm kiss. She'd felt it to the very marrow of her bones. If the doctor hadn't been in the room, she would have kissed him back and never stopped.

"If you recall, Michelina was the one who wanted me to live at the palace, but without her there, it will be better if I move back home with Dad until I have the baby." It was true she and Vincenzo felt too comfortable together. To her chagrin she knew his visits and plans involving her were a distraction that kept him from doing some of his normal functions. All of it needed to stop. A change of residence was the key.

His next comment surprised her. "I was going to suggest it after we got back from our cruise."

"I'm glad we're in agreement about that. I'll still be living on the grounds and can get room service whenever I want. Living with my father will put the kind of distance needed to ease the king's mind." To ease her own mind.

Abby had been thinking of the baby as *their* baby. When he'd kissed her after the sonogram, it had felt so right. She couldn't delude herself any longer. Abby was painfully in love with Vincenzo and felt as if his baby was her baby, too.

"In that case I'll ask some of my security people to move your things back this evening."

"I don't have anything except my clothes, really."

They'd reached the law firm. Vincenzo opened the door for her. She stepped outside, aware that the good news from the ultrasound had been swallowed up in the tension that had plagued them since Michelina's death.

"I'll see you this evening, Abby. Take care."

* * *

After putting in a full day's work, Vincenzo grabbed his phone and left for a run in the palace gym to work off his nervous energy. After a heavy workout, he returned to his suite to shower and shave. His phone rang while he was putting on a polo shirt over cargo pants. He'd asked the sentry guard to alert him when Abby got home from work.

Moving fast, he reached the door to her suite before she did. He wanted to catch her off guard. The second she came around the corner and saw him she stopped, causing the fetching green dress to wrap around her long legs for a moment.

"H-How long have you been waiting here?" Her voice faltered.

"Not more than a minute. I'll help you get packed and we'll have a last dinner here on your terrace. In a little while some of the security men will be here to take your things over."

"No, Vincenzo. I—"

"No?"

She looked conflicted. "What I meant to say is that I'm virtually halfway through this pregnancy and everything has gone fine so far. You don't need to wait on me hand and foot anymore!"

"I *want* to. There *is* a difference, you know. Since you're the only person on this planet who's going to make my dreams come true, would you deny me the privilege of showing my gratitude?"

"But you do it constantly."

He sucked in his breath. "Three-quarters of the time I've been out of the country or occupied with business, so that argument won't wash. All you have to do is tell me that you don't want my company and I'll stay away."

Her eyes flashed purple sparks. "I've always enjoyed your company, but—"

"But what?" he demanded.

"We talked about it in the limo. For the time being, it's best if you and I stay away from each other."

"Best for you, or for me?"

"Best for everyone! From the beginning we knew there'd be gossip. With Michelina's death everything has changed and I'm sure the king is wary of it. You have to know that, Vincenzo." Damn if she wasn't speaking truth. "My going back to live with Father will quiet a situation that's building, but you shouldn't be here helping."

"We've already covered that ground."

"And we'll keep covering it for as long as I'm under-foot here or on the royal yacht!" she cried.

"You *do* have a temper." He smiled. "This is the first time I've ever seen it."

Her face filled with color. "I...didn't mean to snap at you."

He gave an elegant shrug of his shoulders. "Instead of us standing around arguing, why don't you open the door and we'll get started on moving you—baggage and all—out of sight."

She drew closer to him. "Be reasonable."

"I'm offering my services to help. What's more reasonable than that?"

"Because it's not your job!"

The only person who'd ever dared talk to him like this was his father. Abby was even more alluring when she showed this side of her. "What do you think my job is? To sit on my golden throne all day long and order my subjects to fetch and carry for me?"

"Yes!"

But the minute she said it, he could tell she was embarrassed and he burst into laughter that filled the hallway. In another second she started laughing with him. "You're outrageous, Vincenzo."

"My mother used to tell me the same thing. Come on and let me in. After a workout in my golden gym, I'm dying for a cold lemonade."

"The door's open," she said in a quiet voice. "I only lock it at night, but there's really no need to do it, because you've assigned bodyguards who are as far away as my shadow."

CHAPTER SEVEN

VINCENZO OPENED THE door and waited for Abby to pass before he entered. But when he saw the sway of her hips, he had to fight the urge to wrap her in his arms and pull her body into him.

Never in his marriage with Michelina, let alone with the other women in his earlier years, had he known such an intense attack of desire, and without the slightest hint of provocation on Abby's part. She'd done nothing to bring out this response in him.

Somewhere along the way his feelings for her as a friend had turned into something entirely different. Perhaps it was the knowledge that she was leaving the palace tonight that had unleashed the carnal side of his nature. Maybe it was the reality of the baby now that he had the pictures in his possession, knowing it lived inside her body.

Her father was a red-blooded man who'd probably warned her ages ago not to go out on the yacht with him. Vincenzo's own father, a man with several quiet affairs in his background, had no doubt made it easy for Abby's father to leave his service to be certain no misstep was taken.

Vincenzo got it. He got it in spades. But the ache and

longing for her had grown so acute, it actually frightened him.

While she was in her bedroom, he phoned the kitchen to have some sandwiches and salad brought up to the room. "This is Signorina Loretto's last evening in the palace. Tonight she's moving back to Signor Loretto's apartment on the grounds. You'll be delivering her meals there from now on when she requests them."

"Very good, Your Highness."

Having quieted that source of gossip for the moment, Vincenzo hung up and went looking for Abby. "I ordered some sandwiches to be brought. While we're waiting, what can I do to help?"

She had several suitcases on the bed and had already emptied her dresser drawers. "Well...there's not much to take. I left most of my things at Dad's. Maybe if you would empty my CDs and DVDs from the entertainment center. I'll clean out the things in the den myself. The men will have to bring some boxes to pack all my books and Michelina's paintings." She handed him an empty shoulder bag.

She had an impressive collection of operas, from *Madame Butterfly* to *Tosca*. Her choice of movies was as varied as the different traits of her personality. He packed all but one of them and went back to the bedroom. "You enjoyed this?"

Abby glanced at the cover. "*24?* I absolutely love that series. Have you seen it?"

"Yes, and I found it riveting from beginning to end."

Her eyes exploded with light. "Me, too! Did you see the series about the signing of the peace accord?" He nodded. "That was my favorite. Even my father thought it was good, and that's saying a lot considering the kind of work he's in. He only picked apart half of the things in it that bothered him."

A chuckle escaped Vincenzo's lips. "Shall we watch a few episodes of it tonight while we eat and direct traffic?"

"That sounds wonderful."

"Bene."

"Oh—someone's knocking."

"I'll get it."

He opened the door and set the dinner tray on the coffee table.

After she'd emptied the bathroom of her cosmetics, she started on the den. Abby worked fast and it didn't take long. "There!" She came back in the living room. "It's done. Now all your poor slaves can move everything to Dad's."

With a smile he told her to sit in the chair and put her feet up on the ottoman. It pleased him that he got no argument out of her. With a flick of the switch, he sat back on the couch and they began watching *24*.

Again it gratified him that she was hungry and ate her sandwich with more relish than usual. He'd been afraid their little scuffle in the hall had put her off her food, but it seemed that wasn't the case.

The thought came into his head that she was probably excited to live with her father again and enjoy his company. Which left Vincenzo nowhere.

He craved Abby's company. During his trip to France she was all he ever thought about. To his surprise, it wasn't because of the baby. Perhaps in the beginning the two had seemed inseparable, but no longer.

Abby was her own entity. Lovely, desirable. Her companionship brought him nothing but pleasure.

"Don't you think the queen is fantastic in this se-ries? She was the perfect person to be cast in that part. How could the king want that other woman when he had a wife like her?" Abby was glued to the set. Vin-cenzo didn't think her remark was prompted by any other thought than the story itself, but it pressed his guilt button.

In his own way he'd been faithful to Michelina, but it hadn't been passionate love. This need for Abby had only come full force recently. His amorous feelings for her had crept up on him without his being aware.

"She's very beautiful in an exotic way," Vincenzo agreed, but his mind was elsewhere.

"How would it be to have been born that exotically beautiful? I can't even imagine it."

He slanted her a glance. "You have your own attri-butes. There's only one Abby Loretto."

"What a gentleman you are, Vincenzo. No wonder your subjects adore you."

"Abby—"

"No, no." She sat up straight. "Let me finish. All you have to do is look through that scrapbook again to see it."

A burst of anger flared inside him for his impos-sible situation.

"If you're trying to convince me to continue play-ing the role I was born to in life, it's not working. I'm no longer a baby who happened to be the child of a king. I've grown into a man with a man's needs. If I've shocked you once again, I'm sorry."

"I'm not a fool," she said quietly. "I can understand why you balk at the idea of marrying someone you don't love, even if it is your royal duty. After your experience with Michelina, it makes more sense than ever. But I can't believe that someday a woman with a royal background won't come along who sweeps you off your feet so you can take over for your father."

The program had ended. Abby got up from the chair to take the disk out of the machine and put it in the shoulder bag with the others.

He eyed her moodily. "Perhaps that miracle will occur. But we're getting ahead of ourselves. At this point, the birth of our child is the only event of importance in my life. It's all I can think about."

"That event isn't far off now."

No… He had less than six months before she left for the States. Getting to his feet he said, "The men should be here shortly. Come with me. If you're up to a walk, I'll escort you back to your old stomping grounds."

A happy laugh, like one from childhood, came out of her. "That sounds like a plan. I ate an extra sandwich half. The doctor would say that's a no-no. Otherwise at my next appointment I'll weigh in like—"

"Don't say it," he warned her. "I prefer my own vision of you."

She was turned away from him so he couldn't see her reaction. "I'll leave a note to tell them everything is here in the living room ready to go."

Vincenzo waited, then led her down another hall outside her apartment that came out at the side of the palace. They passed various staff as they walked down the steps and out the doors into an early evening.

July could be hot, but the breeze off the Mediterranean kept them cool enough to be comfortable. He'd crossed these grounds hundreds of times before, and many of those times with Abby. But this was different.

If he wasn't fearful of giving her a minor heart attack, he'd reach for her hand and hold it tight while they strolled through the gardens. Her father's apartment was in one of the outbuildings erected in the same style and structure as the palace. At one time it had housed certain members of the staff, but that was a century ago and it had since been renovated.

On impulse he stopped by a bed of hydrangea shrubs in full bloom to pick some flowers. "These are for you." He put them in her arms. "The petals are the color of your eyes. Not blue, not lavender, just somewhere in between."

"Their scent is heavenly." She buried her face in them, then lifted her head. "Thank you," she whispered. "You have no idea how many times over the years I've longed to pick these. Mother called them mop heads. These were her favorite flower and color."

"Maybe it's because she was reminded of them every time she looked into her only baby's eyes." Abby now averted them. "Abby, was there a reason your parents didn't have more children?"

She nodded. "Mom and Dad had me five years after they were married, because he'd been in the military. Two years later they decided to get pregnant again, but by that time Dad had been shot while on duty and it turned out he'd been rendered sterile. They weren't keen on adopting right away. I think it's one of the reasons they decided to move to Arancia, where they could make new memories."

Vincenzo was aghast. "I didn't know. Your father was so devastated when he lost her. I'll never forget."

"No. They were very much in love, but they had a great life all the same."

"And they had you." He was beginning to understand why she and her father were so close.

"Their inability to increase the family size was probably another motivating reason for my wanting to be a surrogate for you and Michelina. It's crazy, isn't it? So many women and men, whether in wedlock or not, seem to have little difficulty producing offspring while others…" Abby didn't finish the rest. She didn't have to.

They continued walking until they reached the apartment where she would live until the baby came. She left him long enough to put the flowers in water and bring the vase into the living room. He watched her look around after she'd set it on the coffee table.

This was the first time Vincenzo had been inside Carlo's suite. Family pictures were spread everywhere. He saw books and magazines her father must have read.

"Is it good to be home, Abby?"

She turned to him. "Yes and no. The apartment at the palace has been like home to me for quite a while. Both Dad and I can be semireclusive without meaning to be. We're both insatiable readers and like our privacy on occasion. He's going to have to put up with me invading his space again."

"Oh, I think he can handle it." Vincenzo happened to know her father had been on a countdown to get Abby out of the country from the time Michelina had died. "I'll stay until the men arrive with your things."

Abby sat down on one of the love seats, eyeing him with some anxiety. "I hope you didn't go to too much trouble to get the yacht ready."

"My father pays the captain a good salary to make certain it's able to sail at any time."

She shook her head. "I don't mean the money."

He let out a sigh. "I know you didn't. Frankly, the only person put out is yours truly, because I had my heart set on taking you to Barcaggio, on the northern tip of Corsica."

"I've never been there. You think I'm not disappointed, too?"

Abby sounded as though she meant it. Her response went a long way toward calming the savage beast within him.

"With your love of history, you'd find it fascinating. They had a unique warning system, with sixty guard towers dating from the fifteenth century, to keep the island safe. At least three towers in sight of each other would light fires to give a warning signal of pirates approaching. The Tower of Barcaggio is one of the best conserved and the water around it is clear like the tropics."

"Don't tell me anything more or I'll go into a deep depression."

A rap on the door prevented him from responding. He was glad the men had come. The sooner they left, the sooner he could be alone with her for a while longer. "I'll answer it."

For the next few minutes, a line of security people walked in with bags and boxes. Vincenzo helped to carry some of her law books into the library. What he saw on the desk gave him an idea. After he'd thanked them and they'd left, he called to Abby.

"Is there something wrong?" She hurried in, sounding a little out of breath.

"I think I've found a way we can be together for meals without leaving our suites."

She looked at him with those fabulous eyes. "How?"

"We'll coordinate our meals for the same time every evening and talk on Skype while we eat. That way I can check on you and know if you're lying when you tell me you're feeling fine."

Her lips twitched. "That works both ways. I'll know if you're in a mood."

"Exactly. Is it a deal?"

"Be serious, Vincenzo."

His heart beat skidded off the charts. "When I get back to my apartment, I'll Skype you to make sure everything's working properly."

"You don't mean every night?"

"Why not? Whether I'm away on business, out of the country or in the palace, we both have to stop for food, and we're usually alone. At the end of a hectic day, I'd rather unwind with you than anyone else. It'll save me having to go through Angelina to find out your condition for the day. Shall we say seven?"

"That'll last about two minutes before you're called away to something you can't get out of."

He decided he'd better leave before her father showed up. Together they walked to the entrance of the apartment. "Shall we find out? How about we give this a thirty-day trial? That should keep the gossips quiet. Whoever misses will have to face the consequences."

Amusement lit up her eyes. "You're on, but a prince has so many commitments, methinks *you'll* be the one who will wish you hadn't started this."

Vincenzo opened the door. "Don't count on it. I'll be seeing you as soon as I get back to my apartment." He glanced at his watch. "Say, twenty minutes?"

"I won't believe it till I see you."

With that challenge, he left at a run for the quick trip

back to his suite. There was more than one way to storm the citadel for the rest of her pregnancy without physically touching her. He didn't dare touch her.

It disturbed him that though he'd been in a loveless marriage, he could fall for another woman this fast. He was actually shocked by the strength of his feelings. To get into a relationship was one thing, but for Abby to be the woman, Vincenzo needed to slow down so he wouldn't alarm her. He knew she was attracted to him. It wasn't something she could hide, but she never let herself go.

Because of her control, he had to hold back, but they couldn't exist teetering on the brink much longer. Thanks to cybertechnology, he'd found a way to assuage some of his guilt. Without others knowing, he could be with her every night for as long as he wanted to satisfy his need to see and talk to her while he focused on the baby.

Vincenzo intended to be a good father, but he was struggling with the fact that he'd fallen for the woman who was carrying his child. What did that say about him?

Abby hurriedly put away her clothes and got settled as best she could before heading for the library. Passing through the living room, she picked up the vase of flowers and carried it with her.

After putting it on the desk, she sat down at her dad's computer, ready to answer Vincenzo's call. The big screen rather than her laptop screen would be perfect to see him, *if* he did make contact. She didn't doubt his good intentions, but she knew from her father that the prince followed a tight schedule, one that often ran late into the evenings.

In her heart she knew the decision to move home had been the right one, but when Vincenzo had walked out the door a little while ago, a feeling of desolation swept through her. Her move from the palace had marked the end of the third journey. Now she was embarking on the fourth into the unknown and had the impression it would try her mettle.

She'd lost Michelina, who'd provided the interference. Now it was all on Vincenzo to support her, but he'd made the wise decision to stay at a distance. So had she, yet already she felt herself in free fall.

Trust that clever mind of his to dream up Skyping as a way to stay in touch without distressing their fathers or the queen. As she was coming to find out, Vincenzo's resourcefulness knew no bounds.

Unable to resist, she leaned over to smell the hydrangeas. She'd never see one again without remembering how he'd just stopped and picked an armload for her.

The way to a woman's heart… Vincenzo knew them all, she admitted to herself in an honest moment. He was in there so tightly, she was dying from the ache. There'd never be room for anyone else. The video-call tone rang out, making her jump.

"Good evening, Abby." She'd put the speaker on full volume to make certain she could hear him. The sound of his deep, velvety voice brought her out of her trance-like state.

His looks went beyond handsome. Adrenaline rushed through her veins. "Good evening, Your Highness."

"You've become very formal since I left you."

"I've got stage fright." It was the truth. No one

in Arancia would believe what she was doing, and with whom.

"Our connection is good. We should have no problem communicating tomorrow evening."

"I might have one problem with the time. Dad is going to be home early for a dinner I'm cooking. Would you mind if we said eight-thirty?"

"I'll make a note on my agenda," he teased.

She smiled. "This is fun, Vincenzo."

"It's not the same as being with you in person, but I'm not complaining. Would you answer a question for me?"

"If I can."

"Did Dr. DeLuca let you know the gender of the baby?"

Her lungs froze. "No. He wanted to obey your wishes. I think you're wise not to know yet. Then your father and the queen would either be planning on a future king or future princess. This way everyone's still in the dark."

He chuckled. "I love the way you think, especially when you read my mind so easily. However, there is one thing I'm curious about. You never talk about the baby."

Pain stabbed at her heart. "I've been taking Dr. Greco's advice—don't think about the actual baby too much. Better to stay focused on taking care of yourself rather than dwelling on a child that won't be yours."

His face sobered. "How's that advice working out for you?"

She took a deep breath. "I'm finding it's very hard to carry out. I have to admit that if you hadn't asked me that question just now, I would know you had a stone for a heart."

"Abby," his voice grated, "you've accepted to do the impossible for me. You wouldn't be human if you weren't thinking about the baby day and night."

"You're right. During the talks I had with you and Michelina before I underwent the procedure, I made a decision to be like the postman who delivers the mail without knowing what's inside the letters.

"If a postman were to open one, he'd probably be so affected he would never make it to the next destination. Getting the ultrasound today was a lot like opening that first letter. I can't not think about the baby, whether it's a boy or a girl, if it will look like you or Michelina or someone else in your families."

Vincenzo turned solemn. "I've told you before, but I'll say it again. I'm in awe of you, Abby. You've taken on a weight too heavy to bear."

"You took on a weight, too. Not every man would trust a stranger with the life of his unborn child."

"You're no stranger," he answered in a smoky tone.

"You know what I mean."

"I don't think you know what *I* mean. You were never a stranger to me. A child in the beginning, of course, but from the beginning always a friend. I feel like I've known you all my life. It seemed a natural thing that you became our baby's surrogate mother."

She moistened her lips. "Depending on when the baby decides to come, we could be halfway home right now." Abby didn't want to think about the big event because of what it would mean. The thought of permanent separation was killing her. "Have you bought any things for the baby yet?"

"I'm glad you brought that up. In a few days I'm

going to go shopping and would like your help to set up the well-furnished nursery."

He couldn't know how his comment thrilled her. "I'd love to be involved."

"I'll send you pictures online and we'll decide on things together."

"Do you know where you're putting the nursery?"

"Either in my apartment or the room down the hall next to it."

"What did Michelina want?"

"We never got that far in our thinking. Her concerns over telling Bianca about the pregnancy overshadowed the fun."

Of course. "Well, it's fun to think about it now. If it's in your apartment, you'll have a nanny coming and going out of your inner sanctum." His low chuckle thrilled her. "When you're up all hours of the night with a baby with colic, will you be glad it's near at hand or not?"

"I'll have to think on that one."

"While you do that, what's on your schedule for tomorrow?"

"You really don't want to know."

"Why don't you let *me* decide?"

His smile was wicked. "Remember that you asked. First I'll do a workout in the pool when I get up, then I'll get dressed and eat breakfast with my father, who will tell me what's on his mind. I'll scan a dozen or so newspapers on certain situations in the world.

"At ten I'll visit the Esposito social enterprise to meet the staff and disadvantaged young people working on a building project at Esposito Ricci.

"At eleven-thirty I'll meet representatives of the San

Giovani Churches Trust, the National Churches Trust and restoration workers at Gallo-Conti.

"At noon I'll meet with the different faith communities at Gravina, where I'll be served lunch.

"At one-thirty, in my capacity as president of business, I'll visit the Hotel Domenico, which has been participating in my initiative to promote the meet-and-greet program in all the hotels. I'll visit the shop, which has been created in the meet-and-greet center, and chat with locals.

"At ten to three, as patron of the Toffoli Association, I'll meet staff and residents working at San Lucca Hospital. At four I'll meet pupils and staff at Chiatti Endowed Schools, where I'll tour the school hall and chapel. The pupils have prepared a brief performance for me.

"At ten to five I'll meet local community groups at the town hall in Cozza, as well as some members of the town council.

"At five-thirty, as president and founder of the Prince's Trust, I'll meet with young people who have participated in programs run by the trust, particularly the team program at the Moreno Hotel in Lanz."

Abby tried to take it in, but couldn't. "You made that up."

He crossed himself. "I swear I didn't."

"You mean that's all? That's it? You didn't have time to ride around in your made-for-the-prince sports car?" she exclaimed. "You're right, Vincenzo. I really didn't want to know and never want to think about it again."

Coming over the Skype, his laughter was so infectious she laughed until she had tears, which was how her father found her when he walked in the den. He could see Vincenzo in all his glory on the screen.

"Abby? Why aren't you talking?"

Her father had leaned over to smell the hydrangeas. "I have company."

Vincenzo didn't blink an eye. "Tell your father good evening."

"I will. *Buonanotte,* Your Highness."

She turned off the Skype. Nervous, she looked over at her dad, who had the strangest look on his face.

"Guilio told me his son has always been perfectly behaved. I wonder what could have happened to him."

Abby got up from the desk, needing to think of something quick. "He's going to be a father."

Carlo gave her a hug. "That must be the reason. Welcome home, sweetheart."

CHAPTER EIGHT

REPORTERS BESIEGED ABBY as she and Signor Giordano came out of the Palazzo di Giustizia in downtown Arancia. She'd won the case for him and it meant some big changes for the country's trade policies. Judge Mascotti had summoned her to the bench after announcing his ruling.

"I realize the palace was interested in this case, but I want you to know I made my decision based on the merits you presented."

Abby couldn't have been more pleased to hear those words.

For court she'd pulled her hair back to her nape and used pins to hold a few coils in place.

She'd worn a navy designer maternity outfit with a smart white jacket. The dress draped from a high waistline and fell to the knee. Her bump seemed quite big to her already, but the jacket camouflaged it well. On her feet she wore strappy white sandals.

Mid-August meant she was into her twenty-third week of pregnancy. Two days ago she'd had her first episode of Braxton-Hicks contractions, but the doctor said it was normal because her body was getting ready.

When Vincenzo found out, he had a talk with Dr. De-Luca and they both decided she should quit work.

Abby wasn't ready to stay home yet. Without work to do she'd go crazy, but she'd made an agreement in the beginning and had to honor it. When she got back to her office there was a celebration with champagne, not only because this case was important to their firm, but because it was her last day at work.

Everyone thought she was going back to the States, so she let them think it. Carolena poured white grape juice into her champagne glass when no one was looking. That was how she got through the party. If some of them realized she was pregnant, no one said anything.

After Skyping with Vincenzo every night from the start, except for the night she'd gone to the hospital about her false contractions, she told Carolena to Skype her at the apartment. Until the birth of the baby, Abby planned to do research for her friend to help pass the time. Carolena had a backlog of work and had gone crazy over the idea.

They drank to their plan and Abby left the office in brighter spirits than before. She walked out to the limo pretty much depleted energywise after her court appearance. Once settled inside, she rested her head against the back of the seat and closed her eyes, still thinking about what the judge had said to her.

She worked hard on every case, but that one had special meaning because it would benefit Arancia. After listening to Vincenzo's schedule for one day, she realized he'd spent his whole adult life promoting the welfare of his country. It felt good to know she'd made a tiny contribution toward his goals.

"Signorina?" She opened her eyes to discover they'd

arrived at the harbor. "Your presence is requested aboard the yacht. If you'll step this way, please."

Her heart thundered in her chest as she climbed out and walked with a security man up the gangplank into the gleaming white royal craft. Angelina was there to meet her.

"The palace heard of your victory in court and wishes to honor you with an overnight cruise. A few of your personal things are on board. Come with me and I'll show you to your cabin. Your orders are to relax, swim, eat and wander the deck at will."

"Thanks, Angelina," she murmured, too overcome to manage any more words and followed her. Strange as it was, this meant she'd miss her nightly conversation with Vincenzo. How crazy was that, when anyone else would be jumping out of their skin with joy at such a privilege?

But she'd lived on the palace grounds for years and inside the palace for four months of that time. She'd learned that if Vincenzo wasn't there, it didn't matter if the whole place was paved in gold. Since the judge's ruling, she'd been living to talk to him about everything tonight. Now she'd have to wait until tomorrow night.

"Is there anything else I can do for you?" Angelina asked from the doorway. The separate cabins were on the main deck, with a glorious view of the sea.

"I'm fine, thanks. Right now I just want to lie down. It's been a long day." She checked her watch. Five to six.

"Of course. If you need something, pick up the phone and the person on the other end will contact me. There's food and drink already on the table for you."

She nodded and closed the door after her. The queen-size bed looked good. After closing the shutters over the windows, Abby went to the bathroom, then removed her jacket and sandals. She ate half her club sandwich and some fruit salad before walking over to the bed. She'd undress all the way later. For the moment she was too tired to take off the sleeveless dress before she simply lay down to close her eyes for a little while.

The last thing Abby remembered before she lost consciousness was the movement of the yacht. When she heard someone calling her name, she thought it was the prince talking to her through Skype. She stirred.

"Vincenzo?"

"I'm right here."

"Oh, good. I wanted to talk to you and was afraid we wouldn't be able to until tomorrow night." But as she sat up in the semidark room, she realized something wasn't right. Abby wasn't at the desk. She was on the yacht and there was Vincenzo standing right in front of her in jeans and a sport shirt.

Her pulse raced. "You're here! I mean, you're *really* here."

"I knocked, but you didn't hear me, so I came in the room to check up on you. You didn't eat a lot of the dinner Angelina brought in."

"I was too tired to eat very much when I reached the room." Abby's hair had come unpinned and fell around her shoulders. "How did you get here?"

"I flew aboard on the helicopter. Are you all right?"

No. She wasn't! Abby hadn't seen him in person in about six weeks. The shock was too much and she was totally disoriented.

"Abby?" he prodded.

"Yes," she said too loudly, sounding cross. He was

much too close. She smoothed the hair out of her eyes. "You're not supposed to be here."

"Don't get up," he admonished gently, but she felt at a disadvantage sitting there and stood up anyway. "You're the loser in our contest, remember? This is the penalty I've chosen to inflict, so you're stuck with me until morning."

Her body couldn't stop trembling. "I confess I didn't think you could stick to it."

"Is that all you have to say?"

She'd been caught off guard and didn't know if she could handle this. A whole night together? "What do you want me to say?"

"That you're happy to see me."

"Well, of course I am." But the words came out grouchy.

"You really do look pregnant now. Will you let me feel you?"

If he'd shot her, she couldn't have been more astonished. That's why he kept standing there? It was a perfectly understandable request. It was his baby, after all. But this was one time when she didn't know what to do. To say no to him didn't seem right. But to say yes...

On instinct she reached for his hand and put it on her bump, to make it easier for both of them. It wasn't as if he hadn't touched her before. Heavens, he'd saved her life. She'd sobbed in his arms.

But there had been a whole new situation since then. The warmth of his fingers seeped through the material of her dress, sending a charge of electricity through her body. She held her breath while he explored.

"Have you felt it move?" he asked in a husky voice.

"I've had quickenings, kind of like flutters. At first I

wasn't sure. They only started a few days ago. But when I lay down a few hours ago, I felt a definite movement and knew it wasn't hunger pains."

"It's miraculous, isn't it?" His face was so close to hers, she could feel his breath on her cheek. He kept feeling, shaping his hand against her swollen belly. "I'm glad you're through working and can stay home, where you and the baby are safe."

She bowed her head. "No place is perfectly safe, Vincenzo."

"True, but you were on television today in front of the courthouse. I saw all those steps and a vision of you falling. It ruined the segment for me."

"Signor Giordano had hold of my arm."

"I noticed. He's recently divorced from his wife."

How did Vincenzo know that? But the minute she asked herself the question, she realized how foolish she was. He always checked out everything she did and everyone she worked with.

"I found him very nice and very committed to his fast-track proposal."

"Has he asked you to go out with him?"

Why did Vincenzo want to know? It couldn't be of any importance to him. "He did when he put me in the limo."

His hand stopped roving. "What did you tell him?"

"What I told everyone at my goodbye party. I'm moving back to the States." If she said it long and hard enough, she'd believe it, but his tension heightened. Being barefoot, Abby felt shorter next to his well-honed physique. She took the opportunity to ease away from him before turning on the switch that lit the lamps on either side of the bed.

He gazed at her across the expanse. "Are you still exhausted?"

No. His exploration of her belly had brought her senses alive and no doubt had raised her blood pressure. If he was asking her if she wanted to go up on deck and enjoy the night, the answer was yes. But she could hear her father saying, "I wouldn't advise it."

They'd both crossed a line tonight. His wish to feel the baby was one thing, but she'd sensed his desire for her. Since her own desire for him had been steadily growing for months, there was no point in denying its existence. Once you felt its power and knew what it was, all the excuses in the world couldn't take that knowledge away. Could you die of guilt? She wondered...

But to give in to it to satisfy a carnal urge would cheapen the gift. She'd told the queen this was a sacred trust. So she smiled at him.

"Maybe not exhausted, but pleasantly tired. I need a shower and then plan to turn in. Why don't we have breakfast in the morning on deck and enjoy a swim? That I would love." *Keep him away from you, Abby.*

"We'll be along the coast of Corsica at dawn. If you're up by seven-thirty, you'll see the water at its clearest."

Part of her had been hoping he'd tell her he didn't want her to go to bed yet, but he was a highly principled man and had made a promise to get her safely through this experience. "I'll set my alarm for that time and join you."

"Good night, then." As Vincenzo turned to leave she called his name.

"Thank you for this unexpected surprise."

"You won the court case and deserve a treat. Everyone in the country will benefit."

"Thank you. But I'm talking about more than a night on this fabulous yacht. I want to thank you for our nightly video sessions. I looked forward to every one of them."

His brows lifted. "They're not over."

"I'm so glad to hear that."

"They've saved my life, too, Abby." On that confession, he left her cabin and shut the door.

To read more into those words would be Abby's downfall. They were both waiting out this pregnancy on tenterhooks in a cage no one else could see. It was an unnatural time under the most unnatural circumstances a prince and a commoner could be in. The closer they got to the delivery date, the more amazed she was that she and Vincenzo had made things work this far.

During the early-morning hours, the sun burned a hole through clouds over the Mediterranean. The ray of light penetrated the turquoise water near the guard tower he'd told her about. Abby had thrown on a beach robe and leaned over the yacht's railing to see how far down it went, causing her braid to dangle.

Vincenzo had done several dives and wore his black trunks, so she could see his hard-muscled body clearly. The dramatically rugged landscape continued underwater in the form of more mountains, canyons, needles, peaks and rocky masses. He clung to some huge rocks below the waterline, then moved downward until he was almost out of sight.

Though he swam like a fish, she was nervous until she saw him come up for air. Abby wished she'd brought a camera to capture him on film, but when she'd left the courthouse yesterday, she could never have imagined where she'd end up.

"I'm envious of you!" she shouted to him. Even though it was August, she'd bet the water was cold this morning, but he seemed impervious to any discomfort.

"One day soon you'll be able to do this," he called back to her.

Not this. Not here. Not with him.

"Is there anything dangerous lurking down there?"

"Only a big white."

"Vincenzo!"

A grin appeared on his striking face. With his black hair slicked back, he was the stuff women's fantasies were made of. "Is breakfast ready?"

She giggled. "Have I told you how funny you are sometimes? You know very well your food is always ready!"

"Well, I'm starving!"

"So am I!"

He swam with expertise to the transom of the fifty-two-foot luxury yacht and came aboard. In a minute they were seated around the pool being served a fantastic meal. Once they'd eaten, Abby took off her robe to sunbathe for a little while. Their loungers were placed side by side. Talk about heaven!

The yacht was moving again, this time around the island. By tomorrow evening her idyll would be over, but she refused to think about that yet.

After the intimacy they'd shared last night when he'd reached out to feel the baby, she decided it didn't matter that he could see her pregnant with only her bikini on. Those black eyes slid over her from time to time, but he never made her feel uncomfortable.

The deck steward brought them reading material in case they wanted it. Vincenzo propped himself on one elbow to scan the newspaper. "You made the front page yesterday. I quote, 'A new star has risen in the legal firmament of Arancia.'

"'One might take her for a film star, but Signorina Abigail Loretto, a stunning blonde with the law firm of Faustino, Ruggeri, Duomo and Tonelli, has a brain and pulled off a coup for import trade in Judge Mascotti's court that had the attorney for Signor Masala already filing an appeal.'"

Vincenzo handed it to her so she could have a look. "Have I told you how proud I am of you?"

Her body filled with warmth that had nothing to do with the sun. "Am I lying here on the royal yacht being treated like a princess by none other than His Royal Highness?"

"I think we need to start a scrapbook for you."

"It will be a pitiful one, since I quit work yesterday. This was it. My one meteoric rise to fame that came and went in a flash. I hope it's all right with you if I help do research for Carolena at the apartment."

"Your life is your own, Abby. My only concern is that you keep your stress level to a minimum, for your sake as well as the baby's."

"Agreed."

His eyes played over her. "You're picking up a lot of sun, but it's hard to feel it with the breeze."

"You're right. I'll cover up in a minute."

"Abby—" She could tell he had something serious on his mind.

"What is it?"

"When you hear what I have to tell you, it will cause you some stress, but it has to be said."

"Go on."

"We've told Gianna about the situation."

Alarmed, she sat up in the lounger and reached for the beach towel to throw over her. "How long has she known?"

"My sister saw you on the evening news. Since she's known you for years, too, she phoned me about it. I was with Father when her call came through. Now that you've been identified to the public, so to speak, we decided it was time she knew about the baby in case word got out and she hadn't heard it first."

"That makes sense, Vincenzo. She'd be hurt if you hadn't told her." Her heart pounded so hard, it was painful. "Did she have the same reaction as your mother-in-law?"

He sat up to talk. "No. She thinks it's terribly modern of all of us—her exact words—but couldn't believe Michelina would go along with the idea."

"Because of the queen?"

"No," he murmured, sounding far away. Abby supposed she knew the real answer deep down.

"Then it was because *I'm* the surrogate."

Vincenzo's silence for the next minute told its own tale. "It's nothing personal," he said in a grating voice.

"I know that."

"She's afraid of how it's going to look when the news gets out. You and I have already discussed this at length, but I wanted you to be prepared when she and her husband come for a visit."

"How soon?"

"Tonight."

Abby's breath caught.

"If she weren't coming, we could have stayed out another night. You don't have to meet with her if you don't want to, Abby. This is none of her business."

"But it is, Vincenzo. She's going to be your baby's aunt. We'll face her together like we faced the queen. Was she good friends with Michelina?"

He nodded. "They were very close. I know for a fact Gianna's hurt because Michelina never confided in her about this."

"Some matters aren't for anyone's ears except your own spouse. Surely she understands that."

"You would think so." He threw a towel around his shoulders and got up from the lounger. "Come on. You need to get out of the sun."

She pulled on her robe and they walked to the covered bar laid out with cocktail tables and padded chairs. Soft rock played through the speakers. One of the stewards brought them iced lime drinks.

"I'm sorry your sister is upset, but I'm not worried about it, if that's what you're thinking. I had my trial of fire with the queen." A smile slowly broke from her.

Vincenzo saw it and covered her free hand with his own. "Then I won't take on that worry." He squeezed it, then let her go with reluctance and sat back. But she still felt the warmth and pressure of his after it had been removed.

"How long will it take us to get back to port?"

"For you, about five hours."

She groaned inside. "But not you."

"No. Another helicopter will be arriving in a half hour to take me back." The yacht had everything, including a landing pad. "Before I leave, I want to dance with you."

Ignoring her slight gasp, he reached for her and drew her into his arms. He moved them around slowly, pressing her against him.

"Do you know how incredible it is to be holding you in my arms while our baby is nestled right here between us?"

Abby couldn't breathe.

"I've needed to feel you like this for a long time. Don't fight me, Abby." He kissed her cheek and neck, her hair.

She felt as if she would faint from ecstasy. The last thing she wanted to do was push him away. For a little while she let herself go and clung to him. "I wish you didn't have to leave," she whispered.

"It's the last thing I want to do." While she was trying to recover from her severe disappointment that he had to go, he brushed his lips against hers before giving her a man's kiss, hot with desire. It spiked through her like electricity.

Close to a faint, she heard the sound of rotors and saw a speck in the sky coming their way. As it grew larger, she felt her heart being chopped into little pieces. Vincenzo had given her a fantastic surprise, but she wished he hadn't. She couldn't handle being around him like this and being kissed like this, only for him to be whisked away. This was torture.

"I'm afraid it will be better if no one sees us arriving together. The paparazzi will be out in full force. Angelina's going to help you leave with some of the staff from the yacht."

"You've had to go to a lot of trouble for me."

"How could it possibly compare with what you're doing for me?" She averted her eyes. "I'll send for you when it's time. We'll meet in the state drawing room as before. It's the only neutral ground in the palace, if you understand my meaning."

She knew what he meant. They couldn't talk to his sister in either of their apartments or his father's.

Though it was painful, she slowly eased out of his arms. "You need to get ready to go, so I'll say goodbye now and take a shower in my cabin."

He moved fast and accompanied her along the deck to open the door for her. But when she went inside and started to shut it, he stood there so she couldn't. His eyes stared at her. The desire in those black depths was unmistakable. She went weak at the knees. A small nerve throbbed at the corner of the mouth she was dying to taste over and over again.

"I'll see you tonight," he whispered in a raw-sounding voice she hardly recognized.

"Stay safe, Vincenzo. Don't let anything happen to you in that helicopter. Your child's going to need you."

"Abby—the last thing I want to do is leave you."

Then don't! she wanted to cry out. "With family coming, you have to."

His face darkened with lines. "Promise me you won't let Gianna get to you."

"She couldn't."

Abby had the feeling he wanted to warn her about something, then changed his mind.

"It'll be all right, Vincenzo."

His jaw hardened. "I'll Skype you at ten tonight."

She'd be living for it. *"A presto."*

Abby shut the door. After the passion in that kiss, this time it had to be goodbye for good.

When Marcello ushered Abby, wearing her jacketed white dress with the brown trim, into the drawing room, she glowed from the sun she'd picked up on her one day cruise. Her blond hair had been caught back with a dark comb. The newspaper had been right. She was stunning. Vincenzo had never seen her looking so beautiful.

"Gianna and I are glad you're here, Abby," he said, welcoming her to come in and sit down.

"I am, too. It's wonderful to see you again, Gianna." Since they'd all known each other for years, Vincenzo had dispensed with the pretense of formality, hoping to put Abby at ease. But he needn't have worried. She had incredible poise. Her self-possession came naturally to her and served her well in her profession.

Gianna, a tall brunette, smiled at her. "Pregnancy becomes you. You look well."

Vincenzo cringed. His sister wasn't pregnant yet and had gone straight for the jugular. So far the two women in his life who'd insisted on talking to Abby since Michelina's death had managed to show a side that couldn't help but hurt her, though she would deny it.

"Thank you. I feel fine."

His sister crossed her slim legs. "I told Vincenzo I wanted a private word with you. Do you mind?"

"Of course not."

He took that as his cue. "I'll be outside," he told Abby before leaving the room. For the next ten minutes he paced before she came out of the double doors. Despite her newly acquired tan, she'd lost a little color. He was furious with Gianna, but since their father had insisted she be allowed to talk with Abby, Vincenzo had given in, knowing it wouldn't go well.

"Are you all right?"

"I'm fine."

"I'll walk you back to your father's apartment."

"Please don't." It was the first time in their lives she'd ever spoken to him in a cold tone. Gianna had to have been brutal.

"I'll call you as soon as I know you're home." When Abby didn't respond he said, "We have to talk. I want your promise that you'll answer, otherwise I'll show up at your door."

"I—I need to go." Her voice faltered before she hurried down the hall and disappeared around the corner.

Tamping down his fury, he went back inside the drawing room. Gianna was waiting for him. He knew that look. "What in the hell did you say to her?"

Ten minutes later he started for the doors.

"Don't you dare walk out on me!"

Vincenzo wheeled around. "I already did." He strode rapidly through the corridors to the east entrance of the palace and raced across the grounds to Carlo's apartment. Once he arrived, he knocked on the door and didn't stop until Abby answered. After closing the door, he took one glance at her wan face and pulled her into his arms.

"Gianna told me what she unleashed on you. I'm so sorry." He cupped the back of her head and pressed it into his shoulder, kissing her hair. "You have to know it was her pain talking. She had to marry a man she didn't love and so far she hasn't conceived. Though she's attractive, she's not a beauty like you and never was. Her jealousy of you and your association with Michelina finally reared its ugly head."

It was like déjà vu with Abby sobbing quietly against him, the way she'd done after she'd been rescued.

"She used scare tactics on you so you'll leave, but don't you know I'd never let you go?"

After she went quiet, she pulled away from him. Her eyes resembled drenched violets. "Maybe I should."

"Abby—how can you even say that?"

She stared at him, looking broken. "The issues she brought up I've already faced in my mind, except for one."

"Which one?"

"Your child. The thought of it growing up with doubts about who its mother really is breaks my heart."

Vincenzo didn't think he could ever forgive Gianna for planting that absurd fear in Abby's mind. "The baby will be a part of Michelina. Michelina had distinctive genes, like her mother and brother. They don't lie, remember?"

She took a shuddering breath. "You're right. How silly of me."

"Not silly, only human in the face of behavior I haven't seen come out of my sister since she was a teenager and threw a tantrum because she couldn't get her own way. But she'll calm down in time, just like the queen. I left her with the prospect that when Father steps down, she'll be the new ruler of Arancia.

"As Dr. DeLuca reminded us, this is a nine-day wonder that will be over for her soon. The good news is, you've walked through your last fire. From now on, we wait until our baby sends you into labor. Does the prospect make you nervous?"

She nodded and put on a smile for him. "Yes, but I'm not frightened, exactly. How could I be, when hundreds of thousands of babies are born every day? It's just that this baby is special."

"After finding out what it's like to be an expectant father, I've learned every baby is special if it's yours, royal or not. If Gianna had given me the chance, I would have told her you've been a blessing to Michelina and me. She would say the same thing if she were here, so never forget it."

"I won't."

"Do you believe me, Abby? It's imperative you believe it."

Her eyes searched his. "Of course I do."

"Thank you for that." Without conscious thought, he brushed his lips against hers. "I have to go and we'll see each other tomorrow night at seven o'clock. Right?"

"Yes."

Before he went back to the palace, he hurried down to their private beach. After ripping off his clothes, he lunged into the water and swam until he had no more strength before returning to his suite.

His phone registered four messages, from Marcello, his father, Gianna, and Gianna's husband, Enzio.

Not tonight.

Normally he didn't drink except on certain occasions. But right now he needed one or he'd never get to sleep. However, even the alcohol couldn't quiet the adrenaline gushing through his system since he'd held Abby. He'd felt every curve of her body.

Tonight he'd felt the baby move against him, igniting a spark that brought him to life in a brand-new way. It was something he'd never expected to feel. The last thing he remembered before oblivion took over was the sweet, innocent taste of her lips. *Abby, Abby.*

CHAPTER NINE

WHEN ABBY COULDN'T reach her father, she left him a message.

"Hi, Dad. I'm just leaving the doctor's office and wanted to report that my checkup went fine. Can you believe my pregnancy is almost over? I'm meeting Carolena for dinner at Emilio's, then we're going to the concert hall to see Aida. Be sure and eat your dinner. It's in the fridge."

This was one night she wouldn't be Skyping with Vincenzo. Last night she'd told him her plans. He wasn't too happy about her sitting through an opera all evening, but she promised to take it easy during the day.

Since the night when everything had come to a head because of Gianna, he hadn't surprised her by showing up unexpectedly. For the last little while he'd been treating her like a friend. She was doing the same. No contact except for technology. It was much easier this way and relieved her of a lot of guilt.

Gianna had forced Abby to face up to the fact that she was desperately in love with Vincenzo. When he'd kissed her before leaving the apartment, it had taken every ounce of her will not to return it. That kiss from him had been one of affection, not passion. It was his way of trying to comfort her.

She loved him for it.

She loved him to the depth of her soul.

During the last scene of *Aida,* she came close to falling apart. Radamès had been taken into the lower part of the temple to be sealed in a dark vault. Aida was hidden there so she could die with him.

When the tenor cried that he'd never see the light of day again, never see Aida again, she told him she was there to die with him. As they fell into each other's arms, Abby choked up. Tears dripped off her chin onto her program because she could imagine a love like that. It was the way she felt about Vincenzo. Before long she'd have the baby and then she'd be gone for good. Thinking of that goodbye was excruciating.

On the way home in the limousine, Carolena teased her that she was full of hormones. Abby attributed her breakdown to the glorious music and voices, but they both knew it was much more than that.

Her dad was at the computer when she walked in the apartment. He lifted his head. "How was the opera?"

"Fantastic."

"You look like you've been crying."

She smiled at him. "Come on, Dad. You know *Aida* is a real tearjerker." They both loved opera.

"Your aunt phoned me today. They've found a house for us near them and sent an email with pictures. Take a look and see what you think. I like it more than any of the others she's sent."

Abby wandered over and stood next to him to check it out. "That's a darling house. I love the Cape Cod style. Let's do it."

Her response seemed to satisfy him. He turned to look at her. "Did you tell Dr. DeLuca about our plans?"

"Yes. He says he has no problem about my flying back to the States within a week of the delivery, provided I'm not having complications. Since Vincenzo is having us flown on the royal jet with a doctor on standby, Dr. DeLuca is fine with it."

"Good."

"He told me something else. Though he hopes I'll go full-term, I shouldn't worry if I start into labor sooner. The baby has dropped and could be born any time now. He says it would be fine. I was glad for that reassurance. My pregnancy has been so free of problems, it's comforting to know that if there's a complication now, the baby will be all right."

"That reassures me, too."

"Dad? Are you having second thoughts about leaving Arancia?"

Their gazes connected. "Absolutely not. There comes a time when you know you're done. How about you?"

"Naturally I'm going to miss it. I've spent more than half my life here, but we have family in Rhode Island and you'll be there. Once I'm settled in a law practice and take the bar, I know I'll be happy."

"I do, too. You'd better get to bed now, honey."

"I'm going. Good night." She kissed his forehead and left for her bedroom.

While she got ready, her mind was on her father. Abby knew he'd had relationships with several women since her mother died, but he seemed eager to leave Arancia. Since she didn't think it was all because of the situation with Vincenzo, she wondered if there was someone back home he'd known before and was anxious to see again.

Once she got under the covers, there was no comfortable position anymore. Then she got hot and threw them off. She'd had backache for the last week and looked like that beached whale. The doctor said she was a good size. Though she'd tried not to think about having to give up the baby, it had kicked her a lot since her sixth month and made her wonder if it was a boy with Vincenzo's great legs.

Abby knew he would have loved to feel it kicking, but by tacit agreement they'd stayed away from each other. She went swimming when he didn't. He didn't pick her up in the limo. Being able to Skype made it possible for them to talk to each other face-to-face and design the nursery, but that was it. Those days would soon be over.

Everything was planned out. Once Abby delivered, she'd be taken to a private place away from any staff or media before the flight back to the States. The contract she'd made in the beginning was specific: no contact with the baby or the parents. Abby's job would be done. That would be it, the end of her association with Vincenzo.

No meetings, no Skyping, no technology to connect them. It had to be that way for the rest of their lives, for the good of the kingdom, for all of them. Vincenzo would be the prince she couldn't forget, but he could never be a part of her life again.

Carolena was getting ready to go to court with a big law case. The work she'd asked Abby to do while she waited out these last few weeks was heaven-sent. Every time she started thinking about the little life getting ready to come into the world, she'd get busy doing more research. But she couldn't turn off her mind in the middle of the night.

Like Vincenzo, this child would be born into that world never knowing anything else. He'd make a marvelous father. She was excited for him, because his whole world was going to change once the doctor put the baby in his arms.

But to never see the baby, to never see Vincenzo again. She sobbed until oblivion took over.

Dr. DeLuca had given her the phone numbers of several former surrogates, but she hadn't felt the need to talk to them. No matter what, every surrogate's experience giving up a baby was different. Hers most of all, since she loved this royal heir and its father with every fiber of her being.

About five in the morning she woke up with lower-back pain. This was a little stronger than usual. She knew it could mean the onset of labor. Then again, it might be because she'd been to the opera last evening and it had been too much for her poor back.

She went to the bathroom and walked around the apartment for a few minutes. The ache subsided. Instead of going back to bed, she sat on the couch with her legs outstretched to watch a Godzilla film in Italian. Her feet were swollen. So were her fingers.

The film put her to sleep, but pain woke her up again. Whoa. She got up to go to the bathroom. Um. It hurt. It hurt a lot.

She went into her father's bedroom. "Dad? Did Mom have a bad backache before I came?"

He shot up in bed. "She sure did. The pain came around to the front."

"Yup. That's what I've got."

"I'll call the doctor."

"Tell him not to alert Vincenzo and tell him no one at the hospital is to leak this to him on the threat of death!"

"You can't ask him that, honey."

"Yes, I can!" She yelled at him for the first time in her life. "I'm the one having this baby and I'm not Vincenzo's wife. This isn't my child." Tears rolled down her hot cheeks. "If something goes wrong, I don't want him there until it's all over. He's been through enough suffering in his life. If everything's fine, then he ca— O-o-h. Wow. That was a sharp pain.

"Dad? Promise me you'll tell the doctor exactly what I said! I've been good about everything, but I want my way in this one thing!

"And make Angelina swear to keep quiet. If she breathes one word of this to Vincenzo, then—oh, my gosh—you'll fire her without pay and she'll never get another job for as long as she lives. I'm depending on you, Dad. Don't let me down."

He put a hand on her cheek. "Honey, I promise to take care of everything." Then he pressed the digit on his phone.

Vincenzo's life had become a ritual of staying alive to hear about Abby's day, but he was slowly losing his mind.

After a grueling session with parliament, he hurried to his apartment for a shower, then rang for some sandwiches and headed for the computer. It was time for his nightly call to Abby. With the baby's time coming soon, he couldn't settle down to anything. The only moments of peace were when he could see her and they'd talk.

Tonight he was surprised because he had to wait for her to tune in. One minute grew to two, then five. He gave her another five in case she was held up. Still no response.

The phone rang. It was Angelina. He broke out in a cold sweat, sensing something was wrong before he clicked on. "Angelina?"

"I wasn't supposed to let you know, but I think you have the right. You're about to become a father, Vincenzo."

What? "Isn't it too soon?"

"Not according to Abby's timetable. She didn't want you to worry, so she didn't want you to come to the hospital until after the delivery, but I know you want to be there. The limo is waiting downstairs to take you to the hospital."

His heart gave a great thump. "I owe you, Angelina! I'm on my way down."

Vincenzo flew out of the apartment and reached the entrance in record time. "Giovanni? Take me to the hospital, stat!"

Everything became a big blur before one of his security men said, "Come this way, Vincenzo." They took the elevator to the fourth floor, past the nursery to one of the rooms in the maternity wing.

"When did she go into labor?"

"Awhile ago," came the vague response. Vincenzo wanted to know more, but a nurse appeared and told him to wash his hands. Then she put a mask and gown on him before helping him into plastic gloves. He couldn't believe this was finally happening.

"Wait here."

As she opened the door, he saw Dr. DeLuca working with Abby. He was telling her to push. His beautiful Abby was struggling with all her might. "Push again, Abby."

"I'm trying, but I can't do this alone. I need Vincenzo. Where is he?" Her cry rang in the air. "I want him here!"

That was all Vincenzo needed to hear. He hurried into the operating room. The doctor saw him and nodded. "He's arrived."

"I'm here, Abby."

She turned her head. "Vincenzo!" He heard joy in her voice. "Our baby's coming! I should have called you."

"I'm here now. Keep pushing. You can do it."

After she pushed for another ten minutes, before his very eyes he saw the baby emerge and heard the gurgle before it let out a cry. Dr. DeLuca lifted it in the air. "Congratulations, Abby and Vincenzo. You have a beautiful boy." He laid the baby across her stomach and cut the cord.

"A *son,* Vincenzo!" Abby was sobbing for joy. "We did it."

"No, you did it." He leaned over and brushed her mouth.

The staff took over to clean the baby. In a minute the pediatrician announced, "The next heir to the throne is seven pounds, twenty-two inches long and looks perfect!"

He brought the bundled baby over and would have placed it in his arms, but Vincenzo said, "Let Abby hold him first."

The moment was surreal for Vincenzo as together

they looked down into the face of the child he and Michelina had created, the child Abby had carried. His heart melted at the sight.

"*Buonasera,* Maximilliano," she said with tears running down her cheeks. "Oh, he's so adorable."

Vincenzo could only agree. He leaned down to kiss the baby's cheeks and finger the dark hair. Carefully he unwrapped their little Max, who *was* perfect, with Michelina's eyes and ears.

"Look, Vincenzo. He has your jaw and the Di Laurentis body shape."

All the parts and pieces were there in all the right places. Vincenzo was overwhelmed.

Dr. DeLuca patted his shoulder. "You should go with the pediatrician, who's taking the baby to the nursery. I need to take care of Abby."

"All right." He leaned down again, this time to kiss her hot cheek. "I'll be back."

An hour later he left the nursery to be with Abby, but was told she was still in recovery. He could wait in the anteroom until she was ready to be moved to a private room. But the wait turned out to be too long and he knew something was terribly wrong.

He hurried to the nursing station. "Where's Signorina Loretto?" He was desperate to see the woman who'd made all this possible. She'd done all the work. She and the baby were inseparable in his mind and heart.

"She's not here, Vincenzo." Dr. DeLuca's voice.

He spun around. "What do you mean? To hell with the agreement, Doctor!"

Vincenzo felt another squeeze on his shoulder and looked up into Carlo's eyes staring at him above the mask he'd put on. "We all knew this was going to be the hard part. Abby's out of your life now, remember?

"Your boy needs you. Concentrate on him. You have all the help you need and a kingdom waiting to hear the marvelous news about the young prince, especially this bambino's grandfather and grandmother."

Vincenzo didn't feel complete without her. "Where is she, Carlo?"

"Asleep. She had back pain around five in the morning. In total she was in labor about fifteen hours. All went well and now that the delivery is over, she's doing fine."

"Tell me where she is," Vincenzo demanded.

"For her protection as well as yours, she's in a safe place to avoid the media."

He felt the onset of rage. "You mean she's been put in a witness protection program?"

"Of a sort. She fulfilled her part of the bargain to the letter and is in excellent health. You once saved her life. Now she's given you a son. Let it be enough."

Carlo's words penetrated through to his soul. What was the Spanish proverb? *Be careful for what you wish, for you just might get it.*

Vincenzo stood there helpless as hot tears trickled down his cheeks.

"Good morning, honey."

"Dad—"

"I'm here."

"This is a different room."

"That's right. You're in a different hospital. You were transported in an ambulance after the delivery."

"I'm so thankful it's over and Vincenzo has his baby."

"Yes. He's overjoyed. I'll turn on the TV so you can see for yourself." Carlo raised the head of the bed a little for her to see without straining.

Abby saw the flash, "breaking news," at the bottom of the screen. "For those of you who are just waking up, this is indeed a morning like none other in the history of the world. There's a new royal heir to the throne of Arancia. Last night at six-fifteen p.m., a baby boy was born to Crown Prince Vincenzo and the deceased Princess Michelina Cavelli by a gestational surrogate mother who we are told is doing well. The new young prince has been named Maximilliano Guilio Cavelli Di Laurentis."

Vincenzo...

"The seven-pound prince is twenty-two inches long."

"Max is beautiful, Daddy." The tears just kept flowing. "He'll be tall and handsome like Vincenzo!"

"According to the proud grandparents, their majesties King Guilio Di Laurentis and Queen Bianca Cavelli of Gemelli, the baby is the image of both royal families.

"We're outside the hospital now, awaiting the appearance of Prince Vincenzo, who will be taking his son home to the royal palace any minute. A nanny is already standing by with a team to ease Prince Vincenzo into this new role of fatherhood.

"Yes. The doors are opening. Here comes the new father holding his son. We've been told he's not going to make a statement, but he's holding up the baby so everyone can see before he gets in the royal limousine."

Darling. Abby sobbed in joy and anguish.

"This must be a bittersweet moment for him without Princess Michelina at his side. But rumor has it that sometime next year the king will be stepping down and the Principality of Arancia will see another wedding and the coronation of Prince Vincenzo."

Abby was dying for Vincenzo, who was being forced to face this. "I can't stand the media, Dad. Couldn't they let him enjoy this one sacred moment he and Michelina had planned for without bringing up the future?"

"Speculation is the nature of that particular beast. But we can be thankful that for this opening announcement, they played down your part in all this. For such forbearance we can thank the king, who told me to tell you that you have his undying gratitude."

Abby's hungry eyes watched the limo as it pulled away from the hospital escorted by security. The roar of the ecstatic crowds filled the streets. Her father shut off the TV.

She lay there, numb. "It's the end of the fairy tale." Abby looked at him. "I can't bear it. I love him, Dad, but he's gone out of my life."

He grasped her hands. "I'm proud to be your father. You laid down your life for him and Michelina and he has his prize. Now it's time for you to close the cover of that scrapbook and start to live your own life."

"You knew about that?"

Her father just smiled. He wasn't the head of palace security for nothing.

Abby brushed the tears off her face. "I gave it to him months ago when he told me he didn't want to be king. I wanted him to look through it and see all his accomplishments."

Her father's eyes grew suspiciously bright. "You've

been his helpmate all along and it obviously did the trick."

She kissed his hand. "Thank you for keeping him away as long as you could. I didn't want him to have to go through any more grief, not after losing Michelina. Forgive me for yelling at you at the apartment?"

"That's when I knew you meant business. As it so happens, I agreed with you, but a man should be at the bedside of the woman who's giving birth to his baby. Evidently Angelina thought so, too. She's the one who told him to get to the hospital quick."

"Bless her. I needed him there."

"Of course you did."

"Lucky for me I was blessed to have you there, too, Daddy."

"Someday you'll get married to a very lucky man, who will be there when the time comes for your own child to be born. I look forward to that day."

Abby loved her father, but he could have no conception of how she felt. Vincenzo was the great love of her life. There would never be anyone else and she would never have a baby of her own. But she'd had this one and had been watched over by Vincenzo every second of the whole experience.

Through the years she would watch Max in secret, because he was her son and Vincenzo's as surely as the sun ruled the day and the moon the night. No one could ever take that away from her.

"Honey? The nurse has brought your breakfast." He wheeled over the bed table so they could eat together. "Do you feel like eating?"

Abby felt too much pain and was too drugged to have

an appetite yet, but to please her father she reached for the juice.

"We haven't talked about you for a long time." She smiled at him. "I want to know the real reason you decided to step down and move back to Rhode Island. Is there a woman in the picture you haven't told me about? I hope there is."

He drank his coffee. "There has been one, but it was complicated, so I never talked about it."

"You can talk to me about it now." Because if there wasn't, then it meant she and her father had both been cursed in this life to love only one person. Now that she'd lost Vincenzo, both she and her dad would be destined to live out the rest of their lives with memories.

"Can't you guess? There's only been one woman in my life besides your mom. It's been you."

"Don't tease me."

"I'm not."

She frowned. "Then why did you decide you wanted to leave Arancia?"

"Because I could see the hold Vincenzo has had on you. Otherwise you would never have offered yourself as a surrogate. If you hope to get on with your life, it has to be away from here."

Abby lowered her head. "I'm afraid he'll always have a hold on me."

"That's my fear, too. It's why we're getting out of Arancia the moment you're ready to travel."

CHAPTER TEN

VINCENZO HAD SUMMONED Angelina to his apartment as soon as he'd returned to the palace with his son. He'd spent time examining Max from head to toe. After feeding him the way the nurse had showed him, and changing his diaper, Vincenzo gave Max to the nanny, who put him to bed in the nursery down the hall. Now there was no time to lose.

"Tell me what you know of Abby's whereabouts, Angelina."

"I can't, Your Highness. Please don't ask me. I've been sworn to secrecy."

"By whom? Carlo?"

"No."

"The king?"

"No."

"Abby?"

She nodded.

He knew it!

"Tell me which hospital they took her to."

Angelina squeezed her eyes tightly. "I don't dare."

"All right. I'm going to name every hospital in Arancia." He knew them all and served on their boards. "All you have to do is wink when I say the right one. That way you never said a word."

"She'll hate me forever."

"Abby doesn't have a hateful bone in her body. She carried my son for nine months and gave me the greatest gift a man could have. Surely you wouldn't deny me the right to tell her thank you in person."

"But she's trying to honor her contract."

"Contract be damned! She's fulfilled it beyond my wildest dreams. If another person had done for you what she's done for me, wouldn't you want to thank them?"

"Yes, but—"

"But nothing. That may have been the rule when Michelina and I signed on with her, but the baby has arrived. There's no more contract. You're free of any obligation. What if I tell you I won't approach her in the hospital?"

After more silence he said, "I'll wait until she leaves. Surely that isn't asking too much. I swear on my mother's grave she'll never know you told me anything."

Still more silence. He started naming hospitals while holding his breath at the same time. Halfway down the list she winked. His body sagged with relief. San Marco Hospital, five miles away in Lanz. Near the airport and several luxury hotels. It all fit.

"Bless you, Angelina. One day soon you'll know my gratitude with a bonus that will set you up for life."

As she rushed away, he phoned his personal driver. *"Giovanni?"*

"Congratulations on your son, Your Highness."

"Thank you. I need you to perform a special service for me immediately."

"Anything."

He'd been doing a lot of undercover services for Vincenzo since the pregnancy. "I hope you mean that. My red sportscar is yours if you do as I say."

His driver laughed. Giovanni came from a poor family.

"You think I'm kidding?"

"You are serious?"

"Do as I say and you'll find out. I want you to round up all your cousins *pronto* and have them drive to San Marco Hospital in Lanz. Signorina Loretto is there recovering from the delivery. She's being watched by her father's security people. Fortunately they don't know your cousins.

"I want them to cover all the hospital exits leading outside. She'll be leaving there by private limousine. I suspect it will happen by this evening if not sooner. When your cousins spot the limousine, they'll follow and report to you when her limo reaches its destination, which I believe will be a hotel, possibly the Splendido or the Moreno. Then you'll phone me and drive me there. Any questions?"

"No, Your Highness. You can count on me."

"There's a healthy bonus waiting for each of them. My life depends on your finding her, Giovanni."

"Capisci."

Vincenzo hung up and hurried down to the nursery to spend time with his precious son before his father and sister arrived. He had to stop Abby from leaving the country. If she got away, he'd track her down, but it would be much more difficult with the baby. He wanted her here. *Now!*

He played with his baby and took pictures with his phone. While the family took turns inspecting the new arrival, he took a catnap. Bianca and Valentino would be flying in tomorrow morning.

At five in the afternoon, his phone rang. He saw the caller ID and picked up. "Giovanni?"

"We've done as you asked. She was driven to the Moreno under heavy guard."

"I'll be right down." After telling Marcello his life wouldn't be worth living if he told anyone where Vincenzo was going, he put on sunglasses and rushed down to the limo in a Hawaiian shirt, khaki shorts, sandals and a droopy straw hat.

Giovanni took off like a rocket. "You look like all the rich American businessmen walking around the gardens. No one would recognize you in a million years, Your Highness," he said through the speaker.

He bit down hard. "If I can make it to her room before someone stops me, it won't matter."

Carlo had made Abby comfortable on the couch in their hotel suite. This would be their home for a few more days before they left the country. The painkillers they'd given her were working.

"Is there anything you want, honey?"

She kept watching the news on TV to see Vincenzo and the baby. "Would you mind picking up a few magazines for me to look at?"

"I'll get them. Anything else?"

"A bag of dark chocolate bocci balls and a pack of cashews." She'd been starving for foods she couldn't eat during the pregnancy. They wouldn't take away her depression, but she needed to give in to her cravings for some sweets or she'd never make it through the next few days.

"I'll have to go down the street for those."

"Dad—take your time. I'm fine and you need a break. Thank you."

A few minutes after Abby's father left, there was a knock on the door. "Room service."

She hadn't ordered anything, but maybe her father had. "Come in."

"Grazie, Signorina."

Abby knew that deep male voice and started to tremble. She turned her head in his direction, afraid she was hallucinating on the medicine. The sight she saw was so incredible, she burst into laughter and couldn't stop.

Vincenzo walked around the couch to stand in front of her. "What do you think?" he asked with a grin, showing those gorgeous white teeth in that gorgeous smile. "Would you recognize me on the street?"

She shook her head. "Take off the glasses." She was still laughing.

He flung them away and hunkered down next to her. His eyes blazed black fire. "Do you know me now?"

Her heart flew to her throat. "Wh-what are you doing here? How did you find me?"

"You'd be surprised what I had to go through. Giovanni's my man when I need him. Did you really think I was going to let you go?"

Tears stung her eyes. "Don't do this, Vincenzo."

"Do what? Come to see the woman who has changed my entire life?"

She looked away. "You have a beautiful son now. We had an agreement."

"I hate agreements when they don't give me the advantage."

Abby couldn't help chuckling, despite her chaotic emotions. "Is he wonderful?"

"I'll let you decide." He pulled out his cell phone to show her the roll of pictures.

"Oh, Vincenzo—he's adorable!"

He put the phone on the floor. "So are you. I love you, heart and soul, Abby."

The next thing she knew, his hands slid to her shoulders and he covered her mouth with his own. The driving force of his kiss pressed her head back against the pillow. His hunger was so shocking in its intensity a moan escaped her throat in surrender.

A dam had burst as they drank deeper and deeper, but Abby's need for him was out of control. She had no thought of holding back. She couldn't.

"For all my sins, I love and want you to the depth of my being, Vincenzo, but you already know that, don't you? I tried not to love you, but it didn't work. Everything your sister said to me that day in the drawing room was true."

His lips roved with increased urgency over her features and down the side of her neck to her throat. "I fell for you years ago when you almost drowned, but I would never admit it to myself because a relationship with you was out of the question. No matter how hard I tried not to think about you, you were there, everywhere I looked. You're in my blood, *bellissima*."

They kissed back and forth, each one growing more passionate. "It seems like I've been waiting for this all my life," she admitted when he let her up for breath.

"We've paid the price for our forbearance, but that time is over. I'm not letting you go."

Abby groaned aloud and tore her lips from his. "I can't stay in Arancia."

"There's no such word in my vocabulary. Not anymore."

"She's right, Vincenzo."

Her father had just walked in the hotel room, carrying some bags. Her breath caught as she eyed him over Vincenzo's shoulder.

"Carlo." He pressed another kiss to her mouth and got to his feet. "I'm glad you're here so I can ask your permission to marry Abby. She's my heart's blood."

Rarely in her life had she seen her father look defeated. He put the bags on the table and stared at the two of them.

"I don't want an affair with her. I want her for my wife. Since you and I met when I was eighteen, you can't say you don't know me well enough."

Her father moved closer. "That's certainly true." He looked at Abby. "Is this what you want?"

"Yes." Her answer was loud and instantaneous.

Vincenzo reached for her hand and squeezed it. "I have no idea if the parliament will allow my marriage to a commoner and still let me remain crown prince. If not, then I don't intend to be in line for the crown and my sister will take over when the time comes."

"Are you prepared to be the targets of malicious gossip for the rest of your lives?"

"If necessary we'll move to the States with our son. He *is* our son. One way or another, she and I have been in communication whether in person or skyping. Max is every bit a part of her as he is of me and Michelina."

Carlo swallowed hard.

"I love Abby the way you loved your wife. The state

you were in when you lost her altered my view of what a real marriage could be. If Abby leaves me, I'll be as lost as you were."

Vincenzo was speaking to her father's heart. She could tell he'd gotten to him.

"I know the king's feelings on the subject, Vincenzo. He was hoping you would follow after him."

"I was hoping I would fall in love with Michelina. But we don't always get what we hope for. If it's any consolation, Gianna always wished she'd been born a boy so she'd be first in line. She'll make a great ruler when the day comes."

"Are you two prepared to face the wrath of your mother-in-law?"

Vincenzo glanced at Abby. "We'll deal with her. When she sees Michelina's likeness in Max, her heart will melt. I know she'll secretly be full of gratitude to Abby, who put her life on the line for Michelina and me to give her a grandson."

"Dad?" Abby's eyes pleaded with him. "What do you think Mom would say if she were here?"

He let out a strange sound. "She always did say it was sinful that Prince Vincenzo had been born with every physical trait and virtue any red-blooded woman could want. Since she loved films so much, she would probably say yours is one of the greatest love stories of this generation and should be made into a movie. Then she'd give you her blessing, as I give you mine."

"Carlo..."

Vincenzo was as moved as Abby, who broke down weeping. He finally cleared his throat. "I want her to move back into the palace tonight in her old room until we're married. Max needs his mother tonight, not a nanny or a nurse."

"In that case a quiet, private marriage in the palace chapel needs to be arranged within a week or two. Just as soon as you've talked to the king."

"I don't want you to take that job back in Rhode Island, Dad."

He broke into a happy smile. "Since I'm going to be a grandpa, I guess I'm stuck here."

"That'll be music to my father's ears." Vincenzo put his hands on his hips. "Do you feel well enough for the trip back to the palace now?" he asked Abby.

She stared at him. "I feel so wonderful, I'm floating. I want to see our baby."

"Do what you need to do while I help your father get everything packed up. Then we'll go out to my limo for the drive back."

"I'll just run to the restroom and grab my purse." Except she walked slowly and looked back at Vincenzo. "I'm waddling like a goose."

His laughter resonated off the walls.

In a few minutes she was ready. When she came back into the room, she found he'd donned his hat and sunglasses. When she thought he would take hold of her hand, he picked her up like a bride, as if she were weightless.

"You and I have done things differently than most of the world. Now we're about to cross the threshold the other way."

"And me looking such a mess." She didn't have on makeup and her hair hung loose, without being brushed.

"You're the most beautiful sight I ever saw in my life." He gave her a husband's kiss, hot with desire.

"So are you," she murmured, resting her head against his shoulder.

Her father opened the door. "The men have the hallway closed off to the exit. Let's go."

After leaving his stunned father and sister in the king's private living room, where he'd announced he was getting married, Vincenzo headed for the nursery. He found Max sleeping and gathered him in his arms. The nanny left for Abby's apartment, wheeling the bassinet on its rollers down the hall. He followed and carried his son through the corridors of the palace. One day their little boy would run on these marble floors.

The staff all wanted to steal a look at Max, but Vincenzo was careful not to let them get too close. Dr. De-Luca had warned him to keep Max away from people during the next few weeks. He found Abby on top of the bed with her eyes closed. After fifteen hours in labor, she had to be exhausted. She was wearing a blue nightgown and robe and had fastened her gilt hair back at the nape.

Their nanny put the bassinet with everything they would need to one side of the queen-size bed and left the apartment. Since both were asleep, Vincenzo put the baby in the little crib on his back. Then he got on the other side of the bed and lay down facing Abby.

It felt so marvelous to put his arm around her. He'd wanted to do this on the yacht and had been aching for her ever since. While she slept he studied the exquisite oval mold of her face. Her lips had the most luscious curve. He had to pinch himself this was really happening. To have his heart's desire like this was all he could ever ask of life.

Abby sighed and started to turn, but must have felt the weight of Vincenzo's arm. Her eyes flickered open.

"Good evening, Sleeping Beauty." The famous fairy-tale character had nothing on his bride-to-be.

Her eyes looked dazed. "How long have you been here?"

"Just a little while. *Viene qui tesoro*." She *was* his darling.

He pulled her closer and began kissing her. Abby's response was more thrilling than anything he'd ever dreamed about the two of them. Vincenzo had promised himself to be careful with her. The kind of intimacy he longed for wouldn't happen until her six-week checkup, but he already knew she was an exciting lover.

They didn't need words right now. There'd been enough words expressed to last months, years. The kind of rapture they derived from each other had to come from touch, from her fragrance, from the sounds of her breathing when she grew excited, from the way she fit in his arms as if she were made for him. She was the fire, giving off life-giving warmth. He couldn't get close enough.

In the throes of ecstasy, he heard newborn sounds coming from the other side of the bed. He planted one more kiss to her throat. "Someone's waking up and wants to meet his mama."

With reluctance, he rolled away from her and walked around to the crib. "I've got a surprise for you, *piccolo,* but let's change your diaper first." Practice made perfect.

Abby sat up higher on the bed, her eyes glued to the baby he placed in her arms. "Oh—" she crooned, bending over to kiss his face. "You darling little thing.

You're already a kicker, aren't you? I've been feeling your father's legs for several months and thought you had to be a boy. Are you hungry? Is that why you're getting all worked up?" Her soft laughter thrilled Vincenzo's heart.

He handed her a bottle. She knew what to do. It fascinated him to watch her feed him as if she'd been doing it every day. A mother's instinct. Deep down he knew she'd been thinking about it from the moment she found out she was pregnant.

"Give him about two ounces, then burp him. Here's a cloth."

What took him awhile to learn she seemed to know instinctively. When she raised Max to her shoulder, their little boy cooperated and they both chuckled. She raised a beaming face to him. "I'm too happy."

"I know what you mean," he murmured emotionally.

"I hope you realize I wanted to talk about the baby for the whole nine months, but I didn't dare."

"You think I don't understand?" He sat down on the side of the bed next to her and watched a miracle happening before his eyes. "We'll take care of Max all night and feed him every time he wakes up."

"I can't wait to bathe him in the morning. I want to examine every square inch of him."

Vincenzo leaned over to kiss her irresistible mouth. "Once the doctor gives you the go-ahead, I'm going to do the same thing to *you*."

Blood rushed to her cheeks. "Darling—"

Abby had just put the baby down in the nursery when her cell phone rang. She hurried out of the room, clutching her robe around her, and slipped back in the bedroom she shared with her husband to answer it. "Carolena!"

"You're a sly one."

Her heart pounded in anxiety. "I was just going to call you. I guess the news is officially out."

"Out? It's alive and has gone around the world. I've got the Arancian morning news in front of my eyes. I quote, 'Crown Prince Vincenzo Di Laurentis marries commoner surrogate mother Abigail Sanderson Loretto in private chapel ceremony with only members of the immediate family in attendance. The question of the prince stepping down is still being debated by the parliament.

'The twenty-eight-year-old first-time mother, an American citizen born in Rhode Island, attained Arancian citizenship six years ago. At present she's an *avvocata* with Faustino, Ruggeri, Duomo and Tonelli.

'Her father, Carlo Antonio Loretto, a native of Arancia who served in the Arancian Embassy in Washington, D.C., for a time, is chief of security for the royal palace. His American-born wife, Holly Sanderson Loretto, is deceased due to a tragic sailboat accident eleven years ago on the Mediterranean.

'Prince Maximilliano Guilio Cavelli Di Laurentis, the son of deceased Princess Michelina Agostino Cavelli of the Kingdom of Gemelli, is second in line to the throne.

'The spokesman for the palace reports that Prince Vincenzo's wife and child are doing well.'"

Abby gripped the phone tighter. "This day had to come, the one the three of us talked about a year ago, when I first met with Michelina and Vincenzo.

But I didn't know then that she would die." Her voice throbbed before breaking down in tears.

"I know this is hard, Abby, but you might take heart in the fact that the paper didn't do a hatchet job on you and your husband. They presented the facts without making judgments, something that is so rare in the media world, I found myself blinking."

"That's because of the publisher's long-standing friendship with the king. I shudder to think what the other newspapers have printed."

"I haven't read anything else except the story in one magazine. Do you remember the one after Michelina's death that said The Prince of Every Woman's Dreams in Mourning?"

"Yes." She'd never forget.

"The quote now reads, 'Hopeful royal women around the world in mourning over prince's marriage to American beauty.'"

Abby groaned. "The truth is, that magazine would have been writing about me if he'd decided to marry Princess Odile."

"But he didn't!" Carolena cried out ecstatically. "Listen to this article from that same magazine. 'Enrico Rozzo, a sailor in the coast guard who was at the scene of the terrible death of Holly Loretto, the mother of then seventeen-year-old Abigail Loretto, said, "Prince Vincenzo thought nothing of his own life when he went in search of Signorina Loretto during the fierce storm. He found her body floating lifeless in a grotto and brought her back to life. His bravery, skill and quick thinking will never be forgotten by the coast guard."'"

Abby's body froze. "How did they get hold of that story?"

"How do they always do it? It's a glowing testimonial to your husband, Abby. He's well loved."

"I know." *By me most of all.* She was blinded by tears, still euphoric after knowing Vincenzo's possession for the first time.

"Just think—he married *you* under threat of losing the throne. Talk about Helen of Troy!"

A chuckle escaped despite Abby's angst. "Will you stop?"

"I always thought you were the most romantic person I ever knew. After what you went through to get that baby here, no one deserves a happier ending more than you."

"I'm not looking very romantic right now." She wiped her eyes. "At my six-week checkup yesterday morning, the doctor told me I'm fifteen pounds overweight. I won't be able to wear that gorgeous yellow dress for at least two months! I look like an albatross!" Carolena's laughter came through the phone.

"A stunning albatross," Vincenzo whispered, sliding his arms around her from behind. She hadn't heard him come in. He was in his robe.

At his touch Abby could hardly swallow, let alone think. "Carolena? Forgive me. I have to go, but I promise to call you soon. You've got to come to the palace and see the baby."

"I can't wait!"

He was kissing the side of her neck, so she couldn't talk.

"Your time is coming."

"When the moon turns blue."

"Carolena, you're being ridiculous."

"A presto."

The second Abby clicked off, Vincenzo took the phone and tossed it onto one of the velvet chairs. He pivoted her around and crushed her against him. "Do you have any idea how wonderful it is to walk into a room, any room, day or night, and know I can do anything I want to you?"

She clung fiercely to him, burying her face in his hair. "I found out how wonderful it was yesterday after you brought me home from my checkup." Heat filled her body as she remembered their lovemaking. She'd responded to him with an abandon that would have been embarrassing if he hadn't been such an insatiable lover. They'd cried out their love for each other over and over during the rapture-filled hours of the night.

"I told the nanny we'd look in on the baby tonight, but for the next eight hours, we're not to be disturbed unless there's an emergency."

"We've got eight hours?" Her voice shook.

His smile looked devilish; he rubbed her arms as a prelude to making love. "What's the matter? It *is* our honeymoon. Are you scared to be alone with me already?"

Her heart was racing. "Maybe."

"Innamorata—" He looked crushed. "Why would you say that?"

She tried to ease away from him, but he wouldn't let her. "I guess it's because the news has gone public about us at last. I don't want you to regret marrying me. What if the parliament votes for you to step down? It's all because of me."

He let out a deep sigh. "Obviously you need more

convincing that I've done exactly what I wanted. Whether I become king one day or not means nothing to me without your love to get me through this life." He kissed her mouth. "Sit on the bed. There's something I want to show you."

While she did his bidding, he pulled the scrapbook from one of his dresser drawers. "I've been busy filling the pages that hadn't been used yet. Take a good long look, and then never again accuse me of regretting the decision I've made."

With trembling hands she turned to the place where she'd put her last entry. On the opposite page were the two ultrasound pictures of the baby. Beneath them was a news clipping of her on the steps of the courthouse the day she'd won the case for Signor Giordano. A quiet gasp escaped her throat as she turned the pages.

Someone had taken pictures of her coming and going from the palace. Pictures of her on the funicular, at the restaurant, the swimming pool, the yacht, the church where she'd worn the hat, pictures on the screen while they'd Skyped. But she cried out when she saw a close-up of herself at the opera. The photo had caught her in a moment of abject grief at the thought of a permanent separation from Vincenzo.

He'd always found a way to her...

Abby could hardly breathe for the love enveloping her. "Darling—" She put the album on the bedside table and turned in his arms. He pulled her on top of him.

"You're the love of my life and the mother of my child. How can you doubt it?" he asked in that low, velvety voice she felt travel through her body like lava, igniting fires everywhere it went.

"I don't doubt you, sweet prince," she whispered

against his lips. "I just want you to know I'll never take this precious love for granted."

"I'm glad to hear it. Now love me, Abby. I need you desperately. Never stop," he cried.

As if she could.

* * * * *

THE PREGNANT
WITNESS

BY
LISA CHILDS

Lisa Childs writes paranormal and contemporary romance for Mills & Boon. She lives on thirty acres in Michigan with her two daughters, a talkative Siamese, and a long-haired Chihuahua who thinks she's a rottweiler. Lisa loves hearing from readers, who can contact her through her website, www.lisachilds.com, or snail-mail address, PO Box 139, Marne, MI 49435, USA.

To Kimberly Duffy-with great appreciation for all
our years of friendship! You're the best!

Chapter One

Gunshots erupted like a bomb blast, nearly shaking the walls of the glass-and-metal building. Through the wide windows and clear doors, Special Agent Blaine Campbell could easily assess the situation from the parking lot. Five suspects, wearing zombie masks and long black trench coats, fired automatic weapons inside the bank. Customers and employees cowered on the floor—all except for the uniform-clad bank security officer.

Blaine had already reported the robbery in progress and had been advised to wait for backup. He wasn't a fool; he could see that he was easily outgunned since he carried only his Glock and an extra clip.

But he left the driver's door hanging open on his rental car and ran across the parking lot crowded with customers' cars. How many potential hostages were inside that bank? How many potential casualties were there, with the way the robbers were firing those automatic weapons? Blaine couldn't wait for help—not when so many innocent people were in danger.

Ducking low, he shoved open the doors and burst into the bank lobby. "FBI!" he called out to calm the fears of the screaming and crying people.

But his entrance incited the robbers. Glass shattered behind him, as bullets whizzed over his head and through the windows, falling like rain over the customers lying faces down on the tile floor. The interior walls, which were glass partitions separating the offices from the main lobby, shattered, as well.

More people screamed and sobbed.

Blaine took cover behind one of the cement-and-steel pillars that held up the high ceiling of the modern building. He held out his hand, advising the customers to stay down as he surveyed them. Except for some cuts from the flying glass, nobody looked mortally wounded. None of the shots had hit anyone. Yet.

"Campbell," the security guard called out from behind another pillar. "You picked the right time to show up." The older man, who was also a friend, had called him here with suspicions that the bank was going to be robbed. Obviously Blaine's former boot-camp drill instructor's instincts were as sharp as ever. He had been right—except about Blaine.

He was too late. The robbers already carried bags overflowing with cash. If only he'd arrived earlier, before they'd gotten what they wanted...

He couldn't arrest them all on his own.

"Stay down!" one of the robbers yelled, as he fired his automatic rifle again.

A woman cried out as another robber tangled a gloved hand in her dark hair and pulled her up from the floor. She was close to one of the wrecked offices, so maybe she worked for the bank or had been meeting with one of the bank officers. She turned toward Blaine, her eyes wide with fear as if beseeching him for help.

But before he could take aim on the robber holding her, the security guard, armed only with a small-caliber handgun, stepped from behind his pillar. "Let her go!" Daryl Williams shouted as he fired at them.

"Sarge, get down," Blaine shouted.

But his advice came too late as a bullet struck the security guard's chest and blood spread across his gray uniform. The woman shrieked—either in reaction to Sarge getting shot or because she was afraid she might be next.

Blaine cursed, stepped out from behind the pillar and fired frantically back. One of the mask-wearing bank robbers spun around, as if Blaine had struck him. But he probably wore a bulletproof vest because he didn't drop to the floor as the guard had. Instead the robber hurried toward the back of the bank with the other zombies. One of them dragged along that terrified young woman. But now she stared back at Sarge instead of Blaine, her gaze full of fear and concern for the fallen security guard. Blaine scrambled over to his friend's side. The man wore his iron-gray hair in a military cut. He may have retired from the service, but he was still a soldier. "Hang in there, Sarge."

"Assist...assist." Daryl Williams tried to speak through the blood gurgling out of his mouth.

"I already called it in when I pulled up and heard the shots. Help is coming," Blaine promised, even though they both knew it would be too late.

Williams weakly shook his head. "Assist...manager..."

"The hostage?"

Daryl nodded even as his eyes rolled back into his head. He was gone.

And so was the woman. Of course Sergeant Williams would want Blaine to rescue her—the civilian. Remembering the stark fear on her pale face, Blaine snapped into action and hurried toward the back of the bank. Alarms wailed and lights flashed as the security door stood open to an alley. If it closed, he wouldn't be able to open it again. That must have been why the robbers had taken their hostage out the back, so she could open the security door for them. But why not leave her? Why take her along?

Blaine caught the door before it swung shut and pointed his gun into the alley. Bullets chiseled chips off the brick around the door as the bank robbers fired at him. If they had a getaway car parked in the alley, they obviously hadn't driven it away yet. He couldn't let them leave with the hostage or else nobody would probably ever see the young woman again. He had barely seen her long enough to give a description beyond dark hair and eyes.

Blaine risked a glance through the crack of the door and more bullets pinged off the steel. But he caught a glimpse of white metal—a van—as the side door opened. Another door slammed. The driver's? He couldn't let them get the hostage inside the vehicle, so he threw the bank door all the way open and burst into the alley. A shot struck him in the chest, but he kept going despite the impact of the bullet hitting his vest.

After his honorable discharge from active duty, he had thought the last thing he would miss was the helmet. He had hated the weight and the heat of it. But he could actually use one now—to protect himself from a head shot. More bullets struck his vest.

He returned fire, his shots glancing off the side of the van before one shattered the glass of the driver's window. Hopefully he'd struck the son of a bitch. But he didn't wait to find out; instead, he reached out for the hostage that one of the damn zombie robbers was pulling through the open side door. He caught the young woman's arm and jerked her backward as he fired into the van. The engine revved, and the vehicle burst forward, tires squealing.

But just in case the occupants fired back at them, he pushed the hostage to the ground and covered the young woman with his body. And that was when he realized she wasn't just terrified for herself but probably also for the child she carried.

She was pregnant.

The van kept going, but someone fired out the open back doors of it. And more bullets struck him, stealing his breath.

MAGGIE JENKINS'S THROAT was raw and her voice hoarse from screaming, but even though the robbers—dressed in those horrible zombie costumes—were gone, she wanted to scream again. She didn't want to scream out of fear for herself but for the man who lay on top of her. His body had gone limp as the breath left it.

He had been shot so many times. But he'd kept coming to her rescue like a golden-haired superhero. And then he'd covered her body with his, taking more shots to his back.

He had to be dead. Why had he interrupted the robbery in progress and risked his own life? He had claimed to be an FBI agent, but why would he have been alone? Why wouldn't he have waited for more agents and for local backup before bursting into the bank?

"Please, please be alive," she murmured, her voice no louder than a whisper. She grasped his shoulders—his impossibly wide shoulders—and eased him back. Something cold and metallic hung from his neck and pressed against her chest. A badge.

So he really was a lawman. But how had he known the bank was being robbed? When the robbers rushed the bank, she hadn't had the time or the nerve to push the silent alarm beneath her desk before bullets had shattered the glass walls of her office.

Maybe one of the tellers or Mr. Hardy, the bank manager, had pushed an alarm. Whatever the FBI agent had driven to the bank hadn't had sirens or lights. She hadn't even known he was there until he pushed open the lobby doors. But, then again, she had hardly been able to hear anything over all of those gunshots. Her ears rang from the deafening noise.

But now she heard his gasp as he caught his breath again. He stared down at her, his face so close that she picked up on all the nuances in his eyes. They were a deep green with flecks of gold that made them glitter. His body, long and muscular, tensed against hers. He moved the hand that was not holding his weapon to the asphalt and pushed up, levering himself off her.

"I'm sorry," he said.

He was apologizing to her? For what? Saving her life? Maybe shock had settled in, or maybe his good looks and his concern had struck her dumb. Usually she wasn't silent; usually people complained that she talked too much.

"Are you all right?" he asked.

Her hands covered her stomach, and something shifted beneath her palm. She sighed with relief that her baby was moving, flailing his tiny fists and kicking his tiny feet as if trying to fight off his mother's attackers.

But it was too late. This man had already fought them off for her. Of course her baby shouldn't be fighting to protect her; it was Maggie's job to protect him or her…

"Are you all right?" the man asked again. He slid his gun into a holster beneath his arm, and then he lifted her from the ground as easily as if she were half her size.

"How are you alive?" she asked in wonder.

He reached for his shirt and tore the buttons loose. The blue cotton parted to reveal a black vest. The badge swung back against it.

She was no longer close enough to read all the smaller print, but she identified the big brass-colored letters. "You really are an FBI agent? I thought you just said that to scare the robbers."

And she'd thought he had been a little crazy to try that when the robbers had had bigger guns than his. But maybe announcing his presence had scared the robbers into leaving quickly because they'd worried that backup would come.

Where was it, though?

"I'm Special Agent Blaine Campbell," he introduced himself.

"How did you get here so quickly?" she asked, still not entirely convinced that he wasn't a superhero. "How did you know the bank was being robbed?"

He shook his head and turned back to the building. "I didn't know that it was being robbed today. Sarge—Daryl Williams—called me a few days ago with concerns."

She gasped as she relived the security guard getting shot, flinching at the sound of the shot, at the image of him falling. He hadn't been wearing a vest, but he'd stepped out from behind that pillar anyway—undoubtedly to save her. "Is Sarge okay?"

The agent shook his head again, but he didn't speak, as if too overwhelmed for words. He had called Mr. Williams *Sarge*, so he must have known him well. Maybe Mr. Williams had once been his drill instructor, as he had been her fiancé's six years ago. The older man worked only part-time at the bank for something to do since he retired from the military.

If only he hadn't been there today...

If only he hadn't tried to save her...

The tears that had been burning her eyes brimmed over and began to slide down her face. She had just lost her fiancé a few months ago, and now she had lost another connection to him because Sarge had really known him. Not only had he trained him, but he'd also kept in touch with Andy over the years. He'd worried about him. He'd known that Andy shouldn't have joined the Marines; he hadn't been strong enough—physically or emotionally—to handle it. He had barely survived his first two deployments, and he had died on the first day of his last one.

Sarge had come for Andy's funeral and never left— intent on taking care of Maggie and her unborn baby since Andy was now unable to.

Strong arms wrapped around her, offering comfort when she suspected he needed it himself. Blaine Campbell had lost a man he'd obviously respected and cared about. So she hugged him back, clinging to him—until tires squealed and the back door of the bank burst open to the alley.

Guns cocked and voices shouted, "Get down! Get down!"

Fear filled her that the robbers had returned. She squeezed her eyes shut. She couldn't look at them again, couldn't see those horrific zombie costumes again. When she and Andy had been in middle school, his older brother had sneaked them into an R-rated zombie movie, and she'd been terrified of them ever since, even to the point where she didn't go to Halloween parties and even hid in the dark so no trick-or-treaters would come to her door.

But they kept coming to her.

Had they returned to make certain she and the agent were dead?

Chapter Two

"Agent Campbell," Blaine identified himself to the state troopers who'd drawn their weapons on him.

While he respected local law enforcement, especially troopers since his oldest sister was one in Michigan, he had met some unqualified officers over the years. So the gun barrels pointing at him and the woman next to him made him nervous. But he refused to get down or allow the pregnant woman to drop to the pavement again, either.

She had already been roughed up enough; her light gray suit was smudged with grease and oil from the alley. Her legs were scraped from connecting with the asphalt earlier. Had he done that when he'd shoved her down? Had he hurt her?

She had also lost a shoe—either in the bank or maybe in the van from which Blaine had pulled her, so she was unsteady on her feet. Or maybe her trembling wasn't because her balance was off but because she was in shock. He kept a hand on her arm, so that she didn't stumble and fall. But she needed more help than a hand to steady her.

"The bank robbers have already left in a white panel van," he continued. "The driver's-side window is broken and the rear taillights have been shot out." He read off the license plate number he'd memorized, as well.

One of the officers pressed the radio on his lapel and called in an APB on the vehicle. "What else can you tell us about the suspects, Agent Campbell?"

Fighting back the grief that threatened to overwhelm him, he replied, "One of them shot the security guard."

"We already have paramedics inside the bank," another officer told him. "They're treating the wounded."

They were too late to help Sarge. The man had died in his arms—his final words urging Blaine to save the assistant bank manager.

"You should have them check out Mrs….?" He turned to the young woman, waiting for her to supply her name. She hadn't offered it when he'd introduced himself earlier.

"Miss," she corrected him, almost absentmindedly. Her dark eyes seemed unfocused, as if she were dazed. "Maggie Jenkins…"

She was single. Now he allowed himself to notice how pretty she was. Her brown hair was long and curly and tangled around her shoulders. Her eyes were wide and heavily lashed. She was unmarried, but she probably wasn't single—not with her being as pretty as she was.

"The paramedics need to check out Miss Jenkins," he told the troopers. "The bank robbers were trying to take her hostage. She could have been hurt." But he might have been the one who'd done it when he had knocked her onto the hard asphalt of the alley.

"She should probably be taken to the hospital," he added. For an ultrasound to check out the well-being of her unborn child, too. But he didn't want to say it out loud and frighten her. The young woman had already been through enough.

The officer pressed his radio again and asked paramedics to come around to the back of the bank. They arrived quickly, backing the ambulance down the alley. A female paramedic pushed a stretcher out the doors and rolled it toward them.

But Miss Jenkins shook her head, refusing treatment. "What about Mr. Williams?" she asked. "He needs your help more than I do."

The paramedic just stared at her.

"The security guard," Miss Jenkins said. "One of the robbers shot him." Her already rough voice squeaked with emotion. "Will he be all right?"

The paramedic hesitated before shaking her head.

Tears spilled from Miss Jenkins's eyes again, trailing down her smooth face. She had cared about Sarge. But Blaine didn't think they could have worked together that long. Sarge had retired from the military only a few short months ago.

Blaine wanted to hold her again, to comfort her as he had earlier. Or had she comforted him? Her arms had slid around him, her curves soft and warm against him. He resisted the urge to reach for her, and instead he released her arm.

"Go with the paramedic," he said. "Let her check you out."

Blaine had questions for the assistant bank manager—so many questions. But his questions would wait until she was physically well enough to answer them.

The troopers immediately began to question Blaine. He had to explain his presence and about Sarge—even while tears of loss stung his eyes. He blinked them back, knowing his former drill instructor would have kicked his butt if he showed any weakness. Sarge had taught all his recruits that a good marine—a strong marine—controlled his emotions. Blaine had already learned that before boot camp, though.

"Why did the security guard call you?" one of the troopers asked.

"I just transferred to the Chicago Bureau office to take over the investigation of the robbers who've been hitting banks in Illinois, Michigan and Indiana." Bank robberies were his specialty. He had a perfect record; no bank robbery he had investigated had gone unsolved, no bank robber unapprehended.

Of course, some robbers were sloppy and desperate and easily caught. Blaine already knew that this group of them—in their trench coats and zombie masks—were not sloppy or desperate. And, therefore, they would not be easily caught. But he would damn well catch them.

For Sarge...

"You think those robberies are related to this one?" the trooper asked.

"I can't make a determination yet." Because he hadn't had a chance to go to the office; his flight had landed only hours ago. But ever since Sarge's call, the urgency in the man's voice had haunted Blaine and made him come here first—with his suitcase in the trunk of a rental car. "I need more information."

And he didn't want to give up too much information to the troopers before he'd verified his facts. He needed to check in with the Bureau, but he couldn't leave the scene yet.

He couldn't leave Maggie Jenkins.

He turned back to where the paramedic had helped her into the back of the first-responder rig. A man in a suit was standing outside the doors, talking to her. He'd come through the back door of the bank, so the troopers must have cleared him.

Blaine recognized him as one of the people who'd been lying on the floor, cowering from the robbers. Instead of checking on her, the man appeared to be questioning her—the way Blaine wanted to. But he wasn't certain she had any more information than he did.

He just wanted to make sure she was all right—that his rescue hadn't done her more harm than being taken hostage had.

MAGGIE WAS FINALLY ALONE. Mr. Hardy, the bank manager, had gone back inside the damaged building to call the corporate headquarters, as she had told him to do. At thirty, he was young and inexperienced for his position, so he had no idea what to do or how to manage after a robbery.

Unfortunately, Maggie did.

She trembled—not with cold or even with fear. She hadn't felt that until the bullet had struck Sarge, and he had dropped to the floor. Before that, when the gunmen had burst into the lobby wearing those masks and trench coats, she had been too stunned to feel anything at all.

Usually just the sight of those gruesome masks would have filled her with terror, as they had ever since Andy and Mark had sneaked her into that violent horror movie. She'd had nightmares for years over it. But for the past few months she'd been having new nightmares. And while they'd still been about zombies, they hadn't been movie actors—they'd been about *these* zombies.

"I can't believe it," she murmured to herself. "I can't believe it happened. Again…"

And it was that disbelief that had overwhelmed her fear—until Sarge had been shot.

"Are you all right?" a deep voice asked.

Startled, she tensed. It wasn't one of the paramedics. Their voices were higher and less…commanding. Agent Campbell commanded attention and respect and control.

He had taken over the moment he'd burst into the bank with his weapon drawn. He had taken over and saved her from whatever the bank robbers had planned for her. And he'd taken over the investigation from the state troopers more easily.

She nodded. "I'm okay," she assured him, worried that he might think she was losing it. I always talk to myself. My parents claim I came out talking and never shut up..." But as she chattered, her teeth began to chatter, too, snapping together as her jaw trembled.

The FBI agent lifted the blanket a paramedic had put around her and he wrapped it more tightly—as if he were swaddling a baby. She had taken a class and swaddled a doll, but she hadn't done it nearly as well as he had. Maybe he had children of his own. She glanced down at his hands—his big, strong hands—but they were bare of any rings. Not every married man wore one, though. Her face heated with embarrassment that she'd even looked. His marital status should have been the last thing on her mind.

"Thank you," she said. "I'm fine, really..." But it wasn't cold out. Why was she so deeply chilled that even her bones felt cold? "I can go back inside the bank and help Mr. Hardy—"

"The bank manager," he said.

She'd noticed that he had stopped Mr. Hardy before letting him back inside the bank. And he'd questioned him. She doubted the young manager had been able to provide many answers.

"Yes," she said. "I need to go back inside and help him close up the bank and take inventory for corporate. There's so much to do..." There always was, after a robbery.

"You need to go to the hospital and get checked out,"

Agent Campbell said as he waved over the paramedic. "You should have already taken her."

"She wanted to talk to you first," the female paramedic replied. She'd told Maggie that she wouldn't mind talking to the agent herself, and her male partner had scoffed at her lack of professionalism.

Maggie hadn't intended to go to the hospital at all—not when there was so much to do inside the bank. And Sarge...

Was he still inside?

She shuddered, then shivered harder. And the baby shifted inside her, kicking her ribs. She flinched and nodded. "Maybe I should get checked out..."

For the baby. She had to protect her baby. She had nearly three months left of her pregnancy—three months to keep her unborn child safe. She hadn't realized how hard that might be.

"My questions can wait," the FBI agent told her, "until you've been thoroughly checked out." He turned toward the paramedics. "Which hospital will you take her to?"

"Med West," the woman paramedic replied. "You can ride along and question her in the back of the rig."

Maggie stilled her trembling as she waited for his reply. She wanted him to agree; she felt safer with him close. She felt safe in his arms...

And after what had happened—again—she would have doubted she would ever feel safe. Anywhere.

"Agent Campbell," one of the officers called out to him. He didn't pull his gaze from her, his green eyes intense on her face. The officer continued anyway. "We located the van."

That got the agent's attention; he turned away from her. "And the robbers?"

The officer shrugged. "We don't know if there's anyone inside. Nobody's approached it yet."

Maggie struggled free of the blanket and grabbed the agent's arm—even though she knew she couldn't stop him. He was going.

"Be careful," she advised him.

She had told Andy the same thing when he had left her last, but he hadn't listened to her. She hoped Agent Campbell did. Or the next time the robbers' bullets might miss his vest and hit somewhere else instead.

Agent Campbell barely spared her a nod before heading off with the state troopers. He had been lucky during his first confrontation with the thieves, but Andy had been lucky, too, during his first two deployments.

Eventually, though, luck ran out...

HIS GUN STEADY in one hand, Blaine slid open the side door with the other. But the van was empty. The robbers had ditched it between Dumpsters at the end of an alley.

"This vehicle was reported stolen three days ago," one of the troopers informed him.

Either they'd stolen it themselves or picked it up from someone who dealt in stolen vehicles. It was a lead that Blaine could follow. Maybe someone had witnessed the theft.

They must have exchanged the van for another vehicle they had stashed close to the bank. They'd had to move quickly, though, so they hadn't taken time to wipe down the van.

They had left behind forensic evidence. Blaine could see some of it now. Fibers from their clothes. Hair— either from their masks or their own. And blood. It could have been fake; they'd had some on their gruesome disguises. But that hadn't looked like this.

This blood was smeared and drying already into dark pools.

"You hit one of them?" a trooper asked.

He hoped he'd hit the one who'd killed Sarge. "I fired at them, but I thought they were wearing vests."

"You must be a good shot," the trooper replied.

More likely he had gotten off a lucky shot. He was fortunate one of them hadn't done the same. If they hadn't been worried that he had backup coming, they probably would have killed him the way they had Sarge.

Blaine sighed. "But the suspect wasn't hurt so badly that he couldn't get away." As they had all gotten away. But at least one of them had not been unscathed.

"Put out an APB that one of the suspects might be seeking medical treatment for a gunshot wound," Blaine said, "at a hospital or doctor's office or med center. Hell, don't rule out a vet clinic. These guys will not want the wound getting reported." And doctors were legally obligated to report gunshot wounds.

So he wouldn't worry that he had sent Maggie Jenkins off to the hospital in the back of that ambulance. He wouldn't worry that one of the men who had tried to abduct her earlier might get a chance to try again.

Again...

What had she been muttering when he'd walked up to the ambulance? Her already soft voice had been strained from screaming, so he'd struggled to hear, let alone understand, her words. But she'd murmured something about not believing that it had happened. Again...

Had Maggie Jenkins been the victim of a bank robbery before?

The same bank robbers?

Hell, Blaine was worried now. Not just that she might be in danger but that he might have let the best lead to the robbers ride away. Had he let her big, dark eyes and her fear and vulnerability influence his opinion of her?

What if Maggie Jenkins hadn't been a hostage but a coconspirator?

Maybe Sarge hadn't been trying to tell him to rescue the assistant bank manager. Maybe he had been trying to tell Blaine to catch her.

Chapter Three

Maggie pressed her palms over the hospital gown covering her belly and tried to soothe the child moving inside her. He kept kicking, as though he was still fighting. "I'm sorry, baby," she said. "I know Mama's not doing a very good job of keeping you safe."

But she'd tried.

Why was it that danger kept finding her? She had already changed jobs, or at least locations, but she couldn't afford to quit. Maybe she should have married Andy one of the times he had suggested it. They had been together since middle school, and she'd loved him. But she hadn't been *in* love with him.

"I'm sorry," she said again. But this time she was talking to Andy.

She should have told him the truth, but he'd enlisted right out of high school and she hadn't wanted to be the heartless girlfriend who wrote the Dear John letter. And when he'd come home on leave, she had been so happy to see him—so happy to have her best friend back—that she hadn't wanted to risk losing that friendship.

But eventually she had lost him—to a roadside bomb in Afghanistan. Tears stung her eyes and tickled her nose, but she drew in a shaky breath and steadied herself. She had to be strong—for her baby. Since he had already lost his father, he needed her twice as much.

A hand drew back the curtain of Maggie's corner of the emergency department. The young physician's assistant who'd talked to her earlier smiled reassuringly. "I had a doctor and a radiologist review the ultrasound," the PA said, "and we all agree that your baby is fine."

Maggie released her breath as a sigh of relief. "That's great."

"You, on the other hand, have some bumps and bruises, and your blood pressure is a little high," the PA continued. "So you need to be careful and take better care of yourself."

She nodded in agreement. Not that she hadn't been trying. That had been the whole point of her new job—less stress. But Mr. Hardy wasn't as competent as the manager at the previous branch where she'd worked. And the zombie bank robbers had hit the new bank anyway.

Maybe she would have been safer had she stayed where she'd been. "I will take better care of myself and the baby," Maggie vowed. "Do you know what I'm having?" She had had an ultrasound earlier in her pregnancy, but it had been too soon to tell the gender.

The young woman shook her head. "I wasn't able to tell."

Or she probably would have pointed it out then.

"But maybe the radiologist had an idea." The young woman's face flushed as she glanced down at the notes. "I'm sorry," she said. "I hadn't realized that you'd been at the bank that was robbed and that paramedics had brought you from the scene."

"That's fine," Maggie said. "I should have told you myself." But she hadn't wanted to talk about it—to remember what it had been like to see those gruesome masks again and to watch as one of them killed Sarge. She shuddered.

"Of course your blood pressure would be elevated," the PA continued. "You must have been terrified."

She had been until the FBI agent had saved her. Where was he? He was supposed to come to the hospital to interview her. Hadn't Agent Campbell survived his second run-in with the bank robbers?

"I'll be okay," she assured the physician's assistant. She had survived. Again. Daryl Williams hadn't been as fortunate—because of her. Maybe Agent Campbell hadn't survived, either.

The young woman nodded. "Considering what you've been through, you're doing very well. But I would follow up with your obstetrician tomorrow and make sure your blood pressure goes down."

"I will do that," Maggie promised. She was taking no chances with her pregnancy. She had already lost the baby's father; she wouldn't lose his baby, too.

"You can get dressed now." The young woman passed over some papers. "Here is your release and an ultrasound picture. There isn't any way of telling his or her gender yet."

Maggie stared down at the photo. She had seen her baby on the ultrasound screen this time and the previous time she'd had one. But this was the first photo she'd been given to keep—probably because he looked like a baby now and not a peanut. He or she was curled up on his or her side, and the little mouth was open. She smiled as she remembered her mother claiming that Maggie's mouth had been open during every ultrasound. She'd been talking even before she'd been born.

"Thank you," she told the PA. But she didn't look up. She couldn't take her gaze from the amazing photo of her baby. The child had already survived so much: the loss of a parent and two bank robberies.

"Good luck, Ms. Jenkins," the young woman replied as she pulled the curtain closed again.

Maggie's smile slid off her lips. She was going to need luck to make it safely through her pregnancy and deliver a healthy baby. He was fine now. And she would do everything within her power to keep him that way.

She dressed quickly so that she could pick up and study the picture again. Maybe she should wait for the FBI agent—to make certain that he was all right. It wasn't as if she could leave anyway. Her purse was back at the bank, so she didn't have any money to pay for a cab. And with Mr. Hardy busy with corporate, the only other person she could have called at the bank to bring it to her was dead.

Sarge...

If only he hadn't stepped out from behind that pillar...

If only he hadn't tried to save her...

Tears blurred her vision, but she blinked them back to focus on the baby picture again. She needed to focus on him or her, needed to keep him or her healthy and safe. The baby was her priority.

She would have to find a phone she could use and call a friend to pick her up. But she didn't really know anyone here in this suburb of Chicago. She hadn't known anyone but Sarge. After the bank where she'd previously worked had been robbed, she had transferred to the branch where Sarge worked—thinking she would feel safer with him there. But the danger had followed her and claimed his life—cruelly cutting his retirement short. The tears threatened again, but she fought them. Sobbing would not help her blood pressure.

The curtain moved as a gloved hand pulled it back.

"I'm sorry," she said, feeling guilty for taking up the

area. "I realize you probably need the bed for someone else…" For someone who actually needed medical attention. "I'm all ready to leave." She just needed someone to pick her up. "I can wait in the lobby."

Nobody said anything, though. But she could feel them standing there, watching her. So then she looked up, and her heart began to pound frantically as she stared into the creepy face of one of those horrible zombie masks. It was her nightmare come to life again.

She would have screamed but for the gun barrel pointing directly at her. She already knew that these people had no compunction about killing. They had already killed once and that had been because Sarge had been trying to save her. She couldn't scream and risk someone else getting hurt again. The only reason they would have tracked her down at the hospital was to kill again.

To kill *her*…

BLAINE CURSED HIMSELF as he flipped screens on his tablet. The Bureau had forwarded him the case file for the bank robberies.

Now he knew exactly what Maggie had been muttering in the back of the ambulance—because it had happened again. A different bank. A different city. But the same witness.

Maggie Jenkins had been robbed before—a couple of months ago—at another bank where she'd been working as an assistant manager. What were the odds that the same robbers, wearing zombie masks and black trench coats, would track her down at another bank in another city? Maybe it was a coincidence, but in his years with the Bureau, Blaine had found few true coincidences.

It was more likely that they knew her. And if they knew her, she knew them. He'd had a lot of questions for

Maggie Jenkins before; now he had even more. And he wouldn't let her tear-damp dark eyes or her sweet vulnerability distract him again.

He dropped the tablet onto the passenger seat and threw open the driver's door. After clicking the locks, he hurried across the parking lot to the hospital. He sidestepped through the automatic doors before they were fully open and flashed his badge at the security guard standing inside the doors. "I'm looking for a witness who was brought here from a bank-robbery scene. Maggie Jenkins."

After waving him through the blinking, beeping metal detector, the guard pointed toward the emergency-department desk. Blaine showed his badge to the receptionist. "I need to talk to Maggie Jenkins—from the bank robbery."

The older woman stared at his badge before nodding. "Nyla can show you where she is."

A young nurse stepped from behind the desk and pushed open swinging doors. "Ms. Jenkins is behind the last curtain on the left."

He followed the woman's directions, past a long row of pulled curtains, and he pulled aside the very last curtain on the left. The bed was empty but for a black-and-white photo. Maggie was gone. He picked up the photo and recognized it as an ultrasound picture. His older sisters had shown him a few over the past ten years. He'd thought they looked like Rorschach tests. They had all prized them.

No matter what her involvement was in the robberies, Maggie Jenkins wouldn't have willingly left that photo behind. He reached for his holster and whirled around to the nurse who'd followed him. "She's gone."

Unconcerned, the young woman shrugged. "She was cleared to get dressed and leave."

"She came by ambulance and didn't have her purse," he said. "She couldn't have left on her own." Not with no car and no money for a cab. At the very least, she would have had to call someone to pick her up. But then, why wouldn't she have taken the ultrasound photo with her? "Did you see anyone come back here?"

Metal scraped against metal as another curtain was tugged back, its rings scraping along the rod. A little girl, propped against pillows in a bed, peered out at Blaine. "The monster came for her."

His skin chilled as dread chased over him. "What monster?"

An older woman, probably the little girl's mother, was sitting in a chair next to the bed. With a slight smile, she shook her head. "It wasn't a monster. Just someone wearing a silly Halloween mask."

"But it's not Halloween," the little girl said, as if she suspected her mother was lying and that the monster was very real.

Blaine was worried that the monster was real, too. "Was it a zombie mask that the person was wearing?"

The woman shrugged. "I don't know."

But the little girl's already pale face grew even paler with fear as she slowly nodded. "It was a really creepy zombie. He was wearing a long black coat."

Blaine's dread spread the chill throughout him. He bit back a curse. One of the robbers had tracked her down at the hospital?

The woman shrugged again. "He put his fingers to his lips, so that we wouldn't say anything. He was just playing a joke."

Apparently the woman hadn't seen any of the news coverage about the zombie robbers.

The nurse shook her head in vigorous denial of the

little girl's claim. "I didn't see anyone dressed like that in this area, and the security guard wouldn't have let him through the front doors."

"What about the back doors?" he asked. "Could someone have come in another way?"

"Only employees can," the nurse replied.

He doubted that employees had to go through a metal detector the way visitors had to. "Show me."

The nurse stepped around the curtain to show Blaine another set of double doors on that end of the emergency department—just a few feet from where Maggie had been. If the robber had come through those doors, no one would have seen him but Maggie and apparently the little girl next to her. He wouldn't have gone through security if he'd come in the employee entrance. The nurse had to swipe her ID card to open those doors. They swung into an empty corridor.

"How would someone get to the parking lot from here?" he asked.

With a sigh of exasperation, as if he was wasting her time, she turned left and continued down the corridor to a couple of single doors. "The locker rooms have doors to a back hallway that leads to the employee parking lot," she said in anticipation of his next questions. "But it's too soon for a shift change, so nobody's back here now."

But a noise emanated from behind one of the doors. A thump. And then a scream pierced the air. Blaine grabbed the nurse's ID badge and swiped it through the lock. As he pushed open the door, shots rang out. A bullet struck him—in the vest over his heart. The force of it knocked him against the door and forced the breath from his lungs.

The nurse cried and ran back down the corridor. Then another scream rang out—from Maggie Jenkins. She had fallen to her knees. But the bank robber had a gloved hand in her hair, trying to pull her up—trying to drag her to that door at the back of the locker room—the door that would lead to the employee parking lot.

How did he know where to take her? How did he have the access badge to do it? He must either be an employee of the hospital or he knew an employee very well.

Ignoring the pain she must have been in from that hand in her hair, Maggie wriggled and reached as she continued to scream for help. But she didn't wait for Blaine's help. She tried to help herself. She grabbed at the benches between the rows of lockers and at the lockers, too, as she tried to prevent the robber from dragging her off. She flailed her arms and kicked, too, desperately trying to fight off her attacker. But then the gun barrel swung toward her face and she froze.

Was the robber just trying to scare her into cooperating? Or did he intend to kill her right here, in front of Blaine?

Chapter Four

Maggie couldn't breathe; she couldn't move. She couldn't do anything but stare down the barrel of the gun that had been shoved in her face.

Agent Campbell had stepped inside the room, but then a shot had slammed him back against the door. Wasn't he wearing his vest anymore? Was he hurt?

Or worse?

She wanted to look, but she was frozen with fear. Because she was about to be *worse*, too. With the barrel so close to her face, there was no way the bullet could miss her head. She was about to die.

In her peripheral vision, she was aware of the gloved finger pressing on the trigger. And she heard the shot. It exploded in the room, shattering the silence and deafening her. But she felt no pain. Neither did she fall. She still couldn't move. Apparently she couldn't feel, either.

But the gun moved away from her face. With a dull thud, it dropped to the floor. And the robber fell, too, backward over one of the benches in what appeared to be the employee locker room.

The robber had forced her to be quiet while they'd been in Emergency—because he'd kept the barrel of the gun tight against her belly. He would have killed her baby if she'd called out for help. But when he'd brought her to this locker room, he'd had to move the gun away to swipe the badge. And so, as the doors were closing behind them, she'd risked calling out.

But she hadn't expected Agent Campbell to come to her aid again. He must have recovered from the shot that had knocked him back because now he started forward again, toward the robber. But he stopped to kick away the gun, and the robber vaulted to his feet. He picked up one of the benches and hurled it at the FBI agent. It knocked Blaine Campbell back—into Maggie.

She fell against the lockers, the back of her head striking the metal so hard that spots danced before her eyes. Her vision blurred. Then her legs, already shaking with her fear, folded under her, and she slid down to the floor.

While the bench had knocked over the agent, he hadn't lost his grip on his gun. And he fired it again at the robber. The man flinched at the impact of the bullet. But like the agent, he must have worn a vest because the shot didn't stop him. But he didn't fight anymore. Instead he turned and ran.

"Stop!" the agent yelled.

But the man in the zombie mask didn't listen, or at least he didn't heed the command in Agent Campbell's voice as everyone else had. He pushed open the back door with such force that metal clanged as it struck the outside wall. Then the man ran through that open door.

Campbell jumped up, but instead of heading off in pursuit of the robber, he turned back to her and asked, "Are you all right?"

The gunfire echoed in her ears yet, so his deep voice sounded far away. She couldn't focus on it; she couldn't focus on him, either.

But his handsome face came closer as he dropped to

his knees in front of her. His green eyes full of concern and intensity, he asked, "Maggie, are you all right?"

No. She couldn't speak, and she was usually never at a loss for words. Her heart kept racing even though the robber and his gun were no longer threatening her. In fact, the more she stared into the agent's eyes, the faster her heart beat. The green was so vibrant—like the first leaves on a tree in spring. Just as she had been unable to look anywhere but the barrel of the gun in her face, she couldn't look away from the agent's beautiful eyes.

"Maggie..." Fingers skimmed along her cheek. "Are you all right?"

She opened her mouth, but no words slipped out. Her pulse quickened, and her breath grew shallower— so shallow that she couldn't get any air. And then she couldn't see Agent Campbell any longer as her vision blurred and then blackened.

BLAINE SHOULD HAVE been in hot pursuit of the robber. He should have been firing shots and taking him down in the parking lot. Instead he was standing over a pregnant woman, waiting for her to regain consciousness. And as he waited, he drew in some deep breaths—hoping to ease the tightness in his chest.

The intern, who had come running, along with the security guards, when Blaine had yelled for medical help, assured him that she was fine. She and her baby were fine. She must have just hyperventilated. And with someone shooting at her, it was understandable—or so the intern had thought.

Blaine wasn't sure what to think. Had she really passed out? Or had she only staged a diversion so the robber could get away from him and those guards that nurse Nyla had called to the locker room?

But then, if Maggie was an accomplice, why had she fought the man so hard? Why had she looked so terrified?

His older sisters had pulled off drama well in their teens. They'd worked their parents to get what they wanted, so he'd seen some pretty good actresses work their manipulations up close and personal. But if Maggie Jenkins had been acting in the locker room, she surpassed his sisters.

"Who are you really, Maggie Jenkins?" he wondered aloud. Innocent victim or criminal mastermind?

Her thick, dark lashes fluttered against her cheeks, as if she'd heard him and his words had roused her to consciousness. She blinked and stared up at him, looking as dazed and shocked as she had when she'd fallen against the lockers.

When he'd inadvertently knocked her against them. A pang of guilt had him flinching, and he fisted his hands to keep them from reaching for her belly to check on the baby. It had been real to him even before he'd seen the picture, but now it was even more real.

"The doctor said you and your baby are not hurt," he assured her. And himself.

"Are you okay?" she asked, and her brown eyes softened with concern.

He shrugged off her worry. "I'm fine."

He would probably have a bruise where the bench had clipped his shoulder, but his physical well-being was the least of his concerns right now.

She stared up at him, her smooth brow furrowing slightly, as if she doubted his words. "Really?"

No. He was upset about Sarge. And he was frustrated as hell that he'd lost one of the leads to Sarge's killer—or maybe the actual killer himself—when the robber had run out the employee exit to the parking lot. But Blaine had another lead—one he didn't intend to let out of his sight.

"I'm worried about you," he admitted. For so many reasons…

She tensed and protectively splayed her hands over her belly. "You said the baby isn't hurt."

"The baby is fine," he assured her. "And so are you."

She stared up at him again, this time full of doubt.

So he added, "For now."

Despite the blanket covering her, she shivered at his foreboding tone.

"You're obviously in danger," he said, "since one of the robbers risked coming here to abduct you from the ER." Or had she called him? Had she wanted to be picked up before Blaine could question her further?

He needed to take her down to the Bureau, or at least the closest police department for an interrogation. But if he started treating her like a suspect, she might react like one and clam up or lawyer up. Maybe it was better if he let her continue to play the victim…

But her eyes—those big, dark eyes—didn't fill with tears this time. Instead her gaze hardened and she clenched her delicate jaw. Angrily she asked, "Why won't they leave me alone?"

"I'm not sure why you were tracked down at the hospital today," he replied.

Could it have been another coincidence? Could the robber have been here to get treatment for the gunshot wound Blaine had inflicted and then stumbled upon her?

But the robber hadn't seemed injured—especially since he'd had the strength to hurl the bench with such force at Blaine. And he'd been fighting with Maggie before that. Maybe he wasn't the injured robber, but had been bringing that one for treatment…

But where was that person?

He'd already lost so much blood in the van.

"Why did one of them come here?" she asked—the same question Blaine had been asking himself. "What do they want with *me*?"

That was another question Blaine had been asking himself. "Maybe you saw or heard something back at the bank," he suggested, "something that might give away the identity of one of them?"

She shook her head. "I couldn't see any of their faces. They wore those horrible masks…" And she shuddered.

"What about their voices?"

"Only one of them spoke at the bank," she said, "and I didn't recognize his voice."

Did the others not speak because she would have recognized one of their voices? And now he wondered about the father of her baby…

But wouldn't she have recognized him despite the disguise? Wouldn't she have recognized his build, his walk, any of his mannerisms? Or maybe she had but wasn't about to implicate him and possibly herself.

Blaine waited, hoping that she would voluntarily admit to having been robbed before. But if she'd been about to confess to anything, she was interrupted when the hospital security chief approached.

The chief was a woman—probably in her fifties, with short gray hair and a no-nonsense attitude. Blaine had been impressed when he'd spoken with her earlier when she'd joined her security guards in the locker room. She was furious that someone had brought a gun into the hospital and nearly abducted one of the patients.

"Agent Campbell," Mrs. Wright said. "As you requested, I have all the footage pulled up from the security cameras."

"Thank you," he said. "That was fast." Hopefully one of those cameras had caught the robber without his hideous disguise. But Blaine hesitated again.

"The security room is this way," Mrs. Wright said, making a gesture for him to follow her from the emergency department.

But he didn't want to leave Maggie Jenkins alone and unprotected. "Do you have a guard that you can post here with Ms. Jenkins?"

Mrs. Wright nodded. "Of course. The police are here now, too. Sergeant Torreson is waiting in the security room to meet with you."

He needed Sergeant Torreson posted by Maggie Jenkins's bed, so that nobody could get to her. And so that she couldn't get away before she finally and truthfully answered all his questions. "Is he the only officer?"

Because he really didn't want to use one of the security guards—not when the zombie robber had to either be an employee or be close friends with an employee. He couldn't trust anyone who worked for the hospital. Not a doctor, nurse or even a security guard...

Mrs. Wright gestured to where a young policeman stood near the nurse who'd brought Blaine back to the employee locker room. He wasn't sure if the man was interrogating or flirting with her, so he waved him over to Maggie's bedside. "I'm Agent Campbell."

"Yes, sir," the young man replied. "We're aware you're the FBI special agent in charge of the investigation into the bank robberies."

Blaine studied the kid's face, looking for the familiar signs of resentment from local law enforcement. But he detected nothing but respect. The tightness in his chest eased slightly. He had backup, and given how relentless the bank robbers were, he needed it.

Of course, he could have called in more agents. Immediately after the robbery, he'd checked in, and the Bureau chief had offered him more FBI resources. But

Blaine had thought the bank robbers gone—the immediate threat over—until he'd come to the hospital and nearly lost the witness. But was Maggie a witness or an accomplice?

"Officer, this is Maggie Jenkins, the woman who was nearly abducted," he introduced them. "I need you posted here to protect her until I come back."

"I'll be fine," Maggie said. "I'll be safe." But her hands trembled as she splayed them across her belly again. She was either afraid or nervous. "I'll be safe," she repeated, as if trying to convince herself.

"We can't be certain of that," Blaine said. After all, the robbers kept returning...for her.

She slowly nodded in agreement, and tears welled now in her dark eyes. The tightness returned to his chest. But, growing up with three older and very dramatic sisters, he should have been immune to tears—especially since Maggie actually looked more frustrated than sad. But something about the young woman affected him and brought out his protective instincts.

But maybe the person he needed to protect when it came to Maggie Jenkins was himself.

"Be vigilant," Blaine advised the young officer. "For some reason these guys keep coming after her." And he intended to find out that reason. But he suspected he could learn more from the footage than he could Maggie Jenkins. She obviously wasn't being forthcoming with him.

So he headed to the surveillance room. But his mind wasn't on the footage he watched or on the police sergeant's questions, either. The hospital was a busy one—with so many people coming and going that it wouldn't be easy to determine which one might have walked in as himself and emerged as a zombie robber.

That was the only footage in which he could positively identify the person—as he burst through the back door and ran across the employee parking lot. But he kept the disguise on even as he jumped into an idling vehicle.

The sergeant cursed. "These guys—with those damn silly Halloween masks—have hit two banks in my jurisdiction."

As the vehicle, another van, turned, the driver came into view of the camera. But they must have known that camera would be there because the driver wore one of those damn masks, too.

"I want you to review your employees," Blaine told the hospital security chief. "Find out who wasn't working today."

"The hospital has hundreds of full- and part-time employees," Mrs. Wright said. "That'll take some time."

"*Your* employees," Blaine said. "I want you to focus on the security staff." He was really glad that he hadn't left Maggie Jenkins in the protection of one of the hospital guards.

"You think it's one of my people?" Mrs. Wright asked—with all the resentment he usually confronted with local law enforcement.

He pointed toward the masked men. "They knew where the cameras are—they knew how to get a gun in and out. They were familiar with employee-only areas of the hospital."

"But…" The woman's argument sputtered out as she grimly accepted that he was right.

Blaine turned toward the police officer. "I'd like you to bring in more officers, Sergeant. And check out anyone on that footage who walked in carrying a bag or a suitcase—anything big enough to carry that disguise and a weapon."

The woman sighed. "There is a metal detector at the front door."

Blaine was well aware of that—since he'd had to have a security guard wave him through it. But he'd wanted the security chief to come on her own to the same realization that he had. It had to be one of her people. But that didn't mean another robber hadn't come through the front door—an injured one.

"It'll still take me some time," she said. "We have three shifts, and since we have some trouble with gangs in this area, we have several guards on staff."

"Check out ex-staff, too," Blaine suggested.

"I'll help you," the sergeant offered.

He wanted the robbers, as well. But he didn't want them as badly as Blaine did. One of them had killed his friend and former mentor. Blaine couldn't let them get away with that—with ending what should have been Sarge's golden years way too soon.

"I have one of your officers helping me now," Blaine told the sergeant. "He's guarding the hostage for me."

The sergeant winced. "That kid's a trainee and easily distracted."

Blaine cursed and rushed out of the security room. He had wasted too much time on footage that had revealed no clues when he should have been interrogating his only concrete lead. But when he returned to the emergency department, he found the young officer flirting with the nurse once again.

And he found the bed where he'd left Maggie Jenkins empty. She was gone. Either she'd been grabbed again, or she'd escaped...

Chapter Five

Even though they had left the hospital a while ago, Special Agent Campbell had yet to speak to her. He only spared her a glare as he drove. The man was furious with her. A muscle twitched along his jaw, and his gaze was hot and hard. Maggie found his anger nearly as intimidating as his devastating good looks. But she couldn't understand why he was mad at her. Unless...

His stare moved off her to focus on the road again. He hadn't said where he was taking her. She had foolishly just assumed it would be to her apartment. Now she wasn't so certain...

Her wrists were bare; he hadn't cuffed her. She sat in the passenger's seat next to him—not in the back. But was he arresting her?

"Do you think I'm involved in the robberies?" she asked. "Is that why you were so upset when you couldn't find me at the hospital?"

That muscle twitched in his cheek again. "When you were gone, I assumed the worst."

The worst to her would have been one of the robbers in the creepy zombie mask returning. But she wasn't convinced that Agent Campbell thought the same.

"Is that really what you thought?" she asked. "That

one of them had come back for me? Or had you thought that I'd taken off on my own?"

"I thought you were gone," he said, which didn't really answer her question. "And I had left that young officer to protect you…"

"I was only using the restroom," she reminded him. "And he couldn't go into the ladies' with me." She had stepped out of the room to raised voices in the ER. For a moment she'd feared that one of the robbers had returned… until she'd recognized the voices.

At first she had been touched that Agent Campbell had been concerned about her. But he hadn't been relieved that she was okay; he had stayed angry. Even after checking her out of the hospital and seeing her safely to his vehicle, he was still angry.

"You do suspect that I'm involved in the robberies," she said, answering her own question.

"Robberies?" he queried, his tone guarded. But then, everything about Special Agent Blaine Campbell was guarded and hard to read—except for the grief he'd felt over Sarge's death. It had been easy to see his pain.

"They've robbed more than one bank," she said. "But you know that…" Or the FBI wouldn't have taken over the case. She suspected he was also aware of something else, too. "You probably know that they robbed the other branch of this bank where I previously worked."

"And then they followed you to the bank where you're working now…" His tone was less guarded now and more suspicious.

Of her?

Her stomach pitched. She hadn't had morning sickness even in her first trimester, so that wasn't the problem. It was nerves. He obviously did suspect that she was involved in the robberies.

"They have robbed a lot of other banks that I haven't worked at," she pointed out.

"How do you know that?" he asked, as if she had somehow slipped up and implicated herself. "How do you know how many other banks have been robbed?"

"From the news," she said. "They've even made national broadcasts. And our corporate headquarters sends out email warnings about robberies at other branches or other banks in the area. So it was just a coincidence that they hit both banks where I've worked."

A horrible coincidence—that was what she'd been trying to tell herself since the robbers, in those grotesque disguises, had burst through the doors of the bank earlier that afternoon.

"They have robbed other banks," he agreed. "But you're the only hostage they've tried taking. They didn't abduct anyone from any other bank."

She shuddered. "That was just today…" They hadn't tried to take her last time; they'd only had her open the security door to the alley. Then they'd left.

"So what was different about today?" he asked.

"You." He was the first thing that came to mind. Actually, since he'd saved her from being kidnapped the first time, Special Agent Blaine Campbell—with his golden-blond hair and intense green eyes—hadn't left her mind. Then he'd saved her a second time…

That muscle twitched again in his cheek, which was beginning to grow dark with stubble a few shades darker than his blond hair. "I wasn't the only thing different about today."

She uttered a ragged sigh and blinked back the tears that threatened as she remembered what else had been different. "They killed Sarge."

"Until today they hadn't killed anyone," he said. "Do you know what that means?"

She shook her head. She didn't know how a person could take another life for any reason. That was why she hadn't been able to understand Andy's insistence on joining the military. He had always been so sensitive. He had never even hunted and had been inconsolable when he'd accidentally struck and killed a deer with his truck.

Agent Campbell answered his own question, his voice threatening. "It means that whoever has been helping them will face murder charges, as well."

So he didn't think she was only a thief; he thought she was a killer, too. Anger coursed through her. She was the one who was mad now.

"Sarge was my friend," she said. "And what today means to me is that I lost a friend. I thought it meant the same to you. I thought you knew him and cared about him."

His teeth sank into his lower lip and he nodded. "That's why I want to find out who killed him and bring them to justice. All of them."

Her anger cooled as she realized she had no right to it. Agent Campbell was only doing his job, and not just because it was his job but because he'd cared about Sarge. And if she were him, she might have suspected her, too. She had been at the scene of two robberies.

She reached across the console and touched his hand. But it tensed beneath hers, tightening around the steering wheel. "I'm sorry," she said. "I understand that you have to question me. I just wish I could be more help for your investigation. I really don't have any idea who the robbers are."

He tugged his hand from beneath hers and reached

for the shifter, putting the car in Park after pulling into a space in the parking lot of her apartment complex.

She breathed a soft sigh of relief. He hadn't arrested her after all. He had actually brought her home. But she wasn't foolish enough to think that he no longer suspected her of being involved.

Was HE BEING a fool? Blaine silently asked himself. Probably.

He should have taken her down to the Bureau or a local police department for questioning. But she was already trembling with exhaustion and dark circles rimmed her dark eyes. He wasn't heartless, but he hoped she wasn't playing him.

Maggie Jenkins had a sincerity and vulnerability that made him want to believe her and to believe that she was just an innocent victim.

Like Sarge...

He flinched over the loss of his friend. Instead of dealing with that death, he'd been busy trying to prevent another—to make sure that Maggie Jenkins stayed safe. He'd believed that was what Sarge had wanted. But what if his old friend had been trying to tell him something else about the assistant bank manager?

That she wasn't just involved in the robberies but maybe that she'd plotted them?

Her fingers trembled as she fumbled with the seat belt. Was she exhausted or was she nervous that he was questioning her? Or nervous that he'd brought her here?

He turned off the car, opened his door and hurried around the car to open hers. She was still having trouble with the seat belt, so he reached across her, brushed her fingers aside and undid the clasp. But now he was too close to her, too close to the curly hair that tumbled around her shoulders, to the big brown eyes staring up at him—to the full breasts that pushed against the thin material of her blouse. He'd never considered a pregnant woman sexy...until now. Until Maggie Jenkins...

Something shifted beneath his arm, which was pressed to her belly, as if her baby was kicking him for the thoughts he was entertaining. He jerked back and stepped away from the car. She slid her legs out first. Since she'd lost her shoe earlier, she wore slippers from the hospital. But she didn't need to wear heels for her legs to look long and sexy.

Remembering how his sisters had struggled to get out of cars while they were pregnant, he reached out to help her. She clutched his hand but barely applied any pressure to pull herself up. And then she was standing right in front of him, so close that her breasts nearly brushed against his chest.

She tugged her hand free of his, and a bright pink color flushed her face. "I—I don't have my purse," she said. "I don't have my keys to get inside."

"You live alone?"

"Now I do," she replied. "But I can get an extra key from my super." She glanced up to the darkening sky. "If he's still awake..."

"You don't live with the baby's father anymore?" He told himself he was asking only because of the case, but he really wanted to know for himself.

She shook her head. "I never did..." And there was something in her voice and her expressive eyes...an odd combination of guilt and grief.

Blaine wanted to ask more questions but Maggie was walking away from him. His skin chilled. It could have been because of the cool wind that was kicking up as night began to fall. It could have been because he had an odd sense of foreboding—the same sense he'd had as he'd driven up to the bank during a robbery in progress.

He glanced around the parking lot. The complex was big—an L-shaped, four-story redbrick building, so there were a lot of vehicles parked in the lot. Quite a few of them were vans. Could one of them have been from the hospital? Could the robbers have followed them here?

He hurried and closed the distance between them, keeping his body between hers and the exposure to the parking lot. His hand was also on his holster, ready to pull his weapon should he need it.

Maggie rapped her knuckles hard against the door of a first-floor apartment. "My super's a little hard of hearing," she explained.

It took a couple more knocks before the door opened. A gray-haired man grinned at her. "Hey, Miss Maggie, what can I help you with?"

"Hi, Mr. Simmons. I left my purse at work," she said but spared him the details of why. "I'm so forgetful these days." She'd actually had other matters on her mind, but again she didn't share those with the older man. "So I need the extra key to my apartment, please."

His gray-haired head bobbed in a quick nod. "Of course I'll get that for you. Who's your friend?" His cloudy blue eyes narrowed as he studied Blaine. Apparently Blaine wasn't the only one in whom Maggie brought out protectiveness.

"Blaine Campbell. He's an old friend," she said, easily uttering the lie.

What else had she lied about?

The older man nodded again, accepting her explanation. "I'll be right back with the key."

After he disappeared, she turned toward Blaine and explained. "I didn't want to worry him. He knows the bank I worked at in Sturgis was robbed, so I told him I left the banking business."

"What does he think you do now?" he wondered.

"He thinks I work in an insurance office," she said, "which isn't really a lie since the bank does offer insurance policies."

Keys jangled as the old man returned to the doorway. "Have you checked on that renter's policy for me yet, Maggie?" he asked.

"Yes," she replied. "I'll bring that quote home tomorrow." She held out her hand for the key, but the gray-haired janitor glanced at Blaine again.

"You're an old friend of hers?" he asked with curiosity instead of doubt.

Blaine just nodded.

"Then you must've known her Andy?"

Andy? Was that the father of her baby? Blaine just nodded again.

"Thought you looked like you might've been a marine, too," the old guy said with another bob of his head.

"I was, sir," Blaine replied, and the admission reminded him of the man who had made him a marine. Sarge... "I served two tours."

"That's how you knew Sarge," Maggie said, softly enough that the older man probably didn't even hear her. "He was your drill sergeant?"

Blaine nodded. As a drill instructor, Sarge had been tough but fair. And he'd been a good and loyal friend.

"Glad you made it home, boy," Mr. Simmons said and reached out to pat Blaine's shoulder. "Too bad her fiancé didn't..."

"Andy," Blaine murmured, and the older man nodded again. Shocked and full of sympathy for her, Blaine turned toward Maggie. Earlier she'd told him that she was single, but she hadn't told him why. She hadn't said that her fiancé died before they could marry.

Her lashes fluttered furiously as she fought back tears over the loss of her baby's father. The hand she held out for the key began to tremble slightly. "Thank you for letting me use your spare, Mr. Simmons."

Finally the old man handed over the key she'd been waiting for. The second she closed her fingers around it, she rushed off toward the other end of the complex.

With a nod at the older man, Blaine hurried after her, careful to keep looking around to make sure nobody had followed them—the way someone must have followed the ambulance to the hospital.

But why?

If Maggie really had no idea who the robbers were, why had they wanted to kidnap her so desperately that they hadn't tried just once but twice?

Blaine stopped at the door where Maggie had stopped, her hand with the key outstretched toward the lock. She gasped. Hearing the fear in her voice, Blaine reached for his gun and pulled it from the holster.

Then he closed his free hand around Maggie's shoulder. She tensed and gasped again. Peering around her, he saw what she had—that the door to her apartment stood ajar. Since Maggie had said she lived alone now, someone must have broken in.

A thud emanated from the crack in the door. Whoever had broken in was still there. Waiting for Maggie…

Chapter Six

Like a rowboat riding on high waves, Maggie's stomach pitched as fear and nerves overwhelmed her. It was bad enough that the zombie robbers had tracked her down at the new bank branch where she worked and at the hospital where she'd been treated after the robbery. But had they now found out where she lived?

"Someone's inside," she whispered in horror.

But Blaine Campbell had already figured that out since he held his gun, the barrel pointing toward that crack in the door. He stood between her and her apartment. Between her and danger. "Go back to Mr. Simmons's apartment," he told her. "And stay there until I come for you."

She would have asked where he was going. But she knew. He had already walked into one robbery in progress today. So why wouldn't he walk into another?

Because he could get killed. Her hand automatically reached out with the impulse to hold him back—to protect him. But he was already pushing open the door a little farther and turning sideways as if to squeeze through. He turned back to her, his green gaze intense. "Go back to Mr. Simmons and call the police."

"Call them now," she urged him. "Don't go in there alone." As he had earlier…

He'd been lucky that the robbers hadn't killed him. If they hadn't been intent on getting away, they may have killed him just the way they had killed poor Sarge. If they'd kept shooting at him, they would have hit him where the vest wouldn't have protected him.

Dismissing her concern, he replied, "I'll be fine."

That was probably what Sarge had thought, too, when he showed up for work that morning. That he would be fine. But he hadn't. And she worried that neither would Agent Campbell.

"I'll be fine as long as you get out of here," he continued. "Now."

She had noticed and admired his commanding presence earlier. Now that it was directed at her, she resented it a bit. And she resented even more that she hurried to obey his command, turning away to head back to Mr. Simmons's apartment.

The minute the nearly deaf super let her inside, she would call the police. But they wouldn't arrive in time to help Agent Campbell. He was already stepping inside her apartment, already facing down danger.

Alone.

As Maggie lifted her hand to knock on the super's door, she heard the scream. It was high-pitched and full of fear.

THE WOMAN'S SCREAM caught Blaine off guard. He'd expected a masked robber. Or at least an armed threat. Instead he walked inside to find a woman—dressed like Maggie in a dark suit—rifling through the drawers of the dresser in what must have been Maggie's bedroom. Instead of being a peaceful oasis, it was full of color— oranges and greens and yellows. It was lively and vibrant, like her personality, except for those times when she'd been too scared to speak. It was also messy, but that might have been because of this woman rifling through Maggie's things.

"Who are you?" he asked, even though the blond-haired woman looked vaguely familiar. Where had he seen her before? The security footage from the hospital?

Could it have been a woman who had tried to abduct Maggie earlier? He doubted that a woman could have hurled the locker room bench with enough force to knock him down, but maybe that was just his ego talking. At the bank there had been one robber smaller than the others. He hadn't given it any thought then, because it could have been a short man. But it could have been a woman.

She just stared at him—her eyes wide with fear and guilt. She didn't hold a gun this time, though. Instead she held a velvet jewelry case in her hand.

"Who are you?" he repeated.

"It's Susan Iverson," another woman answered for her.

Wearing those damn slippers had made Maggie's footsteps silent—so silent that she would have been able to get the jump on him had she been one of the robbers. Hell, he had only her word that she wasn't one of them.

"Susan works at the bank, too. She's a teller," Maggie said, explaining how she knew the woman. "What are you doing here?"

"You left your purse at the bank," Susan replied. "I was bringing it back for you."

"And going through my stuff?"

Maggie was asking the questions he should have been asking. But her sudden nearness had distracted him—not so much that he had lowered the gun, though. He kept it trained on the obvious intruder.

"You used Ms. Jenkins's key to let yourself inside her

apartment?" he asked now. "That's still breaking and entering, you know."

"I used to live with her," Susan replied. She stared up at Blaine through her lashes, as if trying to flirt with him. "You're the FBI agent who rescued us this afternoon from those awful robbers."

"Yes, and you haven't answered the question." She hadn't answered any of the questions—neither had she dropped that little jewelry box.

He'd thought the robbers must have had an inside man. And maybe that thought had been right. Thinking Maggie was their accomplice was what had been wrong.

"You don't live with me anymore," Maggie said. "So you had no right to let yourself into my place." Her voice, usually so soft and sweet, was now sharp with anger and dislike.

"I brought your purse to you," Susan said again, as if she'd been doing Maggie a favor.

"You could have left it with the super," Blaine pointed out, "instead of letting yourself inside. What are you doing here, Ms. Iverson?"

At the moment she was trying to flirt with him—as if that could distract him from what she'd done now and what she might have done earlier. He'd never let a pretty face distract him...before Maggie.

The blonde smiled. "I was searching for clues," she said. "This is the second bank Maggie's worked at that's been robbed. Don't you think that's suspicious, Agent Campbell?"

A hiss accompanied the quick release of Maggie's breath—as if she'd been punched in the stomach. Maybe the baby had kicked her. Or maybe this woman casting suspicions her way had shocked her.

He had come up with suspicions about Maggie on his

own, but he wasn't about to admit it to this woman. At the moment she had become the better suspect. "I think your behavior is questionable right now, Ms. Iverson."

"You caught me—" she fluttered her lashes again "—playing amateur sleuth. I was only trying to help the bank recover the money that was stolen."

He wasn't charmed in the least by her coy attitude. "And you think hundreds of thousands of dollars are in that small jewelry case?"

She glanced down at it, as if just realizing it was in her hand. And she shook her head. Blond hair skimmed along her jaw with the movement. "I—I just found it as I was looking for the money."

Or was that what she'd been looking for? With the hand not holding his gun, he reached for the jewelry case. She held it tightly, but he tugged it from her grasping fingers. He popped open the case and a big square diamond glistened in the dim light of the nearly dark apartment.

Maggie reached out and snapped the case shut, as if she couldn't bear to look at the ring.

"Your engagement ring?" he asked her.

Her beautiful face tense, she nodded.

"I'm sorry," he said. It must have been hard for her to see the ring her dead fiancé had given her—especially after all she'd been through that day.

"Sorry?" the other woman asked with a disparaging snort. "She never even wore that ring. She probably wouldn't have noticed it missing..."

"So you did intend to steal it?" Blaine asked. He needed to grab his phone and call in this attempted robbery, but when he tried to hand the ring case over to Maggie, she drew back as if she couldn't touch it, either. So he shoved it into his pants pocket to reach for his cell. "I'm going to call the local authorities to book you, Ms. Iverson."

"No," Maggie said, reaching out now to grab his arm and stop him from calling. "I don't want to press charges."

"Why not?" he asked. He was furious with this woman, and he wasn't the one she'd been trying to rob.

Maggie just shook her head, and the blonde breathed a sigh of relief.

But Blaine ignored them both. "This needs to be reported and Ms. Iverson needs to be questioned about her involvement in the robberies."

"What involvement?" the woman asked, her already high voice squeaking with outrage. "I have no involvement."

"I'm not so sure about that…" She could have taken advantage of Maggie leaving her purse behind to try to steal the ring. Or she could have been here waiting for Maggie—to abduct her for the others.

"You think I was stealing the ring," the woman said. "Why would I need to pawn that for money if I was helping rob banks for millions of dollars?"

It wasn't quite millions. Not yet. But he worried that it would be if the robbers weren't stopped. And he worried that more people would die. The robbers had killed once, so it would be easier for them to kill again.

Was that what they'd intended to do with Maggie? Kill her? Why? To keep her quiet? And if they needed to keep her quiet, she had something to say—something she hadn't shared with him yet.

But then, there was a lot she hadn't shared with him. Maybe Susan Iverson wasn't the only one who needed to be brought in for questioning…

MAGGIE WAS SO exhausted that all she wanted to do was put on her comfy pajamas, crawl into her bed and sleep for days. But she was still wearing the skirt and blouse from her suit. And this wasn't her bed. It wasn't soft and comfortable. It was hard and cold—kind of like she was beginning to believe Agent Blaine Campbell might be.

Despite her protest, he'd had Susan arrested for breaking and entering, and attempted theft. He should have just let her take the ring.

Susan was right that Maggie had never worn it. She couldn't even look at it without remembering what Andy had sacrificed to buy her that ring. He'd bought it with the bonus for re-upping and volunteering for that last deployment—the one that had taken his life.

And she had never wanted the ring. She should have told him—should have made it clear that she didn't love him the way he had deserved to be loved. Andy had been a wonderful man, and he'd been taken too soon.

Like Sarge.

Could Susan have been involved in the robbery that had claimed his life? If she was, Maggie was certain that Agent Campbell would find out. With just a look he made Maggie want to confess all. But she had nothing to confess.

He didn't look as though he believed her, though. Was he cynical because of his FBI job and all he'd seen on it? Or was being a marine the reason he didn't trust easily?

Of course he had no reason to trust Maggie. He didn't know her.

If he knew her, he would have just let her stay in her apartment. But he'd insisted that she would be in danger in her own home. Susan knew she lived there, and if she were involved with the robberies, some of the others might try to kidnap her again—as they had at the hospital. So he'd had her brought here—to some sort of "safe" house.

But even with an officer standing outside the motel room door, Maggie didn't feel safe.

She had felt safe only with Agent Campbell. But he'd had Maggie brought here, and he'd gone down to the local police station with Susan.

Maggie was surprised that he hadn't taken her to the station, too. She knew he considered her every bit as much a suspect in the robberies as he did Susan. So maybe that officer wasn't posted outside the door for her protection. Maybe he was posted outside the door to keep her inside—to keep her from escaping.

But where would Maggie go?

She had already tried to escape once—when she'd moved from Sturgis to the Chicago suburb where she lived now. But the robbers had followed her.

Was it only the coincidence she wanted to believe it was? After all, the bank she'd worked at before and the one she worked at now weren't the only ones that had been robbed.

But that danger wasn't the only thing Maggie hadn't been able to leave in her past. When she'd let Susan stay with her, the woman had pried into her life. She'd learned about Andy. That was how Mr. Simmons had heard Maggie's sad story. Susan had used it when she'd been late with her part of the rent.

So Maggie hadn't been able to escape her guilt and loss, either. It had followed her, or maybe she was carrying it with her. She clasped her hands over the baby. She didn't want to escape him or her, though. She wanted to protect her baby—the way she hadn't been able to protect Andy. She'd thought that she was saving him from pain by keeping the truth of her feelings from him.

Maybe there was no escape from her past. But what about the danger? Was she really safe here?

Moments later she had her answer as gunfire erupted outside the motel room. She wasn't safe. The robbers had come for her again.

And this time Agent Campbell wouldn't arrive in time to save her...

Chapter Seven

In the dark Blaine fumbled around the top of the door-jamb for the key his friend had left for him. "I found it," he told Ash through the cell phone pressed to his ear. "I can't believe it's still here."

If he'd left a key outside his apartment in Detroit, it wouldn't have been there long; neither would any of the stuff in his apartment. He wouldn't have thought a Chicago suburb would be much safer—especially after he'd found an intruder in Maggie Jenkins's apartment.

Of course, that intruder had been someone she knew. Apparently she hadn't known her that well, though, if she'd ever trusted the treacherous woman. Not only had Susan tried to steal Maggie's engagement ring, but when Blaine searched her purse, he found that she'd helped herself to Maggie's credit and debit cards, as well.

Blaine blindly slid the key into the lock and quietly opened the door. Ignoring Ash's voice in his ear, he listened carefully for any sounds within the small bunga-low. It was the only dark house on the street; that was how Ash had told him to find it.

At this hour everyone else was home—probably watch-ing TV after dinner. What was Maggie Jenkins doing right now?

Eating?

Sleeping?

She'd looked exhausted. Maybe he should have insisted that she stay at the hospital for observation. But then, she hadn't been safe there, either.

"I told the neighbors to expect a tall blond guy to show up at my door within the next couple of days," Ash said.

This was the kind of neighborhood where people watched out their windows, aware of their surroundings and strangers. Because of Ash's warning, they gave Blaine only a cursory glance before their curtains and blinds snapped back into place and they returned to their television shows.

Blaine pushed open the door to a dark and empty house. "Thanks for giving them the heads-up," he said. "And thanks for letting me crash here."

Ash Stryker was also an FBI special agent but with the antiterrorism division, so he traveled more than Blaine did. Right now he was in DC or New York; Blaine couldn't remember which city. Hell, maybe it was neither. Since he specialized in homegrown terrorism, he could have been off in the woods somewhere. Blaine knew better than to ask. Ash was rarely at liberty to say.

"Thanks for calling me about Sarge," his friend replied, his voice gruff with emotion.

Blaine stopped in midreach for the light switch. While he dealt with his emotions over losing Sarge, he would rather stay in the dark, but he hadn't wanted to leave Ash there. He'd had to tell him about their loss. He and Ash went back before the Bureau. They had been marines together, too.

"I'm sorry," Blaine said. "So damn sorry…"

If only he could have done something.

If only he could have stopped Sarge from stepping out from behind that damn pillar.

But Sarge had reacted instinctively to Maggie's scream and had come to her rescue. If the former military man had actually thought she'd been involved in the robberies, he probably wouldn't have tried so hard to save her. But maybe he still would have done it—out of loyalty to her dead fiancé. He suspected Sarge had been Andy's drill instructor, as well.

"I'm going to try to make it home for his funeral," Ash promised. "Let me know when it is."

"Sure thing," Blaine replied. He knew his friend hated going to funerals as much as he did because they had attended way too many. They'd had so many friends who hadn't made it home—like Maggie's fiancé. "I'll tell you as soon as I find out when the arrangements are."

"Thanks," Ash said. "And feel free to make yourself at home."

"I won't be here long enough," Blaine said. He was more determined than ever to catch these bank robbers. He flipped on the switch and an overhead light flickered on, illuminating the sparsely furnished living room.

"I'm not there much, either." Ash stated the obvious. "If my uncle hadn't left me the place, I would probably just rent an apartment or a hotel room for when I'm in the city."

Blaine had wondered why his friend owned a house. Ash was a confirmed bachelor. The only commitment he'd ever made was to their country and the Bureau. "Like me," Blaine murmured.

Ash chuckled. "Well, you have sisters you can crash with when you have the urge to feel domestic."

Blaine groaned as he thought of the noise and chaos of his sisters' households. Kids crying. Throwing toys. His sisters yelling at their husbands. "Staying with them and their families reminds me why I'm single."

But then he thought of Maggie Jenkins and the baby that had moved beneath his touch. Maggie, with her friendly chatter, would fit in well with his family. Hell, she would fit in better than he ever had.

"So I'm warning you," Ash said, "that the fridge and cupboards are probably bare. There are take-out menus in the cupboard drawer by the fridge, though."

Blaine didn't feel like eating. Ever since that bullet had struck Sarge's chest, he had felt sick. Maggie Jenkins hadn't made him feel any better. He'd had local authorities take her into protective custody at a nearby motel. She would be safe.

He didn't need to worry about her. But he was worried. Did the single mom-to-be have anyone she could trust? Even her former roommate had been trying to steal from her. After interrogating Susan Iverson, Blaine believed that was probably the woman's only crime. He didn't think she was smart enough to be able to hide it if she were involved in the bank robberies.

"It's not your fault," Ash assured him. "You know Sarge. He would have never backed down from a fight—not even when he was outgunned."

Blaine sighed. "I know, especially since he was determined to protect the bank's assistant manager." He'd given up his life for hers and the baby's.

A large part of Ash's job was picking up subtext in recorded conversations. That was how he found threats to security. He easily picked up on Blaine's subtext, too. "Sounds like Sarge might not have been the only one wanting to protect this...*woman*?"

"Yes," Blaine admitted. "She's female. She's also young and pregnant." Too young to have already lost her fiancé, her baby's father...

"Married?" Ash inquired.

"No, her fiancé died in Afghanistan." And she must miss him so much that she couldn't even bear to look at the engagement ring he had given her. Blaine patted his pocket, but the ring was gone. He'd handed it over to the local authorities as evidence in Susan Iverson's attempted robbery along with Maggie's credit and debit cards. He would make sure that Maggie got back the cards and the ring.

But he couldn't bring back what she probably wanted most. Her fiancé…

While Blaine had dated over the years, he'd gotten over the breakups easily enough to know that he had never been in love. He couldn't relate to Maggie's pain, losing the man with whom she'd intended to spend the rest of her life. It had been hard enough losing the friends he'd lost over the years and now losing Sarge.

"Was her fiancé one of Sarge's former drills?"

He sighed. "I think so." It would explain why, after retiring from the military, Sarge had taken a part-time job in a bank. Maybe he'd heard about Maggie getting robbed at the first bank, and he'd intended to protect her. Or maybe she had switched to the bank where Sarge was working because she'd obviously known him. Sarge had always stayed in touch with his former drills.

"Then the old man would have been happy he died saving her," Ash said.

Blaine hadn't expected his cynical friend to come up with such a romantic notion. He blinked hard as his eyes began to burn. "Yeah, he would have been…" He sighed. "But the threat isn't over for Maggie Jenkins. One of the robbers tried grabbing her from the ER where the paramedics took her after the robbery."

"You stopped him, though." Ash just assumed.

"This time."

"You'll keep Maggie safe for Sarge."

Blaine wasn't so sure about that. He had that feeling again—that chill racing up and down his spine—that told him all was not well. The thought had no more than crossed his mind when his phone beeped with an incoming call.

"I have to go, Ash." He didn't waste time with goodbyes, just clicked over the phone to take the next call. "Agent Campbell."

"Agent, this is Officer Montgomery," a man identified himself. He then continued, "We have a report of shots fired at the motel where we took the bank-robbery witness."

He cursed, and his stomach knotted with dread. The motel was nearby, but probably still too far for him to get there in time to save her.

MAGGIE STARED AT the locked bathroom door, waiting for somebody to kick it down or riddle it with bullets. But as she listened, an eerie silence had fallen where only moments before gunfire had deafened her.

She'd wanted to press her hands over her ears and hide under the covers in the dark motel room. But this wasn't a nightmare from which she could hide. So she had forced herself to jump out of the bed and run into the bathroom. Once in there she had locked the door and barricaded it shut by wedging the vanity chair beneath the knob. As a barricade, it was flimsy; it wouldn't take someone much to kick open the door and drag her out.

But she wasn't worried just about herself or about her baby. Had the officer who'd been stationed outside the door of her room been hurt or worse? Her stomach lurched with dread because she suspected the worst. If he was fine, wouldn't he have checked on her? Wouldn't he have at least knocked on the bathroom door and assured her it was safe to come out?

But Maggie wasn't even safe in a safe house.

Blaine Campbell was right. Even though she had no idea what it was, she must have seen or heard *something* that could identify at least one of the robbers. Why else would they so desperately want her dead?

Unable to stare at the door any longer, she squeezed her eyes shut. And she prayed. She prayed for that young officer who had only been doing his job. Like Sarge, trying to protect her.

And she prayed for her baby. Her hands trembled as she splayed them across her belly. Nothing shifted or kicked beneath her palms. For once the child slept— blissfully unaware of the danger he and his mother faced.

Was this all Maggie's fault?

Maybe karma didn't think she deserved the baby because she hadn't loved the baby's father the way she should have. Andy had been such a sweet guy; he hadn't deserved to die. And neither did his baby.

Maggie had to keep him or her safe. But there was no window in the bathroom, no way of escaping except through the door she had barricaded. But the shooting had been out front. Whoever had been shooting at the young police officer could already be inside the motel room, just waiting for her to leave the bathroom.

But the gruesomely masked gunman hadn't waited for her to leave the hospital. He had walked right into the emergency department and dragged her from her bed.

If one of those masked gunmen were inside the motel room, he wouldn't wait long for her to come out. He would break down the door to get to her.

To kill her? What else could they want with her?

She had no money to offer them. But after all the

banks they had robbed, they shouldn't need any more money. Some people, however, never thought they had enough. So maybe they wanted to keep robbing banks and for some reason thought she had the knowledge to stop them...

So they wanted to stop her from talking. They wanted to kill her.

As if her fearful thoughts had conjured up one of the men, the door rattled as someone tried to turn the knob. The chair legs squeaked against the vinyl floor, moving as someone wrenched harder on the knob—determined to get to her.

Could she convince them that she knew nothing? That she had no idea who they were?

It was the only chance she had. But she would be able to pull it off only if they still wore the masks. What if they didn't? Then she couldn't look at them—because they would kill her for sure.

The door rattled harder—metal hinges creaking, wood cracking. In case they came in firing, she climbed into the bathtub. She put her face down on her knees and wrapped her arms around the back of her head. Her stance wouldn't protect her or the baby from bullets. But she had no other way to protect herself...

The chair toppled over against the sink, and the door flew open with such force that the wood cracked against the side of the bathtub. Someone must have kicked it in.

But she didn't dare look up. She didn't want to be able to identify any of the robbers. She wanted the danger to end. She actually wanted Blaine Campbell and his protection. But he was too far away to protect her.

"Please leave me alone," she begged. "You don't have to hurt me. I don't know anything about the robberies. And I don't care..."

All she cared about was her baby. She actually hadn't been thrilled when she'd found out she was pregnant. But then Andy had died and she'd been relieved that she hadn't lost him completely.

But now she wasn't just going to lose that last piece of Andy—she was going to lose her own life, too.

Chapter Eight

Guilt had Blaine's shoulder slumping slightly. Or maybe
he'd hurt it when he had broken down the bathroom door.
"Maggie, it's me," he said.

But she kept her arms locked around her head, her
body trembling inside the bathtub. Curled up the way
she was, she looked so small—so fragile—so frightened.

He hadn't dared to say who he was as he broke down
the door...because he hadn't known what he would find
inside. Maggie might not have been alone. One of the
gunmen might have gotten to her and barricaded them
both inside the bathroom when he'd arrived. Or it might
have only been one of the gunmen inside the bathroom
and Maggie might have already been gone.

Blaine hadn't arrived quite in time. The officer outside the door had been shot. Maybe mortally...

Sirens wailed outside the motel as more emergency
vehicles careened into the lot. Hopefully an ambulance
was among them—with help for the young cop and for
Maggie.

Maybe she needed medical attention, too. Had any of
the shots fired at the officer struck her? Blaine looked
into the tub again, but he noticed no blood on the white
porcelain—only Maggie's dark curls spread across the
cold surface.

"Maggie!" He reached out for her.

But she swung her hands then, striking out at him. "Leave me alone! Leave me alone!"

He caught her wrists and then lifted her wriggling body from the tub and into his arms. "Maggie! It's me— it's Blaine!"

Finally she looked up, her dark eyes wide as she stared at him in wonder. "Blaine!" Then she threw her arms around his neck and clung to him.

And his guilt increased. He never should have left her to the protection of anyone else. The young officer had been shot, and Maggie might have been taken if he hadn't gotten there in time. The wounded officer had held off the gunmen until Blaine had arrived.

Then Blaine had fired on them, too. He didn't think that he'd hit any of them, though. And tires had squealed as a van had sped out of the parking lot.

For a long, horrible moment he'd thought that Maggie might have been in that van. That he had been too late to save her. Then he had found the bathroom door locked inside the room, and he'd hoped that she'd hidden away. But Blaine had been doing this job too long to be optimistic. So he had expected the worst—that one of the gunmen had been left behind and barricaded himself alone or, worse yet, inside the bathroom with Maggie.

In a ragged sigh of relief, her breath shuddered out against his throat. She had undoubtedly expected the worst when he'd broken open the door.

He wrapped his arms tightly around Maggie, holding her close. She trembled against him—as if she couldn't stop shaking. She was probably in shock.

"I'm sorry," he said.

But he had to pull away and leave her again—only because he had to make sure that help had arrived for the young officer and for Maggie. He wanted a doctor to check her out again.

He wanted to make sure that she was all right.

How much fear could she and her baby handle?

There was only one way that Blaine would truly be able to protect her, the way Sarge had wanted and died trying to do. And that was to find out who was so determined to grab her or kill her.

Who were the bank robbers?

ONE OF THE paramedics assured Maggie and Agent Campbell that she was fine. Apparently she couldn't die from fear.

What about embarrassment?

She had embarrassed herself when she cried out his name and clung to him. She had acted like a girlfriend when he considered her a robbery suspect.

Or had he changed his mind about that?

Then he took her to his home—although *home* was stretching it. The bungalow obviously belonged to a single man. There were no pictures on the walls. No knickknacks on the built-in shelves. Not even a book or a magazine.

The living room held a couch and a chair while the dining room contained a desk instead of a table. The table was in the kitchen, but it had only two chairs at it. There was a bed in each of the two bedrooms.

Blaine showed her to one while taking the other for himself. Maybe she slept. Maggie wasn't sure. She drifted in and out, occasionally hearing Blaine's voice. She doubted he slept at all. He had been on his cell phone instead.

The house was quiet now. But Maggie knew he hadn't left because she smelled food. Bacon. And coffee. Her stomach grumbled, but she stayed in bed, not eager to face him. Her face heated even now, as she thought of how she'd acted.

Like a girlfriend…

But Blaine Campbell was just an FBI agent doing his job. He probably had a girlfriend somewhere, because a man that handsome was unlikely to be single. Unless Blaine's only commitment was his career…

She had to stop thinking of him as Blaine and remember that he was Special Agent Campbell. That was all he was and all he would ever be to her.

The baby kicked. Apparently they both wanted food. So she tossed back the covers and kicked her legs over the side of the bed. The T-shirt Blaine had loaned her as a nightgown had ridden up, revealing her high-cut briefs. She reached to tug down the hem of the shirt just as someone cleared his throat.

"Sorry," Blaine said, as he had the night before when he'd peeled her off him.

She was the one who should be apologizing—for inconveniencing him as she had. For costing him a friend like Sarge. For making his job harder. But for once she, who usually couldn't stop talking, couldn't find words to express herself and her gratefulness for his saving her over and over again.

"I was just coming up to see if you were awake," he said. "I had some groceries delivered and made breakfast."

The man could cook? He really was perfect.

But perfect wasn't for Maggie—not with the mess her life had become. She pulled the T-shirt down, but it was still short enough that it left her legs bare. And, in her mind, Blaine's gaze skimmed down her legs like a caress.

But that could only be in her mind—her imagination.

The FBI agent couldn't really be interested in her. Not for anything but information...

He proved that a short while later when he picked her empty plate up from the table and started asking questions. "You're sure that you didn't recognize anyone from the robberies?"

"I'm sure," she said. "I only recognized those horrible masks from the robbery at the Sturgis branch where I used to work." She shuddered as she thought of the grotesque masks. They could have come right from that R-rated zombie movie she'd gone to so long ago. "With the masks and the trench coats, I couldn't see any facial features or even body types of the robbers."

"You're not protecting anyone?"

She shook her head. But her hands automatically covered her belly. The baby had stopped moving. Maybe the food had satiated him. The cheesy scrambled eggs, crisp bacon and wheat toast had been delicious—so delicious that Maggie had probably eaten more than she should have.

But then, she could barely remember the last time she'd eaten. Some crackers at the hospital? Before that a breakfast she'd made herself—lumpy oatmeal with too much brown sugar. She would have to learn to be a better cook for the baby. If she lived long enough to cook for him...

"I want to protect my baby," she said. But she feared that she was going to fail, just as she had failed Andy. "That's the only person I'm protecting. So if I knew anything about the robbers, I would tell you."

"You haven't noticed anyone hanging around the bank, casing the place?" he asked.

She shook her head again. "I don't know what casing a place looks like. So I can't say that someone hasn't done it." Obviously they had or they wouldn't have pulled off the robbery so easily—until Blaine had arrived. If only he could have saved Sarge…

Blaine hadn't eaten nearly as much as she had. Most of his food was on his plate yet, forgotten, as he asked his questions. "Nobody came around both of the banks?"

Once again, she shook her head. "The branches are far enough away that they had different customers. I knew most of the clients from Sturgis since I'd worked at that branch since I graduated, but I'm just getting to know the people at this branch." Should she bother? Or should she move on again to another branch, another city?

How would she work there without remembering those robbers bursting in? That was why she'd left Sturgis. Because of the memories. But there were worse ones here; there was Sarge getting shot and dying.

"What about workers?" Blaine asked. "Did Susan work at both branches, too?"

"No," she said. "I'm the only one who worked at both branches." Which was why he had suspected she was involved, and she couldn't blame him for his suspicions. "But I really have nothing to do with the robberies."

He didn't look at her the way he had before, as if he doubted her.

Hope fluttered in her chest like her baby fluttered in her belly, waking up from his or her short nap. "Do you believe me?" she asked.

He uttered a heavy sigh of resignation. "I believe that you're not *consciously* involved."

She should have been happy that he didn't think she was a criminal mastermind, but his comment dented her pride. He clearly thought she was an idiot instead. "I'm not *unconsciously* involved, either."

"You haven't told anyone about your job?" he asked.

"Most people know that I work at a bank," she said, "except for Mr. Simmons."

"Because you don't want to worry him," he said with a slight smile, as if amused or moved.

She sighed. "That was all for nothing after you called the cops on Susan. He probably knows now. But that's all anyone knows about me—that I work there."

"You haven't told anyone any details that might make it easier for them to hold up the bank," he persisted, "to know which days you'd have the most cash on hand?"

"No," she replied, pride stinging at how stupid he thought her. He wasn't the only one who'd thought that. Because she talked a lot, people sometimes thought she was flighty. But her grades in school and college had proved them all wrong. She talked a lot because she really didn't like silence. It made her uncomfortable, so she generally tended to fill it with chatter.

"You don't talk to your family about your job?" he asked skeptically. "You wouldn't share any details with them?"

So now he thought her family members were criminal masterminds? She corrected that misassumption. "For his job, my dad and mom moved to Hong Kong a couple of years ago."

And since Andy's death, all they talked about was the weather—asking about hers, telling about theirs. Their conversations didn't get any deeper; they were probably afraid that they might make her cry if they brought up something that would remind her of Andy. Or maybe it would make them cry because they'd loved him like a son.

"You don't have any brothers or sisters?" he asked.

"No." And because she was sick of being the only one

answering questions, she started asking some of her own. "What about you?"

"I have three older sisters," he replied, and his lips curved into a slight smile as his green eyes crinkled a little at the corners.

Growing up, she had wanted sisters. But her father had been busy with his career, and her mom hadn't wanted to raise more than one child alone. Maggie would really be raising her baby alone.

She shook off the self-pity before she could wallow and asked, "Any brothers?"

"Just in arms," he replied.

Fellow marines. Andy had called them brothers, too. She sighed.

"Do you have any *friends* that you're really close to?" he asked. "Anyone that you would talk to without realizing that you might have let some information slip?"

He really thought she was an idiot. But maybe she had been—because she had told someone more than she should have.

Since he watched her closely, he must have caught her reaction as her realization dawned. "There is someone," he concluded. "Who?"

"It doesn't make a difference now," she said.

"Who is it?" he asked, his voice sharp as if he thought she was protecting someone.

"Andy," she said. "I told Andy everything…" Since they were kids, he had been her best friend, her confidant.

His blond head bobbed in a sharp nod. "Of course…"

But then she realized that she'd lied to the agent. She hadn't told Andy everything, or she would have told him the truth—that she didn't love him as anything more than her best friend. Maybe she'd told him so much about the bank because, as with her parents just discussing the weather, she had preferred to talk to Andy about her job than about her feelings or their future. She hadn't seen one for them, but not because she'd thought he was going to die.

"But Andy's gone," she said. "So there's no way he could have had anything to do with the bank robberies."

"Can I ask...how did he die?"

For once she was short with her words. "He drove a supply truck. An IED took out the whole convoy."

He flinched. "I'm sorry."

She nodded. It was her automatic reaction to everyone's condolences. Condolences she didn't feel she really deserved, just the way she felt she hadn't deserved Andy.

"Would Andy have told anyone what you told him?" Blaine asked.

"Why?" While he had listened to her, Andy really hadn't cared about her job. He'd been proud that she'd gone to college, that she'd gotten her degree in finance, but he'd thought that she would quit working once they got married and started having kids.

Andy really hadn't known her at all. Or he would have guessed that, while she loved him, she wasn't in love with him. So if Andy hadn't known her that well, maybe she hadn't known him, either.

"I can think of hundreds of thousands of reasons why he might have told someone," Blaine replied.

Maggie defended her friend. "Andy didn't care about money."

"But that was quite a ring he bought you..."

He hadn't just paid for that ring with money; he'd paid for it with his life, too. "He used his bonus—for re-upping and for his last deployment..."

Blaine nodded as if she'd answered another question—

one that he hadn't actually asked. "Maybe he didn't realize that he was revealing anything."

She hadn't realized that something she'd said could
have led to those robberies, to Sarge's death. She hoped
Blaine was wrong because she already had too much
guilt to live with; she didn't need any more.

Chapter Nine

Maggie insisted on going to the bank, and Blaine agreed. The bank wasn't open for business, though. Not yet. Repairmen were working on replacing the broken windows and fixing the damaged walls and furniture. So Blaine took her around the back, through the security door that the robbers had dragged her out.

That was hard enough—watching her face drain of color as she relived those moments. She probably hadn't thought she was going to get away from the robbers. And for a few moments Blaine hadn't thought he was going to get her away from them—then or later at the hospital or the motel.

He relived all those moments and found his arm coming around her thin shoulders. "Maybe this was a bad idea," he murmured.

"I need to go to my office," she said. "And make sure I didn't leave anything out yesterday."

"The manager closed up the bank yesterday," he assured her. "I'm sure he locked up whatever paperwork you might have had out."

He did not want her going to her office. Since her walls were glass, it had also been damaged from the gunfire. And in the lobby was the outline where Sarge's body had been. She didn't need to see that, and neither did he.

Maggie shook her head. "No, Mr. Hardy wouldn't have done it himself. He probably let Susan do it and that's how she got hold of my purse."

Blaine hadn't been that impressed with the manager—especially when the guy had been firing questions at her while the paramedics were trying to assess her condition. It was obvious that most of the day-to-day administration had fallen on Maggie's slim shoulders. "She got your purse, your keys and your credit cards."

She sighed. "I should cancel my credit cards."

"She already used a couple of them," he said. While Maggie had been at the hospital, the greedy woman had used her cards. "Why did you ever have her as your roommate?"

Maggie shrugged hard enough to dislodge his arm and stepped away from his side. Maybe he had offended her by implying that she wasn't the greatest judge of character. "She was really nice to me when I first started working here," she said in defense of their relationship, "so I agreed to let her move in when her boyfriend kicked her out and she had nobody else to stay with."

He wondered if that had been a ruse. Maybe he had underestimated Susan Iverson's intelligence. He would take another look at her. But first he wanted Maggie to look at something; that was why he had agreed to bring her down to the bank.

He had also wanted to get out of Ash's small house before he lost all objectivity where Maggie Jenkins was concerned. She was too damn beautiful for his peace of mind. He couldn't lose the image of her hair tangled from sleep, her body all soft and warm and sexy. When she'd tossed back the blankets and revealed her bare legs and the shapely curve of her hips, he had been tempted to crawl into bed with her.

She sighed again. "But I learned quickly why her boyfriend had kicked her out."

"The woman can't be trusted." Blaine wondered if this one could. He wanted to trust Maggie Jenkins; he wanted to believe she was every bit as sweet and innocent as she seemed.

But he couldn't rule out any possible suspects yet. And she was a possible one—even after the attempts on her life. Or maybe because of them. Her coconspirators could be trying to prevent her from giving them up.

He led Maggie to a back office, near the rear exit, where he had had the bank security footage set up across six small monitors. He pressed a remote and started it rolling.

"What is all this?" she asked.

"Security footage." Sarge's security footage. "I want you to watch it."

"All of it?" She sounded overwhelmed. The six monitors probably were a bit daunting.

Blaine was used to it, as he often watched days, sometimes weeks or even months, of security footage when he was investigating bank robberies. But this time while they watched the monitors, he saw only Maggie—her full breasts and belly pushing against his old T-shirt. Those long, bare legs...

How would they feel wrapped around him? How would she feel when he buried himself inside her?

He shook his head, shaking off the thoughts. *They* would never happen. She wasn't just pregnant with another man's child; she was still in love with that man. It didn't matter that Andy was dead. A love like theirs—where she had told him *everything*—was deep and enduring.

Blaine had never had anyone in his life to whom he'd told *everything*. He had learned at a young age that if he told his sisters anything they would tell *everyone*. So he'd been keeping his own counsel for a long time—which was good because he had no intention of sharing his thoughts about Maggie with anyone else. In fact, he wanted to forget all about them.

So he focused on the video screens playing out on the monitors in Sarge's office. It might have been hard to be there, if Sarge hadn't been like Blaine and Ash—too nomadic to personalize any space. It wasn't as if they would be there long enough to put down roots anyway. If Ash hadn't inherited that house in the Chicago burbs, he would have just had an apartment like Blaine had in Detroit—something devoid of decoration and sparsely furnished.

Days of security footage passed before his eyes in a blur—slow enough to pick out faces but fast enough that hours passed in minutes. His head began to pound—maybe more from his mostly sleepless night than from watching the footage.

If staring at those monitors had affected him, he worried how it was affecting Maggie. "Are you okay?" he asked her.

Maggie nodded. "I'm fine." But her fingers touched her temple and she closed her eyes.

"We can take a break," he offered.

"I don't understand why we're watching *these* videos," she said as she gestured at the screens. "All of this happened a week or more ago."

Had she expected him to show her the footage of the robbery? That would have been too much for her—to relive those terrifying moments, to relive Sarge getting killed…

He may have already told her. So much had happened

that he couldn't remember exactly, so he asked, "Do you know why I showed up when I did yesterday?"

"Because you're working those bank robberies."

That was what he'd told the state troopers in the alley. "Sarge called me," Blaine said. "He told me that he thought the bank was going to be hit."

She gasped in surprise. "He knew?"

"Yeah, he must have realized that someone was casing the place." And hopefully that someone had been picked up on the security footage.

She shrugged. "But *I* don't know how to tell who's casing the place."

"I do," he said. While he'd worked his way up in the Bureau through other divisions, he specialized in bank robberies now. To date, his record was perfect; he always caught the thieves.

Always…

And this time he had even more incentive than his record and his career. He had Sarge. And Maggie…

"So what am *I* looking for?" she asked.

"Someone you know."

She laughed as if he'd said something ridiculous. "I know a lot of these people."

He could tell. Even though she hadn't been at this branch that long, she often stepped out of her office to talk to bank clients, her face breathtakingly beautiful as she smiled welcomingly at them. They all smiled back, charmed by her friendly personality.

But he stopped the footage on one monitor as he noticed that one man smiled bigger than the others. And he hadn't left his greeting at a smile. He had gone in for a hug—a big one that had physically lifted Maggie off her feet. She hadn't looked happy, though; she had looked uncomfortable.

"Who's that?" he asked.

She stared at the screen, her eyes wide and face pale as if she'd seen a ghost. "I always forget how much he looks like Andy..."

"Who is he?"

She released a shaky breath. "Mark—that's Andy's older brother, Mark."

"Does he have accounts at the bank?"

She shook her head. "No, he just came by to see me. To check on me."

Blaine's senses tingled as he recognized a viable lead. "Did he use to come by the other branch you worked at?"

"Sometimes."

He nodded.

"It's not what you think," she assured him.

She had no idea what he was thinking. People rarely did. He wasn't even thinking of the case. He was thinking that the man wasn't just looking at her with concern or familial affection. He was looking at her with attraction. The way Blaine looked at her...

But in the footage she wasn't looking at the man at all. Like the ring, it was as if she couldn't bear to look at him. Because he looked so much like her dead fiancé?

He was a good-looking man. With their frequently inappropriate comments, his sisters would've gone on and on about his dark hair and light-colored eyes. And Andy had looked like that?

A weird emotion surged through Blaine—anger or resentment? Jealousy?

He was jealous of a dead man...

"WHAT AM I THINKING?" Blaine was asking her, his voice gruff with a challenge as if he doubted she could read him.

Few people probably could. The man was incredibly

guarded. But he'd let that guard down, briefly, to mourn the loss of his friend and former drill instructor. So Maggie felt as if she had found a tiny hole in his armor.

"You're thinking that Mark is involved in the robberies," she replied. "And that's ridiculous."

Blaine turned back to the monitor and studied the frozen frame of Mark lifting her off her feet. That muscle twitched in his cheek—almost as if it bothered him that another man was holding her.

But her thought was even more ridiculous than his thinking that Mark Doremire was a robber. Blaine Campbell was not jealous of another man touching her. Blaine had no interest in her beyond helping him figure out who the robbers were.

"Why is it ridiculous?" Blaine asked.

"Because he's Andy's brother."

A blond brow arched, as if that made Mark guiltier. Because of what she'd told Andy? If only she'd kept her mouth shut...

Maybe her mother had been right—she talked too much. Or, in this case, she'd written too much.

Once again, she defended her best friend. "Andy was the most honest person I've ever known."

Blaine didn't challenge her opinion of Andy. He just pointed out, "That doesn't mean that his brother is honest, too."

"I understand their personalities being different. But not their fundamental beliefs. They were raised by the same parents—raised the same way," she said. "How could they be that different?"

"You are obviously an only child." He laughed. "I have three sisters, and they are very different from each other."

"How?" she asked. She had always wished she'd had siblings. But her dad's career was demanding, and he hadn't been around that much to help her mother. So Mom had won the argument to have only one child.

He laughed again. "Sarah is a car salesperson—with that over-the-top bubbly personality. Erica is a librarian—quiet and introspective. And Buster..."

"Buster?" She'd thought he'd said they were all sisters.

"Becky is her real name," he explained. "She's in law enforcement, too. She's a county deputy. So my sisters are absolutely nothing alike."

"Maybe not personality-wise," she said. Mark and Andy hadn't been that much alike, either. Mark had liked to tease and joke around, and Andy had always been so sensitive and serious. "But morality and ethics..."

"Sarah sells cars," he repeated. "I'm not so sure about the ethics..."

She laughed now. From the twinkle in his green eyes, it was obvious how much he loved all of his sisters—even the car salesperson.

"Mark has been coming around *because* of his ethics," she said, "because he made a promise to Andy—the last time Andy left for a deployment—that he would take care of me if something happened to him."

That blond brow lifted again with a question and suspicion. "How is he taking care of you?"

If he was asking what she thought he was...

She shuddered in revulsion. "Not like *that*. Mark is like my brother, too. We all grew up together."

Blaine clicked the remote and unfroze Mark's image. Andy's brother kept smiling at her...before Susan walked up and started flirting with him. "What about with her?" he asked. "Is he brotherly with Susan Iverson?"

She hoped not. "Mark is married. He's not interested in Susan." But as she watched the footage, she wondered. "Maybe he's just a flirt..." Sometimes it felt as if he was

flirting with her, which always made her extremely uncomfortable. Because she really thought of Mark as a
big brother and only a big brother.

"I need to talk to Mark," Blaine said. "Where can I
get hold of him?"

"I think I have his address somewhere in my office.
He and his wife invited me to dinner before." But she
had politely declined because it was so hard to see him.
"I can call him…"

She would really prefer calling him to seeing him.

But Blaine shook his head. "I'll get his address from
your office. Then I'll put you back into protective custody."

"Because that worked out so well last time?" she asked.
"How is that young officer?" Before they had left the little bungalow for the bank, Blaine had called the hospital
to check on him, but all he'd told her was that the young
man had made it through surgery.

"He's still in critical condition," he said.

"Then just let me call Mark," she urged, her heart beating fast with panic at the thought of being separated from
Blaine again. "You can talk to him—you'll know that he
had nothing to do with the robberies."

But Blaine shook his head in refusal. "No, I have to
see him face-to-face."

So he had to leave her again.

And every time he left her, there was another attempt
to grab her. One of these times the attempt was destined
to be successful.

Would this be the time?

Chapter Ten

Every time Blaine left her alone or in someone else's protection, Maggie Jenkins was in danger. He didn't want to risk it again. It was better that she stayed with him. So she sat in the passenger seat of the FBI-issued SUV that had replaced his rental sedan as he drove to her almost brother-in-law's address.

But now was he the one putting her in danger?

He shouldn't have brought her along with him. But he couldn't risk a phone call that might have tipped off Mark Doremire to his suspicions. If the man was one of the robbers, he certainly had enough money to escape the country—to one where there was no extradition.

Hell, he was probably already gone.

But then, who kept trying to grab Maggie or kill her? And why? If she could identify them, wouldn't it be easier to escape now than to stick around to try to kill her?

"This trip is a waste of time," she remarked from the passenger's seat. "Mark won't be able to help you, either— just like I couldn't help you this morning at the bank."

She had helped him. He'd found a possible suspect. She just didn't want to see that her dead fiancé's brother could be a suspect.

"I watched all that footage and I didn't notice anyone *casing* the bank," she said, her soft voice husky with frustration. "I didn't notice anything out of the ordinary. And I didn't at the first bank that was robbed."

He should have brought up that footage, too. But she'd already admitted that Mark Doremire had been at that bank. Both banks had been robbed—it was a coincidence that was worth checking out.

But he should have checked it out alone. "You really shouldn't be along with me," he said regretfully.

"No," she agreed, even though it had been her comments that had talked him out of risking her safety to someone else's responsibility. "I don't want to see Mark. And I really don't want to see one of those zombie robbers again." She shuddered with revulsion. "Maybe I should go stay with my parents in Hong Kong."

His pulse leaped in reaction to her comment, to the thought of her going away where he couldn't protect her, where he couldn't see her. "You can't leave the country."

"Why?" she asked, her voice sharp with anger. "Am I still a suspect?"

He wasn't sure what she was. Entirely too distracting. Entirely too attractive...

He couldn't let her leave. "Right now you're a material witness."

"Some witness," she said disparagingly. "I can't help you at all. I didn't see anything on that footage. And during the robberies I only saw what everyone else saw— trench coats and zombie masks." She shuddered again at mention of the disguises.

She obviously hated those gruesome masks.

"You heard one of them speak," he reminded her.

She shrugged. "But I didn't recognize his voice."

So it hadn't been Mark Doremire who'd spoken. But it could have been someone he knew—a friend of his. "You might if you were to hear it again."

She sighed with resignation. "That's true. I doubt I'll forget him announcing the robbery the minute they walked into the bank."

Like the guns and disguises hadn't given away their intentions.

Announcing a robbery made them seem more like rookies than professionals. But then, they hadn't been robbing banks that long. Less than a year—barely half a year, actually. Blaine would catch them before they went any longer. If he had his way, the last bank they robbed would be the one at which Sarge had died.

"Which house is it?" he asked as he turned the black SUV onto the street on which Mark Doremire lived. The SUV would probably give away Blaine's identity, but he tucked his badge inside his shirt.

"I don't know," Maggie replied. "I haven't been here before." She leaned forward and peered at the numbers on the houses. "That one…"

This neighborhood wasn't like Ash's. Nobody looked out the windows. They probably looked the other way. The houses were in ill repair, with missing shingles and paint peeling off. If Mark had stolen any of the money, he hadn't spent it yet—at least not on his house.

"I'll stay in the car," she offered.

Blaine turned toward her. Her face was pale, as if she'd already seen a ghost. "I can't leave you in the car."

"Why not?"

"Someone could have followed us."

She glanced around fearfully. "Did someone?"

He doubted it; he had been too careful. "I don't know. But I don't want you out of my sight."

He didn't want her walking into the line of fire, either. So he handed her his cell phone. "Call him."

"But we're already here…"

If she tipped Mark off now and he ran, Blaine was close enough to catch him. He'd also radioed in his intentions to speak to a possible suspect. So other agents and the local authorities knew where he was and there was a deputy in the vicinity.

"Call him."

She sighed but looked down at the piece of paper that had Mark's address and cell phone. Then she punched in a number. "It didn't even ring. It went straight to his voice mail. Do you want— Oh, his voice mail is full." With another sigh, of relief, she hung up the phone.

Straight to voice mail? That wasn't a good sign—especially since the house looked deserted. Maybe he had already left. Just then an older car, with rust around the wheel wells and on the hood, pulled up across from them and parked at the curb in front of the house.

"That's his wife," Maggie said as a red-haired woman stepped from the car.

Nobody else was inside the vehicle, so seeing no threat to Maggie's safety, Blaine opened his door. "Mrs. Doremire."

She jumped as if startled. But then, in a neighborhood like this, it probably was strange for someone to call out her name. It was probably strange for anyone to even know her name. She slowly turned around and stared at him. "Yes?"

"Tammy," Maggie called out to her.

The woman peered around him and noticed Maggie inside the SUV. She smiled and waved. "Hi, there. Mark will be thrilled that you finally came over to visit."

"Is he here?" Blaine asked.

Tammy turned her attention back to him, and her brow furrowed with confusion. "I'm sorry…"

"Blaine." He introduced himself with his first name

only. If the press had mentioned him in any reports about the bank robbery, it would have been as Special Agent Campbell. "I'm a friend of Maggie's."

And, really, friendship was all he could expect from her—even though he wanted so much more. He wanted *her*.

"I'm sorry," Tammy Doremire said again, as she crossed the street to the SUV. "Mark isn't here right now."

"Where is he?"

She sighed. "He's at one of his folks'—probably his dad's."

"Dad's?" Maggie asked. "Mr. and Mrs. Doremire aren't together anymore?"

"They split up after Andy died," she said. "It was too much for them. So Mark keeps checking on them, like he checks on you, Maggie. He's trying so hard to take care of everybody since Andy's gone."

Maggie's voice cracked as she apologized now. "I'm sorry…"

It wasn't her fault that Andy had died. It was who-ever had set the damn IED where the convoy would hit it. But Mark's wife didn't absolve her of guilt. She only shrugged.

"Sometimes he'll stay the night at his dad's," she said, "so you'll probably want to come back tomorrow."

Maggie nodded in agreement. But Blaine had other plans.

"It was nice meeting you, Mrs. Doremire," he said as he slid back behind the wheel.

She nodded, but her brow was furrowed again—as if she'd realized she hadn't really met him. He had only told her his first name.

"We'll come back tomorrow, then," he lied.

"Why?" Maggie asked after he'd closed his door. "You can tell Mark has nothing to do with the robberies. He's too busy taking care of everyone."

"Where does Andy's dad live?" he asked.

She shook her head.

"You don't know?"

"I didn't even know they had gotten divorced," she pointed out, and that guilt was in her voice again, as if she considered herself responsible, "so how would I know where either of them is living now?"

"One of them might have kept the house where they lived before Andy died," he said. "You know where that is."

He felt a flash of guilt that it might have been the house where Andy had grown up—a house where she and Andy had shared memories. It would be hard for her to go back to that.

"I know," she admitted and then confirmed his thoughts when she added, "but I don't want to go there."

He wished he didn't have to take her there. But he had to find Mark before his wife had a chance to warn him that a man, a friend of Maggie's, was looking for him. Because then the man would run for sure…

BLAINE CAMPBELL CARED only about his job. He didn't care about her or he wouldn't have made her give him directions to Andy's childhood home in southwestern Michigan. He wouldn't have kept her in the car to go with him. He wouldn't have made her keep revisiting her past and her guilt.

Everything had fallen apart since Andy's death. And that was all her fault. If she had told him the truth earlier, he wouldn't have reenlisted. He wouldn't have needed the money for the damn ring she had never wanted.

Blaine Campbell had taken it as evidence against Susan Iverson. She hoped he never returned it.

Maggie stared out the windshield at the highway that wound around the Lake Michigan shoreline. She had always liked this drive—until she had traveled it up for Andy's funeral. Then she had vowed to never use it again.

She hadn't wanted to go back. It wasn't home without her best friend. She had to make a new home for herself and for her baby. But she was afraid that she hadn't found one yet—at least, not one where they would be safe.

"Andy's been gone awhile," Blaine remarked.

"Nearly six months," she said. But sometimes it hadn't sunk in yet. Sometimes she still looked for his letters in her mailbox or an email in her in-box or a call...

"Did you even know that you were pregnant when you learned that he'd died?"

She nodded. Since her cycle had always been so regular, she'd taken a test on her first missed day. She hadn't been happy with those test results because she'd known that Andy would insist on marrying her. He had always been so old-fashioned and so honorable. But now he was dead...

Blaine's gaze was on the road, so he must have missed her nod. She cleared her throat and replied, "Yes, I had just found out."

"You're strong," he said.

She nearly laughed. Had he already forgotten how she'd screamed her head off that first day they'd met? She wasn't nearly as strong as she'd like to be. If she was, she might have saved Sarge. "Why do you say that?"

"Some women might have lost the baby," he explained, "because of the stress."

"I was fine." She hadn't had any problems then; she hadn't even had morning sickness. She was more afraid of losing the child now.

As if he'd heard her unspoken thoughts, he reached across the console and squeezed her hand. "I'll keep you safe," he promised. "I'll keep you both safe."

Andy had made promises, too. He'd promised that he would return from his last deployment. So Maggie knew that some promises couldn't be kept. She suspected that the promise Blaine had just made was one of them.

He didn't believe that, though. He thought it was a promise he could keep and his green eyes were full of sincerity as he shared a glance with her. Then he turned his attention back to the road and to the rearview mirror. His hand tensed on hers before he released it and gripped the wheel.

"Hold on!" he warned her as he pressed harder on the accelerator.

Maggie instinctively reached out for the dashboard, bracing her hands against it, just as the SUV shot forward. "What's going on? Why are you driving so fast?"

She had felt safe with him earlier. But not now.

"Just hold on," Blaine said again, as he sped up some more.

Tires squealed as he careened around a curve.

"What are you doing?" she asked again—with alarm.

But then more tires squealed and metal crunched as another vehicle slammed hard into the rear bumper of the SUV. The SUV fishtailed, spinning out of control toward where the shoulder of the road dropped off to the rocky lakeshore below. Nobody had ever broken a promise to her as fast as Blaine just had.

Maggie screamed in fear as the SUV teetered on two tires, about to roll over and plummet to that rocky shore.

Chapter Eleven

Blaine cursed and jerked the wheel, steering the SUV away from the shoulder. Gravel spewed from the tires as the SUV fishtailed, the back end sliding toward that steep drop-off to the rocky shore below. He needed all four tires on the pavement before he could accelerate. But before he could regain complete control, the van struck again. Metal crunched on the rear door of the passenger's side.

Too close to Maggie and her baby.

He had just promised that he would protect them. It was a promise that he'd had no business making. As a marine, he knew that there were promises that couldn't be kept—the way all his fallen friends had promised their families they would come home again. It was a promise that Maggie's fiancé had probably made to her when he'd given her that ring.

Blaine was not about to break his promise. At least not yet.

He pressed on the accelerator, taking the curve at such a high speed that a couple of the tires might have left the asphalt again. The black cargo van skidded around the corner behind him, its tires slipping off the pavement onto the gravel shoulder. So close to that dangerous edge, the van slowed down, and Blaine increased the distance between them.

He had grown up driving on roads like this—roads that curved sharply around lakes. But there had been mountains to maneuver, too, in New Hampshire. So he wasn't fazed. But neither was the driver of the van as he regained control and closed the distance between them again.

Blaine wanted to reach for his gun; he wanted to shoot out the van's tires and windshield. He wanted to do anything he could to stop the van from slamming into them again. But he needed both hands on the wheel to keep the SUV from plummeting over the rocky shoulder, and he didn't want Maggie trying to use his weapon.

He didn't want Maggie doing anything but hanging on—especially as the van made contact with them again. But the SUV absorbed the impact better than the van did.

In the rearview mirror, Blaine caught sight of a dark cloud as smoke began to billow from beneath the hood of the vehicle behind them. The rear bumper of the SUV was probably mangled, but so were the front bumper and the grille of the van.

If the radiator was ruined, it wasn't going to get far. He could just wait for it to stop running and try to apprehend the driver and whoever else was riding with him. But Blaine had no idea how many people were inside the van or how much firepower they had.

Even if he hadn't just made that promise to protect them, he couldn't risk the safety of Maggie and the baby. So he accelerated again and took the curves at breakneck speed. Maggie's hands were still pressed against the dashboard as she braced herself and her baby for another hit.

But the van didn't catch up again.

Blaine slowed down and, using his cell, called in the attempt to run them off the road. He described the van and then he asked for the nearest hospital.

"Do you think one of them was hurt?" Maggie asked as she peered behind them. But the van was no longer in view.

It might be where Blaine had left it smoking. Or the driver might have turned it around and tried to get somewhere they could hide it—the way they had tried to hide the getaway van between those Dumpsters in the alley.

He doubted blood would be found inside this van. He hadn't been able to take any shots at them. So he explained, "I'm taking *you* to the hospital."

She shook her head. "I'm fine."

Her face was eerily pale, and he could see the frantic beat of her pulse pounding in her throat.

"No, you're not fine," he argued, as he followed the directions the local dispatcher had given him to the hospital.

If there was something wrong with her or the baby, it was his fault. He should not have brought her along with him. He hadn't been any better at protecting her than the young officer the night before. Even with the van chasing them, he should have driven more carefully.

He slowed down on his way to the hospital. But he wanted her checked out. He wanted to make sure that she and the baby were fine.

Before he left them…

BLAINE HAD INTENDED to leave as soon as a doctor had taken Maggie into the ER to be checked out. But before he could cross the waiting room to the exit doors, another FBI agent, badge dangling down the front of a black leather jacket, showed up at the hospital.

"Agent Dalton Reyes," the dark-haired man introduced himself, hand outstretched. He didn't look much like the proverbial men in black since he wore a jacket and jeans instead of a dark suit.

But Blaine wasn't wearing a suit, either—just black pants and shirt. Since interrupting the robbery in progress, he hadn't had an opportunity to even take his suits out of their dry-cleaning bags.

"Reyes?" Ash had mentioned the young agent before. The Bureau had recruited him from an undercover gang task force with the Chicago PD. "You work organized crime?"

The dark head bobbed in a quick nod. "Yeah. Right now I'm working on a car-theft ring. The black cargo van that just tried running you off the road was recovered. It's one these thieves grabbed yesterday. This ring is very organized and very professional. You put in a request, and they'll steal the vehicle you want."

Blaine had put out a request himself—for information on a ring just like this. "Thanks for getting back to me about this, but you could have just called…"

Reyes grinned. "I could've, but then I wouldn't have gotten a chance to meet the infamous Blaine Campbell."

"Infamous?" Blaine asked. He didn't think that adjective had ever been used for him before.

"You've got quite a reputation."

He groaned. "What has Ash told you?"

Dalton laughed. "Ash doesn't talk. But he's damn good at getting other people to talk."

He was new to the Chicago Bureau, so people were bound to talk about him. To wonder what his story was, to worry that he might move up ahead of agents who had been there longer. He didn't care to move into management; he just wanted to take criminals off the street. He had never wanted to put anyone away more than these suspects. They'd already killed Sarge and were determined to kill Maggie, too.

"How about you?" Blaine asked, turning the conversation back to what he really cared about: the case. "Can you get these car thieves to tell you who's been putting in the requests for these vans?"

"I've got an inside man," Dalton said. "So I've got confirmation that the bank robbers have been paying—and paying big—to get disposable vehicles for the bank heists."

"Who?" he asked. "Who the hell are these robbers?"

Dalton shrugged. "My guys aren't the kind who care about names. In fact, they would probably rather *not* know. The only thing they care about is cash."

Blaine cursed as frustration overwhelmed him. He needed a lead and some hard evidence. "Does your inside man at least have a description of the guy ordering the vans?"

"Good-looking guy with dark hair and light eyes," Dalton replied with a chuckle. "My inside man is actually a woman."

That description matched the man from the security footage—the man who'd lifted Maggie into his arms. "I'll send you a picture to see if she can confirm it's my guy."

Blaine would forward him a screen shot from the security cameras as well as Mark Doremire's DMV picture. If he was the man, Blaine could link him to the vans and therefore the robberies. Maggie would have to accept his involvement.

But then it would probably be like losing Andy again— to lose another piece of him when she realized his brother wasn't the man she'd thought he was.

He hadn't been checking up on her as his brother had requested. He'd been casing the banks where she worked.

Dalton nodded. "Send me the photo. I'll get it to my informant right away. Whatever you need to get these guys, let me know. I'm happy to help."

He obviously knew about Sarge. Blaine sighed. "Ash must've talked some."

Reyes nodded again. "Yeah. He said this one's personal for you both."

It was, but not just because of Sarge. It was personal because of Maggie, too.

"He thinks it might be extra personal for you, though," Reyes continued, "because of the witness."

He glanced toward the ER, where Blaine kept looking, wondering how Maggie and the baby were.

"Ash talks too damn much," he said.

Reyes chuckled. "He's worried about you. He thought I should tell you about another agent who works out of the Chicago Bureau, Special Agent Bell. He works serial killers."

"Maggie's not a serial killer," Blaine said. She was not a criminal at all. "She's a victim."

"Yeah, Bell got too *personally* involved with a victim's sister," Reyes said. "It's the case he never solved. The serial killer he never caught."

Would these suspects be the ones that Blaine never caught—because he cared too much?

"You can't go!" Maggie exclaimed as she clutched at Blaine's arm, panicking at the thought of being separated from him. Since the first moment she'd met him, she'd thought him a golden-haired superhero, and every time he saved her life he proved that he was her hero.

"There are local authorities here," he said, gesturing with his free arm to where two police officers stood near the nurses' station. "You'll be safe."

She shook her head in protest. He couldn't pass her off to someone else again. He couldn't leave her. She was afraid that she wouldn't be able to protect her baby without him. "I'm not safe anywhere. Except with you."

"Not even with me."

"You kept me safe," she said. "They were trying to run us off the road. We would have been killed if you hadn't driven the way you had."

His voice gruff, he brushed off her gratitude. "But I could have hurt you…"

"The doctor said that the baby and I are both fine," she reminded him. "I can leave now. They don't need to keep me for observation." Blaine was the only one who wanted her to stay in the hospital with the local deputies guarding her. "I can leave with you now."

He wouldn't meet her gaze, just shook his head. "I don't think that's a good idea."

"Why not?" she asked. "Where are you going? Have they found the van?" She'd seen the smoke from under the hood. It probably hadn't gotten very far.

"The van has already been recovered," he said. "Empty. And it had been stolen."

"So you're not going there," she said. "So where are you going?" That he didn't want her along. Had he found another lead he was pursuing? Was he going to put himself in danger?

The thought of that scared her as much as being without his protection. She didn't want anything happening to Blaine. Maybe it was just the danger and the fear that had her so attached to him, but she had never felt like this before. She had never been as drawn to another person.

"I'm going to Andy's dad's house," he said. "I confirmed that he is still living in the house where Andy grew up."

She hadn't wanted to go back there, now that Andy was gone. "I thought you wanted me to go along."

"I was wrong to even consider taking you there," he said. "It's too dangerous."

"It's Andy's dad—"

"And maybe his brother."

If they believed Tammy...

Maggie wasn't so sure that they should. While Mark had always been caring and friendly, sometimes too friendly, Tammy had always seemed cold to her—even at Andy's funeral. Maybe that was just because Mark had been too friendly.

But Tammy wasn't at the dad's house. "They're not going to hurt me," she said. "I've known his dad for years." But, truthfully, she hadn't known Andy's parents that well. They had usually hung out at her house or around town more than at Andy's.

"Maybe his dad wouldn't hurt you," Blaine said. "But you're wrong about his brother. The description of the guy who ordered the stolen vans matches Mark's description."

"Dark hair? Blue eyes?" She shrugged. "A lot of guys look like that." Except for Blaine. She had never seen a man as attractive as he was, but it wasn't just his looks. It was his protectiveness and his courage and his intelligence that she found even more compelling than his physical appearance.

"I sent someone a picture of Mark for a positive ID," he said.

"It won't be," Maggie said. She refused to accept that Andy's big brother could be robbing banks. "Mark wouldn't hurt me." He had promised Andy that he would take care of her. He would never break his promise to his brother.

Blaine sighed as if exasperated with her. Maybe that was why he wanted to leave her at the hospital. He was tired of her. "Don't you think it's strange that we were run off the road shortly after leaving his house?"

Her heart—that had finally slowed from a frantic beat—started pounding hard again. "No…" She really didn't want Mark involved. "That van could have followed us from the bank."

"I doubt it," Blaine replied. "I was too careful. I didn't see anyone following us. I think Mark was either in that house or his wife called him and told him where we were heading."

"But you didn't say where," she reminded him. "You said that we would come back to their house the next day. If they were involved, wouldn't they have just waited for us to come back?"

"Or they'll make damn sure they're gone before tomorrow." He pushed a hand through his disheveled blond hair. "Hell, they could be gone now. I have to go."

She didn't release his arm. "You can't go without me." She hadn't wanted to go back to Andy's house, hadn't wanted to relive the past. But now she was more afraid of the future. She didn't want to be separated from Blaine and she wasn't sure it was just because she was scared.

"I can't put you in danger again," he said.

"I won't be in any danger," she said. "This is Andy's family. I'm carrying Andy's baby. They're not going to hurt me." They wouldn't want to lose that last piece of Andy any more than she did.

His mouth curved into a slight grin. "What about me?"

"They're not bad people," she said. "They won't hurt you, either."

"That wasn't what I meant." He stared at her, his green

gaze tumultuous with regret. "I'm worried that I'm going to hurt you."

"You've saved my life again and again," she reminded him. She would never forget how he had protected her and her baby. Maybe gratefulness was the feeling over-whelming her and making her panic at the thought of him leaving her. But it didn't feel like just gratitude. "You're not going to hurt me."

Physically—he wouldn't. She knew that he would pro-tect her from physical harm. He had proved that over and over again.

But he was only doing his job. And she had to remem-ber that. She had to remember that, when he caught the robbers, Blaine would move on to his next assignment, and he would leave her.

For good.

So he probably would hurt her. Emotionally. If she let herself fall for him...

But she wouldn't do that. She wouldn't risk her heart on anyone right now. She was going to save all her love for her baby.

Chapter Twelve

Maggie was getting to him in a way that no one had ever gotten to Blaine before. He couldn't even draw a deep breath for the panic pressing on his chest.

What had he been thinking to bring her along? He shook his head in self-disgust.

"What?" she asked from the passenger seat of the battered SUV.

"I shouldn't have brought you..."

"I told you that I won't be in any danger."

Maybe she wouldn't be. But he was worried that *he* was in danger. He was in danger of falling for her. And that would be the biggest mistake he'd ever made.

It wasn't that he still believed she was involved in the robberies. But he would be a fool to totally rule out the possibility. Even though there were attempts being made on her life, it could be to silence her, so that she wouldn't reveal her coconspirators. But he doubted that. If she actually knew anything about the robbers, she would have told him by now; she was too scared to keep secrets any longer.

The reason it would be a mistake for him to fall for Maggie Jenkins was because she was in love with another man. He suspected she would forever love her dead fiancé.

That was why she had insisted on coming along with him. To protect Andy's family from him.

"I really don't believe they're involved," she insisted. And he wondered now if she was trying to convince herself or him.

"Andy could have told them what you had shared with him about the bank," he said. "What did you share with him?" And how did it tie in to the robberies?

"I rambled on," she said, "like I usually do since I talk so much. I complained about working harder than the manager. I told him what my duties were—how I handled the money deliveries and pickups—how I knew the security code for the back door and the vault."

That information had definitely been used in the robberies. Even at the other banks, the robbers had threatened the assistant managers and never questioned the managers.

"It sounds like Andy shared that information with his brother." And Mark had used it to rob all the banks.

She shook her head, tumbling her brown curls around her shoulders. "Andy wouldn't talk to anyone about my job."

"Why not?" he asked, and he wondered about her dismissive tone.

She shrugged. "It's not very interesting."

"It's not?"

"Most of the time it's very boring," she said.

Had Andy thought her job boring and uninteresting? "But you told him about it anyway?"

"I wrote about it," she said. "I guess my letters to him were kind of like writing in a journal. I complained about stupid policies and procedures."

"You wrote him letters?"

"Yes," she said. "Didn't I tell you that before?"

"Not about the letters—just that Andy was the only person you'd told about your job," he said. Because she told Andy everything. He'd thought that had been in person, though. "Where are the letters now? Did you get them back?"

She shook her head. "No. I don't know what would have happened to them after he…after he…" She trailed off, unable to talk of his death. Of her loss…

"His personal effects would have been returned to his family," Blaine said. He was definitely right about Andy's family; they had to be involved in the robberies.

Maggie sucked in a breath, as if she had just realized it, too. "But they wouldn't have read his personal letters…"

"If they miss him as much as you do," he pointed out, "they might have."

"But those are letters that *I* wrote to him," she said, her voice cracking with emotion. "They're not the letters he wrote to me. They're not about Andy and his life."

"I'm sorry," he said. She had every right to be angry. "Those letters should have been returned to you. They're your personal thoughts and feelings. Hell, you were his fiancée. You should have gotten everything."

She shook her head in denial. "We weren't married. So his personal effects should have gone to his family."

"You're family—you and his baby," Blaine said. "His parents and brother should have at least given you those letters."

"Maybe they just didn't have time…" She kept defending them.

Maybe she was naive. Maybe she just tried to see the best in everyone. But that was how she had wound up with Susan Iverson as a roommate. She didn't need protection just now; she needed it every day. She needed protection from her own sweetness and generosity.

"His brother's been checking on you," he said. The image from the security footage of him hugging her hadn't left his mind. "He could have brought the letters to you then. He's had six months to get them to you." Unless he had been using them for something else—to help him plan the bank robberies.

"We're here," she said with a sigh of relief as he pulled the battered SUV to the curb across the street from the brick Cape Cod.

He could have sworn earlier today that she hadn't wanted to come back here. Of course, she thought she was going to prove to him that Andy's family wasn't involved. But with every new thing he learned, his suspicions about them grew. He didn't even need confirmation from Dalton Reyes that Mark Doremire was the one ordering those stolen vans.

He was so convinced that Doremire was involved that he'd had a local officer watching the house before they arrived. The car was parked a little way down the street. Too far down the street if Doremire and his father were armed. The other men from the bank could be there, too.

Maggie reached for her door handle, but Blaine caught her arm and held her back from opening the door. With his other hand, he grabbed his cell and checked in with the officer.

"Nobody's come or gone, Agent Campbell," the officer assured him.

So what did that mean? That they had holed up in the house with weapons? At least the driver of the van, and whoever else might have been riding inside, couldn't have joined them. They wouldn't have had time to ditch the van for another vehicle and drive up without the officer seeing them.

Blaine clicked off the cell and turned back to Maggie. "I want you to stay here until I check out the inside of the house."

"Mr. Doremire may not let you in unless he sees me," she warned him. "Andy's parents kind of kept to themselves when we were growing up. They didn't socialize much. So he's not going to open his door to a stranger."

Blaine tugged his badge out of his shirt. He wasn't hiding it this time. "This will get him to open the door," he said. Or he would knock down the damn thing. "You need to stay here until I determine if it's safe or not."

He waited until she reluctantly nodded in agreement before he stepped out the driver's side. But moments later Mr. Doremire proved her right. When Blaine knocked on the door, a raspy voice angrily called out, "Go away!"

"I am Special Agent Campbell with the FBI," Blaine identified himself. "I need you to open up this door, sir. I need to talk to you about your son."

"It's too late for that!"

That was what Blaine was afraid of. That Mark was already gone—that he'd taken off to some country from which he couldn't be extradited. But then, who had tried running them off the road on the way here? Only Mark would have known they had stopped at his house looking for him. Only Mark would have known where they'd been heading.

"Go away!" the older man yelled again.

"Let me try," a soft voice suggested as Maggie joined him at the solid wood door to the Cape Cod. It was painted black—like the shingles on the roof. And there was no welcome mat.

"I told you to stay in the vehicle," he reminded her.

Even with the squad car not far away, she wasn't safe; someone could have taken a shot at her as she had crossed the street.

Ignoring him, she knocked on the door. "Mr. Doremire, it's me—it's Maggie. Please let us in…"

Inside the house, something crashed and then heavy footfalls approached the door. It was wrenched open, and a gray-haired man stared at them from bloodshot eyes.

Blaine could smell the alcohol even before the man spoke. "Have you heard from him?" he demanded to know.

"Mark has been by to see me," she said. "At the bank. Is he here?"

"Mark?" the older man repeated, as if he didn't even recognize the name of his eldest son. "I'm not talking about Mark."

Did the man have other boys? Maybe there were more Doremires involved than Blaine had realized. Maybe they made up the entire gang.

But Maggie's brow furrowed with confusion, and she asked, "Who are you talking about?"

"Andy," Mr. Doremire replied, as if she was stupid. "Have you heard from Andy yet?"

She reached out and clasped the older man's arm and led him back inside the house. "I'm sorry, Mr. Doremire," she said as she guided him back into his easy chair. A bottle of whiskey lay broken next to the chair. But no liquor had spilled onto the hardwood floor. He'd already emptied it.

She crouched down next to the old man's chair and very gently told him, "Andy's dead. He died in Afghanistan."

"No!" the gray-haired man shouted hotly in denial.

"He didn't die. That's just what he made it look like. He's alive."

She shook her head, and her brown eyes filled with sympathy and sadness. "No…"

"I've seen him," the man insisted. "He's alive!"

"No," she said again. "That's not possible. His whole convoy died that day. There's no way he survived." And her voice cracked with emotion and regret.

Mr. Doremire shook his head in denial and disgust. "That boy wasn't strong enough for the Marines," he said. "He had no business joining up. He got scared. He took off. He wasn't part of that convoy."

Why was Andy's father making up such a story? Just because he couldn't handle his son being dead?

"They wouldn't have reported that he was dead if they hadn't been certain," Maggie continued, patiently. "They wouldn't have put us through that and neither would Andy."

"None of the remains recovered have actually been identified, so there is no way of proving that he was part of the convoy," the older man insisted. "They never even recovered his dog tags."

"They are still working on DNA," Maggie said with a slight shudder. "But they know that Andy's gone…" And from the dismal sound of her voice, she knew it, too.

Blaine hated that she was reliving Andy's last moments. Or had those actually been his last moments? Was Andy's father right? Was Maggie's fiancé still alive? Mr. Doremire had claimed that he'd seen him.

If so, Blaine had another suspect for the robberies— one who had definitely read her letters and knew about the bank's policies and procedures, and the duties and responsibilities of the assistant manager.

"Will you be okay in here?" Blaine asked Maggie.

She nodded. "Of course."

But she stared up at him with a question in her eyes as if wondering where he was going...

"I have to make a call," he said.

From his years as a marine, he had connections, people he could call to verify if Andy Doremire had been identified among the convoy casualties. Maybe they hadn't identified the remains immediately after the explosion, but in the past six months they would have. And he couldn't trust that Mr. Doremire's drunken claims were valid. Or was Andy alive and robbing banks?

MAGGIE BIT HER bottom lip to stop herself from calling out for Blaine. She didn't want to be left alone with Andy's dad and his outrageous story. He was drunk, though. That had to be why he was talking such nonsense.

"He's calling someone in the military," Dustin Doremire said. "He's going to talk to some marines."

Blaine had been a marine. He would know whom to talk to.

"Probably," she agreed. "He's wasting his time, though." Andy was dead. Therefore, he was not robbing banks—as Blaine probably now suspected.

"They're not going to tell him anything," Mr. Doremire said with a derisive snort. "It's a cover-up."

So he was drunk and paranoid. "What are they covering up?" she asked. She wasn't even sure who "they" were supposed to be. First Andy had faked his death and now someone else was covering it up?

"You know what they're covering up," he accused her, suddenly turning angrily on her.

She edged back from his chair, not wanting to be so close to him. "I don't know what you're talking about." That was definitely the truth.

"Andy told you everything," he said. "You know..."

But now she wondered. Had Andy told her everything? He had never mentioned his father drinking so much. Maybe it had started only after his death. But now she wondered—because she hadn't come over to Andy's house very often. He had always come to hers. And if his car was broken down and she had to pick him up, he met her on the street.

Maybe she hadn't been the only reason Andy had joined the Marines. Maybe he hadn't done it just to support her, the way he had old-fashionedly claimed he'd wanted to do. Maybe he had also joined to escape his father.

"That boy loved you so much," Mr. Doremire continued. "He was crazy about you."

Andy had loved her. If only she could have loved him the same way...

The older man uttered a bitter laugh. "The boy was such a fool that he couldn't see you didn't feel the same way about him."

"I cared about Andy," she insisted. "He was my best friend." And she would forever miss him and she would regret that his son or daughter would never know him—would never know what a sweet guy he'd been.

"But you didn't love him," the older man accused her, as if she'd committed some crime. "It's your fault, girl. It's all your fault."

"What's my fault?" she asked.

"It's your fault he joined the Marines, trying to prove he was man enough for you." Mr. Doremire shook his head. "He wasted his time, too. You never looked at him like you're looking at that man..." He gestured toward where Blaine had gone out the open front door.

"That man is an FBI agent," she said. "He's investi-

gating the robberies at the banks where I've worked."
He had to have heard about the robberies; they'd made
the national news.

But the older man just stared bleary-eyed at her. Had
he even known she worked at a bank?

"I don't care who the hell he is," Mr. Doremire replied.
"He's not going to be raising *my* grandchild."

She hoped Blaine had stepped far enough away from
the open door that he hadn't overheard that. But her face
heated with embarrassment that he might have. She assured the older man, "Agent Campbell is not going to be
raising my child."

She knew that once the robbers were caught he would
move on to his next case. She was nothing more than a
witness and possible suspect to him.

"That's Andy's child!" Mr. Doremire lurched out of
the chair and reached for her as if he intended to rip the
baby from her belly.

She jerked back to protect her baby. She didn't even
want his hands on her belly, didn't want him hurting her
child—before he or she was born or after—the way he
must have hurt Andy had he ever spoken to him the way
he'd spoken of him.

"Mr. Doremire," she said, "please calm down." *And
sober up.*

"Andy won't be letting some other man raise his kid,"
he ominously warned her. "You'll see. He'll show himself to you, just like he's shown himself to me."

She wondered how many bottles of whiskey it had
taken for Andy to show himself. She suspected quite
a few.

"Andy is gone, Mr. Doremire," she said. "He's dead."

His hand swung quickly, striking her cheek before

she could duck. Tears stung her eyes as pain radiated from the slap.

"That's what you want," Mr. Doremire said. "You want him dead. But he's not! He's not dead!"

"Okay, okay," she said, trying to humor the drunk or deranged man. "He's alive, then. He's alive."

He had no idea how much she really wished that Andy was alive. Then she wouldn't have lost her best friend. She wouldn't feel so alone that she was clinging to an FBI agent who was only trying to do his job.

Maybe she was as crazy as Andy's dad to think that Blaine could have any interest in her beyond her connection to the bank robberies.

The older man started crying horrible wrenching sobs. "If he's dead, it's your fault," he said again. "It's all your fault!"

She nodded miserably in agreement. Maybe it was…

If he hadn't wanted to buy her that damn ring…

If he hadn't wanted to take care of her…

"You're the one who should be dead!" He swung his arm again.

And, realizing that the man wasn't just drunk but crazy, too, she cried out in fear that he might actually kill her.

Chapter Thirteen

Maggie's scream chilled Blaine's blood. He dropped his phone and ran back into the house—afraid of what he might find.

Why the hell had he left her alone? He hadn't even checked the house. Mark Doremire could have been hiding somewhere, waiting for his next chance to grab Maggie.

But when he burst into the living room, he found only the older Doremire and Maggie. She was backing up, though, and ducking the blows of the man's meaty fists.

Blaine jumped forward and caught the man's swinging arms. He jerked them behind his back. "Dustin Doremire, I am placing you under arrest for assault."

"No," Maggie said. "You don't need to arrest him." But her cheek bore a red imprint from the older man's hand.

Blaine jerked Doremire's arms higher behind his back, wanting to hurt him the way he had hurt Maggie. The old drunk only grunted. After all that whiskey, he was probably beyond the point of feeling any pain. Only inflicting it...

"He hurt you," he said. And Blaine blamed himself for leaving her alone with Andy's drunken father.

"He's hurting," she said, making excuses for the man's abuse. "He misses his son."

Blaine had placed a few calls. But nobody had really answered his questions about Andy Doremire. In fact, they'd thought he was crazy to even ask. Of course the man was dead. His family wouldn't have been notified if his death hadn't been confirmed.

Otherwise, he would have been listed as missing. Blaine knew that. But for some reason he had wanted to think the worst of Andy Doremire. He'd wanted proof that her dead fiancé wasn't the saint that Maggie thought he was—he wasn't a man worth loving for the rest of her life.

But he was a better man than Blaine was. Andy wouldn't have willingly left her alone and in danger.

"Are you all right?" he asked her. "How badly did he hurt you?"

She brushed her fingertips across her cheek and dismissed the injury. "It's nothing. I'm fine."

She wasn't fine. He could hear the pain in her voice. But he wasn't sure whether it was physical or emotional pain. He suspected more emotional. She hadn't wanted to come here—to Andy's childhood home. And now he understood why.

"He needs to be brought in," he said. "I need to arrest him." Actually he only intended to hand him over to the officer outside to make the arrest and process Mr. Doremire.

"Please don't," she beseeched him, her big brown eyes pleading with him, too.

"You never want me to arrest anyone," he said. "You make it hard for me to do my job." He had ignored her and arrested Susan Iverson anyway. He was tempted to do the same with Mr. Doremire. "I need to question him."

"Let *me* question him," she said.

He settled the older man back into his chair. The guy collapsed against the worn cushions. The chair was one of the only pieces of furniture left in the nearly empty house. In fact, the Cape Cod made Ash's little bungalow look almost homey.

Blaine had no intention of letting Maggie question him. But before he could ask, she already was. "When did you see Mark last?"

"Mark?" The older man blinked his bloodshot eyes, as if he had no idea whom she was talking about.

"Mark is your oldest son," she prodded him. "His wife, Tammy, said he was here—visiting you."

He shook his head in denial. "I haven't seen that boy for months. He's not like Andy. Andy keeps coming around to check on me."

Did he have his sons confused? Even Maggie thought they looked a lot alike. He shared a significant glance with her as they both came to the same realization.

"When was Andy here last?" she asked. "When did he come see you?"

Doremire's eyes momentarily cleared of the drunken bleariness, and he stared at her with pure hatred. "You have no right to say his name."

The old man would have reached out again; he would have swung his arm if Blaine hadn't squeezed his shoulder and held him down onto the chair.

"She has every right to say his name," Blaine insisted. "They were engaged."

The older man shook his head. "She never would've married him. She didn't care about him…"

"That's not true," Maggie said, but her voice was so soft she nearly whispered the words.

"She loved him," Blaine said. "You know that. You have the letters she wrote to your son. Where are they?"

The drunk blinked in confusion, the way he had when she'd asked about Mark. "Letters?"

"*My* letters," she said. "The ones I wrote to Andy when he was overseas. Do you have them?"

He shook his head. "His mother probably took them— like she took everything else when she left."

Blaine could see that she had taken most everything. And he could see why she had left, too, if the man had been like this with her. If he had been abusive...

"Where did Mrs. Doremire go?" Maggie asked.

"She took all Andy's life-insurance money and bought herself a condo."

That money should have gone to Andy's fiancée and his unborn child, but Andy must not have listed her as his beneficiary yet. Knowing she was carrying Andy's child, his family should have given her the money, though. It would have been the right thing to do.

But this family obviously didn't care about what was right. Or honorable. Or legal.

He had to find Mark Doremire—had to catch him before he got beyond Blaine's reach.

"Where is her condo?" Maggie asked.

Andy's father named some complex that had her nodding as if she knew where it was. "It's not that far from here," she said. "We can go there now."

Blaine had no intention of taking her anywhere but to a bed. To rest...

But the thought of a bed reminded him of that morning, of her flicking back the covers to reveal all her voluptuous curves. The woman was so damn sexy.

"Tell that witch that she didn't break me," Mr. Doremire said. "Tell her that I'm fine..."

He was anything but fine. The former Mrs. Doremire was probably well aware of that, though.

"I hope you will be," Maggie said. After how the man had treated her, how could she wish the best for him?

Blaine had met few women as sweet and genuine as Maggie Jenkins.

But the old man stared up at her again with stark hatred. "I hope you get what you deserve."

It wasn't so much what he said but the venomous tone with which he said it that had Blaine protesting, "Mr. Doremire—"

"And you, Mr. Agent, I hope the same for you. Maybe you two deserve each other..."

Blaine knew that wasn't true. Maggie deserved a better man. He should have protected her better than he had. So, finally, he guided her toward the door.

"But don't go thinking you're going to be raising that baby together," Mr. Doremire yelled after them. "Andy's going to take that baby. He's going to raise his son himself."

Maggie sighed. "Andy's gone..."

"He's not dead," the older man drunkenly insisted. "You're going to see when he comes for his baby boy. You're going to see that he's not dead."

Maybe he wasn't dead—in his father's alcohol-saturated mind or in Maggie's heart. Blaine wished he was man enough to deserve her love. But he suspected she had none left to give anyway.

ONCE BLAINE SAID it was too late to see Mrs. Doremire, Maggie feigned falling asleep in the SUV. She didn't want to talk. She didn't want to even look at Blaine. Her face was too hot, and not from Mr. Doremire's slap but with embarrassment over all the horrible things that old drunk had said in front of Blaine.

Maybe he hadn't heard everything; maybe he'd been outside during the worst of it. But he had come running back when she'd screamed. He had saved her—as he always did.

Mr. Doremire hadn't been wrong about how she looked at the FBI agent. Despite not wanting to fall for him, she was falling. She had more love to give than she'd realized. But Blaine wouldn't want her love—or anything else to do with her, for that matter—once the bank robbers were caught.

The SUV drew to a stop. Then the engine cut out. A door opened and then another. Hers.

Blaine slid one arm under her legs and another around her back, as if he intended to lift her up the way he would a sleeping child. She jerked back.

"Sorry," he said. "I didn't mean to scare you. I just didn't want to wake you up."

"I'm up," she said.

But he didn't step back; he didn't give her any room to step out of the SUV. He was too close, his green gaze too intense on her face.

Her skin heated and flushed. She wished he wouldn't look at her. She lifted her hand to her face.

But he beat her to it, bringing his hand up to cup her cheek. "I don't think it'll bruise," he said.

She shrugged. She couldn't have cared less about her face. The man's words had hurt far more than his slap. "It's fine."

"I'm sorry," he said.

"You're sorry?"

"I shouldn't have left you alone with him." Blaine pushed a hand through his disheveled hair. "I knew he was drunk. I never should have stepped outside."

"You called someone about Andy," she said. It wasn't a question because she knew that he'd done it. She had watched the new suspicions grow in his green gaze. "To make sure that he's really dead."

Finally he stepped back and helped her from the SUV. Then he escorted her from the street up to the little bungalow where they had spent the night before. He hadn't taken her back to the hospital or to a hotel.

Her chest eased a little with relief.

"Are you going to ask me what I found out?" he asked, opening the door.

She shook her head as she passed him and entered the living room. "No."

"So, you're sure he's dead?"

"I know it." Even before Mark had called her, she'd known. She'd seen the news of the explosion—of the casualties—and she had known Andy was among them.

"But they didn't even recover his dog tags," Blaine said.

She shrugged. "I don't know what was recovered or not. I don't know if my letters were even sent back. You should have let me talk to Mrs. Doremire."

"It's been a long day for you already," Blaine reminded her as he flipped on the light switch. "We went back to the bank and watched all that footage. Then we saw Mark's wife and nearly got run off the road."

She shuddered at the reminder of those harrowing moments when she had thought the SUV was going to flip over and crash onto the rocky shoreline.

"And if that wasn't already too much for you," he said, "then you were assaulted by a crazy drunk."

"He is crazy," she agreed. "Thinking that Andy's alive…"

"That makes sense, actually," Blaine said, "that he doesn't want to let his son go."

She sighed. "I guess that is his way of dealing with his grief—denial and alcohol."

"How about you?" he asked.

She stared up at him in confusion. She had dealt with her grief months ago and neither alcohol nor denial had been involved. "What do you mean?"

"Are you going to be able to let Andy go?"

"I don't think he's alive," she assured him. "I'm not seeing him anywhere." She didn't see ghosts. Regrettably, she did keep seeing zombies—in person and in her nightmares. She would probably rather see ghosts.

"That's not what I meant," he said.

"What did you mean?" she wondered.

Instead of explaining himself, he just shook his head. "It doesn't matter."

She thought that it might, though—to her. Did he want her to let Andy go? Or was he like her almost father-in-law and not entirely convinced that Andy was dead?

"What did the people that you called tell you?" she asked. She already knew, but she didn't want to leave him yet. As tired as she was, she didn't want to climb the stairs and go to bed. Alone.

"They said that Andy's dad's claims were crazy," he replied. "They're not covering up anything…"

"Mr. Doremire said a lot of crazy stuff," she said. Hoping to dispel her embarrassment, she continued, "Like that nonsense about us…"

"Nonsense?"

Her skin heated again and not just on her face; she was warm all over. "Of course. All his drunken comments about you and me. That was just craziness…"

"What was so crazy about it?" he asked.

She drew in a deep breath to brace herself for honesty. "It's crazy to think that you'd be attracted to me."

"It is?" That green gaze was intense on her face and then it slid down her body.

Now her warm skin tingled. "Of course it is," she said. "I'm so fat and unattractive…" And he was the most beautiful man she'd ever met.

"You're pregnant," he said. "And you're beautiful."

She laughed at his ridiculous claims; they were as outrageous as Mr. Doremire's. "I wasn't fishing for compliments. Really. I know exactly what I look like—a whale."

He laughed now as if she were trying to be funny. She had just been honest. He was not being the same as he replied, "I would not be attracted to a whale."

"You're not attracted to me." She wished he was. But it wasn't possible. Even if she wasn't pregnant, she knew he would never go for a woman like her—a woman who talked too much and didn't think before she let people get close to her.

He stepped closer to her, his gaze still hot on her face and body. "I'm not?"

She shook her head. But he caught her chin and stopped it. Then he tipped up her chin and lowered his head. And his lips covered hers.

Maybe he had intended the kiss as a compliment or maybe it was just out of pity. But it quickly became something more as passion ignited—at least in Maggie—and she kissed him back.

She locked her arms around his neck and held his head down for the kiss. Her lips moved over his before opening for his tongue. He plunged it into her mouth, deepening the kiss and stirring her passion even more. Making her want more than just a kiss…

Chapter Fourteen

It had just been a kiss. But even though it had happened hours ago, Blaine still couldn't get it out of his mind. Probably because it hadn't been just a kiss. It had been an experience almost profound in its intensity.

And he hadn't wanted to stop at just a kiss. He had wanted to carry her upstairs to one of the bedrooms and make love to her all night long.

But he'd summoned all of his control and pulled back. His cell had also been ringing with a summons from the Bureau chief to come into the office for an update on the case.

"You've lost your objectivity," the chief was saying, drawing Blaine from his thoughts of Maggie.

"What? Why?"

"The witness," Chief Special Agent Lynch said.

Blaine glanced at the clock on the conference room wall. He had left her alone too long. Of course, he hadn't actually left her alone. He had left her with two agents guarding Ash's house—one patrolling the perimeter and one parked in a chair outside her bedroom door. They were good men, men for whom both Ash and Dalton Reyes had vouched. They weren't special agents yet; they were barely more than recruits. But Truman Jackson had been a navy SEAL and Octavio Hernandez had worked in the gang task force with Reyes.

She should be safe…

But he had thought that when he'd left the local authorities to protect her.

"The witness is in danger," he said. "That was proven today—" he glanced at the clock again and corrected himself "—*yesterday* when someone tried running us off the road."

"The van was processed."

"Any evidence?"

"Not like in the first one," the chief replied. "No blood."

"Have you gotten a DNA match yet?"

The chief shook his head. "We'll check some other databases—see if we can find at least a close match."

"Good—that's good."

"What leads have you come up with?" the chief asked. "Or have you been too busy protecting the *witness*?"

"She is the best lead," Blaine insisted.

"You checked to see if her fiancé is really dead," the chief said. "She's leading you to a dead man as a suspect?"

"She didn't think he was alive. It was the man's father who raised some questions…"

"You think her fiancé's family is involved in the robberies."

He sighed. "Her fiancé's brother is a viable suspect. Reyes even confirmed him as having bought the van recovered after the robbery. The one in which the blood was found." Someone else had ordered the black cargo van. Why? Was Mark already gone?

"Where is he?" the chief asked, as if he had read

Blaine's mind. "Why haven't you brought Mark Doremire in for questioning?"

"We haven't found him yet."

"We?" the chief asked. "You're having the witness help you do your job?"

"I have an APB out on him," he said. "The witness is helping me figure out places where the man could be hiding. We checked out his dad's house."

The chief studied him through narrowed, dark eyes. "So you're only using her to lead you to a suspect?"

Blaine tensed as anger surged through him. "I'm not using her. I'm trying to keep her and her baby from getting killed."

"Is it the pregnant thing that's getting to you?" the chief asked.

If this was the way this chief ran this Bureau, Blaine wasn't sure he would want to stay in Chicago after all. And he'd considered staying here, putting down roots. Chicago wasn't that many miles from his sister Buster, who had settled in west Michigan.

"What?" he asked, offended that his professionalism was being questioned.

"I've read your history. I know you have a few sisters. Is that it?" the chief persisted.

He didn't feel at all brotherly toward Maggie Jenkins. And he suspected that neither did Mark Doremire. "The robbers keep trying to grab her. One of these times that they're trying, we'll be able to catch them."

"So you're using her as bait."

He tensed again. Furious and offended. "You may have read my file, but you don't know me."

"Ash Stryker does," the chief said. "He vouched for you. Says you're the best."

Although Blaine appreciated his friend's endorsement, he added, "My record says that."

"I'm still worried about the witness."

So was Blaine.

"You no longer think she's personally involved in the robberies?" the chief asked, as if he wasn't as convinced.

"She didn't plan the robberies." Blaine was certain of it. "She didn't recruit the other robbers."

"What evidence do you have of that?" Chief Lynch asked. "Her word?"

"The attempts on her life," he replied.

"Coconspirators have never tried killing each other?" The chief snorted. "You've been doing this job long enough to know better than that."

"No honor among thieves," Blaine murmured.

"Or loyalty."

"If that were true, she would have given them up," Blaine pointed out. "If she knew who they were, the fastest way to stop them would be to tell me who they are."

"You really believe that she doesn't know?"

He nodded. "But the robbers don't realize she doesn't. They must think that she can identify them somehow. That's why she's our best lead to them. It's also why she's in so much danger."

"But guarding her isn't the best use of *your* time or talents," the chief said. "We'll put other agents on her protection duty. We can keep Jackson and Hernandez on her."

Blaine was used to butting heads with local authorities trying to run his investigation. Usually the Bureau respected his handling of a case. But maybe the chief was right. Maybe he had lost all perspective where Maggie Jenkins was involved.

Maybe it would be better for him to trust her protection to someone else…because he couldn't trust himself where Maggie Jenkins was concerned.

BLAINE HAD BEEN gone so long—all night and all morning—that Maggie doubted he was ever coming back. And she felt sick to her stomach because of it. Maybe that was why the baby was restless; maybe it was because he missed him, too.

Him? Andy's dad had called him a boy. Sometimes she thought her baby was, too. But she didn't care if she had a boy or girl; she just wanted a healthy baby. That was all she wanted.

She didn't want Blaine Campbell. *Liar,* she chastised herself. She had wanted him, the night before, when he'd kissed her senseless. But when he'd pulled back, and her senses had returned, she'd recognized his kiss for what it was. A balm for her battered ego. Pity…

So she didn't want Blaine Campbell anymore. All she wanted was a healthy baby. And she couldn't have that with someone trying to kill her. So she gathered her courage and picked up the phone one of the agents had let her borrow. She dialed a number she had looked up online. Andy's mom was listed.

"Hello?" a friendly female voice answered on the first ring.

"Mrs. Doremire?"

"Maggie? Is that you?" the older woman asked. "Is everything all right? Is the baby all right?"

"Yes." For now…

"Oh, thank God." The woman released a sigh of relief that rattled the phone. "What can I help you with, honey?"

Honey. She didn't hate her like Andy's dad did? "I stopped by your old home yesterday…"

The woman drew in a sharp breath. "I'm sorry that you did that. Was it…unpleasant?"

Maggie's cheek hadn't bruised, but it was still sensitive to the touch. "I understand that he's very upset about Andy's death."

"What death?" she asked.

And that sick feeling churned harder in Maggie's stomach. Was Andy's entire family crazy?

"My ex-husband refuses to accept that Andy's dead," Janet Doremire continued.

"Is that why he's drinking so much?"

"It's his new excuse to drink," Janet replied. "But he always had one."

Why had Andy never told her what he'd gone through at home? They had been best friends. But apparently neither of them had really told each other everything.

"I'm sorry…"

"He refuses to accept Andy's death because then he'll have to admit his blame for it."

"Blame?" Someone besides her blamed himself for Andy's death?

"He's the reason Andy joined the Marines," Janet explained. "Dustin told him that it would make a man of him."

But Maggie and Sarge had been right. Andy hadn't had the temperament for it. He wasn't like Blaine Campbell, who hadn't hesitated over firing his weapon or risking his life.

Mrs. Doremire sighed again. "Instead it killed him."

Was that why Andy's mom had left his dad? Because she blamed him, too? Or was it over the drinking? Maggie didn't want to pry.

But Mrs. Doremire willingly divulged, "Andy's death showed me that life's too short to waste. I wasted too many years with my ex. I didn't want to spend another minute in that unhappy marriage. Andy would have wanted me to be happy."

"Yes, he would have," Maggie agreed. He had loved his mother very much. But now she realized he had never said that much about his father.

"Andy would have wanted you to be happy, too," Janet Doremire continued.

Tears stung Maggie's eyes, but she blinked hard, fighting them back. He would have wanted her to be happy because that was the kind of man he'd been.

"I know you're carrying his baby, but you need to move on, Maggie," Janet Doremire continued. "You and Andy only ever dated each other. You got too serious way too young—like me and Andy's father had. You should get out there." The woman chuckled. "Well, once the baby's born."

"Mrs. Doremire, I can't—" Maggie couldn't have this discussion with Andy's mother. She couldn't talk about dating someone else. "That's not why I called you…"

"I'm sorry, honey," Mrs. Doremire said. "Why did you call me?"

"I was wondering if you had the letters I wrote to Andy—if they'd been returned in his personal effects…?"

"I don't know," Mrs. Doremire said. "I never looked through his stuff."

"Do you have it?"

"No. I left it and the rest of my past at the old house. I don't want to wallow in it. You shouldn't, either," Mrs. Doremire said. "You don't need those letters, honey. Let them and Andy go."

The baby shifted inside Maggie, kicking, as if in protest. Would Mrs. Doremire even want anything to do with her grandchild once he or she was born? Or was she determined to forget everything about Andy?

That was obviously her way of dealing with her grief. And Andy's dad chose to wallow in alcohol. Since his ex hadn't taken everything, as he'd claimed, he must have either broken it or sold it. What had he done with her letters?

"Thank you, Mrs. Doremire..." But she spoke only to a dial tone. The older woman had already hung up. "But I really do need those letters..."

"We just need to know who has them," a deep voice remarked.

She turned to find Blaine standing in her bedroom doorway. She hadn't even heard him open the door. How long had he been there?

"She says her ex-husband," Maggie replied with a sigh. "I don't want to go back there, but I really want those letters."

"I'll send an agent with a warrant for Andy's personal effects," he said. "We'll get them."

Her face heated with embarrassment. "I wish nobody had to see those letters."

"Nobody cares about the personal parts," Blaine said. "Just the parts that relate to the bank procedures."

"That's what I worry about someone reading," she admitted. "I was such a fool to share those details with anyone. I'll probably get fired when it gets out that it's all my fault."

"We don't know that it is," Blaine said. "Maybe nobody read those letters. And as you've pointed out, other banks were robbed."

"Other banks that probably follow the same procedures we do," she said with a sigh. "I'll get fired and be unable to get a job anywhere else." And then how would she support herself and her baby?

"Don't panic," Blaine said. "We'll figure this out."

No, he would. And once he figured it out, he would be gone.

"Where have you been?" she asked. Then her face grew hotter as she realized she sounded like his wife or girlfriend, like someone who actually had a right to ask him where he'd been.

"Bureau chief wanted an update on my progress," he replied easily, as if he felt she had a right to ask.

"You were gone a long time," she said. "You must've had a lot to tell him." He had probably told the chief about her letters and Andy's brother and dad.

"He had a lot to say, too," Blaine said with a sigh. "He thinks that I'm losing my objectivity where you're concerned."

"Because he thinks you should still consider me a suspect?" Maybe Blaine did; he had never really said that he no longer had any suspicions about her.

"Chief Lynch thinks that I shouldn't be the one protecting you," he said.

That explained the other agents who'd guarded her last night and today. But the thought of losing Blaine's protection panicked her. She wasn't just frightened for the baby's safety or hers; she was panicked at the thought of no longer seeing Blaine. "I don't understand. You've saved me. You've kept me safe."

"He's right," Blaine said. "I should not be protecting you. I have lost my focus."

"So you're going to send me away—to one of those *safe* houses again?" She was losing him already. She had been right to not fall for him. But despite her best intentions, she was afraid that it was already too late.

"Not yet," he said. And he stepped inside the room and closed the door behind himself. "Not tonight..."

"Blaine...?"

"This is why I shouldn't be the man protecting you," he said, "because I want you. Because I'm attracted to you, and when I'm around you, I can barely think, let alone keep you safe."

She must have fallen asleep; she must have been dreaming—because he couldn't be saying what she was hearing. Testing her reality, she reached out and touched his face. His skin was stubbly and sexy beneath her palm, making her fingers tingle.

"You're attracted to me?"

"I showed you last night," he reminded her, "with that kiss."

"I thought that was pity."

He laughed. "That wasn't pity."

"Then why did you stop?" She'd lain awake all night—wanting him. Needing him...

"I thought I was taking advantage of you," he said, "of your vulnerability."

She shook her head. "You weren't..."

"I want to," he said. "I want you..."

She wanted him, too, so she tugged him down onto the bed with her. And she kissed him with all the desire he had awakened in her the night before—all the desire she had never felt before. It coursed through her again as their lips met.

He kissed her back. And it was definitely not with pity but with desire. He touched her, too, his hands moving gently over her body.

Her pulse pounded madly. She wanted him to rip off her clothes, but he removed them carefully, slowly, as if giving her time to change her mind.

She had never wanted anything—anyone—more. She didn't take off his clothes slowly; she nearly tore buttons and snaps in her haste to get him naked. When all his golden skin was bare, she gasped in wonder at his masculine beauty. His body was so sleek but yet so muscular, too.

He made love to her reverently, moving his lips all over her body. He kissed her mouth, her cheek, her neck before moving lower. He nibbled on her breasts, tugging gently on her nipples.

She moaned in ecstasy, her body already pulsing with passion. She pushed him back on the bed and he pulled her on top of him, gently guiding his erection inside her.

"This is all right?" he asked, his hands holding her hips—holding her up before she took him all the way inside her. "For the baby?"

She bit her lip and nodded. Even though she had told her doctor it wouldn't be an issue, the female obstetrician had assured Maggie that sex wouldn't jeopardize her pregnancy at all. "It's fine."

He pulled her down until he filled her. And she moaned again.

"Are you okay?" he asked.

"Not yet," she said, as she began to move again—rocking back and forth—trying to relieve the inexplicable pressure building inside her. "But I will be…"

He helped, guiding her up and down—teasing her breasts with his lips and gently with his teeth—until ecstasy shattered her and she screamed his name. Then he thrust and called out as he joined her in ecstasy.

She collapsed on top of him, their bodies still joined. He clasped her to him, holding her tightly in his arms. His heart beat heavily beneath her head, and his lungs panted for breath. Finally his heart slowed and his breathing evened out, and she realized he'd fallen asleep beneath her.

She would have been offended if she wasn't aware that he'd had no sleep the past two nights. And maybe even more nights before that. She hadn't had much more sleep, so she began to drift off, too.

Until her eyes began to burn and her lungs…

At first she blamed guilt. But Mrs. Doremire was right. Andy would have wanted her to be happy, so she couldn't use him as an excuse. But as it became harder for her to breathe, she realized what the real problem was.

Smoke. Someone had set the house on fire.

Chapter Fifteen

"Blaine!"

The sound of his name—uttered with such fear and urgency—jerked him awake as effectively as if she'd screamed. He coughed and sputtered as smoke burned his throat and lungs.

Soft hands gripped his shoulders, shaking him. "The house is on fire! We have to get out!"

They pulled on clothes in the dark and Blaine grabbed up his holster and his gun. He couldn't believe that he hadn't awakened earlier. The fire must have been burning for a while because there was a lot of smoke—so much that it was hard to breathe. Hard to see. But there wasn't much heat.

Maybe the smoke was just a ruse to get them out of the house—where Maggie could be grabbed. Or shot. But the smoke, growing denser and denser, could kill her, too.

She coughed and sputtered. But she didn't speak. She must have been too scared.

So was Blaine. He was scared that he had failed her and the baby—that he had broken his promise to her that he would keep them safe. He shouldn't have let his desire for her distract him. He shouldn't have crossed the line with a material witness.

"We have to stay low," he said as he helped her down

to the floor. He reached forward and touched the door, his palm against the wood. It wasn't warm—at least, not as warm as the floor beneath his knees.

Maggie must have felt it, too, because she gasped and started to rise. But Blaine caught her arm and pulled her back down as she began to cough.

Getting out wouldn't be easy, especially if the whole first floor was engulfed as he suspected. But he didn't have time to devise a plan. He had to act now—before the floor gave way beneath them.

So he opened the door to the hall. The smoke was even thicker than in the bedroom. He crossed it quickly to the bathroom, grabbed towels from a shelf and soaked them under the tub faucet. Maggie was still in the hall as if she hadn't been able to see where to go. He wrapped Maggie's face and body in the wet towels, and then he picked her up in his arms.

"Blaine…"

He coughed, and his eyes teared up from the smoke. But there was no time. And maybe there was no escape. He couldn't jump out a second-story window—not without hurting Maggie and her baby. So he ran toward the stairs. The bottom floor was aglow from the flames, but none licked up the steps. So he ran down them—wood weakening and splintering beneath them from the heat and the fire.

The house creaked and groaned as the flames consumed it. And the smoke overwhelmed him, blinding him to any exits. But he remembered where the front door was.

But had it been barricaded? Or were those gunmen waiting outside it to make sure they didn't escape?

As he headed toward it, the door burst open, and men in masks hurried into the house. These weren't those horrible zombie masks. These masks had oxygen pumping into them and were attached to hats. Firemen had arrived. Of course one of Ash's neighbors would have called the police. They would have noticed the flames—unlike Blaine.

He shouldn't have sent the other agents away. But he had wanted one last night alone with Maggie. That night might have cost her life or her baby's life. Her body was going limp in his arms.

One of the firemen took Maggie from him and carried her out. Blaine should have fought the man. He should have made certain that he really was a fireman. What if it was one of the robbers in another disguise?

Blaine hurried after him, but the smoke was so thick in his lungs now that he couldn't draw a breath deep enough. He couldn't breathe. And before he could hurry after Maggie, the house shuddered as the second story began to fall into the first...

MAGGIE'S THROAT BURNED. From the smoke and from screaming. Over the fireman's shoulder, she had seen the roof collapse and the house fold in on itself...and on Blaine. She'd pounded on the fireman's shoulders, but he hadn't released her.

And for a moment, she had stared up in fear that the mask wasn't any more real than the zombie masks had been. She'd worried that it had just been a disguise.

And she'd reached for it. But she'd been too weak to pull it off. Too weak to fight off the man as he carried her away. He put her into the back of a vehicle, and it sped away with her locked inside. Sirens wailed and lights flashed, but she still did not trust where it would take her. She didn't trust the oxygen either that a young woman gave her in the back of that van.

What if it was a drug or a gas? What if it knocked her out? She tried to fight it, but she didn't have the strength to pull off the mask. And then it began to make her feel better, stronger.

So when the doors opened again, she was strong enough to fight. To run. But the doors opened to a hospital Emergency entrance. She pulled off the oxygen mask and asked, "Where's Blaine?"

The paramedic stared down at her as she pushed the stretcher through the sliding doors of the ER entrance. "Who?"

"Agent Campbell," she said. "He was in the house…" She coughed and sputtered, but she wasn't choking on the smoke. She was choking on emotion. "He was in the house…when the roof caved in…"

The paramedic shrugged. "I don't know…"

"Do you know if anybody else got out?"

Blaine hadn't been the only one inside; there had been other firemen, too. Real firemen, she realized they were. They would have saved him. Right? They would have made certain Blaine got out alive.

"I don't know, miss," the female paramedic replied. "We were told to get you to the hospital right away because of the baby."

Maggie had one hand splayed across her belly, feeling for movement. Was he okay? She hoped the smoke hadn't hurt him. She was scared to think of what it might have done to his heart. His brain…

"That's good," she agreed. "We need to check out the baby."

"And you, too," the paramedic said. She leaned back as doctors ran up.

But Maggie grabbed the young woman's arm. "Was

there another ambulance there?" Was there someone who could help Blaine?

Because after seeing the roof collapse, she had no doubt that all of the people still inside would need medical help. Maggie was glad that she and her baby had been brought to the hospital so quickly. But she also wished they would have waited for Blaine—to bring him in with her.

Then she would know how badly he'd been hurt. Or if he had survived at all...

The young paramedic didn't have a chance to answer her question before doctors and nurses whisked Maggie's stretcher into a treatment area. They hooked her to another oxygen machine and an IV. There was also a heart monitor for the baby and an ultrasound.

She breathed a sigh of relief when she heard the fast but steady beat. "He's alive..."

"His heart sounds good," a doctor agreed.

"And his lungs?"

"Did you ever lose consciousness?" someone asked. "Did you pass out from the smoke?"

Maggie shook her head.

"We'll administer some prenatal steroids to help the development of his lungs," the doctor said, "to make sure everything's fine..."

But everything wouldn't be fine until she learned if Blaine had made it out of the burning house.

"He's active," the doctor said as he watched the ultrasound screen.

He. The picture on the ultrasound confirmed what Maggie had previously only suspected. She was carrying a baby boy. She wanted to share that news with her best friend. But he was gone. She wanted to share that news with the man she loved. But Blaine was gone, too.

Maybe the IV contained a sedative because she must have drifted off despite her worry. She didn't know how much time had passed, but when she awoke, she was no longer in the emergency department. She was alone in a room but for the man—tall and broad-shouldered—who stood in the doorway.

Hope burgeoned in her heart. "Blaine?"

The man stepped forward…into the light that glowed dimly from another doorway, perhaps to the bathroom. The man's hair was dark and his eyes were light, not gold and green like Blaine's. Disappointment made her heart feel heavy in her chest. "You're not Blaine."

But the man who had purchased those stolen vans had been described as dark haired with light eyes. This man matched that description as much as Mark Doremire had.

Could he be one of the robbers? And if he'd forgone the zombie mask, then he had no intention of letting her live.

"Who are you?" she asked. She didn't recognize him. She would have had no way of identifying him as one of the suspects in the robbery.

"I'm not Blaine Campbell," he agreed with a short chuckle. "My name is Ash Stryker. I'm also an FBI agent and a friend of Blaine's."

"Is he okay?" she asked. "Is he here?" She struggled to sit up, ready to jump out of bed and go to him.

Ash shook his head. "No. He's not here. That's why he asked me to stay with you."

"But is he okay?" she asked, and her panic grew. Had Blaine asking Ash to stay with her been his deathbed request? Was that why he wasn't there?

Because he was gone? Dead and gone?

Ash nodded, but he had that same telltale signal of stress that Blaine did. A muscle twitched in his cheek.

Maybe that twitch wasn't just betraying his stress but his lie—like a gambler's tell in a poker game.

"No," she said, her voice cracking as hysteria threatened. "I don't believe you. I saw the roof collapse. He couldn't have gotten out of there without some injuries."

Serious injuries.

Fatal injuries.

The man flinched as if he'd felt Blaine's pain. "He has some bumps and scratches," he admitted. "And a couple of small burns. But he's fine. Or I wouldn't be here."

Even though Blaine had asked him? But then, he would have been too distraught over the loss of his friend to worry about her.

Maybe Blaine wasn't gone.

The dark-haired man sighed. "Of course, I have no place to go right now…"

"It was your house he was staying at," she realized. And that Blaine had let her stay at, as well. He should have taken her to a motel. It might not have protected her, but it would have protected Ash Stryker's house. "I'm sorry…"

"It wasn't your fault," he assured her.

"But whoever set the fire is after *me*," she said. "So I feel responsible." She felt responsible for the house and for those injuries Blaine had suffered. How badly had he really been hurt?

Agent Stryker moved closer to the bed and assured her, "You're not responsible for any of this."

"I wish that was true," she said. "I shouldn't have stayed at your house. I shouldn't have stayed with Blaine." Or made love and fallen in love with Blaine.

He chuckled. "Blaine was right…"

"What was he right about?"

"He said that you couldn't possibly have anything to

do with the robberies," Ash said. "He said that you're too good a person to be consciously involved."

He thought she was a good person?

"I figured Blaine was only thinking that because he grew up with sisters and has this whole chivalry thing going on," Ash said.

She nodded. "He is very chivalrous and protective." The man was a hero like she had never known.

"I also guessed that you're pretty," he said.

She didn't feel pretty now. She felt bedraggled from the smoke. Maybe it was good that Blaine wasn't there. He would have regretted sleeping with her.

Maybe he did regret it. Maybe that was why he wasn't here—with her. Had he even checked on her?

"Where is Blaine?" she asked.

Ash sighed. "He's determined to end this," he said. "He wants these guys caught."

"He wants to avenge Sarge's death," she said. "Sarge is—"

"I knew Sarge, too," Ash said with a grimace of regret and loss. "He was also my drill instructor."

"I'm sorry."

"Stop apologizing," he said. "None of this is your fault. Blaine is going to prove that. He's going to find out who the hell is responsible and bring them to justice."

She breathed a small sigh of relief. He had to be okay, then. He had to be strong enough to want revenge. But her breath caught again as she realized that he was putting himself in more danger.

"You should be with him," she said. "You should make sure he's really all right. The doctors wanted to keep me here because they're worried about my lungs having a delayed reaction to all that smoke. I think it's called hypoxia." That was why they were keeping her on oxygen.

Blaine wouldn't have oxygen with him. He wouldn't have anyone to help him if hypoxia kicked in, depriving his body of oxygen. He could die.

He wasn't just in danger from whoever was trying to kill them. He was in danger from his own body shutting down on him.

That muscle twitched in Ash's cheek again. He was worried, too. Blaine must have checked himself out against doctor's orders.

"Have you heard from him?" she asked.

He shook his head.

Maybe it was already too late to help Blaine.

Chapter Sixteen

Maggie was okay. So was her baby. Blaine hadn't left the hospital until he'd learned that. He hadn't left the hospital until Ash had shown up. He wouldn't have trusted anyone else to protect her. He probably shouldn't have trusted Hernandez and Jackson since he wasn't sure how the robbers had discovered where Maggie was staying.

He'd been so careful to avoid being followed—to avoid anyone discovering where he had hidden her. But he hadn't kept her safe. Ash would. Or at least he would try…the way Sarge had tried.

Maggie was in too much danger. She and her baby had survived this time. But eventually their luck would run out.

Blaine had to focus on finding the robbers. He couldn't think about her—or what they'd done right before the fire started. He couldn't think about anything but suspects.

He was determined to find the one who had so far eluded him. So he went back to Mark Doremire's house.

His wife opened the door and stared at him through eyes wide with surprise. At first he thought it might have been because of the hour; it was barely dawn. But she was looking at him instead of the sky.

"Are you all right?" she asked.

He felt as if a roof had fallen on him. But then, it had.

He'd been fortunate to come out with only a few scrapes and light burns. The firemen had used their own bodies to protect him. His lungs burned, though, from all the smoke he'd inhaled. The doctor hadn't authorized him to leave the hospital. He'd wanted to keep Blaine for observation—something about a delayed reaction to smoke inhalation.

But Blaine felt time running out since each attack on Maggie had been harder for her and for him to survive. So he had refused to stay and checked himself out against the doctor's orders.

"No, I'm not fine," he admitted. "I'm about to arrest you for obstruction of justice if you don't tell me where your husband is hiding."

She shrugged but continued to block the doorway to the kitchen the best she could with her thin frame. "I can't tell you what I don't know."

He could have pushed her aside and searched her house. But he'd had someone watching it—someone with thermal imaging who'd detected only one person inside the house. Mark really wasn't there. "You don't know where your husband is?"

She shook her head. "I figured he was following Maggie around like his brother used to. But it seems as though you're doing that now."

"I'm just doing my job," he said. But it was a lie. Protecting Maggie had less to do with his job than with his heart. He had fallen for her.

And just as Dalton Reyes and his boss had warned him, he'd gotten distracted. Because of that, he had nearly lost his life and hers, as well. He had to put aside his feelings for her and focus only on the case. He wasn't going to be like Special Agent Bell and leave this case unsolved.

The younger Mrs. Doremire snorted derisively as she recognized his lie. "So you've let sweet Maggie get to you, too," she said. "Something about her makes a man feel more important, more manly. That's what killed Andy. That dumb kid actually thought he could be a soldier—for her."

"That was Andy," Blaine said. "What about his brother? He's *your* husband." He wanted to goad her—to piss her off at Mark—so that she would give up his whereabouts.

"But I don't need him like dear sweet Maggie does," Tammy replied. "It doesn't help that before Andy left for his last deployment he asked Mark to watch out for her. Why do you think we moved here?"

Blaine shrugged even though he could have guessed. The robberies...

"Because she moved here," Tammy said. "I left behind my friends and family for Maggie."

"You hate her."

She laughed. "That's the thing about Maggie. You can't hate her. She's too sweet. But she's also manipulative as hell. She'll suck you in and ruin your life."

"Has she ruined yours?" he asked, wondering why the woman resented her so much.

"She ruined my marriage. I haven't seen Mark in days," she said. So she blamed Maggie for all the problems in her marriage instead of blaming her husband. "I have no idea where he is. So if you want—arrest me. Take me in for questioning. Drug me with truth serum. I'm not going to be able to tell you what I don't know."

"Who would know where he is?" Blaine wondered.

Tammy sighed and leaned wearily against the doorjamb. Her red hair was tousled, and she wore a robe. But somehow he doubted she'd had any more sleep than he had. "Like me," she said, "Mark left his friends behind in Michigan. Maybe his mom or dad would know where he's gone."

"His dad only talks about Andy," Blaine admitted.

"Everybody loved Andy. He was sweet—like Maggie," she said. "But genuinely sweet. He was a good man who died too soon."

"What about Mark?" he asked. "Is he a good man?"

She shrugged again.

"Could he be involved in the bank robberies?"

She gasped in surprise.

He narrowed his eyes skeptically at her surprise. "You didn't figure out that's why I'm looking for him?"

"I had no idea why you're looking for him," she said. "I thought you were just a friend of Maggie's."

He was so much more than just friends with her.

"I'm a special agent with the FBI," he said. "And I'm working the bank robberies—the one where the suspects wear zombie disguises."

She sighed. "Mark wouldn't have gotten involved in the robberies on his own." She laughed now. "God knows he's no criminal mastermind. He would have only gotten involved because someone asked him—or manipulated him—into getting involved."

He suspected what she would say next, on whom she would place the blame, but still he had to ask, "Who?"

"Maggie, of course."

"You think she's a criminal mastermind?" He could have laughed, too, at that thought. Not that Maggie wasn't smart. She was. She was also too honest and open to take anything from anyone.

She hadn't even been willing to take a compliment from him. But then she'd taken his desire—his passion. She'd made love with him, too.

"I think she's a desperate single woman who's about

to be raising a baby alone," Tammy Doremire said. "She just might be desperate enough to start stealing."

He doubted Maggie Jenkins was a bank robber.

And Mrs. Doremire must have seen that doubt because she added, "She's not above stealing, Agent. Even you think she probably stole my husband."

He doubted that, too. She thought of Mark as an older brother. But maybe Mark didn't think of her as a little sister. Maybe he saw her for the sweet, desirable woman that Blaine did.

He pressed his business card into the woman's hand. "If you see your husband, give me a call. I need to talk to him."

"If anyone knows where he is," she said, "it'll be Maggie. You should ask her where he is."

"If Maggie knew where he was, I wouldn't be here," he said with certainty. He had wasted his time talking to her.

Tammy Doremire glanced down at the card he'd handed her, then called after him when he started walking toward his SUV, "Be careful, Agent Campbell. The most danger you're in is from Maggie Jenkins."

He couldn't argue with her because he suspected she was right. Maggie was dangerous to him—to his heart. But somebody else was a danger to her, and Blaine wouldn't be able to leave her until he found out who and stopped that person.

"IF YOU DON'T find him, I will," Maggie threatened as she struggled to escape her bed. But the oxygen line tugged at her nose and face. And the IV held her like a manacle.

Ash stretched out his hands, as if trying to hold her back. "Maggie, you have to stay here for observation."

"*You* don't," she said. "Go find him."

"I'm here for observation, too," Ash said. "I'm here to observe you."

"I don't need observation," she said. "I need to know that Blaine is really all right. And if you won't find out for me, I will find out myself." She struggled to sit up again.

"Blaine will kill me if I leave you," Ash said. "I promised him I'd watch out for you."

"Have someone else stand outside the door," she suggested. "A deputy or another agent."

"I'll send one of them to look for him."

She shook her head, rejecting his offer. A stranger wouldn't know where to look for Blaine. "You're his friend. You care about him. I trust you and only you to find him and make sure he's okay."

Ash replied, "I am his friend. And that's why he trusted me to protect you."

"You're not protecting me," she said. "I'm not supposed to get upset because of my blood pressure." She had been warned that she had to watch it, that she had to make sure that it didn't stay high. "And not knowing if Blaine is all right is upsetting me."

"Maggie…"

"Please, go find him," she urged his friend. "That's what you can do to protect me." Because not knowing whether or not Blaine had really survived the fire was the greatest risk to her health.

Ash sighed in resignation. "Damn it, if he's okay, he's going to kill me for leaving you. But I'll make sure the man who replaces me on protection duty can be trusted."

She wasn't worried about herself right now. She wasn't even that worried about the baby. The doctors had assured her that he was fine. Now she needed assurance that Blaine was, too.

Just knowing that Ash was looking for him eased her mind some—enough that she eventually drifted off to sleep. And Blaine popped vividly into her mind.

Naked, his golden skin stretched taut over hard muscles. He had made her feel emotions she had never felt before: lust, passion and love.

She hadn't wanted to fall in love with him. But it was too late. She had lost her heart to Special Agent Blaine Campbell. And now she may have lost him.

He should have stayed in the hospital—stayed where they could give him oxygen and monitor him to make sure he had no serious aftereffects from the fire. But he'd gone off on his own to track down killers.

Those zombie-masked men had been dangerous enough when Blaine was in full superhero mode. But in his weakened state, with his injuries…

She shuddered to think of what might have happened to him. But she clung to hope the way she clung to the memories of their lovemaking. With her eyes closed, she relived every kiss, every caress.

Her skin grew hot. But not with passion. She smelled the smoke again and felt the heat of the flames. And in her mind those flames began to consume Blaine…

She jerked awake with a scream on her lips. But a hand covered her mouth, holding that cry inside her. So that she couldn't alert anyone to his presence?

With the lights out, even the bathroom one, she saw only a big, broad-shouldered shadow looming over her. This couldn't be whoever Ash had asked to take his place protecting her. An agent or a deputy—a real one—wouldn't have been standing over her in the dark.

Who was this person?

What were his intentions? To smother her with a pillow? Or simply with his big hand?

She reached up, trying to fight him off. And she smelled the smoke again. This time it wasn't just a vivid memory. This person had been at the fire, too.

Chapter Seventeen

"I'm sorry," Blaine said, his voice gruff from the smoke that still burned in his throat and saturated his hair and clothes. "I didn't mean to scare you." He slid his hand from her lips. But he wanted to cover her mouth again—with his. He wanted to kiss her.

Maggie sat up and threw her arms around his neck. "You did scare me—so badly," she said as she trembled against him. "I thought you didn't make it out of Ash's house."

"Where is Ash?" he asked, furious that his friend hadn't been the one guarding her door. Dalton Reyes had been standing outside, and while Blaine admired what he'd done with the Bureau, he wasn't sure he could trust him, even though Ash obviously did.

"I begged him to look for you," she said.

Begged or manipulated? He shook off the thought, angry with himself for letting Tammy Doremire get to him. She was probably the real manipulator. "Why?" he asked.

"I wanted to make sure that you hadn't had aftereffects from the smoke," she said.

"I'm fine." But he wasn't. He was in even more danger than her almost sister-in-law had warned him about. He was in love with his witness.

"Then where were you all this time?" she asked, her eyes glistening in the darkness as she stared up at him.

Guilt and regret tugged at him for leaving her alone. After the fire, she had to have been terrified. But apparently she'd been more concerned about his safety than hers or she wouldn't have sent her protection away. She wouldn't have sent Ash out to find him.

Anger at Ash flashed through him, but then, he couldn't blame the man for letting her get to him. She had gotten to Blaine, too.

"I was working the case," he said. "Trying to track down a suspect."

"Mark?" she asked. From her tone it was obvious that she was still reluctant to believe Andy's brother could have anything to do with the robberies.

"I went to see Tammy Doremire to see if she'd heard from her husband yet." Mark was definitely one of the robbers—probably the mastermind, no matter that his wife thought he was an idiot.

"Has she heard from him?" she asked with more concern than suspicion.

He shook his head.

"He's her husband," she said. "How can she not know where he is?"

"I don't think their marriage is that great," Blaine said. His sisters would have killed their husbands if they'd gone hours, let alone days, without checking in with them. Hell, Buster probably knew where her husband was every minute of every day.

"Is he seeing someone else?" Maggie wondered.

"Maybe." He was thinking of Susan Iverson, but he added, "She thinks *you* know where he is."

She gasped. "I don't."

"She thinks you two may have been involved." He

could believe that Mark had been interested in Maggie. But he believed that she thought of the man only as an older brother—maybe as a link to her dead fiancé.

She gasped. "That's crazy." And she drew back from him. "Do you think that, too?"

"No." He trusted her. He believed her.

But then he worried that maybe he was being a fool. Maybe she had manipulated him just as Tammy had warned. Maybe Maggie had manipulated Blaine into falling in love with her. Or maybe he was just scared that for the first time in his life he'd fallen in love and he worried that she would never be able to fully love him back. Not when her heart still belonged to her dead fiancé.

BLAINE WAS STANDING there right in front of her, right beside her hospital bed, but Maggie felt him pulling away from her. Whatever Tammy had said must have gotten to him—must have gotten him doubting her.

She felt like a suspect again.

"If I knew where he was, I would tell you," she said. Not because she thought Mark was guilty of anything, but to prove his innocence. Then Blaine would be able to focus on who was really involved in the robberies.

"His wife thinks you know…"

"His wife is paranoid," she said. Tammy had never been nice to her; she was the kind of woman who couldn't be friends with other women. "She's delusional, too, if she thinks I'm having an affair with her husband."

"Maybe there's another reason you might know where Mark is," Blaine said. "Maybe he's hiding someplace that Andy might have gone. Did he have an apartment or a house of his own?"

Everything kept coming back to Andy and those damn

letters she'd written him. If only she'd had something to tell him about other than her job.

If only she'd had the guts to tell him about her feelings, her true feelings…

She shook her head. "No, it would have been crazy for him to have a house or apartment when he was hardly ever home. Andy stayed with his parents whenever he was home on leave—which hadn't been that often since he joined the Marines after high school."

"He wasn't home much?"

After seeing how mean a drunk his father was, she understood why he hadn't come home a lot. "No."

Then she remembered that he hadn't always come home. "He did sometimes stay somewhere else…" She should have thought of it earlier, but it was a place she'd wanted to forget.

That muscle twitched in Blaine's soot-streaked cheek. "Your place?"

"No." As much as she had missed her best friend when he'd been gone so long, she hadn't wanted him to stay with her. She hadn't wanted him to think they were more than they were. She should have said no when he asked her to marry him; she should have refused that ring.

"Then where else had he stayed?" Blaine asked.

"The Doremires have a cabin near Lake Michigan— at least, they had it before Andy died," she said. "I'm not sure if they kept it after they divorced. I can call Mrs. Doremire and ask…"

He shook his head. "No. Let me check it out. I don't want anyone tipping off Mark before I can track him down."

"I'm not so sure his mother would call him." Especially since she hadn't seemed to want anything to do with her life before Andy's death.

Janet Doremire was right—that life was too short to waste. The fire had proved that to Maggie. She was lucky that she hadn't lost her baby and Blaine.

"I don't want to take that risk. Where is the cabin?" he asked.

"It's north of where they live," she said. "Close to Pentwater. But I don't know the name of the actual road. I would need to show you where it is."

He shook his head. "I can't take you along with me. I'll be able to find it. I know that area."

"But you sound like you're from out East," she said.

"New Hampshire," he said. "But my sister lives near Pentwater."

"Which sister?"

"Buster."

She wanted to meet all of his sisters, but most of all Buster because he talked about her with the most affection and exasperation.

"It's good you have family within a four-hour drive." Her family was too far away to offer much support. "So maybe you will stay here even after you find these robbers?"

He shrugged. "I can't think about that until I finish up this case."

Probably because he would be moving on to the next case.

"I need to find that cabin," he said.

"It's really remote and hard to find," she warned him. Even if she could talk Blaine into taking her along, she wasn't certain that she would be able to find the cabin again. She had gone there only a couple of times with Andy—one summer during high school and most recently when he had proposed to her. She shouldn't have gone then. She should have known what he was going to ask her.

"It sounds like the perfect place to hide," Blaine murmured. "He has to be there."

Maybe he was. "But just finding Mark won't prove him guilty of the robberies."

"I'm hoping to find more than Mark. I'm hoping to find the guns, the cash. Hell, if it's so remote, it might be their hideout."

And that meant that he might find not just Mark there, but the other robbers—if Mark really was involved.

"You can't go alone," she warned him. "Not if there's any chance that it's their hideout..."

Because they weren't going to want to be found. Blaine hadn't died in the fire, but that didn't mean that he was safe—especially since he kept willingly risking his life.

BLAINE COULDN'T TAKE her along for so many reasons, but he missed Maggie when she wasn't with him. He worried about her. The doctors had assured them that she was fine. They had even released her.

In his opinion, that had been too soon. But then, keeping her in the hospital wouldn't have ensured her safety. Someone had nearly abducted her from an ER. Had nearly burned her up in the home of an FBI agent.

Maggie wasn't safe anywhere.

Hell, he couldn't even trust her safety to a friend like Ash. She'd gotten to him. So he'd left her in the protection of the one person he knew who could not be sweet-talked or manipulated.

Maggie would be safe.

But as his SUV bounced over the ruts of the two-lane road leading to the cabin, he wondered about his own safety. The place wasn't just remote. It was isolated. He had seen nothing but trees for a long while. This was the kind of place where serial killers would bring their victims, so nobody could hear their screams for help.

Blaine shuddered with foreboding. But maybe he was just overreacting, as Maggie kept insisting. Maybe Mark wasn't involved. Maybe he was just taking a time-out from his jealous wife and his drunken father and the loss of his brother...

Maybe the guy really had nothing to do with the robberies, and Dalton Reyes's informant had identified the wrong guy. As Maggie had pointed out, a lot of guys looked like Mark Doremire. Andy had. Hell, even Ash did.

Even though he would have to start all over looking for suspects, Blaine almost hoped Mark had nothing to do with the robberies. If he didn't, Blaine could just check in with him and make sure that everything was all right with the man.

Then he could return to Maggie and ease her worries about her letters to Andy inspiring the robberies. She already took on too much responsibility for everything that had happened. Maybe that was his fault, too—for being so suspicious of her. Maybe he should have told her that he trusted her.

Instead he had pulled away from her. Physically and emotionally. He needed distance. He needed perspective. Hell, maybe if Mark wasn't at the cabin, Blaine would hang out for a while. He would try to regain his lost perspective.

But he worried that time and distance wouldn't change his feelings for Maggie. He would probably always love her. And she would probably always love Andy.

Finally some of the trees gave way on one side of the two-track road, making a small space for a little log cabin. Blaine couldn't see any vehicles. Only a small space of the dense woods had been cleared for the cabin, so he doubted there were any vehicles parked around the back.

Maybe Maggie had been right. Mark wasn't here. Coming here had probably been a waste of Blaine's time. Because no matter how much distance he gained, he was unlikely to gain any new insights.

Still, he shut off the SUV and stepped out of it. He would take some more time to enjoy the silence.

To clear his head.

But the silence shattered as gunfire erupted. And Blaine worried that he was more likely to lose his head than clear it.

Chapter Eighteen

Maggie had wanted to meet Buster, but not like this—not riding along in the Michigan state trooper's police cruiser. At least Buster had let her ride in the passenger's seat and not the back.

The woman had pulled off into a parking lot, and now she studied Maggie through narrowed eyes that were the same bright green as her brother's. She was blonde, too, but most of her hair was tucked up under a brown, broad-brimmed trooper hat, so it wasn't possible to tell if it was golden, like his, or lighter.

She was older than he was but not more than a few years. And she was even less approachable. Maggie, who usually had no problem making conversation, had no idea what to say to the woman, so an awkward silence had fallen between them—broken only by an occasional squawk of the police radio.

Finally Buster cleared her throat and remarked, "Blaine has never asked me to guard anybody for him."

"I'm sorry for being such an inconvenience," Maggie said. "I know you're too busy for babysitting."

"I have four hyper kids and an idiot husband," Buster shared, "so I'm used to babysitting."

The heat of embarrassment rushed to Maggie's face. She hated feeling so helpless and dependent.

But then Buster continued, "*This* isn't babysitting. Nobody is trying to kill my kids or my husband—except for me when they piss me off too much. You're in real danger."

Maggie felt safe, though, with Blaine's older sister. She had an authority about her—the same authority that had Blaine easily taking over the bank investigation and her protection duty.

"Blaine is the one in danger now," Maggie said, as nerves fluttered in her belly with the baby's kicks. "He's trying so hard to track down those robbers."

"That's his job," Buster said. "He's been doing it for a while. And he's been doing it well."

Maybe he was right about Mark, then. Maggie hadn't wanted to believe Andy's brother capable of violence, but she was on edge and it had less to do with how Buster was studying her and more to do with the danger she felt Blaine was facing. "I'm still worried about him."

"I see that..."

With the way she had been staring at Maggie, she had probably seen a lot. More than Maggie was comfortable with her seeing.

Buster continued, "I see that you love him."

Maggie's breath shuddered out in a ragged sigh. She could have lied—although she sucked at it—and said Buster was mistaken. But she wasn't a liar. And maybe it would relieve some of the pressure on her chest—and her heart—if she admitted to her feelings. "Yes..."

"You could have denied it," Buster said.

"Why?"

"Because you haven't told him yet," his sister replied. "And he's the one you should have told first."

Maggie shook her head. "I can't tell him at all." Ever. "Why not?"

"Because he doesn't have the same feelings for me that I do for him," Maggie said. "And I would just embarrass him." The way she had at the hospital when she'd clung to him, refusing to let him leave without her.

"Blaine doesn't embarrass easily," Buster said. "Trust me. I've tried." She chuckled. "He has three older sisters. He may not get embarrassed at all anymore."

Maggie laughed, too, as she imagined a young Blaine enduring his siblings' teasing and tormenting. He had probably handled it as stoically then as he handled everything now. Her laughter faded. "It may not embarrass him, but it would make it awkward for him. He's only doing his job—"

"He has never asked me to protect anyone for him before," Buster repeated as if that was monumental.

As if it meant something.

Could he return her feelings?

Maggie shook her head. "That's because I'm in a lot of danger," she said. "People have been trying to kidnap and kill me."

"People?"

"He thinks the brother of my…" She didn't know what to call Andy. While she had accepted his proposal, she'd done it only to avoid hurting him, not because she'd ever intended to actually marry him.

"Baby daddy?" Buster supplied the title for her.

Maggie laughed again. But Andy would have been appalled at that title, especially since he'd been trying so long to get her to marry him. He'd wanted to marry right out of high school, but she'd told him she wanted to go to college first. And then when she'd graduated, he had suggested they get married. But she'd put him off, saying that she wanted to get her career established first.

Poor Andy…

Buster reached across the console and squeezed her hand. "You cared about him."

"We were friends since sixth grade, when my family and I moved to town. He was the first person who was nice to the new girl in class." Because he had been nice to her, she had latched on to him, declaring them best friends. But Andy hadn't wanted to be just a friend.

Buster nodded as if Maggie's words had given her sudden understanding. "So he's the only boy you ever dated?"

"Yes," Maggie replied.

"It must have been hard losing him and finding yourself alone," Buster said, "with a baby on the way."

Did Buster think that Maggie was afraid to be alone? That that was why she'd fallen in love with Blaine? Because he'd been nice to her? Maggie knew that he was only doing his job, though. He didn't want more than friendship from her; he probably didn't even want friendship.

"But that's not why I…" she began defensively, "…why I have feelings for your brother." She couldn't say it— couldn't express those feelings.

"That's not why you've fallen for my brother," Buster said, as if she didn't doubt her.

"He might not believe that, though," Maggie said. "Or he might think I'm just grateful for all the times he has saved my life and the baby's."

"May I?" Buster asked, as she moved her hand from Maggie's arm to her stomach. She smiled as the baby kicked beneath her palm. "You should tell Blaine how you feel about him. That's the only way you're going to know what he thinks and how he feels about you."

Was it possible that he could return her feelings? He had made love with her. He'd wanted her…

"My brother has never been an easy man to read," Buster said. "Hell, he wasn't even easy to read when he was a little boy. It's always been hard to tell what Blaine is thinking or feeling. So don't assume that you know."

Maggie had been making assumptions. But it wasn't based so much on what she thought of Blaine but more on what she thought of herself. She didn't believe that she, especially pregnant, could ever attract a man like Blaine Campbell. The gorgeous FBI special agent was more of a superhero than a regular man. "But—"

"Do you want any more regrets?" Buster interrupted. "It seems like you already have a few."

About Andy. About never telling him the truth…

"I don't regret my baby," Maggie said, anger rushing over her.

"I know," Buster said. "And I am a firm believer in everything happening for a reason. So stop beating yourself up about the baby's daddy."

Apparently Maggie wasn't very hard to read at all.

Buster patted Maggie's belly. "Remember—everything happens for a reason."

Because she carried his child, Maggie would always have a piece of Andy with her. She hadn't completely lost her best friend.

"You're right," Maggie agreed.

But she didn't have a chance to tell Buster exactly what she was right about because the police radio squawked again—interrupting them. "Shots fired during FBI raid on cabin. Possible casualties…"

She grabbed Buster's hand and clutched it. Possible casualties? Was one of them Blaine? Had he been shot?

"WE DIDN'T FIND the shooters," Trooper Littlefield reported to Blaine. He was one of Buster's coworkers.

He had provided backup—along with a couple of FBI agents—in case the cabin had been the robbers' hideout. But they had arrived early and hidden in the woods so that it would look as though Blaine had come alone.

Blaine had even felt alone in the middle of the woods. These law-enforcement officers were so good that he hadn't seen a single one of them—until the gunfire had erupted. Then they'd stepped out of their hiding spots and returned fire—giving him cover so that none of the shots had actually struck him.

"They had a vehicle parked on a two-track gravel road that led to another cabin, and before we could block them in, they'd gotten away," the trooper said regretfully.

Blaine sighed. They had eluded him so many times that he wasn't surprised. "In a van?"

The trooper nodded.

Dalton Reyes stepped up to him. "Another stolen one," he confirmed with a curse. "The guy who ordered this one isn't the one that my informant ID'd, though. She claims she hasn't seen him again."

Blaine had a bad feeling that Mark Doremire was already gone. But still he held out hope. "You sure you can trust your informant?" he asked. Mark was a flirt; maybe he'd turned the woman to his side.

"I don't really trust anyone." Reyes shrugged. "Maybe she's been lying to me."

"Do you think any of the guys you're after could be involved in the robberies?" Blaine asked. "There were five guys at the bank." But more could have been involved.

He had no idea how many had been shooting at him in the woods.

Dalton shrugged again. "I'm not sure. I didn't get a look at any of the shooters."

"And the guy inside the cabin?" Blaine asked, as he

walked back into the run-down log structure. He'd already been inside but Agent Reyes hadn't. He hoped Dalton recognized the corpse because Blaine was afraid that he did.

Dalton checked out the scene and cursed. The guy was slumped over in a wooden chair, a pool of blood dried beneath him. His clothes—a camo shirt and pants—were also saturated and hard with dried blood. Bloody bandages were strewn across the table in front of him.

But those weren't the only things on the table. A pile of envelopes, bound with a big rubber band, sat atop the scarred wooden surface, too.

Maggie's letters…written to her fiancé. Blaine hadn't looked at them; he probably wouldn't be able to look at them. But he knew they were hers.

"What the hell happened to him?" Dalton asked.

"I think I killed him."

Dalton snorted. "This guy has been dead for days. You didn't do this."

"I think I did. During the bank robbery," he said. "That first van that was recovered had blood inside, and I did get off some shots during the robbery."

Ash stepped into the cabin behind Dalton. "Is he the one?"

Blaine nodded. "Yeah, I'm pretty sure this is the guy who shot Sarge."

Ash patted his shoulder. "You got him!"

"I wasn't sure I hit him. They were wearing vests…"

This guy's vest was lying on the floor near his chair along with the zombie mask and the trench coat. He had definitely been one of the robbers. Was he the one who'd killed Sarge?

When Blaine had fired back, he'd thought that he shot the one who'd hit Sarge.

"He must not have had his vest tight on the sides," Dalton said as he leaned over to inspect it. "Looks like it was too small for him—probably left a gap."

So Blaine had gotten a lucky shot into the guy's side. "There was a smaller robber—maybe their vests got mixed up..."

"I don't care what happened," Ash said. "I just care that you got him—for Sarge."

But who was he? Blaine stepped closer to the body, intent on tipping back the guy's head to get a better look. But then a glint of metal caught his eye, and he saw the dog tags dangling from the chain around the corpse's neck.

He picked up the tags and read, "'Sergeant Andrew Doremire...'"

"Who the hell is that?" Ash asked.

"A dead man," Blaine replied. He tipped up the face—he looked like the man on the security footage from the bank. Maggie had said that Andy and Mark looked eerily similar.

Dalton snorted. "Obviously..."

"No, he's Maggie's dead fiancé."

Dalton Reyes cursed. "Do you think she knows he didn't really die in Afghanistan?" Of course he would ask that; he'd already said he didn't trust anyone.

"No way," Blaine said with absolute certainty. Maggie carried too much guilt over his death, probably because she hadn't been able to talk him out of joining the Marines. But she hadn't been to blame for Andy's death.

Blaine was.

Apparently Dustin Doremire hadn't just been a delusional drunk. He'd been right. Andy wasn't dead—or, at least, he hadn't been until Blaine had shot him.

"He was one of Sarge's drills," Ash said. "He must

have been worried that Sarge had recognized him. That's why he killed him."

Or because Sarge had been trying to kill *him*…

Blaine pushed a hand through his hair. "That must have been why they were trying to take Maggie along with them—they probably thought she recognized him, too."

But she hadn't. She had refused to accept that even the brother of her childhood sweetheart could have had anything to do with criminal activities. She would never believe that Andy had.

So who were the other robbers? Definitely Andy's brother—unless the informant had mistaken Mark's picture for his younger brother. But if his brother hadn't been involved, where the hell was he?

Maybe even Andy's father was involved. That could have been why he'd been drinking so heavily when they'd gone to see him—because he'd known that Andy wasn't going to survive this time.

Blaine had killed him. Would Maggie be able to forgive him? Would she be able to forgive herself?

Chapter Nineteen

He was alive!

Blaine was alive.

Her heart leaped for joy the moment she saw him walk through the door of his sister's sprawling ranch house. When he'd asked Buster to protect her, he hadn't wanted her to take Maggie to her home—he hadn't wanted her to put her family at risk. Neither had Maggie.

But when they had been waiting to hear about Blaine, Buster had insisted on bringing Maggie home with her. In case the news was bad, Buster had probably wanted to be close to her family.

Her kids had gathered around them. She had three boys and one little girl—the opposite of Buster and her siblings. The boys had lost interest in Maggie quickly and gone back to playing with trucks in the living room while Maggie and Buster waited in the big country kitchen. Although shy, the little blonde girl had crept close to Maggie and pressed pudgy little fingers against her belly.

"Baby?" she had asked, though she was little more than a baby herself.

"Yes," Maggie had replied. And she had even managed a laugh when the baby kicked and the little girl had jumped away in surprise.

But fear for Blaine's safety had pressed heavily on

Maggie until he walked through the door. His bruises and scrapes were from the night before—from the fire. Otherwise he was unscathed from the shooting. Maggie had never been happier to see anyone in her life.

But she didn't dare launch herself into his arms the way she wanted to. He had that wall around him—that wall he'd put up back at the hospital. Something was wrong. Maybe it was just that he'd realized he had lost perspective with her, and he was trying to be more professional.

Buster pulled Blaine into a tight hug. "Thank God, you're all right. We were going crazy worrying about you."

"Why?"

"We heard the call on the radio," Buster said, "about the shooting and a possible casualty."

The little girl tugged on her mama's leg. "What's a castle tea?"

Buster pulled back from her brother and picked up her daughter. "It's nothing…"

But it wasn't. Maggie saw the look of regret on Blaine's face. Then he leaned forward and kissed his niece's cheek. "Hey, beautiful girl…"

"Hey, Unca Bane…"

Buster chuckled.

The boys abandoned their trucks and rushed into the kitchen, launching themselves at Blaine the way Maggie wished she had. She wanted his arms around her like they were around his nephews and niece.

"They're so many of you," he murmured. "You have your own Brady Bunch, Buster."

"There are only four—five counting Carl," she said. "But he had to go to work."

"Is that why you came home?"

She bit her lip and shook her head.

"It's because of what you heard on the radio?" He glanced at his niece. "About the castle tea?"

Buster nodded.

"I'm fine," he said. "I had no idea you would have heard…" He stopped himself. "That's right—there was a trooper along for backup."

"Since you're fine, us troopers must be good for something, huh, Mr. Special Agent?" Her green eyes twinkled as she teased him.

He shrugged. "I had a couple other special agents along," he said. "That's why I'm fine."

She gently punched his shoulder. Then she turned to where Maggie sat on the kitchen chair, watching them and wishing she was part of their loving family. Buster must have seen that longing because she reached out for Maggie's hand and tugged her up from the chair. Buster sighed and remarked, "You are so beautiful pregnant. If I'd looked like you, instead of a beached whale, I might have had a couple more."

"God help us," Blaine muttered.

He already had as far as Maggie was concerned, since he'd brought Blaine safely back to his family. And her…

But she wasn't hers. He had yet to even look at her. Maybe he was mad that she was at his sister's home—endangering his sister's beautiful family.

"I'm sorry," she said. "I know you didn't want me here. We can leave now."

Buster stared at her with wide eyes, urging her to tell Blaine her feelings. But Maggie shook her head. It was obvious to her that he didn't want her love. Why couldn't his sister see the emotional distance he'd put between himself and Maggie?

"We'll leave in a little while," he said, finally speaking

directly to her. But still, he wouldn't look at her. Instead he turned back to Buster. "Can we have a few minutes alone? Maybe in the sunroom?"

Buster nodded. "Of course."

He took Maggie's arm and drew her from the kitchen through a set of French doors off the family room. He pulled the doors closed behind him, shutting them alone in a solarium of windows. But the sun had already dropped, so the room was growing dark and cold.

Maggie shivered.

"If you're cold—"

"No, I'm fine," she said. "Why do you want to talk to me privately?" Did he want to yell at her for endangering his family? "I told Buster it was a bad idea to bring me back here."

"Buster rarely listens to anyone but herself," he replied. "Poor Carl..."

She suspected that Carl was a very lucky man, and that he was smart enough to know it. No matter how much she joked about her husband, it was obvious that Buster loved him very much.

The way Maggie loved Blaine...

"Why did you want me alone?" she asked again. She tamped down the hope that threatened to burgeon—the hope that he wanted to tell her his feelings.

But that hope deflated when he finally replied, "I have to show you something."

Instinctively she knew it wasn't something she would want to see. He didn't even *want* to show it to her. He *had* to...and even without his choice of words, she would have picked up on his reluctance from the gruffness of his voice.

"Did you find the letters?" she asked. If they'd been at the cabin and if it had been used as a hideout, then the robberies were her fault. She shouldn't have talked so much about the bank. Her mother was right; she had always talked too much. Even though she hadn't given out security passwords or anything, she'd talked too much about her duties as the assistant manager. And it wasn't as if Andy had actually been interested; she'd just rambled.

"Yes, I found your letters," he replied. But he didn't hold them out for her to look at; he held out a photograph instead.

She didn't look at it. First she had to know, "What's this?"

"You tell me," he said as he lifted it toward her face. "Is it Andy?"

Her heart leaped again. Was it possible that Andy was alive? But then she looked at the picture. The man in it wasn't alive. And he wasn't Andy, either.

"Why would you think that was Andy?" She'd thought he had realized that Mr. Doremire had been drunk and delusional when he'd made those wild claims about Andy faking his death and the Marines covering it up.

"He had on Andy's dog tags."

The dog tags that his father claimed had never been found. No wonder Blaine had thought it was Andy. She shook her head.

"He must have been mistaken," she said. And with as much as he drank, it would be understandable.

"The dog tags must have been in his personal effects along with the letters," she explained. "His brother must have taken them when he took the letters."

"Now you think Mark took the dog tags?" he asked.

She pointed at the photo. "That's Mark, so he must have, since he was wearing them when he died."

"You're sure that's Mark?"

"I'm sure," she said. "I'm surprised you didn't recognize him from the security footage." But he did look different dead. He didn't look like the smiling man on the television monitor.

Blaine released a ragged breath as if he had been holding it for a while, maybe since he'd found the body and had thought it was Andy. "I think he's the robber I shot at the bank."

Shock and regret had her gasping. She remembered that horrific moment—remembered Blaine firing back at the man who'd shot the security guard. "You think he's the one who killed Sarge?"

Mark had been like her big brother, too. He had always seemed as sweet and easygoing as Andy had been, and he had adored his younger brother. How could he have killed a man that Andy had loved? A man she had loved, as well?

Sarge had been so kind and supportive after Andy's death. He had kept checking on her. Maybe he had made a promise to Andy. Mark must not have. Or, if he had, it was a promise he'd broken.

Blaine nodded. "He was wearing a vest that was too small for him. I got a shot into his side. He bled out from the wound."

"Nobody got him help?" she asked, horrified that his coconspirators would have just let him bleed to death.

Blaine shook his head. "No. They got him to the cabin, but they couldn't stop the bleeding."

"He wasn't the one who tried grabbing me at the hospital, then," she said. "That man was healthy and strong." It gave her some relief that Mark hadn't been trying to hurt her. "He couldn't have been behind any of those other attempts on our lives."

"No," Blaine agreed. "It must've been whoever he was working with."

There had been five of them. So four other men were still out there, apparently still determined to kill her and Special Agent Blaine Campbell.

BLAINE HUSTLED HER quickly out of his sister's house. It was less for his family's safety and more for hers. He wanted to protect her. He also wanted to comfort her because he had seen the fear on her face when she'd realized that she was still in danger.

"We'll be safe here," he said, as he locked the motel room door behind them. He could have driven her back to Chicago. But night had already fallen, and she was obviously exhausted. She trembled with it and maybe with cold. He turned up the thermostat as she shivered.

"I thought you weren't going to protect me anymore," she said. "Didn't your boss tell you that you shouldn't?"

He nodded. "And he's right."

"You said that last night…"

Before he had made love to her. What the hell had he been thinking to take advantage of her that way?

"I'm sorry," he said. "About last night…"

"You didn't start the fire," she said.

"But I should have been awake. I should have been alert," he said. "My boss was right. You will be safer with someone else protecting you."

"I feel safe with you," she said, and she turned back to him and stared up at him with those chocolaty brown eyes.

There was such an overall glow about her. Maybe it was the pregnancy. But he suspected it was just her— just Maggie's warm personality. She had even won over Buster and that was never easy to do.

"Maggie, I have to focus on the case," he said. He hoped she would understand that he couldn't let her distract him any longer. "I have to dig deeper into Mark's life and find all of his associates."

"I can help you," she said.

"You know his friends?"

She shook her head. "He was older than me and Andy, so I don't know who he hung out with." She nibbled her lower lip. "I guess I can't help you."

"You need to focus on yourself and your baby," he said. "Stay healthy. Stay well."

She touched her belly with trembling hands. "Yes…"

"I will find them all," Blaine promised. "I'll stop them." He just hoped he could stop them before they tried to kill her again. They obviously cared little for human life since they had let one of their own die instead of getting him help. To save themselves…

So, even dead, Mark could lead him to the others. That must have been the reason they hadn't sought out medical attention or wanted his body found.

"Thank you," she said.

"I haven't done anything yet," he said.

"You've saved my life," she reminded him. "Many times. Thank you for that."

He shrugged off her gratitude. "I was just doing my job." But it was so much more than that, and they both knew it.

"And thank you for last night," she said, "for making me feel desirable. Wanted…"

He wanted her again. But he kept his hands at his sides. He wouldn't reach for her again.

But she reached for him. Sliding her arms around him, she pressed her voluptuous body close to his. And the tenuous hold he'd had on his control snapped. He couldn't resist her sweetness, her passion.

She rose up on tiptoe and pressed her lips to his, sliding them across his mouth—arousing his desire. He kissed her back.

She eased away from him but only to ease her hands between them and undo the buttons of his shirt. He helped her take off his holster. And his jeans...

She gasped, as she so often did, as she stared at his nakedness. "You are the most beautiful man."

Maggie's words filled him with heat and pride.

She touched him, her fingers caressing his skin. "You were hurt last night."

He had some scrapes, a couple of first-degree burns. "It's nothing."

She shuddered. "When that roof caved in, I thought you were gone. And then when we heard that radio call..."

"About the castle tea?" he teased.

But she didn't laugh. In fact, her eyes glistened with tears. "I was so scared."

He drew her against him and held her close. "I hate that you were scared."

But he was scared, too. He was scared that he'd irrevocably fallen for her.

"Make me forget my fears," she challenged him. "Make me forget about everything but you. Make love to me..."

He couldn't refuse her wishes. He helped her off with her clothes and then helped her into bed. Joining her, he kissed and stroked every inch of her silky skin. And with every kiss and every caress, she gasped or moaned and squirmed beneath him. Then she caressed him back, running her soft hands over his back and his hips and lower. She encircled him with those hands. He nearly lost his mind, but he fought for control. He wanted to give her pleasure.

So he made love to her with his mouth. She cried out. But this was a cry he loved to hear from her—a cry of pleasure as she found release. Then, carefully, he joined their bodies. He tried to move slowly and gently.

But she arched and thrust up her hips. And her inner muscles clenched around him, tugging him deeper inside until he didn't know where she ended and he began. They were one. And as one, they reached ecstasy—shouting each other's name.

He held her close as they both panted for breath. He held her and waited—for the next attempt on their lives. He didn't know if it would be another fire or more shooting. He didn't know what it would be; he just knew that it would happen. As if on some level he had known that he would fall for Maggie Jenkins.

She had taken his heart. Now he just had to hold on to his life…

Chapter Twenty

Maybe it had been only days. But it felt like weeks since Maggie had last seen Blaine. She knew he was busy working the case. He had explained that he had to hand off her protection to someone else so that he could focus.

Had she distracted him?

She was working again, too. But she was preoccupied by thoughts of Blaine. It wouldn't matter how long she went without seeing him; she knew she would never *not* think of Special Agent Blaine Campbell.

A noise at her office door startled her, and she jumped.

"Sorry," the bank manager said. "I didn't mean to frighten you."

"It's not your fault," she assured him. Even though no attempts had been made to kidnap or kill her the past few days, she was still on edge. Still waiting for the robbers in their hideous masks to burst through the bank doors or into her apartment with their guns drawn.

"Has everything been all right?" he asked.

She nodded instead of uttering a lie. Because everything was not all right—not without Blaine. She ached for him.

"Things are back to normal now," Mr. Hardy said with a sigh of relief as he gazed around at the bank. The glass had all been repaired. Everything was back in its place as if the robbery had never happened. "And with one of the robbers found dead, maybe the others have gone into hiding."

"Agent Campbell will catch them," she said with unshakable confidence.

"Hopefully," he said, but he sounded doubtful. "I understand that the robber that was found dead was related to you."

"No," she said.

"Well," he said again, his voice rising with a slight whine, "he would've been had your fiancé not died."

She wouldn't have married Andy, though—even after finding out she carried his child. She hadn't wanted friendship love in her marriage; she'd wanted passionate love. She had wanted to be in love, not just to love someone. She had finally found that with Blaine, but he didn't want the instant family he would have with her. He probably didn't even want a relationship. He was totally focused on his career—so much so that she hadn't even heard from him.

Mr. Hardy was looking at her strangely. Then Maggie recognized the suspicion. "I was not involved in the robberies," she said. "I had nothing to do with them."

Except for those damn letters she'd written. Did he know about those, too?

He nodded. "Of course you didn't..."

But she heard the doubt in his voice. "I need this job, Mr. Hardy. I wouldn't have done anything to jeopardize it."

"Susan Iverson thinks you may have been involved with that man."

"Susan may have been," Maggie said. "But I wasn't. He's just someone I used to know." And apparently she hadn't known him nearly as well as she'd thought she had. "Like Susan, he proved to be someone I couldn't trust."

"She claims that the agent totally misread the situation when he found her in your apartment—"

"Stealing my engagement ring," she said.

"She assured me she wasn't stealing it," he defended the blonde bank teller. "That she was only looking for evidence that you were involved in the robberies."

Maggie shook her head. She'd had enough of people lying and scamming her. "She used my credit cards," she said. "She can't explain that away."

"You owed her rent money."

Anger surged through her, and she stood up. "That's a lie. And if you choose to believe her lies over me, maybe I don't need this job as much as I thought."

He held out his hands. "Calm down, Maggie. I know this is an emotional time for you. Susan needs her job, too, and if you drop the charges against her, I think you could work together again."

Blaine had caught the woman in the act of stealing. It wasn't up to Maggie whether or not charges were pressed. But she didn't bother explaining that.

"Why are you defending her?" she wondered. And then, as color flooded his face, she realized why. He was involved with the young teller. "Oh..."

"I don't know what you're thinking," he said fearfully, as if he actually did know, "but you're wrong."

"No, *you're* wrong." Especially if he had betrayed his wife with the blonde opportunist. "There actually is evidence against her, and she will be prosecuted. I couldn't drop the charges even if I wanted to."

Maybe Susan had been involved in the robberies, too. Maggie wouldn't put anything past the woman. She was a user. Mr. Hardy would figure that out soon enough.

Disgusted with him, she grabbed her purse and said, "I'm going home."

"Yes, get some rest and think about it," he suggested.

Maybe Maggie needed to return to the branch where she had previously worked. She couldn't work for Mr. Hardy anymore. She couldn't work with Susan Iverson. Maybe she needed to join her parents in Hong Kong. It wasn't as if Blaine would miss her. He had gone days with no contact.

As she headed out the door, her new protector followed her. The burly young man, Truman Jackson, was something with the Bureau—maybe a new recruit. Since there had been no recent attempts to grab her, she doubted they would have wasted a special agent on babysitting duty. She had been lucky to have Blaine as long as she had.

"Are you all right, Miss Jenkins?" the young man asked as he helped her into his unmarked vehicle.

"Maggie," she corrected him as she had the past few days. "And I'm fine."

"But you're leaving early…"

She hadn't done that the past couple of days. In fact, she had worked late, trying to catch up from the time the bank had been closed for repairs.

"I'm tired," she said. And that was no lie. She was exhausted. From looking over her shoulder. From worrying.

From missing Blaine.

"So you want to go right back to your apartment?" Truman asked.

"Yes, please," she said, and happy that he was driving, she closed her eyes and relaxed as much as she could.

"Do you think I'll need protection much longer?" she asked. If no more attempts were made on her life…

"I couldn't say, Maggie."

"Do you know if Special Agent Campbell has gotten any closer to apprehending the other bank robbers?" She wanted to know what was going on with the case, but most of all she wanted to know what was going on with Blaine.

Was he okay? Had he recovered completely from the fire? Had anyone tried to kill him again?

Truman shrugged his broad shoulders; one of them nudged hers. "I don't know," he replied. "Do you have his number? Could you call and ask?"

No. She hadn't been given his number. He had barely looked at her as he'd passed off her protection to someone else.

"I don't want to bother him," she said. And that was true. She didn't want to distract him anymore. He had a job to do, and she had only been part of that job to him.

Truman had lost interest in their conversation, his attention on her apartment door as he pulled into the parking lot. He reached for his holster. "Who is that?"

A woman stood outside the door. She wore dark glasses that obscured most of her face, but Maggie recognized the bright glow of her red hair.

"It's my…" almost sister-in-law? "…friend." But Tammy had never really been her friend—not even when they were younger. Like Maggie and Andy, Tammy and Mark had dated all during high school. Tammy had actually been there when Mark had sneaked her and Andy into that horror movie. She had thought Maggie's fear funny—as Mark had. And recently Tammy had been suspicious and resentful of Maggie. She had even suspected her of cheating with Mark.

Was that why she'd come here? To lash out some more in her grief? Maggie wasn't certain how much more she could take today.

BLAINE GRABBED AT his tie, struggling to loosen the knot. He felt suffocated within the walls of his new office, and he felt buried beneath the files atop his new desk. He would rather be out in the field, physically tracking down solid leads instead of fumbling through piles of paper.

He would actually rather be with Maggie, making certain that she was safe. There had been no new attempts on her life. But he was not a fool enough to think that it was over, not with so many of Mark's associates out there yet. Blaine was only a fool for Maggie—for falling for her.

As he'd had to so many times over the past few days, he pushed thoughts of Maggie from his mind and focused on the case again. He grabbed a file from the stack and read over the names of Mark Doremire's friends and family. Was old man Doremire one of the robbers?

Hell, was Andy? Maybe the guy wasn't really dead.

Blaine shook his head. He was losing it. Andy was gone. But another name on his list looked familiar. He shuffled through the other folders for the report from the security chief at the hospital, and he pulled out her list of employees. One of the names matched.

Mark Doremire's brother-in-law worked security at the hospital. Hadn't Tammy Doremire told him she had no friends or family in the area? Why had she lied to Blaine?

Had she been trying to protect her brother since she must already have known that she'd lost her husband? If her brother had been in on the thefts, she would have known that Mark had been hurt.

Maybe she had even been along for the robberies. Blaine touched his tablet and played some of the security footage from the holdup. There had been a robber who was smaller than the others. It was the one who'd dragged Maggie to the back door of the bank, the one who'd pulled her into the van.

Tammy Doremire wasn't just related to a couple of the robbers. She was one of them.

He just had to find the other two. They might be associates of her brother's. Or...

His phone rang, drawing his attention from all those files. He clicked the talk button. "Campbell."

"Special Agent Campbell?"

"Yes."

"This is Truman Jackson," a male voice said.

"You're the guard on Maggie." Blaine's heart slammed against his ribs as fear overwhelmed him. Before letting Truman protect her again, he had made certain that the man had not been compromised—that he could be trusted. Ash Stryker had vouched for him, so Truman had been chosen as her new protector. Had he failed his duty?

"Is she okay?" Blaine anxiously asked. "Has there been another attempt on her life?"

"No, no," the man quickly assured Blaine. But there was concern in his voice.

That concern had Blaine grabbing his keys and rushing out of his office. But even outside the confining walls, he couldn't breathe. Now panic and concern suffocated him.

"What's going on?" he asked. What had compelled the man to call him?

"I brought Maggie home from the bank," Truman relayed, "and there was a woman waiting at her apartment door."

At least she had been at the door and hadn't let herself inside the way Susan Iverson had. But maybe Susan had learned her lesson about doing that.

"Who was she?" Blaine asked.

"Maggie," he said, "told me that the woman was a friend but…"

"But what?"

"I don't know," the man replied. "But I didn't pick up the friendship vibe from her. Maggie insisted on speaking alone with the woman, though, so I left them together in Maggie's apartment."

Blaine clicked the lock on his SUV and jumped behind the wheel. "Did you check the woman for a weapon before you left them alone?"

"Of course," the man replied, as if offended. "She wasn't armed. And she's too thin to do any physical harm to Maggie."

That didn't ease Blaine's fears any. "Who is she?"

"A red-haired woman," Truman replied. "I checked her license."

Blaine didn't even need her name for confirmation. He knew who was with Maggie.

"Tammy Doremire…"

The robber from the bank—the one who had tried bringing Maggie along. Probably the only one who really wanted her dead…

Chapter Twenty-One

Maggie handed Tammy a cup of tea. Brewing it had bought her some time to gather her thoughts since she had no idea what to say to the new widow.

But Tammy must not have wanted the tea because she set the cup on the coffee table in front of her. Maggie kept hers in her hands, hoping the heat of the mug would warm her. But she still shivered—maybe more with nerves than cold.

"You still have a bodyguard," the other woman said.

It hadn't been a question, but Maggie nodded in reply. Truman had searched Tammy to make sure she carried no weapon, so of course she would have realized he was a bodyguard.

"But there haven't been any attempts lately," Tammy said. "It seems like the FBI wouldn't want to waste manpower."

"I don't know," Maggie replied. She had no idea why Tammy cared about the bodyguard or the FBI, let alone how she would have known about the attempts on Maggie's life.

Unless…

No, she refused to suspect the worst of everyone; she refused to be as cynical as Blaine had been. But Blaine had been right about Mark…

"Having protection for you is probably Agent Campbell's idea," the woman continued, her voice sharp with bitterness as she said his name. "I'm surprised that he's not still personally protecting you."

"He's busy," Maggie said. At least that was what she was telling herself to salve her wounded heart.

Tammy sighed. "It doesn't matter."

But it did matter to Maggie that she hadn't heard from Blaine—that she didn't know exactly what he was doing. Or feeling.

Since the mug was beginning to cool, Maggie set it beside Tammy's on the coffee table. But she didn't join her on the couch or settle onto one of the chairs across from her. Maggie didn't feel comfortable enough with this woman to sit down with her.

But she should have gone to see her earlier out of respect. "I'm glad you came over," Maggie said.

"You are?" Tammy asked skeptically.

"Of course. I've been wanting to talk to you, wanting to tell you how sorry I am about Mark." Of course she hadn't known how to express sympathy for a man dying in the commission of a crime—of a murder. If only Mark hadn't been involved in the robberies...

Both he and Sarge would be alive. How could Maggie express sympathy for that?

The woman ignored her remarks and pointed out a box that sat on the end of the coffee table. Wrapping paper with little rubber ducks covered the box, and a bright yellow bow topped it. "What's that?"

"I don't know," Maggie said. She hadn't noticed it earlier. Tammy hadn't had it with her when Truman had searched her body and her purse. He would have found the brightly wrapped package. "It wasn't here this morning."

"Maybe it was delivered today," Tammy suggested.

Maggie shook her head. "Then it would have been left outside the door." Not on her coffee table.

"Maybe your elderly janitor brought it inside for you."

Maggie's skin chilled as she realized that Tammy wasn't offering a possible explanation but a fact. She knew because she had given it to Mr. Simmons to bring inside for her. Why?

"This is yours?" Maggie asked. "You brought this for me?" Despite what she'd told Truman, they weren't friends. Why would the woman have brought her a baby gift?

"Yes," Tammy replied. "But let me open it for you." She tore the ribbon and easily slipped the top off the box. Then she smiled and lifted a gun out. "Now tell me how sorry you are about Mark."

Fear slammed into Maggie as she stared down the barrel of that gun. She covered her belly with her palms—even though she knew there was no way to protect her baby from a bullet. "What are you doing?"

"I'm going to do what we should have done at the first bank so you wouldn't have time to figure out it was us and report us to the FBI," Tammy said. "I'm going to kill you."

"But the guard is just outside the door," Maggie reminded her. "Truman is going to hear the shot. You won't get away with this. He might even shoot you."

"You think I have anything to live for?" Tammy asked, her face contorting into a mask of pain and hatred nearly as grotesque as those zombie masks. Tammy must have chosen them; she had found it funniest that Maggie had been so afraid during that movie. "Mark's dead because of you."

"I didn't shoot him," Maggie said.

"No, your FBI agent shot him," Tammy said. "I had

hoped that he was the one protecting you. That he would be here, so that I could kill you both."

"You've got your wish," a deep voice murmured as the apartment door opened with a slight creak of the hinges. "I'm here."

Maggie had spent the past few days missing Blaine and longing to see his handsome face again. But not now. She would rather have never seen him again than to have him die with her.

BLAINE HAD EXPECTED the gun because he'd met Mr. Simmons at the door. The older gentleman had wanted to make certain that Maggie got the baby gift that he'd put in her apartment for the red-haired woman. He'd thought the box was heavy for a baby-shower gift.

Of course it held no gift for Maggie or her baby. It had held the gun.

Tammy was clever—so clever that she had probably been the one who had actually plotted the bank robberies. She had probably been the one who'd read Maggie's letters.

"This is perfect," the widow said with a smile of delight as she stood up with the gun clutched in her hands. At least the barrel was pointed at him instead of Maggie, who stood trembling on the other side of the coffee table from the deranged woman.

"This is stupid," Blaine corrected her. "There's nothing specifically linking you to the robberies. No evidence that you were aware of the crimes your husband and your brother were committing. You could have gotten away with it all."

Her smile vanished off her thin lips. "My brother?"

The woman obviously didn't care about herself right now—not when she planned to shoot two people with another federal agent posted right outside the door. But maybe she cared about her sibling.

"He was the one who tried abducting Maggie from Emergency," Blaine said. "He's a security guard at the hospital."

Tammy shook her head in denial. "The fact that he works there doesn't prove anything."

"His security badge will prove he was the one who opened the back door of the employees' locker room when he tried to kidnap Maggie." At least Blaine hoped it would. He needed evidence—not just suspicion—linking the man to the crimes.

"No…" But the conviction was gone from Tammy Doremire's voice as it began to quaver. "You can't tie him to the robberies…"

Maybe he wouldn't be able to, but he wasn't going to let her think that. "I have a team working on it right now. They're getting search warrants. They're digging into all of his financials. They're checking all his properties for any evidence linking him to the robberies. I'm pretty sure they'll find something. Aren't you?"

Her thin face tightened with dread and hatred. She knew that her brother wouldn't have gotten rid of all the evidence—or at least not the money. He could see she was torn, tempted to call and warn her brother about the warrants.

So he stepped closer, prepared to grab her weapon from her hands. Her eyes widened with alarm as she noticed that he'd closed some distance between them.

"Get back!" she yelled. "I'm going to kill her. You're not going to stop me this time."

"Why do you want her dead?" he asked. "If you hadn't sent your brother to the hospital after her, I wouldn't have linked him to the crimes." He was sure that her brother had acted on her orders; all the men probably had.

"It's all her fault!" Tammy yelled, as if she thought that saying it loud enough would make it true. "If she hadn't written those damn letters to Andy..."

A noise emanated from Maggie, but she'd muffled it with a hand over her mouth. She had already held herself responsible for the robberies; she didn't need this crazed woman compounding her guilt.

But making her feel guilty wasn't enough torment for Tammy Doremire. She intended to kill her, too.

"Who read them?" Blaine asked, stalling for time—hoping to distract the woman enough for Maggie to escape. He had left the apartment door open. Maybe Truman could get off a shot.

"I—I did," Tammy admitted.

As he'd suspected, she was the mastermind behind the robberies. He acted shocked, though, as he edged closer to her and that damn gun she gripped so tightly. "You read her personal correspondence to her fiancé?"

She snorted. "Personal? There hadn't been anything very personal about them. They were not *love* letters—not like I would have written to Mark—" her voice cracked with emotion, with loss "—if he'd been in a war zone."

She had loved her husband. The grief and pain contorted her face.

"Why didn't you take Mark to a hospital when he was hurt?" he asked. "Why did you drive him instead to that cabin in Michigan?"

"He—he wanted to go there," she said. "He knew he was dying—because of you. Because you shot him!" She pointed the gun at Blaine's chest.

And he was glad; it wasn't anywhere near Maggie

now. Maybe she could escape. Instead, she gasped in fear for him.

And her gasp drew Tammy's rage back to her. She whirled the gun in Maggie's direction. "But we wouldn't have been there if it wasn't for her. Mark just couldn't stay away from poor, sweet Maggie. She caused his death—just like she caused Andy's."

"That's bull." Blaine called her on her craziness. "I killed Mark—not Maggie. I pulled the trigger. Not Maggie."

She swung the gun back to him, and her eyes were wild with rage and grief. "It was your fault!"

"I shot him, but the vest should have protected him," Blaine said. "But he wasn't wearing *his* vest. He was wearing *yours*."

Tears began to streak down the woman's face as her own guilt overwhelmed her. She knew why her husband had died. But she couldn't accept her own part in his death. It was easier for her to blame him and Maggie.

She sniffled back her tears. And as she tried to clear her vision, he edged closer yet. "No…" she cried in protest of her guilt more than his nearness. "He shouldn't have died…"

He was counting on her not noticing how close he was to her. But she wasn't looking at him anymore; she had swung the gun back toward Maggie.

"Mark killed an innocent man," Maggie said in defense of Blaine shooting him. Of course she would defend him as she did everyone. "Why? Why would you two resort to stealing and killing?"

"Mark and I needed that money," Tammy said, desperately trying to justify their crimes. "We needed it to start our family."

"Hundreds of thousands of dollars?" Blaine scoffed.

He wanted to irritate her, wanted her to shoot at him instead of Maggie. He wore a vest. Maggie was completely unprotected.

"I—I couldn't get pregnant. I need—needed—fertility treatments. Or in vitro. All that's so expensive, and Mark lost his job." Now she wasn't just pointing the gun at Maggie but at her belly, and jealousy twisted the woman's face into a mask nearly as grotesque as the zombie one. "But this one—she easily gets pregnant."

Maggie held her hands over her belly, trying to protect her unborn baby. But her hands would prove no protection from a bullet.

"You don't want to hurt the baby," Blaine said, as horror gripped him. Maggie's baby was a part of her, and because he loved Maggie, he loved her baby, too. He couldn't lose either of them.

"She doesn't deserve that baby," Tammy said. "She never wanted it. She never wanted Andy. She didn't love him like I loved Mark. It's not fair."

"Life's not fair," Blaine commiserated.

But the woman didn't hear or see him anymore. It didn't matter that he was the one who'd fired the shot that had killed Mark. She hated Maggie more—she hated that the woman had what Tammy wanted most. A baby...

And she intended to take that baby from Maggie before she took her life. He had to protect them. So Blaine did two things—he kicked the coffee table into the woman's legs and he grabbed for the gun.

But it went off. And a scream rang out. Maggie's scream.

Chapter Twenty-Two

Pain ripped through Maggie; she felt as if she were being torn in two. She patted her belly, but she felt no stickiness from blood, just an incredible tightness. She hadn't been shot. She'd gone into labor.

Blaine dropped to the ground beside her. "Where are you hit?"

She shook her head. "No..."

His hands replaced hers on her belly, and his green eyes widened. "You're in labor?"

"It's too soon," she said, as tears of pain and fear streamed down her face. "It's too soon. You have to stop it. I can't have the baby now."

Or Tammy Doremire would get her wish. Maggie wouldn't have the baby the woman didn't think she deserved. Maybe she was right.

Maggie probably didn't deserve her baby. But she wanted him. With all her heart she wanted him.

"We're going to get you to the hospital," Blaine said. "We're going to get you help." But his hand shook as he dialed 911, and his voice shook as he demanded an ambulance.

He was worried, too. Somehow Maggie found that reassuring, as if it proved he cared. If not about her, at least he cared about her baby. He showed he cared when he climbed into the ambulance with her and let Truman take Tammy Doremire into custody.

He took Maggie's hand, clasping it in both of his. "Everything's going to be okay," he promised. "Everything's going to be okay."

"Thank you," she managed between pants for breath. "Thank you."

His forehead furrowed and he asked, "For what?"

"You saved my life again," she said. And she hoped that he had saved the baby's, too.

But when they got to the hospital, it was too late. The doctors couldn't stop the labor. Her little boy was coming. "It's too early..."

"He'll be fine," Blaine assured her. "He's tough— like his mama."

Was she tough? Maggie had never felt as helpless and weak as she did at that moment. She couldn't stop her labor; she couldn't stop him from coming.

"Push," a nurse told her.

"I can't..." She shouldn't. But the urge was there—the urge to push him out. A contraction gripped her, tearing her apart again. There had been no time for them to administer an epidural. No time for them to ease her pain. She didn't care, though. She cared only about her baby. "It's too soon..."

"We'll take care of him," the doctor promised. "Push..."

Blaine touched her chin, tipping up her face so that she met his gaze. "You need to do this, Maggie. You've taken care of him as long as you could. Let the doctors take care of him now."

So she pushed, and her baby boy entered the world with a weak cry of protest.

"He's crying—that's good," Blaine assured her. "He's going to be okay."

But the doctors whisked him away, working on him. Were his lungs okay? Were they developed enough? Maggie had so many questions. But she didn't want to distract the doctors from her son, so she didn't ask any of them.

Blaine stroked his fingers along her cheek. "He'll be okay. He'll be okay. He's tough—just like you are."

Even though he'd repeated his assurance, Maggie couldn't accept it. She didn't feel tough. She felt shattered. Devastated. And Blaine must have seen that she was about to fall apart because he pulled her into his arms. And he held her. He held her together.

And not just then but over the next few days. He stayed with her at the hospital, making sure that she and the baby were all right. Maggie fell so far in love with him that she knew she would never get over him.

She didn't want to get over him. She wanted to be with him always. She wanted to be his wife—wanted her son to be his son, too.

The doctors already thought he was the little boy's father. They called him Dad, and Blaine never corrected them. But it wasn't his name on little Drew's birth certificate—it was Andy's as the father. He deserved that honor. He deserved to be with his son.

Andy was gone. Maggie had accepted that, but she wanted to honor him by giving his son his name. Blaine was with Maggie when the nurse brought in the baby from the neonatal unit. "He's breathing on his own, Mom," she said. "No more machines. He can stay in here with you."

"He's so tiny," Blaine said with wonder as he stared down at the sleeping infant.

"Drew's going to be a big boy," the nurse assured them. "He's doing very well for a preemie." She handed the baby to Maggie before leaving the room.

Her heart swelled with love as he automatically snuggled against her, as if he recognized her even though she hadn't carried him as long as she was supposed to.

"He's so tiny," Blaine repeated, still in awe.

"He's doing well, though," Maggie assured him.

"Drew?" Blaine asked.

Maybe she should have run the name past him first. But he had never indicated that he wanted a future with her and her son. So she hadn't wanted to presume.

She nodded.

"That's good. It's a good name," he said, his green gaze on the baby in her arms.

"I'm glad you think so," she said. She wanted him to be part of their lives. But even as she contemplated asking, he started pulling away.

He stood up. "Now that you're both okay, I need to get back to work on the case," he said. "I need to find the other robbers and make sure they don't try to go after you or Drew."

She shivered, and the baby awakened. But not with a cry. He opened his eyes just a little and stared calmly up at her. She had been in danger for too much of her pregnancy. She appreciated that Blaine wanted to make sure that they would finally be safe. But she wasn't sure that was really the reason he was leaving.

Or if he just wanted to get away from her. Maybe he didn't like that everyone had assumed he was the baby's father. Maybe he didn't want to be an instant daddy.

Before he left, he leaned over the bed, and he pressed a kiss to her lips and another to the baby's forehead. "I have a guard posted at the door. Truman will protect you. You'll be safe," he assured her.

"What about you?" she asked.

He grinned. "I'll be fine."

She couldn't help but remember that Andy had promised the same thing when he'd left for his last deployment. Would Blaine not return, as well?

BLAINE WOULDN'T PUT it past Tammy Doremire to set a trap for him. He interviewed her at the jail. In exchange for a lesser sentence, she gave him an address—not just for her brother but for the two coworkers who'd helped them pull off the robberies. He doubted she actually cared how much time she spent behind bars; she just wanted to make sure that Blaine was dead—like her husband.

"What did Maggie have?" she asked, as if she actually cared.

His blood chilled with a sense of foreboding. But he had guards posted at the hospital. They weren't hospital guards, either. Once he'd realized a hospital security guard had been involved in the robberies, he hadn't trusted any of them. Truman was inside Maggie's room, personally protecting her and Drew. He felt so bad about Tammy getting her alone that he would give up his life before he would let anyone hurt her or her baby again.

"A boy," he said.

"Of course," she said, as if she should have known. "Boys run in the Doremire family."

"She named him Drew," he said.

She shrugged, and her red hair brushed the shoulders of her orange jumpsuit. She looked nearly as bad as she had in the zombie mask. "Maybe she loved Andy more than I thought."

Maggie had loved her fiancé. He saw it in her face whenever she talked about him. She missed him.

Could Blaine fill the void Andy had left in her? He loved her so much that he wanted to try. But did he love her enough for both of them?

He had no idea how she actually felt about him. She had turned to him for protection—for comfort. But who else had she had now that Andy was gone?

Who else could she trust now that the family that had almost been hers had turned on her?

"That's too bad for you, huh?" Tammy remarked. "Since you love her…"

Blaine hadn't told Maggie his feelings; he wasn't about to tell this woman. He stood up and gestured toward a deputy to take Tammy back to holding. As they led her away, she turned back and smiled a sly smile.

She had definitely set a trap for him. So he was ready. He took Ash Stryker and Dalton Reyes with him as backup, along with some Michigan troopers. According to Tammy, her brother and his friends had gone back to the cabin. Supposedly she and Mark had stashed the money there. After finding the body, the dog tags and Maggie's letters, Blaine hadn't taken the time to search the entire area. Maybe the money was hidden there.

But Blaine suspected he wouldn't find just the money. Or the robbers.

"We could have called in more troopers," Ash remarked as he pulled his weapon from his holster.

But if Blaine had requested more, he might have had to use his sister, and he didn't want to put her in danger, too. He wanted her to be there to help Maggie and the baby in case he couldn't. He wanted Maggie to have a friend she could trust—unlike Susan Iverson or Tammy.

"You face down terrorists every day," Dalton Reyes teased him. "You're afraid of a few zombie bank robbers?"

"Some of the worst terrorists I've dealt with have been the homegrown kind, holed up in remote spots just like this one," Ash warned them. "They could have an arsenal in there."

Blaine sighed. "Oh, I'm sure that they do…"

He had no more than voiced the thought when gunfire erupted. It echoed throughout the woods, shattering the windows of the cabin and the windows of the vehicles he and the other agents had driven up.

He gestured at the others, indicating for them to go around the back as he headed straight toward the cabin. He was the one that they wanted—the one that Tammy Doremire wanted—dead.

Maggie had already lost one man who loved her. She shouldn't lose another—especially when Blaine had yet to tell her that he loved her. He should have told her…

He was afraid now that he might never have the chance. The gunfire continued. They had to have automatic weapons—maybe even armor-piercing bullets. The vest probably wouldn't help him—neither would the SWAT helmet he and the other agents wore.

Ignoring the risk, he returned fire. He had to take out these threats to Maggie and the baby. He had to make sure that they couldn't hurt her or Drew ever again. One man, wearing the zombie mask and trench-coat disguise, stepped out of the cabin. Blaine hit him, taking him down, but as the man fell, his automatic weapon continued to fire.

And Blaine felt the fiery sting as a bullet hit him. He ignored the pain as another robber exited the cabin, aiming straight for him. Even as his arm began to go numb, he kept squeezing the trigger. The zombie fell, but so did Blaine. He struck the ground hard.

His ears ringing from the gunshots, he could barely hear the others calling out for him. "Blaine! Blaine!"

"Are you hit?" Reyes asked.

"Where are you hit?" Ash asked.

He didn't even know—because what hurt the most

was his heart—at the thought that he might never see Maggie again. "Tell her…"

But he didn't have the strength to finish his request. Like Mark Doremire, he was afraid that he was about to bleed out in the woods.

All he managed to utter was her name. "Maggie…"

Chapter Twenty-Three

Maggie had suspected the worst even before Ash Stryker and another man walked into her hospital room. Their faces were pale with stress, and their clothes were smeared with blood that wasn't theirs. They looked unharmed but yet devastated.

"No…"

He couldn't be dead. Blaine couldn't have died without learning how much she loved him. How much she needed him…

He had always been there when she had needed him. Why hadn't she been there when he had needed her?

She was already out of bed, standing over Drew's clear bassinet. She stepped away from it, so that she wouldn't startle the sleeping baby. But her legs trembled, nearly giving way beneath her. Truman grabbed her, steadying her with a hand on her arm.

Ash shook his head. "He's not dead, Maggie," he said. "He's not dead."

"But he's hurt." They wouldn't look the way they did if he wasn't. "How badly?"

Ash shook his head again. "I don't know."

"Where was he shot?" she asked. "How many times?"

"What the hell happened?" Truman asked the question before she could add it to her others.

"We went back to that cabin," the other agent replied. "The woman told us the others were there getting the money she and her husband stashed somewhere on the property."

Maggie gasped. "Tammy wouldn't have helped Blaine. She wanted him dead."

"It was an ambush," the agent confirmed.

"But Blaine was expecting it," Ash said. "We got them all. It's over, Maggie."

But so might Blaine's life be over. "Where was he shot?" she asked again. "How many times?"

"Just once," the other agent replied. But from Mark's and Sarge's deaths, she knew once was enough to kill. "The bullet grazed the side of his neck."

"It nicked an artery," Ash said. "He lost a lot of blood."

"But he's alive," she said, clinging to hope.

Ash nodded but repeated, "He lost a lot of blood, though."

"The doctors aren't sure he's going to make it," the other man added. "After they stabilized him, they flew him here."

"Why?" There were hospitals closer to the cabin. Good ones.

"The last thing he said was your name," Ash told her.

So they'd thought he wanted to be with her? He had probably only been worried that Tammy had set a trap for her as well as him. She'd wanted them both dead.

But Maggie didn't care why they had brought Blaine here. She had to see him. She turned to Truman. "Can you keep an eye on Drew while I go see Blaine?"

"Of course," the big man replied, but he looked nervously at the tiny baby as if afraid that he might awaken.

"This way," Ash said, as he guided her down the hall

to an elevator. They took it to the ground floor and the intensive care unit.

"Only one person at a time," the nurse at the desk warned them.

Ash waved her forward, so she followed the nurse to Blaine's bedside. Her golden-haired superhero looked so vulnerable and pale lying there. An IV dripped fluids—maybe plasma—into him, probably replacing the blood he'd lost. A bandage covered the wound on his neck. The injury had been treated.

Now he just had to fight.

"Please," she implored him as she grasped his hand. "Please don't leave me." Tears overflowed her eyes, trailing down her face to drop onto his arm. "I can't lose you. You have to fight. You have to live."

Panic had her heart beating frantically, desperately. What could she do to help him fight? How could she lend him some of her strength, as he had always given her his? She wouldn't have survived without him. Even with all the robbers dead or in jail, she wasn't sure that she could survive now without him.

"Please," she implored him again, "please don't leave me."

His hand moved inside hers, his fingers entwining with hers. He squeezed. She glanced up at his face and found his green-eyed gaze focused on her. He was conscious!

Embarrassed that he'd caught her crying all over him, she felt heat flood her face. "I'm sorry," she said.

"Sorry?" he asked, his voice a husky rasp.

"I—I'm crying all over you," she pointed out. "And I'm making assumptions."

"Assumptions?"

"I shouldn't have assumed that you're with me," she

said. "I know that you've just been protecting me—that you've just been doing your job—"

He tugged his hand from hers and pressed his fingers over her lips. "Shh…"

The man was exhausted, and here she was, rambling away. She had always talked too much.

"I'm sorry," she murmured again—against his fingers.

He shook his head—weakly. "You're wrong…"

Before he could tell her what she was wrong about, the nurse stepped back into the area. "He's awake? Mr. Campbell, you're conscious!" She leaned over and flashed a light in his eyes.

Blaine squinted and cursed. "Yes, I'm conscious."

"I have to get the doctor!" the nurse exclaimed as she hurried off.

"I should go," Maggie said. "I should tell Ash that you're awake." His friends had been worried about him, too.

"I think he probably heard," Blaine pointed out, as the nurse's voice rang out.

"Then he'll want to see you," Maggie said. She tugged on her hand, trying to free it from his so that she could escape before she suffered even more embarrassment. But before she could leave, a doctor hurried over with the excited nurse.

But even while the doctor talked to him—telling Blaine how lucky he was—he wouldn't release her. While she loved the warmth and comfort of his hand holding hers, she dreaded the moment when they would be alone again. Because even though he hadn't died, she suspected he would still be leaving her.

BLAINE WAS GRATEFUL to the doctor for saving his life, but he couldn't wait to get rid of him and the nurse. He wanted to be alone with Maggie again.

But the doctor wouldn't stop talking. "You're going to need to take it easy for a while and let your body recover from the blood loss. We're going to keep you in ICU overnight. You really need your rest."

"I should leave," Maggie said again as she tried to tug her hand free of his.

He wouldn't let her go, though. He was strong enough to hang on to her. She gave him strength. Hearing her sweet voice had drawn him from the fog of unconsciousness. She'd made him want to fight. Had made him want to live…

For her.

With her.

"No," he said. "I need to talk to you." And he gave a pointed look to the doctor and nurse, who finally took his not-so-subtle hint and left them alone.

"It's okay," she said. "I understand. You don't have to explain to me that you were just doing your job— protecting me and Drew. I know that you don't feel the same way about me that I do about you."

He reached out again and covered her silky soft lips with his fingers. "Sweetheart, you do talk too much." She'd said it herself, but until now he hadn't agreed with her.

"Sweetheart?" She mouthed the word against his fingers.

"But that's the only thing you're right about," he said. "You're wrong about everything else."

She stopped trying to talk now, and she waited for him to speak. That had never been easy for him—to share his feelings. He'd been hiding them for too long.

And obviously he'd hidden them too well from Maggie because she had no idea how he felt about her.

"You were never just a job to me," he said. "If you

were, I wouldn't have had to protect you myself. I would have trusted you to Truman or someone like him way before I had to—"

"But you did," she murmured against his fingers.

"I had to," he said, "or I was never going to figure out who was trying to hurt you and the baby. But it killed me to not be with you every day." And when he'd had to leave them again—after Drew had been born—it had literally nearly killed him. "I don't want to be away from you and Drew again."

Tears began to shimmer in those enormous brown eyes of hers. "Blaine…?"

He knew what he wanted to say, but he didn't know how to say it. "I don't have a ring…"

He couldn't forget the size and shine of the diamond Andy had given her. But Andy was gone. She had accepted that; Blaine needed to accept it, too.

"And I can't get down on one knee right now…" Hanging on to her hand had sapped all his strength. If he tried getting out of bed, he would undoubtedly pass out at her feet.

"I don't need a ring," she said. "I don't need any gestures. I just need to know how you feel about me."

"I'm not good at expressing my feelings," he said apologetically.

"Just tell me…"

"I love you," he said. "I love your sweetness and your openness. I love how you worry and care about everyone and everything."

"You love me?"

He nodded. "I know I'm not your first choice and that you'd promised to marry another man. But Andy's gone. And I'm here. And I will love you as much as he would have—if not more. I will take care of you and Drew. I will treat your son just like he's mine, too, if you'll let me."

The tears overflowed her eyes and spilled down her cheeks. "I don't deserve you," she said. "And I didn't deserve Andy. Tammy was right about that. I didn't love him like I should have. I loved him because he was my best friend. I didn't love him like a woman should love the man she wants to marry. And I didn't want to marry him. But I didn't know how to say no to his proposal without hurting him."

And with her big, loving heart, she would have given up her own happiness to ensure someone else's. He didn't want her doing that for him.

"You won't hurt me if you tell me no," he lied. It would hurt him. But he'd heard what she'd said when she'd thought him unconscious. He didn't think she would tell him no. But he wanted her to say yes for the right reasons. "You'll hurt me if you say yes and don't really love me."

"I love you," she said. "I love you like a woman loves a man. I love you with passion. I love you like a soul mate, not just as a friend."

The tightness in his chest eased, and he grinned. "I love how much you talk," he said. "I really do...especially when you're telling me how much you love me." But then he realized what she had yet to say. "But you haven't answered my question."

"Did you ask me something?" she asked with a coy flutter of her lashes.

"I will get out of this bed," he said, but they both knew it was an empty threat at the moment.

"I don't need the bended knee or the ring," she said. "I just need the question."

So he asked, "Will you marry me, Maggie Jenkins? Will you take me as your husband and as Drew's father?"

"Yes, Special Agent Blaine Campbell," she replied. "I will marry you."

He used their joined hands to tug her closer, to pull her down for the kiss to seal their promise.

Someone cleared his throat above the sound of a baby crying. "Excuse me," Truman said. "But someone was looking for his mama…" The burly agent carried the tiny fussing baby over to Maggie.

She laid the little boy on Blaine's chest, and the baby's cries stopped. He stared up at Blaine as if he recognized him. "Here's your daddy," she said.

Blaine had a perfect record—every case solved with the FBI, every criminal caught—but this—his family—meant far more to him. This woman and their child was what made his life special now and for always.

* * * * *

MILLS & BOON®
By Request

RELIVE THE ROMANCE WITH THE BEST OF THE BEST

A sneak peek at next month's titles...

In stores from 14th December 2017:

- **Bound by a Baby** – Maureen Child, Tessa Radley *and* Yvonne Lindsay

- **A Proposal Worth Waiting For** – Raye Morgan, Teresa Carpenter *and* Melissa McClone

In stores from 28th December 2017:

- **The Montoros Affair** – Kat Cantrell, Jules Bennett, *and* Charlene Sands

- **New Year, New Man** – Michelle Major, Ally Blake *and* Natalie Anderson

Just can't wait?
Buy our books online before they hit the shops!
www.millsandboon.co.uk

Also available as eBooks.